Sarah rose, beckoning for him to follow

"I missed you," she said, twining her arms around him, her breath sweet and eager.

Hutch felt a spasm. He could just as easily have come home to find her dead, something he'd never thought about before. "Maybe I shouldn't go away so much."

"Hush," she said, reaching for him.

It was a moonless night, the sky streaked with clouds, and they had wandered into a grove of trees whose branches shut out what little starlight there was. Sarah took his hand and pressed it to her breast. Hutch felt smooth skin and realized that her nightdress was lying in a pool at her feet. A prickle of excitement raced along his spine, raising the hairs on the back of his neck. And as she unfolded beneath him, a feeling so full and aching welled up inside him that it blotted out everything else. Only later, when her head lay still on the crook of his arm and he believed she was asleep, did he dare whisper it aloud to her.

"I need you, Sarah," he said, and to his surprise she turned, burrowed against him, and whispered the words she'd been waiting to tell him all along...

LONE STAR RISING

LONE STAR RISING

SUE ANN WAGGONER

WARNER BOOKS

A Warner Communications Company

For the *Challenger* and her last crew:
Greg Jarvis
Christa McAuliffe
Ron McNair
El Onizuka
Judy Resnick
Dick Scobee
Mike Smith

Be silent, friend,
Here heroes died
To blaze a trail for other men.

— Alamo inscription

Prologue

Her eyes, darker than white man's coffee, skimmed off across the horizon. The land stretched like the undulating hip of Earth Mother herself, forever and away without limit. Yellow Fawn had never seen such land before.

She looked toward the hardwood grove that edged the river. The oaks and maples reminded her of home, their leaves light green against the sky, their branches quaking gently in the breeze. An immense field of grass stretched before her and Yellow Fawn waded hip deep into it, the movement of her body and the steadily blowing wind setting the grass in motion. It tossed and tumbled around her and she laughed, alone in the great grass lake, her laughter carried by the wind.

The wind was the spirit of this new land, Yellow Fawn decided. It was Earth Mother's hand stretching out to sweep them up. The wind had been blowing the day the Cherokee arrived and chose a site for their village. It had been blowing still the day the white man, Chase, came to them for the first time. Their lodges were half-built by then but their supplies were low. Chase came like a god among them, bringing a trader and three pack animals laden with goods.

Yellow Fawn stood apart from the excitement caused by their arrival. In Georgia, white men had killed her father and her husband. A great white man named Jackson had

issued the letter that drove them from their land. She would
not swarm forward with the others, eager for goods she did
not need. There was no man to adorn herself for, no man to
obtain a gift for, no man who might surprise her, in turn,
with the gift of a mirror or a length of calico. She was
utterly alone, and while the others clamored around the
white men, she went stubbornly about her work.

But all the while she watched from the corners of her
eyes. These men brought none of the worthless trinkets she
associated with whites. Chase was not a trader himself but a
man who led traders. The things offered for barter were
worthy things, cooking pots and medicine and well-woven
cloth. Soon Yellow Fawn was looking up, looking at the
white man against her better judgment.

Chase was a tall and sinewy man with light hair and gray
eyes that seemed almost blue against his tanned skin. His
height and the way he carried himself made him seem older
than he was, Yellow Fawn realized. He caught her studying
him and smiled, a smile open and uncalculating, a smile
with surprising power. Later she discovered that he was
from that part of the east shared by her Cherokee grandfa-
thers, and this made him even more memorable to her.

Chase came often to Spotted Turtle's village, sometimes
with a trader, always a trader who would not cheat them,
but sometimes only to visit. His stature rose among them
and it became customary for Yellow Fawn to return his
gaze, to nod her head to him, to serve him food in her
uncle Spotted Turtle's lodge. Little by little it became
customary for her to do these things for him in her own
lodge, the lodge she thought would never know a man
again.

The wind had tossed and sighed around them the first
time he came to her and the first time they lay locked in
each other's arms. She felt Earth Mother's hand around
them, wrapping them together in this land without signposts
or limits.

Beyond the river, Chase told her, the wind blew stronger
still and the land sloped up to meet the sky. Trees ceased to
grow and grass stretched in an endless, rippling ocean,
turning and dipping with the earth's curve. Where the ocean

ended no one knew, for the way was barred by savage Comanche, people who had no written language and whose most permanent home was the back of a horse. Yellow Fawn listened to Chase speak of these wonders, but when he finished she shook her head with a disbelieving smile.

Now she waded free of the grass and began climbing the soft, low hills cradling the river where maples and green live oaks mingled with willow trees to form a dense thicket. Yellow Fawn slapped a buzzing insect and listened to the wail of mourning doves. High above her a hawk glided, wings motionless, head alert. She crested the hill and saw red-brown glistening below her. The Red River, named for the color of its waters, flowed from the west, a great hunter's bow spanning more than a thousand miles.

Somewhere along the river's southern curve, somewhere the water could take her to, was Chase. Yellow Fawn thought of his gray eyes and of his long-fingered hands. She was older than he, she ought to be beyond such things, but she thought of him nevertheless. He had been seen three days to the south, according to Bull Calf, the messenger. And he had sent word: he was guiding a party of traders, he was bringing them to Spotted Turtle's village, he would stay a week or more. Yellow Fawn smiled, knowing the message was for her. Above her the gliding hawk sighted its prey, cried once, and vanished in a downward plunge.

PART I

Chapter One

Sarah Kincaid Bell opened her eyes against the yellow ceiling of her bedroom. Outside it was a cloudy day in late winter but the walls of the room, with their stenciled border of green and gold pineapples, glowed as if washed by sunlight.

In the mirror above the bureau, Sarah could see the pineapples reflected. They marched away in a long, perfect line. Cautiously, not wanting to wake her husband, she moved her legs beneath the sheets. Such luxury! Until she'd married and come here she'd never, in all her fifteen years, known the caress of sheets or the pleasure of painted walls. Her parents' cabin, on a worn-out section of land set well back from Caney Fork, was mud daub and chinking and Sarah, oldest of ten, had slept in a lean-to with the cattle.

It still seemed a miracle that she'd arrived here, like the story the peddler told about the elf girl who was swallowed by a carp and transported, alive, to the kitchen of the king's palace. Like the elf girl, Sarah was ready to jump from the belly of the carp and dance for the king's delight, if only she might be allowed to remain in the palace. For her father had made it clear: *if 'ee fail to please him, Saree, don't think 'ee can come home again; we've enough mouths to feed.*

No one had made mention of her husband's pleasing her,

though in Sarah's eyes he did. She knew very little of men and had no one to compare him to. There was the oldest Chase boy, Hutch, who'd caught her fancy as a child. But he'd since disappeared across the Sabine River into Texas, heedless of her secret liking. Since she'd come of courting age, no one had so much as glanced her way. Fragile and reedlike in her looks, Sarah's parents could offer no more than a sack of corn as a dowry. And that, for a girl who looked likely to die in her first childbed, was no dowry at all.

So when Arden Bell, thirty years her senior, had favored her at a wedding supper and called on her at home the week afterward, Sarah's mother had all but rushed into the woods to gather flowers for her daughter's wedding. Sarah was removed from the cattle lean-to and brought back into the cabin. She was given extra milk to drink in hopes that her jutting collarbones and flat cheeks wouldn't frighten her suitor away. Two months to the day later, Sarah left on her honeymoon.

It was on the honeymoon that Sarah discovered her husband's moods. Sometimes he wanted her just as she was, a girl of fifteen who knew nothing of the world beyond Caney Fork. There were nights when he gathered her fine-spun hair in handfuls and made her pretend, over and over again, to be the virgin she'd been on their first night together. He would gasp and ease himself into her, trembling with desire, while she lay stretched like a rose upon a trellis.

But there were other times when his mood turned dark and he lashed out at her with sudden fury. Her first taste of this had come one morning in the hotel breakfast room. They were to rent a buggy and ride out to view the fresh, incomparable scenery of the Blue Ridge. Sarah dressed in peach-colored muslin, smoothed her auburn hair with the toilet water provided by the hotel, and hurried down to join her husband. Arden didn't stand to pull her chair back for her. Sarah would always remember that detail clearly. When she sat down she saw that his face was dark.

"What has kept you?" he demanded, as if he'd been waiting for hours. Then he called for paper and pen and wrote, with a sour and elaborate flourish, a note for two hundred dollars. "I bet the gentleman over there that you would not be more than five minutes coming down." A Tidewater planter in cream-colored trousers smiled genially across the room at them, as if this sort of thing was done every morning.

Sarah was speechless. She'd seen her husband take a seat at cards, had twice fallen asleep waiting for him to come up to her, but a wager like this was beyond her understanding. "Arden, I . . . you should have . . . have warned me."

"Shut up," he snapped. He was furious. She could feel his anger reaching toward her from across the table. "Don't ever tell me what I should have done!"

Sarah looked down at her plate, at the eggs that had just arrived, swimming in grease. Vomit rose in her throat; she pushed her chair back and ran up the stairs to their suite. The room still smelled of toilet water, a scent that would forever after make her nauseated.

Arden pounded into the room behind her. "What's got into you?" he asked, catching her arm. "Didn't your folks teach you anything about being a wife? Don't you know not to run out of a room—make a fool of me—that way?"

He turned her loose and she spun away from him. His fingers left marks on her arm, peach-colored marks that matched her dress. The next day the marks turned dark blue, and she wore long-sleeved dresses for the rest of her honeymoon, though Arden never mentioned the incident again and she sometimes wondered if it had ever happened.

After two weeks in the Blue Ridge, Arden brought her home. He made a show of carrying her across the threshold and of setting her down in the newly papered parlor. The paper had been put up just for her, he said. Sarah had never seen wallpaper before and she stared at the huge, blooming roses that seemed almost to breathe in her presence. Nor had she seen a mirror like the long, beveled glass that hung on the wall. She walked up to it and laid her hand against its cool, smooth surface. "Arden," she said, and his reflection appeared behind her.

"I want you to meet Sally," he told her, taking her hand. Sally, it turned out, was the old black cook. She grinned and bobbed at her master and new mistress, revealing strong white teeth in a withered face. "Leave all the fuss work to her. That's what God made niggers for, I reckon, to do the fuss work. They sure ain't good for anything else." He drew Sarah down onto his knees, opened each hand, and kissed her upturned palms.

At such moments Sarah felt cherished beyond imagining. The other times, times when her husband's rage rose up around her, she pushed into a corner of her mind. Whatever triggered his fury, she believed, was her fault. It was something she did that brought on his anger. In time she would learn, be better, and then each of their moments would be pierced with sunlight.

Arden stirred in the bed beside her, his hand clasping her pale breast and his dark beard, streaked with gray, furring her shoulder. During the night he'd clung to her with shaking need, caressing her and promising her a hundred gifts. Outside a light drizzle had begun.

The drizzle, thought Creath Chase, was going to make Bell's mill a crowded place today. Wet weather always brought folks around to the smaller tasks in life. But the mules were already harnessed when the drizzle began, and Creath searched for a canvas to cover the corn.

"Can't I go along?" Jane begged, balancing on the wagon wheel to help spread the cover. "Please?"

Creath looked at his sister. Jane, fifteen and bursting from her child-bodiced dress like ripe cotton from the bole, was so insistent that he wondered if there was someone she'd gone sweet on and hoped to see.

"No, you can't go," said Jane's twin, Samuel. "Mill ain't no place for a girl."

"How can it be no place for a girl," Jane whimpered, "when Sarah Bell lives there, and she's scarce three months older'n me?"

Now their father joined the conversation. "Sarah is Arden Bell's wife," he reminded. Like his two oldest sons, Hutch and Creath, John Chase was a tall man and spare, with gray eyes and hair the color of sun-washed sand.

Creath took the wagon seat and grinned down at Jane.

"Just think," he said, "if you would have married Arden Bell instead of letting Sarah Kincaid get him, you could spend *all* your time at the mill."

"Arden Bell!" Jane snapped saucily, wrinkling her nose in disgust. Then she added, with a hint of womanly knowing, "I pity Sarah."

"Sarah made her bed," John said. "See you don't do the same."

"I'm not marrying anyone at all," Jane replied, but a faint blush showed in her milk white cheeks.

Sam, as pale-skinned as Jane and sharing her black hair and blue eyes, climbed up beside Creath. "I'll tell Ly Owen you said as much," he called down, sending Jane off in exaggerated anger.

So it was the middle Owen boy who'd caught Jane's fancy, Creath thought, and the Owens with as many sons and as little land to divide among them as the Chases themselves. Creath wrapped the reins around his fist.

"Watch Bell so he doesn't cheat you," his father warned. "He's a hand at that." Creath nodded and the wagon, heavy with shelled corn, creaked forward.

At eighteen, Creath stood six feet two, an inch shorter than Hutch had been at the same age when he left home three years ago, according to marks gouged inside the door frame. With Hutch's leaving, new responsibilities had settled on Creath's shoulders and though his brother's infrequent letters, marking a trail into distant and foreign lands, filled him with excitement, Creath had no intention of joining him.

He thought with envy of those long-ago times when Grandpa Chase was a boy and when the first Chases came down from the New River into the middle basin of the Cumberland. The land was wild and open then, free for the claiming. Now it was like a pieced quilt, with every corner stitched down tight.

The bench of land settled by Grandpa Chase so many years ago had worn thin, and though more had been cleared and parcels added, the acreage could not keep up with the family's needs. John and Mary Chase raised a brood of nine, all of them living and six of them boys. After Hutch and Creath came Jane and Samuel, then Johnny, Joseph, Ellen, Alice, and Andrew. Even if the girls married well and one or two of the boys headed west as Hutch had done, more land would still be needed. And land, in this well-settled country, cost a thumb of gold.

It was the question of land that occupied Creath's mind this morning. He had been dickering for a section of good acreage all week, only to find, at the last minute, that Arden Bell had bought it out from under him.

The lost deal gnawed at Creath. Already, Bell's mill occupied a prime place on Caney Fork, catching the water as it pulsed over a necklace of rapids in its boil toward the Cumberland. All around the mill spread Bell's holdings, crowned with a house that far outdid the neighborhood.

What did the man need with so much land? Creath wondered. Surely he didn't mean to become a full-fledged planter. The idea of a Tidewater-style plantation straddling Caney Fork brought a smile to Creath's lips. There was no telling, though. A man who married a girl one-third his age and paraded her to the Blue Ridge on a honeymoon might intend anything at all.

Bell's mill sat well away from his house, which occupied the rise of land above it. There were even two roads these days, a high one and a low one. Creath took the low one that led down to the mill. It was still early in the day, but already a line of wagons could be seen.

"It'll be a wait to get ground today," Sam said. Then, before they'd even reached a full halt, he sprang down from the wagon.

Creath understood Sam's eagerness. So many wagons meant more than the ordinary share of jokes and rough stories. Most of what Creath knew of life—of men and women anyway—had been learned here, in the days when he'd tagged along with Hutch and stood in the shadows listening. Here he'd tasted his first corn whiskey and seen his first hand of cards played, for cards, with their promise of easy winnings from whiskey-muddled farmboys, were Arden Bell's passion. That thought, light as chaff from a kernel of corn, blew into Creath's mind and stayed there.

*   *   *

Sarah heard the creak of wagons but did not wake her husband. Instead she eased herself from his grasp, wound a shawl around her shoulders, and padded down into the kitchen. Sally had started the fire and the glow lit the kitchen to its corners. "You go away, Sally," she said. "I mean to cook breakfast myself today."

Sally, who knew all the signs of poverty, doubted if Sarah knew much of cooking anything but mush. She shook her head once in disagreement but took herself off without saying a word. If that child wanted to make breakfast for the master, that child could surely try.

A bowl of eggs stood on the table. Sarah cracked three of them into a tripod skillet and set the skillet over the fire. The hem of her nightdress brushed the hearthstones and the stones warmed her bare feet. She was filled with happiness as she fumbled her way through the unfamiliar kitchen. This was one of the things she must learn, she told herself, one of the tasks she must master. One by one, her command of wifely duties would keep her husband's anger at bay. *If 'ee fail to please him, Saree, don't think 'ee can come home again.*

The eggs were sticking. Sarah hurried to place cold roast meat beside them in the pan, hoping the fat would drizzle them loose. Because she'd never been allowed in the kitchen, she didn't know that Sally began the cooking with a dollop of lard in the pan. She only knew how the eggs looked when they came into the dining room, yolks round as suns and shiny with grease. Hastily, her hair curling against her flushed forehead, Sarah dropped a chunk of butter onto each yoke.

But the eggs still stuck and when she tried to lift them, the yolks broke and the whites tore apart. Suddenly, she remembered the plate of eggs set before her in the Blue Ridge hotel. The plate of eggs, the scent of toilet water, her husband's rage. It all came back to her, sweeping her happiness into a ball that burned to ashes in the hearth fire. Improvising, Sarah chopped at the eggs with the edge of the turner, lifting and stirring. But the mess that resulted bore no resemblance to the fluffy scrambled eggs Sally often made.

Just then she heard Arden's footsteps behind her. Somehow, the sound stopped her panic. He was her husband. He loved her. He had clung to her all night long. He would not send her home for three ruined eggs.

Sarah stood and faced him, brushing a feather of cinnamon-spice hair back from her forehead. Years later the memory came back to her. She must have looked a fool, standing above the ruined eggs with an idiot's smile on her face. She yearned for Arden to come forward and embrace her, maybe even sweep her upstairs to make love again beneath the gold and green pineapples.

But thoughts of lovemaking were far from Arden Bell's mind. He'd awakened, found himself alone in the bedroom, and breathed a sigh of relief because of it. His desire for his young wife's body was torture to him, his need for her a shameful secret.

Better if he'd never laid eyes on her, he thought, though it was too late for that now. Sarah had consumed his thoughts from the first moment he saw her, a burning white candle of a girl whose breast buds, he knew, would stand out like strawberries against her pale skin, whose silky body hair would be tinged copper red. He'd had no rest until he owned her and now, it seemed, she was the one who owned him.

Arden had sat in the bedroom for several minutes before getting up, legs flung over the side of the bed, shoulders hunched like a drunk's. Finally he'd roused himself, poured water into the basin, and tried to wash his wife's scent from his hair and beard. Even now, dressed and awake, he fancied that the smell of her clung to him like myrrh.

When he came into the kitchen, the smile she gave him seemed full of calculated seduction. "What's this?" he asked roughly, striding across the kitchen floor to the smoking pan.

"Breakfast," Sarah said, feeling the first stirring of uneasiness.

"Where's Sally? I got to have something to eat, and that in the pan ain't fit for hogs."

"I sent Sally off," Sarah told him. "I thought we could . . . just the two of us—" She stopped. Her crinkly hair fanned about her shoulders; her brown eyes were full of quiet pleading.

It was that look that fired his rage. No matter how he tried to free himself, she was always tangling him up, tying him to her. He felt as if weeds had reached up from the bottom of a pond to draw him under. Suddenly his hand struck out, skimming her shoulder. "Didn't your folks teach you anything at all? You think this is some play-party game? Damn, I should'a got a woman for a wife, not a girl whose nose I got to wipe every time she turns around."

He reached down and grasped the skillet by its handle. The cloth potholder was still there, where Sarah had left it. He brandished the burned hash of eggs in front of her, holding it so close she felt warmth against her face. Sarah might have stepped back. She had stepped back during his other rages, had waited on shore for the sea storm to pass. But this time she held her ground and when her husband thrust the skillet forward, the heated metal caught her under the jaw.

Searing pain curled the length of her throat but she didn't cry out. She only gasped and felt a strange release. It was Arden who sobbed first, in anguished surprise. He had come to depend on Sarah's stepping back, on her leaving a clear field for his anger. He flung the skillet aside and collapsed at her knees. Then he was up, running for water and a rag.

"How could I have done such a thing?" he cried, dabbing at the red mark that swooped from beneath her jaw to the collar of her nightdress. "How could I have?" He wrapped his arms around her and pulled her away from the awful scene. He carried her into the parlor with its rose-papered walls. "You know I didn't mean it, don't you, Sarah? You know I didn't."

He begged her for a word of forgiveness but she didn't give her one. Something wouldn't let her. Maybe it was the pain that sealed her throat tight, hurting every time she swallowed. Maybe it was a strange, mean selfishness within her, she thought. Her mam had ever said she was a selfish one.

They sat for a long time in the front room, locked

together, saying nothing. The discreet sounds of Sally tidy-
ing the kitchen came to them, and the impatient jingling of a
harness. "I got business down at the mill," Arden said,
sliding her from his lap.

Sarah sat for a long time after he left, her gaze falling
straight ahead on the familiar pattern of roses on trellises.
The roses, blood red against blue, seemed to throb in the
mid-morning light. Sarah lifted her hand to her jaw. It was
the first time he'd hit her, she thought. Though likely not
the last.

Chapter Two

The shanty that housed the large millstones had been full
since Creath and Samuel arrived. That had been three hours
ago, but their sack of raw corn still waited, with four others
ahead of it. Milling grain was only a sideline for Arden
Bell, who was more interested in the social benefits of
running a mill than in the work to be done. As a consequence the massive millstones were chronically neglected,
the grooved surfaces allowed to wear smooth between dress-
ings, making it necessary to send each batch of grain
through twice to achieve the desired result. Creath was in no
hurry, though, and Sam would be content to linger in the
millhouse all day.

"Have you heard anything from old Hutch?" Tom Wilson
asked, tipping back on his chair, a cast-off from the house,
and propping his boot against the shanty wall.

Everyone in the county knew that Hutch Chase had gone
to Texas, and that act of far-flung adventuring earned him
the affectionate nickname "old Hutch" in spite of his youth.

Creath smiled. He'd always been more comfortable
answering questions about his older brother than about
himself. "He's in the Red River trade," he replied, enjoying

the feel of the distant river's name on his tongue. "Shows traders the way up from Nacogdoches."

At first Arden Bell appeared not to hear him, shifting his attention to the ground meal funneling down into its cache. He poured it into a coarse-woven sack, tied the opening with a piece of twine, and handed it to the owner. "That's fifty cents, John." A steep price, to be sure, but the next nearest mill was thirty miles away. John Parker handed him the money and shouldered the sack. "Who's next?" Bell asked and, taking up the sack indicated, began funneling its corn into the eye of the turning stones. Then, in a quiet voice, he asked, "Are there many white folks in Texas?"

The question was casual but Creath felt Bell's eyes studying him. Something in him drew back, though he wasn't sure why. He'd always been shy of people, maybe because he'd grown up with Hutch doing the talking for both of them. But it was more than that. There was something hidden in Bell's offhanded question. "Not so many," Creath replied, paring his words. "A few settlements, I expect."

"That's only in the north," Sam broke in, his face glowing with enthusiasm. If Hutch was Creath's friend, he was Sam's idol, someone whose very footsteps were to be studied. Sam had managed to learn more about Texas than Hutch's sparse, months-apart letters told them. "There's more families going all the time. It's getting right crowded in some parts."

Bell's eyes flicked from Sam to Creath. "Looks like your whole family's been took with Texas fever," he said, his lips drawing back in a smile.

In spite of the smile, Creath saw that Bell's eyes remained calculating, as if he were measuring the weight and worth of new milled grain. "Well, Hutch an' Sam may've been touched," Creath replied. "Me, I'm not planning on going anywhere."

Behind his seamless smile, Creath studied the mill owner. Bell had been drinking ever since they arrived, passing the jug freely but always taking two swigs to others' one. The drinking had smoked out something raw and jagged in him, though Creath doubted if any of the others caught it. "How about you?'' he asked the mill owner suddenly. "You thinking of selling out and heading west?''

Bell's laugh was too hearty. "Me? God, boy, I got everything I want right here." He surely did, Creath thought. And the new land across the Fork on top of it. "But if I was you," Bell advised, "I'd be right interested in getting some of that prime Texas land.''

Creath shrugged. Bell was pushing toward something, but it would take time to come to light. "You go ahead of us if you want, Mose," he said, turning to Moses Boone, who'd come after them. "Sam 'n me ain't hurrying, so long as the jug's full.'' Bell smiled his keen smile and Creath made a show of reaching for the whiskey.

When a second jug was opened, Bell snapped a deck of cards onto the shaky tabletop. "Who's for a friendly game?'' he asked.

"High stakes or low?'' Tom Wilson asked.

Bell smiled. "Any way you like.''

The drizzle outside had thickened, keeping them on to drink and talk. It was the kind of situation Bell liked best. Of the eight men there, four were eager to part with their money. Of course, he'd take corn in place of cash, or anything else they had clear title to. "How about you, Creath? You in?''

Creath wasn't a gambler by nature. He was about to get his grain and go, disappointed that this was the point of the afternoon, when something in Bell's eye caught him. "No limit wagers?'' he asked.

Bell pushed back a chair. "Like I said," he replied, "choose your poison.''

Creath sat down and the other players shuffled into place around the table. "What the hell're you doing?'' Sam whispered at Creath's elbow.

"Just stand behind Bell," Creath told him. "I don't trust him.''

"But—''

"Do like I said.'' Creath's eyes were serious, so Sam found a spot against the wall behind Bell. He'd never seen anyone cheat at cards and he hoped he'd know what to look for.

Bell saw the boy slip behind him but, with the whiskey working in him, he paid no heed. Farmer boys, he thought, smiling as he dealt around. The pain of this morning was starting to dim. These boys around him—taking their money was going to be like grabbing a sugar tit from a baby. Maybe he'd buy Sarah a present with his winnings. Of course he would, and she'd come to him with that adoring look in her eyes again. Probably, she'd already forgotten what had happened, was up in the house washing her hair with fresh rainwater, waiting for him to come . . . "Where's that jug?" he asked, his spirits rising.

Each time the jug came around Creath lifted it and threw his head back, balancing it on the crook of his arm. But he pushed his tongue over the rim as he bobbed his Adam's apple up and down, letting no more than a drop into his mouth. As a consequence, he'd managed to stay in the game with Bell long after the others had grown careless, lost their stakes, and dropped out. He was feeling confident, a small pile of winnings before him, when he drew a poor hand and tried to bluff his way through. He glanced up at Sam and in that single, unguarded moment Bell guessed his situation and called his bluff.

"Handful of nothing's what you got there, boy, and that don't ever beat two pair." Bell smiled as he raked Creath's coins toward him. "Tell you what, though, I'll grind your corn on credit if I've wiped you out."

Sam, standing behind Bell's shoulder, saw his brother's brow furrow. Creath was furious with himself for being so easy to read. Then, through an effort of will, his brow smoothed. "No, I'm not wiped out." He reached into his pocket and pulled out a stack of gold eagles, money he'd earned and hoarded, money he'd intended for the land across the Fork. "How about another hand, Arden? My pile against yours."

The atmosphere in the mill shanty changed, charged by the sight of the gold on the table. A nervous laugh bubbled up and evaporated. Neither Creath nor Bell took note of it. Their eyes were intent upon each other. "If it's another hand you want . . ." Bell said, reaching for the cards.

"It's young Chase's deal," someone said behind them.

Creath felt a jab of pride. *Young Chase*. It was what they had called Hutch before he went west.

Sam, straining his eyes, saw two queens appear in Bell's hand. Lord, how did they get there? he wondered. *What if he cheated and I didn't see him?* A trickle of sweat started down the back of Sam's neck and his stomach clamped down when Creath raised the ante. He'd had no idea his brother possessed so much money, more money than he had ever seen at one time before; money that was, surely, about to become Arden Bell's. Sam bit his lip when the two men turned over their hands, bolting forward with jubilation at the sight of the three kings Creath held.

"You got him," Sam said, and the others, who'd been watching just as intently, murmured their approval. Having been beaten by Arden Bell themselves, they'd let Creath take their revenge for them.

"I reckon Sam and me'll be going now," Creath said quietly. "If you can see your way clear to grinding my corn."

A muscle in Bell's jaw worked. "Just a minute here. You're going to give me a chance to even up, aren't you?"

Creath pushed the pile back to the center of the table and reached inside his shirt for three more eagles to add to it. "You got cash too, of course?"

Now the mill shanty grew quiet, the only sounds the grinding of the great millstones. The men leaned forward, tension knotting them together. Bell was caught. All he had was on the table before him. Acquiring a wife and new property had stripped him clean. But his mouth watered for his lost cash and for Creath's gold eagles. "I'll make you an offer," he said. "My wagon and harnesses . . . *and* horses."

Creath leaned back in his chair. "I already got a wagon," he said. "A good one, too."

"A nigger, then. Sally's a good cook, though past breeding."

"My family don't keep niggers." Creath reached for the stack of coins. He didn't put them away, just lifted them and let them clink down through his fingers. "Tell you what," he said slowly, "I'll take the deed to that piece of land you bought last week."

Sam's heart beat hard, a pulse that jumped in his veins

like fire. He'd known his brother had been eyeing a piece of bottomland and that Bell had beat him to it. Now he understood that this had been Creath's purpose all along, to drive Bell to a bargaining point and force him to use the land as a wager.

"The deed to the land I bought last week?" Bell echoed. His face was flushed but his mind worked rapidly. It might work . . . it might just work at that, the young fool. He suppressed a smile. "Why don't you all have a drink while I go get that paper?" he suggested, greed thickening his voice.

Sarah was no longer in the front room when Bell entered the house. Probably she was upstairs, he thought. He didn't call her name. Instead he rummaged hastily for the deed. He could almost feel the weight of those eagles in his hand.

When he returned to the shanty he laid the folded paper in the center of the table. Creath nodded, pushed in his gold eagles, and the game went on. Bell lifted the jug with each card dealt him, no longer bothering to pass it to anyone else. The millstones ran dry, grinding with no corn between them, but Bell ignored the damage being done. He'd become obsessed with the notion of winning.

Creath was easily the favorite in the little shanty, and when he won the hand there was a murmur of approval. He swept the money to one side and picked up the deed. "What the hell is this?" he asked, frowning as the paper unfolded in his hands.

Bell tried to muster a blameless look. "Land title," he said.

"This is a claim for land somewhere in Texas. I wagered for the land you bought last week."

"That's land I bought last week," Bell told him. "Look at the date."

Too late, Creath realized that Bell had foreseen the possibility of being beaten, even in his hazed condition, and crafted a no-lose hand for himself. The gold eagles winked up from the table. Slowly, methodically, Creath began arranging them in rows. "Well, Arden, that was pretty sharp of you.'' He gestured toward a chair. ''What say we play again?''

Bell started to decline, but the pressure in the room stopped him. Everyone felt he'd cheated young Chase. Refusing the hand would be risky, for this was a country where memories ran long and grudges deep. Bell took his seat again. ''I—it'll be a small-stakes game, boy. You've cleaned me out.''

Creath picked up his cards one by one. ''You've got that land across the Fork,'' he said quietly. ''Bet that.''

Bell wanted to roar in anger. His head throbbed in the close, musty air of the shanty. Everyone was watching him, pinning him with their eyes. A familiar feeling came over him, the feeling of being trapped. Where had it last been . . . ? Yes, this morning with Sarah. She made him feel the same way, pulling and clutching at him with her soft young body.

Creath pushed a stack of coins to the center of the table. ''What've you got to match against it?'' he asked, raising his eyes to meet Bell's.

Bell took a long sip from the jug. He'd be damned if he'd let them push him into risking his new bottomlands. They were all alike, the men and Sarah, all clutching and pulling at him. ''I've got a wife,'' he said. ''I'll bet her.''

From his watching place against the wall, Sam's head snapped up. He leaned forward expectantly, and everyone else in the shanty with him. If the millstones had stopped turning and Caney Fork had stopped flowing, they would have been the last to know.

''Do you accept the wager?'' Bell asked. ''Or do we call it a draw?''

How could a man do such a thing? Creath wondered. How could a man wager away his wife? And Sarah Bell, from what he'd seen of her, was a sweet thing, big russet eyes in the kind of heart-shaped face a man would be glad to wake up beside. He felt something stretch inside him, sympathy for one so easily cast off.

Creath's eyes were steady on his opponent's face. ''I'll accept if the lady is willing,'' he said. ''If she isn't, you put up the land instead. Deal?'' Bell nodded and Creath glanced over his shoulder. "Would somebody go up to the house and fetch Mrs. Bell?"

No one in the shanty said a word from the time Sam left until the time he returned. They looked down, they looked away from each other, like men sharing a guilty secret. All but Creath, who rose as Sarah crossed the doorstep.

She looked like a deer shined in the woods, he thought. It was an old hunter's trick, shining deer at night. He and Hutch had done it often, one of them swinging the lantern while the other brought down the startled deer. That was how Sarah looked to him, her eyes wide and luminous, her skin damp from the rain. Creath fancied he saw raindrops clinging to her lashes. He wondered how much Sam had told her on the way down from the house.

Sarah swept by him to her husband. "I hear you've made a wager," she said, her voice surprisingly strong for someone so small. If she were to stand next to him, in the fold of Creath's arms, her head would not top his shoulder. "Is it so?"

Arden Bell's face lost its florid red. It became heavy and pallid, reflecting the ashen light of the afternoon. "If you're agreeable," he replied. "Only if you're agreeable. That's the condition."

Sarah's cheeks burned. It was like him to put her in this position, just as it was like him to expect her to step away from the raised frying pan. The wave of rebellion, risen in her that morning, hadn't subsided. Arden was mistaken to think it had. She glanced at the men gathered in the shanty. Then her gaze went to Bell and remained there. "I'll stand by my husband's bet," she said.

The men caught their breaths. None of them had expected her to comply. "Saree," Arden said. His eyes were bloodshot, his voice contained the whisper of shame.

"Your husband's had a mite to drink and a run of bad luck," Creath said. "Maybe you'd like to change your mind. No one'll think the worse of you."

Sarah had wound a strip of lace around her throat and fastened it with a cameo pin. Her face, rising above the lace, was small and determined. "No need to think. I'll agree to whatever bet he's made."

She sat down while the cards were dealt, sweat starting from the back of her knees. The thought of leaving the safety of her papered parlor and the small share of happiness she'd known there terrified her. Yet the door had swung open and she stood looking out of it. Her heart beat wildly because she was young and because she longed to remake her life.

For the first time she realized that it was Creath Chase she'd been wagered to. He was so much like Hutch in looks it took her by surprise. Long-boned and fair-haired, both of them, with eyes like gray quartz. But there were differences, too. Hutch was taller and rangier in her memory, with a hard jaw and mouth. Creath's mouth was wide and gentle, his hands the blunt-fingered hands of a blacksmith.

The rules of cards eluded her, but Sarah followed the expressions on the men's faces. Creath's face was calm and smooth, her husband's strained and ashen. *Chase is going to win,* she told herself, trying to prepare herself, to think ahead; *Arden has gambled me away.* She knew at once, when the hands were revealed, that the ace spots on Creath Chase's cards had bested the knaves in her husband's hand.

"I'll get my things," she said, rising to her feet. She felt light inside, almost hollow, but sure of herself nonetheless.

Creath put the gold eagles back in his pocket and picked up the thickly folded piece of paper with scrolls of ink decorating it. He was slow to meet her eyes, but when he did, he nodded reassuringly.

Arden caught her by the wrist before she reached the shanty door. "Now, Saree, 'twas a jesting wager. I doubt Creath'll force you to go."

She pulled her wrist free. "He won't need to force me. I only want to get my things."

"And go with him?"

" 'Twas your idea, Arden."

"But—" his tongue worked laboriously in his mouth. *"You cannot go, Sarah!"* She ignored him and started toward the door again. Lurching forward, he caught her by the shoulders and spun her violently around. Then his hand flashed through the air and crashed against her jaw. Flames leaped up in her burned skin, tears rocked in the corners of her eyes. He wasn't so drunk that he couldn't aim the blow where it would hurt most, she thought.

Creath sprang forward. "I'm all right," she gasped, waiting for the pain to subside. Two men wrestled Arden away from her and held him pinned against the wall. Pain gnawed at her throat and her blood was hot against her temples. She walked swiftly out of the shanty and down to the tangle of wagons. "Which one is yours?" she asked when Creath caught up with her.

He pointed and climbed up. "Sam'n me'll wait while you get your things," he said. "The boys'll hold your husband 'til we're gone."

"I've changed my mind," she said as she climbed onto the seat beside him. "There's nothing I need."

In the back of the wagon, Sam settled between the sacks of fresh cornmeal. He was struck with admiration for his brother, whose wide-shouldered back towered beside Sarah's slight one. "What are you going to tell ma?" he asked, but Creath ignored the question.

On the way home the drizzle slackened and a stiff breeze sprang up in its place. Sarah shivered.

"He'll simmer down by tomorrow," Creath told her. "I'll take you home then."

"No," she said, shaking her head.

"You might change your mind, once you sleep on it."

"I won't."

Creath looked at her profile, firm and fine beneath a crinkly halo of hair.

She'd already begun to take hold of him; he felt that even before the wagon reached home. When he got her bedded down with Jane and got his parents reconciled to the idea of having her, he went outside and sat alone in the clean night air. He watched the miraculous turning of the stars and thought of fetching a lantern and rifle and going off to shine deer. But it was her face he wanted to see. Her face, at once fragile and determined, with its luminous russet eyes.

The next morning when her husband came around, shouting

for his wife, Creath stood him off while Sarah waited inside
the house. "Thank you," she said afterward, and went back
to helping his mother cut dried apples for pie. When the pie
was served she smiled as she handed it to him, smiled for
the first time, and the room lit up around her.

One afternoon Creath was shoeing mules in the forge and
Sarah brought his lunch to him. "I don't imagine I was
what you wanted from Arden," she said, leaning against the
wall to watch.

He half smiled as he drove nail holes into the iron shoe.
"Not exactly," he answered. "There was some land I
wanted. Your husband fooled me on that account though.
Before I won you, I won a deed to someplace in Texas."

"Texas?" He nodded. She watched his arm, steady as a
pendulum as it swung the mallet down on the punch. "You
reckon to go there?"

He glanced at her, at the quick, light fire in her eyes.
Until now, he'd thought of the deed as so much paper.
"What I reckoned to do," he said, "was get more land
here. We've a houseful, if you haven't noticed."

"I've noticed," she answered. She was working at her
life as forcefully as he was working at the iron, struggling to
bend it to her needs. Cast off from her moorings, she'd
begun to grow bold and daring. She had no choice to be
otherwise. "Couldn't you do just as well in Texas?"

Creath laid the mallet and punch aside. "I couldn't
manage alone," he said. "And my brother out there, Hutch,
he isn't one for farming."

Sarah came away from the wall and stood beside him.
"You needn't manage alone," she said, drawing a breath.
"Not if you take me with you."

She put her hand on his and waited for her words to
settle. The hot metal smell of the forge would always be, to
her, the smell of new life.

Chapter Three

Two months later, at sunset on a Sunday in May, Creath and Sarah made Galveston Bay, arriving on the *Talent*, a creaking and storm-slowed schooner that had taken twice as long as promised from New Orleans. Skiffs darted like dragonflies over the bay, occupants calling out for news of the States and warning the newcomers that no lodgings were to be had ashore.

Sarah said nothing to this, though the idea of another night cooped up with the smell of bilge water brought a wave of nausea to her. She'd suffered with seasickness the whole time out and longed for the feel of land beneath her feet.

"We'll go ashore anyway," Creath assured her, his hand stealing shyly around her waist. It was hard to believe she'd ever been wife to another man, hard to believe that even now Arden Bell might still be looked on as her legal husband. She seemed to have been waiting just for Creath, just as his hand seemed carved and whittled to fit the curve of her waist.

"I'd like that," she answered, her voice taut with enthusiasm, her eyes catching the last rays of the sun. She burned with such internal fire that sometimes he feared she'd burn herself up.

"We don't have much to unload, at least," he said. Their farm tools, purchased in New Orleans against the high prices of the west, had been in the rush of crates jettisoned during a storm.

Sarah touched the bodice of her dress to hear the rustle of paper. "We have our deed still," she said. They'd decided it would be safest with her, in the women's quarters of the ship where theft was less likely.

Once on shore they learned that those in the skiffs had been right: the little settlement was full to the gills, so

chock-a-bloc with emigrants that ships in port were renting
sleep space to those who'd arrived on foot.

Sarah spied a woman struggling to hang a quilt tent from
the branches of a tree. Breaking away from Creath, she
walked over to her. "My man will help you," she said, her
voice shy over the words *my man*, "if you share your space
with us."

Elva Roberts nodded and made way for the couple,
pushing bundles and children aside with her foot. She'd
come a long, hard way, from Kentucky she told them, and
would never forgive her husband for dying on her. She
meant to quit Texas as soon as she could. There'd be no
squandering money on a burial stone on the way out, either.

Creath mistrusted Elva. A woman who wouldn't spare
headstone money for her own husband might be capable of
anything. Besides, he wanted to put a roof over Sarah's
head. "We can't stay here," he said when the quilts were
stretched into a serviceable canopy. He'd worked up a light
sweat, a sweat that showed off the fine-grained quality of
his skin. "A man told me where to get a room."

But Sarah was already arranging their bundles at the base
of the tree, using one side of the tent as a wall. "If there's a
room anywhere," she said, "it's bound to cost dear." She
couldn't read or write, add or subtract, but she'd an uncanny
memory for numbers. She knew that most of Creath's gold
eagles had been left with his parents. Of the money he'd
kept, so much had been spent on stagecoach fare, so much
more on the dashing steamer that took them south, so much
for food, so much for passage on the schooner, so much for
the lost plow, axes, and scythes. The eagles that remained,
she thought, would be huddling together for warmth soon,
and there were things they needed. "It's just for a night or
two," she added confidently. She unfurled a quilt and was
hidden for a moment in a blaze of colors. Then she
reappeared, smiling above the calico border. "Please, Creath."

He took up the ends of the quilt and helped her lay it
down in the shape of a bed. "All right, Sarah. Just to please
you." But later, lying with her head against his shoulder and
stars winking through the tree leaves, Creath realized that it
was she who'd pleased him, whether she knew it or not.

* * *

Sarah enjoyed Elva Roberts even if Creath didn't. She liked the fury that fueled and polished the woman's movements and gave machinelike energy to her hands. Elva's fingers were as hard and shiny as acorns, capable of thumping a misbehaving child on the back of the head with force and surprising speed. Her hair was a hard, knobby bun and her eyes, swift as a bird's, caught Sarah watching her. "You know how to use a metate?" she asked.

Sarah shook her head and Elva showed her how to grind corn between the two flat stones. It was Mexican corn, large and white and soft, and Sarah's mouth watered when Elva cooked it into bread on the griddle. Elva did not offer her a mouthful of the cooked bread and Sarah did not ask for any. She went on grinding while Elva went on cooking and soon saw the purpose in it: people passing by, drawn by the smell, bought the sweet, heavy bread as soon as it was lifted off the griddle.

When the last of the corn was used up, Elva counted out a share of the coins and handed them to Sarah. "We'll buy more corn tomorrow," she said, "if you're of a mind to help."

Sarah nodded quickly and pocketed the coins, counting them with her fingers. Creath had gone off to see about their land and to ask if anyone knew the whereabouts of his brother Hutch. As soon as he came back she would show him the money, the first they'd earned in Texas.

Creath, in the little land office that represented the majestic Republic of Mexico, could scarcely credit his ears. "What do you mean *worthless*?" he asked. "I won the deed fair and square."

Don Ybarra smiled indulgently, even sympathetically. "I do not doubt your word, señor. But it is nevertheless worthless." He pointed to the signature. "See? A forgery."

Creath countered by pointing to the seal of Mexico, stamped in indelible ink. "Is this a forgery too?"

"No," Don Ybarra replied. He folded the deed and handed it back to Creath. "What you have won, señor, is a claim in the misfortune of Don Padillo." When Creath looked at him questioningly, he went on. "Until last year, Don Padillo was the land commissioner at Nacogdoches.

Regrettably, he fell in love with the wife of one of his assistants. Far from Saltillo, such things happen. The character weakens. In Don Padillo's case, it weakened so much that the beautiful woman's husband met with an accident. Don Padillo himself was imprisoned for the murder. His papers, blank deeds among them, fell into the hands of a fraud.'' Don Ybarra paused and looked up at the shafts of light that sifted through the log roof of his domain. "Such is the air of this land," he said. "It breathes corruption. Check the coordinates, señor. You will see that your land lies in the ocean."

Creath leaned forward slightly. "What about the colonies, then? Austin's or DeWitt's? Who has the best land?" Creath knew, from Samuel mostly, all about the *empressarios*, the men who were licensed to settle colonists on vast tracts of land.

Again Don Ybarra shed a sympathetic smile. "Regrettably, señor, that is no longer a possibility. On April 6 the government of Mexico passed a decree prohibiting any further colonization of our lands by Americans. You are exactly one month too late."

Creath turned away from him, out into the street that was barely a street, his fist clenching in a spasm of anger. Beyond the thin row of buildings stretched land, more land than he'd ever seen, land that had never known seed or plow. Yet it couldn't be claimed. He was as land-starved here as he'd been back home. Only here he had Sarah to break the news to, a thought that was both a comfort and a source of shame.

He waited until the next night to tell her, whispering it into the darkness that engulfed them. Her hand, white as a dove, floated out of that darkness to light on his shoulder. "Never mind," she soothed, her voice soft as wind. "We'll manage." She rolled against him, a rag doll bundled in clothes. She smelled of leaves and smoke, for she'd progressed from the metate to the griddle and had spent all day poised over a mesquite fire. "There's the money I've earned with Elva, and you can get a job. We'll manage." Her hand was no longer a dove but a wave hurrying him along, filling him with desire, driving disappointment from his mind.

Sarah closed her eyes at the sweetness of it, at the touch of Creath's hands, at the tickle of night air against her skin.

She trembled at the revelation of the magic hidden within their bodies and drew him to her to share her happiness. She wondered if he knew her thoughts, if he knew that here, beneath the tree, Elva Roberts's quilts rising above them like starlit sails, he was all the land she knew or needed.

From Elva, Sarah learned to cook. "You've a hand for it," the older woman said, "and no butter and egg notions to get over, either."

If Sarah *had* had butter and egg notions, she would have been hard pressed to cook anything at all, for here cows and hens did not exist and flour was as dear as gold dust. Instead there were oysters and mullet pulled from the bay, corn and sweet potatoes bought on the streets, turkey, antelope, and buffalo brought in from the prairie. And there was the inevitable settlers' staple, dried venison sopped in honey. The sweet taste of honey soon became intolerable to Sarah and she experimented by adding vinegar and wild spring onions to the fare, an innovation that proved so popular she and Elva sold it and tripled their profits.

One day as Creath was returning from the blacksmith's where he'd found work, he looked down the road and saw Elva's canopy tent hanging in disarray. His heart jumped, fearing some misfortune had overtaken the women, and he began to run.

"I'm safe as a ring in a sailor's ear," Sarah assured him with a little laugh. "It's just that Elva's going. She's got enough money for the passage." Then, leaping ahead to catch his next thought, she added, "We can stay put a while yet, so long as the weather holds." She knew that Creath had scoured the port for lodgings, just as he'd scoured it for news of his brother, and neither were to be had.

But the large, branchy tree was lonely without Elva and her quilts and her children and Creath began to worry about leaving Sarah alone during the day. "Maybe we ought to go back," he said one evening.

Her eyes opened wide. "Back to Caney Fork? Have you forgotten about Arden? He might try to snatch me back from you, Creath."

"I don't think he could. It was a gambling bet, Sarah. There were witnesses."

But she shook her head and burrowed against him, her chin sharp against his chest. "No. This is our home now. We'll get land here if we just hold on."

She knew no more than he did about the complexities of getting land, but Creath felt oddly reassured by her words. He fell asleep with his hand tangled in her hair, thoughts of going back vanished from his mind forever.

The next day Sarah put their belongings in a safe hiding place and went exploring the port herself, looking for a place to live. The few rooming houses—crude, knocked-together affairs built above and beside saloons—had no room at any price.

"It's not just money I'm offering," she told the owner of a large, two-story cabin called the Baywater House. "I can cook. What your lodgers don't eat, we can sell for profit."

The man looked at her and dim recognition dawned in his eyes. "You're the one under the tree," he said. Sarah nodded. "You cook alligator? Man brought me a whole alligator this morning. You cook it up so it don't gag anyone, you got yourself a place to stay."

"Well, alligator meat, that'll be just fine," Sarah heard herself saying. It couldn't be much different from other meat, she reasoned. Meat was meat. You cooked it with honey and vinegar and whatever vegetables you could get hold of. She spent the rest of the day in the lean-to kitchen and got back to their tree to find Creath wild with panic. "Where were you?" he asked, worry lines creasing his forehead. His fair skin had scorched under the Texas sun and when she put her arms around his neck it was as hot as fire.

"I got us a place," she told him.

"A place to stay?" He let out a whoop of pleasure and hugged her, spinning her off the ground.

"It's just for a little while, Creath. We'll be living on our own place soon enough."

He didn't argue or remind her of the decree against colonization for he had begun, already, to trust her vision of the future as much as he trusted his own.

Chapter Four

Yellow Fawn came awake to the sound of hooves, her heart filled with expectancy because it was rumored again that Chase was coming. One small detail rose in her mind. A deerskin shirt she'd been working on as a surprise for him was not finished and she should rise and put it away before he chanced to see it. Instead she turned in half sleep, her black hair wrapping her like silk, the thought of the shirt swept aside by the memory and the anticipation of the man himself.

But a moment later her pulse quickened in alarm. The hooves were menacing and insistent and, above their din, cries filled the air. For a moment she held herself still in the murky light, straining to recognize voices. Then she bolted from her sleeping pallet, grabbed a knee-length tunic, and jerked it over her head. She didn't bother with a skirt, for already the smell of smoke hung thick in the morning air.

Yellow Fawn was not a tall woman nor was she particularly athletic, but life had removed any trace of fear from her nature. She raced from her cabin, legs elastic beneath her garment, feet bare and hard against the ground.

Outside all was confusion. Half-clad men and women poured from their lodges, children and dogs clamoring at their heels. The corn and bean fields bordering the eastern edge of the village had been set on fire along with many of the lodges, and flames leaping from rooftop to rooftop gave a strange luster to the dawn. The furious bellowing of a bull filled the air then collapsed in a wet gasp as the animal's throat was cut.

Yellow Fawn watched in horror as a rider swooped down on a running child, snatched it by the shoulders, and rode

off with it slung before him like a sack of flour. As the rider
flashed by, Yellow Fawn saw his face, painted ghostly
white with a grotesque vermilion ring circling his mouth.
These were the ones Chase had told her about, she realized;
the ones who lived to the west and made no permanent
camps.

The startled Cherokee were now beginning to group
against the attack and Yellow Fawn glimpsed her uncle,
Spotted Turtle, grasping his gun. But the raiders were too
fast and too formidable to defend against, for the fleetness
of their ponies, the smoke that clouded the air, and the
confusion they created afforded them almost supernatural
protection.

A clamor rose from the horse corral and now Yellow
Fawn's legs propelled her in that direction. Before she could
reach the animals they came streaming toward her, mounted
attackers driving them on. An ancient white mare, recogniz-
able to all in the village, lagged behind the herd and was
brutally dispatched. At this a cry burst from the throat of
Cattail, Spotted Turtle's wife. The horse was hers, a gift
from her husband. It had carried her faithfully over the years
and had seemed, to the old woman, to weep tears of human
sadness at leaving their home in the eastern mountains. Bent
on revenge the old woman ran forward with a fleshing knife
in her hand, slashing the thigh of the brave who'd killed her
horse.

The Indian showed no sign of pain but simply shifted on
his horse, caught the old woman's wrist, and kicked his
mount into a swift canter. With a snap, Cattail's arm was
wrenched from its socket. She staggered, feet slipping
beneath her, as the warrior grinned and tightened his
grip.

Recognizing the cry that burst from her aunt's throat,
Yellow Fawn searched through the confusion for her. Most
of the lodges were burning now and smoke curtained the air
like heavy fog. When at last she saw Cattail, the brave had
carried her almost beyond the edge of the village. Yellow
Fawn overtook them with surprising ease, realizing only as
she came abreast of the brave that he had deliberately
slowed his pace. Swiftly, he released Cattail and seized

Yellow Fawn instead, grabbing her arm just above the elbow.

Yellow Fawn felt herself lifted in a viselike grip. Her feet danced off the ground until she was looking at a face that was hard and fierce beneath streaks of black and yellow paint. A second later she was flung backward as the brave abruptly abandoned his plans to capture her.

Despite her lean legs and taut body, he saw she was not young. He could do better farther up the river, in the camps of the Tonkawa and Wichita. "*Puste!*" he hissed, which, in his tongue, meant *old woman*. Yellow Fawn was thirty-one.

Yellow Fawn spun through the air and struck the ground on her hands and knees. By the time she reached her aunt, Cattail's breath was jagged and sweat beaded her forehead. The dislocated shoulder jutted at an odd angle and Yellow Fawn probed beneath the old woman's cotton tunic, feeling with her fingers for the socket and the ball end of the bone. She'd set dislocations before and once, alone, had pushed her own thumb back into place.

"Shall I help you?" she asked, bending over the old woman. Cattail nodded and screwed her eyes shut. In one firm motion Yellow Fawn forced the bone to its socket, ignoring the halting gasps that escaped Cattail's drawn lips.

Cattail opened her eyes and Yellow Fawn, running her fingers over the top of the shoulder, nodded assurance. As the eyes of the two women met, something troubling passed between them. "Caddo?" the old woman asked, not truly believing that the neighbors who'd made way for them so peacefully would launch such an attack.

Yellow Fawn shook her head. "Comanche," she replied. Turning her head she glanced back at the village. Only now did she see her own lodge in flames. She pictured the inside as she had left it—the loom whose massive beams had taken more than a year to season, the half-finished deerskin shirt, the clothes and personal goods hung on pegs to hide the grayness of the walls. And, hidden deep at the bottom of a chest, the silver gorget that had been her husband's.

Rising, she pushed the memory of all these things from her mind because, for her, they existed no more.

Spotted Turtle was an old man who had lived many years in honor and made many decisions for his people. Now he sat alone, his shoulders hunched against the ever-present wind. For the first time in his long life, his people had no lodges. Their horses were gone and their cattle lay in slaughtered heaps. The very possessions necessary for civilization—inkwells, clothing, cooking utensils, tools, bedding, guns, books, medicines—all were gone, taken or despoiled by the Comanche. And seven young ones also, children whose laughter would not be heard again. Spotted Turtle had been surprised by this enemy sweeping out of the west and, because he'd been surprised, he felt he'd failed his people.

Late in the day the white man Chase arrived, bringing with him a trader named Findley Ware. Spotted Turtle was ashamed to have a stranger see his people in such a state and ordered a hasty lean-to to be built. There he welcomed the two men with as much dignity as possible, his niece Yellow Fawn going among them with the few refreshments that had been salvaged and his wife Cattail sitting to one side, her mouth closed in bitter silence.

Like many Cherokee, Spotted Turtle's family tree was whorled with white blood and he spoke fluent English. In a few vivid sentences, he described the savage warriors to Chase, concluding with a conviction his niece had expressed to him earlier: "Yellow Fawn thinks they were Comanche."

Hutchinson Chase had learned to sit quietly and now his only movement was to scratch the underside of his jaw with his thumb. His gray eyes, habitually narrowed from days in the sun and already showing fine lines at the corners, rested on the graceful form of Yellow Fawn. She was sitting with legs folded to one side, her profile in bright relief against her hair. It was a wonder, her hair, always worn straight and unbound, always blown by the wind and tumbled by his fingers, yet it never tangled. "Seems as she's right," Hutch said, returning his gaze to Spotted Turtle. "Comanche have been riding the blood trail all east of here."

Spotted Turtle nodded. Without seeming to observe, he noted the way the young man's eyes darted to Yellow Fawn at the mention of her name. She was the old chief's last living blood relative and in the smoke of the morning he had foreseen a day when he would no longer be able to protect her. But the tall and raw-boned white man who had come among them and learned their ways, the man they called *Chase* because its meaning fit him—he could protect her. Spotted Turtle saw now that he would do so, and the tightness in his chest eased.

Turning over his pipe, which Cattail had found among the smoldering ruins of their lodge, he tamped willowbark tobacco into the bowl. He lit it, drew, and handed it to the trader. "We cannot remain here," he commented almost casually, his eyes shifting from the trader to Chase.

"No," Hutch concurred. He knew the Comanche well enough to know that once they'd found fat quarry they would return again and again. Comanche saw no need to farm when others grew vegetables for them and the sad, unaccountable barrenness of their women would always send them out in search of children to capture. "Where will you go?"

A bitter smile crept over Spotted Turtle's face. "When first we saw the white man he came among us and said, 'This is a fine land and we will live on it, but where will you go?' We crept into a corner of our land, giving all else to the white man, and built again our homes and farms. Then the white man came among us again, saying, 'These are fine houses and fine farms and we will live in them and tend your fields, but where will you go?' Now we have come here, to a land promised to us, but find it too dangerous to live upon. And if the white men of the east were to know this, they would say, 'That is too bad, but where will you go?' "

There was a long pause as the pipe passed from hand to hand and Cattail grunted approval of her husband's words. Findley Ware, a short and robust man, felt eminently uncomfortable.

"We will go farther north," Spotted Turtle said at last. "There is more protection there. Perhaps we will learn to hunt buffalo or perhaps, in time, we will live like the Comanche themselves, moving with the wind.''

Spotted Turtle's eyes sagged with weariness and he passed his hand briefly over them. The Cherokee were not primitive people but one of the Five Civilized Tribes, with a written language and constitution. In the east they had lived in communities nearly indistinguishable from those of their white neighbors, operating farms, sawmills, smithys, and schools. When the whites had begun to clamor for their lands, he had urged his people to remove voluntarily, believing the promise of an Indian territory inviolate to white encroachment. In the space of a few years, he had seen his people slip from civilized prosperity into life in a harsh wilderness.

Hutch remained thoughtful. ''Do you have horses left?'' Spotted Turtle shook his head. ''Cattle?'' Again, the old man shook his head. ''I'll show you how to make dog travois tomorrow.''

Spotted Turtle chuckled softly. ''We have nothing to move, friend.'' Then, for the first time, he looked at the trader. ''And nothing to trade with, either.''

Disappointment flashed in Findley Ware's eyes, for he'd brought a cache of goods with him. Hutch turned to him, cutting him off before he could speak. ''I'll vouch for Spotted Turtle's people. Leave your goods now and work out a deal, so much extra next time you come. Sound fair enough?''

Findley Ware was uncertain. Indians had a slippery reputation in his book and the old squaw looked as mean as a buffalo cow ousted from her wallow. Nevertheless he had no longing to pack his goods back to Nacogdoches, and Hutchinson Chase's word was as good as any man's. He looked at Spotted Turtle. ''Fair enough,'' he said.

They left Spotted Turtle and Cattail by their fire and Findley Ware unfurled his bedroll beside his packs. Hutch slipped softly along beside Yellow Fawn. ''Chase,'' she said, her English simpler and less perfect than her uncle's, ''I have no more lodge.''

In the darkness it was her scent that reached him, warm and clean and slightly smoky. He put his hand out and stroked her hair. "I'll make us a *wikiyap* for tonight," he said.

"What's that?"

"Little house made of grass. You'll like it." His voice was soft in the darkness, as it often was, and she knew he was smiling.

She shifted closer to him. "No bed?"

"If you want."

"I do want," she answered, her hand venturing out to touch his. She had never been so bold with her Cherokee husband, but that had been long ago, when she was a young girl, and Chase had always encouraged her sudden caresses. Now he responded quickly in the darkness, folding his arms around her and burying his face in the clean-animal smell of her hair. It made her feel like a girl again and, mindful of the sorrowing village, it was all she could do to stifle the joy that welled in her throat.

Hutch stayed with Spotted Turtle's people for over a month and Findley Ware with him, for the trader could not find his way back to Nacogdoches alone. Despite Spotted Turtle's words, there was enough salvage to transport, and Hutch spent patient days showing the Cherokee how to make travois for the dogs. He loaded Yellow Fawn's goods himself, and her heart swelled to have a man again by her side.

What she had saved Hutch could not make out, for she packed and folded it out of his sight in hastily made containers. Only one thing he knew of, and that was a melted lump in silver unearthed from a chest whose charred timbers fell apart at her touch. She cradled it in her hands and pressed it to her cheek as if it were a living thing. Hutch knew she'd had a Cherokee husband once, a man named White Fox who'd been killed by the Creeks, but she never spoke of him and he knew only because Spotted Turtle had told him. When he saw Yellow Fawn caressing the melted silver he decided it must have been some gift from White Fox to her, an armband or brooch or buckle. It was then he decided on a gift of his own, though he didn't give it to her until the ruined camp lay far behind them.

The band moved north along the tributaries of the Red River into a sandy-soiled land thick with pine and white oak. Insects were thicker here and gnats and mosquitoes swarmed out of the still-water bayous in clouds, even at night when smudge fires were lit to keep them away. But the forests were thicker here too and that would protect the band from the Comanche, for those restless lords of the plains depended on the grassland avenues as routes of attack and escape.

Spotted Turtle's people found a home beside a nameless little stream which came, in time, to be called Cutfoot Creek. The stream's banks were a webwork of trees and vines, with maples and cypress rising from the clear slow waters and the occasional flicker of an alligator gliding in their camouflage. Spotted Turtle directed his village to be set well back from the stream, beneath the dense canopy of the forest.

Yellow Fawn loved to wake to the sight of that canopy, vaults of pine and white oak tangled with magnolia, beech, and holly. This was a better place than the site of the first village, she thought; it was closed and protected and reminded her of their lands in the east.

"See up there?" Hutch asked one morning, pointing to a squirrel that jumped from branch to branch above them, distinguishable by its truncated tail that stood up in a short, stiff plume. Yellow Fawn nodded, her head on his shoulder. "I nicked that squirrel's tail way back home. He came here over the treetops, didn't even touch the ground."

He glanced at her, his long gray eyes alight, and Yellow Fawn lifted herself on one elbow. "What about the big river?" she asked. "How could he get over?" She smiled as she settled back against him. "I don't believe you, Chase." But to her too it seemed as if the woods stretched in one unbroken band from the east, interrupted only by the Mississippi. From treetop to treetop, leaf trembling against leaf, she was connected to her home.

Hutch stayed with Yellow Fawn six weeks, longer than he ever had before, the days slipping by faster than he could count. He built a lodge for her, setting it up off the ground to guard against snakes and the damp, and from a loblolly pine he cut pieces for a new loom. With the other men he cleared field space which Yellow Fawn and the women planted with squash, corn, and beans. In time they would add tobacco and cotton as well.

Hutch and Yellow Fawn reached out to embrace the routine of these days. The simple fabric of life, difficult or mundane to others, was as rare as golden cloth to them. For the first time, Hutch fully grasped the solitary nature of her life without him and, as the seasons swung from late spring to summer, she sensed restlessness ripening in his bones.

"You're going soon?" she questioned one night.

Surprised, he caressed her lightly. "I been thinking on it. Thought maybe you might want me to stay, though."

Yellow Fawn was glad for the darkness that hid her face, for she could not keep her true thoughts from showing. Yet she would not tie him to her and said in a soft voice, "No. No, you go, Chase."

"I've got something for you," he said.

She watched the play of firelight on his back and longed to pull him back to her. It was always like this for her, the time before his leaving worse than the hours of stillness that followed.

He rummaged through his gear and came back with a burlap sack that he handed to her. Yellow Fawn slid the rough cloth back to expose what seemed to be a smaller, dimmer version of the sun, a polished copper cooking pot. Firelight gleamed along its curved sides and, holding it up, she saw her own face, long and large-eyed with prominent cheekbones and strong brows.

"I wanted to get you something better," Hutch said, remembering the melted silver she'd swept up from the ashes, "but this was the best Ware had with him. Next time I come from Nacogdoches—"

She stopped his words, touching her fingertips to his lips. "I like this, Chase," she said. "There is no need for anything better." And, putting her arms around him, she drew him back to her.

In Nacogdoches Findley Ware replenished his trade goods and bought an extra mule. From the Cherokee he'd learned the locations of several likely Caddo camps, and he was eager to expand his circle of trade. He'd just stood Hutch to a drink and was about to bring up the subject of another foray into the woods when the owner of the rough-hewn public house leaned across the counter to them. "Either of you named Chase?" he asked, having studied the trader and guide for several minutes.

"I am," Hutch answered, his hand automatically sliding toward the hilt of his knife.

The man held out a paper folded in thirds and addressed to *Hutchinson Chase, Guide on the Red River.* "This is for you, then," he said. Hutch reached for the paper, but the man pulled it back. "For two bits," he added. Hutch glared at him, for messages were customarily passed and carried through the wilderness without fee, but the man hung firm. "How else'll I know it's really you, 'less you're willing to pay?"

Hutch dug into his pocket and produced the two bits— wedge-shaped pieces of silver that had been cut, pie-fashion, from a single silver coin. Unfolding the paper, he read the brief message written a full two months earlier: *Hutch, I am in Galveston Bay and looking for you. Ask at the Baywater House for me. Creath, May 28, 1830.*

It was one of dozens of messages Creath had sent out with whoever chanced to be going into the wilderness. His first letters had been long and talkative, full of greetings and the news that Sarah was with him. But as he wrote message after message, Creath trimmed his sails and cut back to mere essentials.

Hutch studied the paper, refolded it and, grinning, tucked it into his shirt. "What say to another round, Findley?" he asked. "My treat."

The trader took the bottle and poured eagerly. The afternoon was flowing the way he wanted it to and he wasn't about to disturb things by asking what the paper had contained. Ware saw the future opening before him and began to understand the itch that kept men like Hutch Chase returning to the scattered settlements of the Red. For a moment he fancied a deep and close kinship between the two of them. "What say we go upriver again?" he asked.

But Hutch, having finished his drink, stood up. "Not me, Fin. I'm going south to see my brother."

"When will you be back?"

Hutch shrugged, unused to such questions. "See you next season maybe," he replied, then turned and left, his height momentarily blocking the doorway and snuffing out the daylight. Ware watched him go, at once envying and disliking a man who could slip so easily from one world into another.

Chapter Five

In July the slapped-together port of Galveston began to wither and wilt in the face of humid breezes blowing in from the ocean. Creath came home from the smith's shop each night soaked in sweat from standing at the hot forge, a white salt line ringing the collar and underarms of his shirt. His appetite waned and he grew thinner, almost as thin as his beanpole brother Hutch, he joked. Sarah urged him to stay in bed, saying she could work for both of them, but he continued to rise each morning before dawn and go to the forge. Blacksmiths were rare and in high demand, he told her, and he felt as if he were minting money instead of shoeing horses and banding wheels. Sarah escaped the heat of the lean-to kitchen by spending more and more time selling her wares in the streets. She soon became a familiar figure in the port town, her crinkly hair tied back with a strip of cloth, a basket of food in either hand. Even after she shared out the money with her employer and her suppliers there was a sizable sum left to add to the money Creath earned. This was true even after she diminished the money one more time by hiring a black woman named Nell Dawkins to tend the kitchen in her absence.

Nell was a runaway who'd fled the States when her husband was sold to a Mississippian who intended to start a cotton plantation on the banks of the Brazos, that unaccountably long river that ran through thirteen hundred miles of Indian-haunted wilderness to empty into the Gulf a day's ride south of Galveston Bay. Nell kept communications with her husband alive by word of mouth and stinted herself on food and lodgings, saving against the day when she could buy him away from the man she called Marse Downy. "Maybe then we go live 'mongst the Injuns," she told Sarah. "Injuns gen'lly like black folks."

Everyone in Galveston knew about Nell and from time to time some self-styled entrepreneur would hatch a scheme to return her to her owner in the States. But on closer examination the plan always proved more trouble than it might be worth and Nell was left unmolested to glean and beg such jobs as she could. She felt she'd found a treasure ship in Sarah, who looked the other way when she began to sleep, free of charge, in the shanty kitchen of Baywater House.

The arrangement might have gone on indefinitely if the House's owner, Sam Kendall, had not stumbled outside at 3 A.M. one night to vomit up the vile whiskey a Santa Fe trader had bestowed on him in exchange for lodgings. Nell was a towering woman, strong and solid as a man, and when she stretched in sleep her feet protruded past the open door of the shanty. Sam tripped over them in the darkness, realized the abuse of his good will, and sobered instantly. Burping righteous indignation, he threatened to take Nell back to Mississippi himself.

Sarah wakened to the raised voices of employer and employee, ran for the stairs, and arrived in time to put an end to the dispute by saying that if Nell went, she did too. Sam grew silent and, finally, placating, for he'd grown accustomed to sharing the revenue of Sarah's sales.

When Kendall left them alone, Nell turned to Sarah. "You sure did good by me, Missy," she said. "I won't forget it." Suddenly she laughed. "Marse Kendall, he sure gulp when you say you be gettin' out with me. He see all that money fly away from him and he 'bout choke!"

In the same way she'd taken to Elva Roberts, Sarah took to Nell, though the woman was something of a mystery to her. How Nell maintained her strength on the meager pickings she allowed herself was a marvel, almost a natural wonder. Nell was also a repository of physical and meta-physical lore, much of it helpful and just as much of it nonsense, and when Sarah awoke one stifling night and found Creath delirious and bathed in sweat beside her, Nell was the first person she turned to.

"Just the acclimatin'," Nell said, sponging Creath's forehead by the light of a tallow lamp.

"How long will it last?" In the flickering light Sarah's eyes were dilated with worry.

"Maybe a week. But it bound to come back again, better and worse, 'til the country does its work on him, gettin' him acclimated." Nell paused. "Summertimes is the sick times mostly. I shake and sweat three seasons 'fore I get healthy."

"Three *seasons*?" Sarah asked in astonishment, looking from her husband to Nell.

"This is a place what tests its folks. You likely get the fever too, Missy, but don't worry—since you such nice folks, you just get the light fever like this. The devil, he keep his worst for someone else. Tomorrow you lay hold of some calomel to dose him with."

Creath kept to his bed for several days and rose saying that hell could be no worse than having intermittent fever in Texas in July.

Sarah urged him to wait a few days before going back to the smith's shop. "You don't know what you're risking," she said gravely. "If anything happened to you, I'd—"

"You'd be fine," Creath said. He thought of her industry, her bustling thrift and the food she produced in the crude kitchen. "You'd be well fed, anyway. You could open an inn of your own with Nell."

Sarah replied with a soft snort of indignation. "Well fed isn't everything. I'd get to be another Elva Roberts, hard and bony." She came up and put her arms around him. "It's you that keeps me soft, don't you see?"

In the end he put her cautions aside, anxious to keep adding to their store of money. He kept a closer watch on Sarah's health than he did on his own, but as the days passed she seemed to grow stronger, not weaker.

Between bouts of fever Creath began to fill their room with farm things—broken augers and saws and bores bought cheap and mended by him at the smithy. It was a good distraction for both of them, hoarding up goods, for it kept their minds from the question of land. The prohibition against colonization, aimed at halting the flow of Americans into Texas, was still in effect. Word had gotten back to the States, slowing emigration so noticeably that the port was no longer the jumping-off place it had once been. But whenever Sarah opened her eyes in the morning and saw the curved blade of a scythe glinting in the sunlight that fell against the wall, she felt a rise of hope.

Then one day Creath chanced to fix the wheel rim of a settler who'd come down from Stephen Austin's colony complaining of the lack of workmen there. "Got lawyers to beat the band but not a smith or a wheeler in the lot. Feller like you'd be a welcome addition." Seeing that he'd caught Creath's attention, the older man looked appraisingly at him. "My name's Ogden. Jack Ogden. You lookin' to settle a piece of land?"

The metal rim was heated through and Creath reached for a pair of tongs to lift it with. Unbidden, Ogden found a second pair of tongs and helped him fit it over the wheel.

"I tried to settle," Creath replied, dousing water over the new-banded wheel to cool the hot metal, "but I got here after the decree."

Ogden cracked a grin. "Every law's got a loophole somewhere, and Austin's lawyers've already found him one. You take my advice and hurry on up to San Felipe 'fore the Mexicans find a way to stitch it shut again." Creath remained cautious, as he always was with strangers at the outset, but his heart was pumping eagerly and he wished Sarah were here with him.

"Married?" Ogden asked, and Creath nodded. "You and your wife list as stock raisers when you get there. Farmers only qualify for one *labor*, a hundred and seventy-seven acres of land. But if you list as a stock raiser, you can claim a whole *sitio*."

"How much is that?"

"Four, five thousand acres."

Creath felt a tingle at the back of his mouth, a tingle that until now he'd felt only in Sarah's arms. He thought of her again, thought of walking with her through knee-deep grasses that swirled past them to the horizon. The tire was cool and he began to heft the wheel up. Again he found Ogden willing to help him.

"You think on what I said," Ogden advised. "I can't keep runnin' down here ever' time I got a busted wheel."

Creath left the smithy shortly after Ogden's wagon rolled away. It was still day out and he kept his eye alive to any vehicle that might be a sound purchase. Four thousand acres, when at home he'd been brokenhearted over the loss of a hundred! Enough for all of them, once it had been broken, enough to tell those back on Caney Fork to come on west. But it was Sarah he wanted it for mostly. Ever since he'd fallen sick, a second fever had burned in him, a fever to get her away from these swampy lowlands. Light-footed, he climbed the stairs of the Baywater House two at a time.

Sarah whirled around when she heard him unlatch the door. "You're sick again," she said, eyebrows peaked in alarm.

But he swept her up in his arms, feeling in his mind the tug of grass around their knees. "We can get land in Austin's colony," he said. "Man told me about it today, man named Ogden." He paused, suddenly playful, and grinned. " 'Less you've decided you want to head back east instead. 'Less you've got like Elva Roberts in your thinking."

"Just in my cooking," Sarah answered, her eyes full of the russet glow that had first drawn him to her. Then she was out of his arms, rooting for the crockery jar that held their money. "How much is land?" she questioned.

"*Un medio*," he said. "One dollar to Austin for every eight acres. Here." He lifted the jar for her and emptied it onto the bed, a great splash of copper and silver topped by the few gold eagles that had been the first to go in. Heaped in a pile, it was more than either of them had thought. "We'll leave right away," Creath said. "Soon as I can buy a wagon and a team."

It was Sarah who sobered first. "We'll need a cow and a calf at least," she said. "And setting hens and seed corn and potatoes and house plunder."

"Well?"

"Well, you've time to pick out a good wagon."

Hutch hadn't been back to Galveston since he'd landed in an autumn storm three years ago. Then there had been only a bare spit of land, nothing at all like the teeming settlement that boasted the likes of Sam Kendall's Baywater House. As he approached the two-story log establishment his eye was caught by a woman, a girl really, the first white woman he'd stopped to look at in a long time, perhaps because she was looking at him.

"Hutch Chase?" she asked, shading her eyes against the sun as she approached. She set down a basket of food that appeared, to his eyes, heavier than she was. "You don't know me?"

He shook his head and, mindful of her old crush on him, Sarah felt a twinge of disappointment. *He never noticed me,* she realized with surprise, for she'd believed that even in her skinny, bare-kneed poverty he'd valued her in some secret way. She swept the bit of childish vanity aside and smiled. "I'd know you anywhere, Hutch. You and Creath are two alike. Come up with me and wait, he'll be home soon enough."

An hour later Sarah watched with amused surprise as Creath, her steady and protective Creath, turned into a pup at the sight of his older brother. The two danced into each other's arms and Creath, tall as a tree from her point of view, was lifted off the ground by Hutch. The two men brought out hidden facets in each other; she saw at once that it was ever to be so. For Hutch, Creath laid out not only his plans but also his fears, something he had never done for her alone.

"I'm thinking of hiring a man to ride to San Felipe with us," Creath said. "I hate to part with the money, but I keep thinking, what if the Indians catch us out alone, just me and Sarah?"

Hutch glanced toward the other side of the room, where Sarah was scraping food scraps into a basin. Once he'd heard the name Kincaid, he'd understood why she'd seemed familiar; he remembered her, albeit dimly, from his Caney Fork days. Half as old as Yellow Fawn, he thought, and

light as milkweed down. It took no effort at all to see why
his brother was concerned. Then he remembered the way
she'd approached him, calm and unhesitating, the heavy
basket of food carried, not pulled, over the ground. "Can
she shoot?" he asked.

"I can shoot," Sarah responded without turning around,
and Hutch laughed.

"I guess there's no reason I can't ride up to San Felipe
with you," Hutch said. "And out to your land until you get
settled. That makes three of us, and two of us Chases. I
reckon that'll do against any Indians you care to name."

Sarah turned in time to see relief wash across Creath's
face.

Nell knew of their going days before Sarah told her,
through magic, Nell insisted, although Sarah suspected it
was more likely through astute observation. Either way, the
element of surprise was on Nell's side when she cornered
Sarah in the shanty kitchen one afternoon and said, "You
got to help me 'fore you go, Missy. You been so good to
me, an' I might never meet no one like you again." Digging
in the bodice of her dress, she produced a rag-wrapped
hoard of money. "You got to get your man to buy my Jonah
away from Marse Downy. I try an' do it myself, he just
laugh an' switch me off his place."

Sarah looked at the money in her open palm. "Oh Nell,"
she said, "this isn't nearly enough."

"I know that, Missy. But you an' your man just add to it
a little, me an' Jonah come with you and help 'til it's
worked off. My Jonah, he's good and strong, not as strong
as me, maybe, but he'll put in a good day's work for you."
Nell looked at her unswervingly. "Please, Missy."

Sarah realized that she was caught at the center of a
carefully constructed plan, a plan the black woman had been
spinning for days, maybe weeks. "I doubt I *can* help you,
Nell," she answered. "Creath isn't one for slave-holding."

"I know that too, Missy. It ain't like he's buying a slave
hisself. He's just helpin' me get my Jonah back an' addin' a
bit extra to get a good worker. You put it to him that way
an' use a little woman-honey on him, he go along with us."
Sarah hesitated and Nell hammered the final nail. "You do

like I say, you have another woman for comp'ny. You leave me here, you likely be wishin' the other way when the first baby come 'long.''

Sarah nodded. "I'll ask him, Nell," she said, closing her fingers over the money.

It was easier than she'd expected to talk Creath into the plan, for although he had no special interest in freeing slaves, he had a deep and long-held dislike for slave owners. They were the ones who kept small landholders out of the competition, he believed, and he leaped at a chance to steal a march on one of them. Hutch went with him, to give him lessons in narrow-eyed dickering, he said. They returned three days later with Jonah, a light-skinned mulatto who was taller than either of them.

"I sure thank you," Nell said after she'd hugged her husband and found him still sound.

Creath pulled a piece of paper from his pocket. "It's written down right here, how much extra I put in and how long it'll take to work off."

"No need worry 'bout that. Me an' Jonah, we work our hardest for you, Marse Chase."

Creath frowned. "Don't call me Marse."

But Sarah slipped up beside him. "She calls all white men Marse," she explained. "Leave her be."

The grant given to Stephen Austin by the Mexican government put him in control of some thirteen million acres of land. It was a vast and challenging wilderness, bordered by the Gulf on the south, the La Vaca River on the west, and the tributaries of the San Jacinto River on the east. Its northern limit was El Camino Real, the ancient Spanish road that connected Mexico City and Saltillo in the south with San Antonio de Bexar and Nacogdoches in the north.

The original inhabitants of the land were Indians, alligators, and moving clouds of insects, forces that had combined to defeat all previous attempts at colonization. But Austin's grant also included two important rivers, the Colorado and the Brazos de Dios, whose rich bottomlands held infinite appeal for men like Creath Chase, especially when sold at one-tenth the price of land in the States.

Austin's Americans were a tough and rigorous breed, not about to be run off by Kronks, as they called the warlike Karankawas. As a people they were mostly southern, mostly literate, mostly Anglo-Celt; they loved freedom and did not mind purchasing it with hard work. Any family who did not meet these requirements was quickly weeded out, for Austin's agreement was to settle the land with people who would take root, creating a buffer between the Mexican settlements and the Indians.

Other *empressarios* had received grants as well—DeWitt and De Leon to the west, Burnett and Vehlin to the north and east—but none had succeeded so well as Austin. By 1830 he'd settled more than one thousand families, acting as their guide, lawyer, partner, and parent, and when he saw the Chase brothers standing before him, his eyes lighted. They were the same sort of rangy, energetic borderers who were already thriving on his land. Even the fragile-looking woman with them conveyed a kind of resilience.

"You're claiming as stock raisers, both of you?" he questioned. "The full amount?" He was a fine-boned man, dark and slight and unmarried despite his thirty-seven years.

"Not me," Hutch said quickly. "I've just come to help my brother set up."

Austin felt a flicker of disappointment, then wiped it away as he turned to Creath. "You then, a full *sitio*?"

"I've not enough to pay for that much," Creath said. "But if I could add to it later . . ."

Austin smiled diplomatically. "I've never turned an honest man away for lack of money. If you've a serious mind to settle, we'll work something out."

Creath frowned. He didn't like the idea of owing. You bought something outright and it was yours, but if you didn't buy it outright its status was confusing. Because Jonah owed him, Jonah's freedom wasn't completely his own. Creath resisted the idea of putting himself in a similar position with Austin.

It was Sarah who settled the matter by saying, "We'd be obliged for the consideration." A look of understanding passed from Sarah's eye to Austin's. He was no mere land seller, she saw, but someone with a vision. "You won't be sorry."

Once outside Creath turned to her. "Why'd you do that? It'll take the rest of our lives to pay off that land."

"I can't think of a better way to spend the next fifty years. Can you?" She smiled impudently, her hair whipping around her face in the steady wind. Then she drew near and looped her arm through his. "Oh, Creath, don't worry so. This is what we're here for, isn't it?"

"Yes. Yes, I guess it is." He dropped his voice below anyone else's hearing and smiled. "That and a few other things."

She looked up in surprise, taken aback by his boldness. Then she began to laugh, putting one hand over her mouth when Hutch turned to give them a puzzled glance. Her other hand, with a life of its own, brushed against Creath's thigh.

The lands Austin portioned them were along the Brazos, the river whose full name meant arms of God. To reach them the party had to travel south from San Patricio, retracing much of the road they had just traveled. It was deep summer, the air so thick with blister flies and mosquitoes and sand gnats that it was almost impossible to sleep at night. Sarah spun thread from the fur of the rabbits the men shot for food.

"I never knew you could get thread off a rabbit," Creath said, watching her.

"You never knew what poor was, then," Sarah replied without interrupting her spinning. "When you build me a loom, I'll weave us mosquito barring."

Hutch looked on, Sarah's mention of a loom reminding him of the one he'd built for Yellow Fawn. It would be time for him to go back soon, for he missed the woman and his life along the Red; it made him chafe some, knowing he was moving through a patch of land so hellbent on civilizing itself.

The drop spindle, suspended from a length of thread, turned as Sarah pulled and pinched the fibers of rabbit fur. He watched the hypnotic turning of the spindle and the play of firelight over her face. She was different from Yellow Fawn, as different as a dewdrop from a dusky bayou, but they both had a way of holding a man. Creath had never spoken of his feelings for her, but he had no need to; Hutch could see for himself how his brother felt about Sarah.

Suddenly the sound of raised voices broke through the wilderness. "They're at it again," Hutch said, bemusement turning up the corners of his mouth. Nell and Jonah, devoted lovers apart, could not keep the peace in reunion. Their camp, always at a distance from the Chases, rocked with spirited discourse almost every night. "Guess they've got a lot to talk over," Hutch had once observed, bringing a peal of laughter from Sarah.

Creath was more inclined to resent the intrusion on his domestic tranquility. "They crabble and crack more than a river full of alligators," he said.

"It's just their way," Sarah put in calmly and, forestalling any plans to jettison the pair, added, "I'd be lost without Nell."

Indeed I would, she thought. Besides the vast quantities of work performed by the couple, Nell had dosed Sarah with some plant whose grindings, she swore, would keep her free of child. Sarah tried it, found it didn't make her too sick, and kept taking it. She didn't want a baby now, with so much work to do and nothing put by. Hutch would leave before autumn and though the higher ground seemed to have cured Creath's fevers, there was no being certain. Sarah might have to slip into Creath's yoke as well as her own, and she couldn't do it with a rounded belly.

But it was something more than this that kept her from wanting a child, she realized, something she didn't like to think of outright. It was the fact that she was still married to Arden Bell. All these months she had lived with Creath she had done so without a nod from church or state. Not that she was religious: guilt was not her problem. But what if her children were found out as bastards and what if, because of it, all their lands and holdings were taken from them? She'd heard the story in her own family, set in another time and place, but it seemed the kind of story that was likely to repeat itself. She frowned slightly as she spun on, wondering how to seal her children's birthright for them.

* * *

They lived at first in a half-faced camp, a crude, three-walled structure whose open side Sarah covered with mosquito barring. Here she and Creath slept at night, listening sometimes to the screech of owls and sometimes to the screech of Nell and Jonah in the clearing beyond. Hutch slept outside, to guard the horses he said, but also because he valued solitude. He was different from his brother, Sarah had come to see; quieter and not nearly as easy to read. Sometimes she felt as if she were watching him through a pane of glass, as if he moved and thought and spoke in a world separate from their own. His heart isn't with us, she often thought with a twinge of sadness.

"I reckon Hutch has a woman somewhere," she told Creath one night.

His surprise came to her through the darkness. "Did he say something?"

She shook her head. "He said nothing. But words aren't everything, especially to him."

Creath couldn't imagine his footloose brother trailing a woman's love behind him, but if Sarah sensed it, it might well be so. She had an uncanny knack of sensing things, a knack he was rapidly coming to rely on. One night soon after their arrival, before the loom was built or mosquito bars woven, he'd suggested sleeping on the riverbank, where the breeze would blow off the insects. But Sarah had tossed and turned beside him and at last pestered him into moving away from the water. Looking back, he'd seen the gleam of alligator eyes behind them.

Another time Sarah had been pounding hominy when she paused, looked at him, and smiled. "We've neighbors now," she said.

"What tells you?"

"I just feel it. Things feel different." Not many days after, a man named Robey came riding through the woods to tell them he and his family had settled not far off. So if Sarah insisted that Hutch had a woman, it was likely so. Creath stroked her hair in the moonlight.

"I hope he stays a while yet, woman or no," he said, and Sarah nodded. Hutch might not have the massive physical strength Creath had, for he had never built his muscles at a smith's forge, but he had just as much persistence and an even broader knowledge of the land. Often he would disappear at night, going off alone to hunt and bringing back deer, turkey, and a bear whose hide Sarah had taken charge of for a rug. He even turned his hand to homesteading, helping Creath and Jonah clear a garden plot and, now that that was done, burn over the cane breaks along the river bottoms.

While the men worked in the bottoms, Sarah and Nell started the garden. It rained after the first day's planting, a heavy rain that turned the freshly cleared earth to waxy mud. When Sarah's shoes became mired she took them off, tucked up her skirt, and kept working, not minding at all the warm ooze that sucked at her feet.

"Best keep those shoes on, Missy," Nell said. "This is snake country, so Jonah say."

Sarah straightened up. "Not where it's clear here, Nell." She looked at the shoes, set atop a tree stump for safe keeping. Creath had bought them for her in Galveston when her old pair wore out, paying three times what he would have in the States. "They're the only pair I have and I can't ruin them."

But Jonah had told Nell stories of immense snakes rising up in the unlikeliest places. "You hear a hiss," she said, "you step back quick."

Sarah worked on, interrupting her row only when a stump stood in her path. She disliked a garden pocked with stumps and one day she would see them all pulled out, she thought. Thick mud was drying on her hoe and she swung it against a stump to shake it loose.

Something danced over her foot and Sarah looked down. The tap of her hoe had knocked scorpions loose from their nesting place under the bark. One of them writhed on the top of her foot. It was a female, carrying translucent hatchlings on her back. Repulsed and terrified, Sarah raised her foot to shake it off. In a flash she saw the tail straighten and whip forward. The sting she never felt at all.

Creath's eyes were as fever-bright as Sarah's and he wouldn't leave her side. He'd been the first one up to the camp in response to Nell's howl, and that had been two days ago.

"You take yourself off while I sponge her fever down," Nell said gently. But Creath took the bucket and rag from her himself and pushed her out of the open-faced shack.

This was what he'd feared most for Sarah, that she'd burn up and away from him like a comet, filling him with light only to leave him in darkness. "You can't go now, Sarah," he whispered hoarsely. "You've got to stay by me."

Outside, Hutch and Nell heard him talking. "He 'bout to lose his mind," Nell commented sadly. It was one of the rare times in her life when she felt truly helpless. She'd done her best by Sarah, had nicked open the puncture with her thumbnail, sucked and spat, sucked and spat until the foot had bloated in her hands and she'd screamed for the men to come. "Ain't there more we can do? Hearing him talk to her like that, an' her not even hearin' . . . ."

Her voice trailed off as Hutch made no response. He'd seen Yellow Fawn's people chanting over their near dead, and chanting seemed to pull them through about as often as anything else. Who was to say? he thought. All of life was a mystery sometimes, his own brother, whispering in a shanty at the edge of the wilderness, was the biggest mystery of all.

Sarah's body, in spite of the swelling, looked startlingly fragile and her skin was glazed with sweat. She was delirious, Creath knew, and past hearing what he said. But he talked on, his words disappearing into the night like pebbles sinking beneath the surface of a pond.

Through the walls of her fever Sarah grabbed at his words, clutching at them as they drifted down to her. But always they floated just beyond her comprehension, her effort to capture them unbalancing her, sending her spinning and adrift.

At first she thought she was on the *Talent* again, sailing toward Galveston Bay. She was seasick, she was going to vomit, she was in a storm watching their crates being thrown overboard. But even the sun-blazed deck of the *Talent* hadn't tortured her like this. There must be some other source of heat, some other . . . ah, she remembered it now, a searing pain that cut along her jaw. Ruined eggs and a hand snatching her up. *Sarah Bell. You are Sarah Bell, married still. If 'ee fail to please him, Saree, don't think 'ee can come home again.*

You can't go, Sarah. Creath's words came to her again. Far away and indistinct they still were, but now she could detect their sound and shape, and their meaning became as clear in her mind as in his own. Cool water was caressing her, sluicing over her body the way the waters of Caney Fork sluiced over their rapids. She felt a great millstone turn, its reverberations pulsing through her.

Be easy, she wanted to tell him. *Be certain I won't leave.* She opened her mouth to speak but found herself too weak to do more than gasp.

"Sarah?" he questioned. Her eyes, sunken and circled, did not drift away but held his gaze. He touched the back of his hand to her forehead and found it cooler.

She tried to speak again, gave up, and settled for a thin smile. But she must have made herself clear for he lay down beside her, taking her in his arms and murmuring "Ssh, ssh now." He stroked her hair away from her forehead with his fingertips and soon—no, it was not her imagining—she felt dampness where his cheek rested.

A great and overwhelming tenderness filled Sarah, a river of tenderness that would roll down the years, flowing through her long after the fever that had channeled its path disappeared. "Creath," she said softly. But his fingers had stopped moving and he was asleep against her, the world made whole again.

Chapter Six

As Hutch crossed and recrossed Texas in the early 1830s he saw changes alter the face of the land. Mere shadows they were at first, chasing themselves along the horizon, but he

saw, long before anyone else, that the wild and empty land
he'd come to in 1827 was about to disappear forever.

Despite the ban on immigration, Americans continued to
flow into the country, latecomers who had no legal status, no
chance of securing land, and not the least desire to return to
the States. From this pool came restless adventurers like
Sam Houston and Buck Travis, men who would take a hand
in the future of things. And from this pool too came Ripley
Paxton, the young Tennesseean who traveled with Hutch
during the winter of 1831.

The day they met would long be vivid in Hutch's mind.
He'd come up from the Brazos in September, his hands
blistered from having helped Creath and Jonah build a new
cabin, the second in as many years. The new cabin was a
twenty-foot square with front and back doors, bars across
the doorsills to keep the hogs and chickens out. Creath had
set it on a rise of land to catch the breeze and Sarah had dug
and hauled wild peach trees to plant on either side of the
door. The first year's cabin, half as large in size and set too
far in the lowlands, went to Nell and Jonah while the
half-faced shack became Creath's smithy. "We're a proper
plantation," Sarah had said, lifting her skirt with one hand
as she crossed the high-barred threshold, her eyes bright as
autumn leaves.

The fever of a year before had polished her from the
inside out, Hutch thought, while the bond between her and
Creath seemed stronger each time he came back to them.
Their contentment shed a light of its own, touching the
ladles and noggins, the graters and needles and harnesses
and commonplace things of life with warmth. Now when
Hutch rode away, he always had the sense that he was
leaving something of importance behind.

That same sense of sadness invaded him at Nacogdoches
that year, for the town had changed, like a friend gone away
and come back again with different clothes and a different
outlook on life. The place was awash in soldiers, toughs
recruited from the lowest ranks of Mexican society and
shipped north to the frontier. They swaggered through the
streets, bullies on a holiday with bayonets atilt, arresting
anyone who chanced to look at them crosswise. Hutch kept

his distance and took refuge in the public house, where his sentiments were roused by a young Tennesseean vociferously lamenting the military presence. The Tennesseean's complaint centered around the waste of a prime horse, one he'd arranged to buy from an Indian named Teal Duck.

"D'you know, afore we could make the swap some damned Mescan soldier shot Teal Duck dead? The Indians, they sent my horse into the hereafter with him. Ruin of a damned good horse, far's I can see. Mescan army's half outlaw, half idiot. If they hadn't a shot old Teal Duck, I'd be a fine-mounted man today." The Tennesseean raked his hand through his curly dark hair and, looking up, chanced to see Hutch's sympathetic grin. "Howdy, name's Rip Paxton. Rest yourself." With one foot, he pushed out a chair for Hutch to sit on.

Paxton's family, Hutch learned, had come into Texas early that summer, led by the rumor that land was being granted to latecomers. With a knot of other settlers they'd formed a town called Liberty, only to have the town officially abolished and the district put under military rule. Disgusted by the dictatorial bent of the Mexicans, Paxton had broken off from his father and brothers to roam Texas on his own.

"Damned Mescan soldiers everywhere," Rip protested. "Goliad, Velasco, San Antonio—everywhere I've been, there's been a mess of soldiers to keep me company."

Hutch rocked back in his chair. "Well, you won't have to worry about them for long."

"Why not?"

"Talkin' the way you are, you're bound to get yourself shot sooner than not."

Rip didn't get himself shot but put in with Hutch for a winter of trade along the Red. Hutch congratulated himself on this turn of events, figuring he'd not only found a partner he liked but also had saved a life in the bargain.

In recent years a road, the Trammels Trace, had been blazed north from Nacogdoches to accommodate the increased traffic of the area. In addition to the Indians, whites had begun to trickle into the country, pocketing themselves along wooded streams and open parklands. That winter Hutch ventured farther west than he ever had before, finding

settlements in places that had been unmapped only a few
years ago. At the season's end the two men worked their
way back south and east, along a necklace of rivers and
villages that led them, in the middle of a howling storm, to
Cutfoot Creek and Spotted Turtle's village.

Yellow Fawn had counted the days, gouging them on a
stick with her knife, waiting for him to come that year. She
had not seen him since early summer and her longing had
ripened like a living thing within her.

The first sign of trouble had come with the Mexican
soldiers, riding into the camp in midsummer with gifts of
silver. These were not the bullies Hutch had seen on the
streets of Nacogdoches but officers, men of rank and refine-
ment who could trace their ancestry back to Spain. They
had approached the Cherokee ceremoniously, presenting
Spotted Turtle with a silver-chased pipe to mark their new
era of friendship and giving to the other men gorgets,
earrings, and *conchos*, half-domed silver disks that found
their way onto the clothes of men and women alike.

Yellow Fawn had burned with curiosity to know what
their mission was and what they were discussing with
Spotted Turtle and the others under the brush arbor at the
edge of the village. That her uncle would use wise judgment
she had no doubt, but since the Comanche had ridden
against them a new force had risen in the tribe to challenge
him.

At the head of this group was Walking Bird, a fierce and
resolute brave popular because of his boldness and willing-
ness to lead. He had implied, if not openly stated, that
Spotted Turtle's decisions could no longer be relied upon,
for why else were they living here, cut off from their lands
and people, cut off from the mountains that were the source
of their power?

Even Yellow Fawn had to admit that Spotted Turtle had
not truly been himself since the morning the Comanche
attacked their old village. He was quieter, more withdrawn,
as if some spark had gone out within him.

That Walking Bird and his faction sat with Spotted Turtle
and the Mexican officers gave Yellow Fawn cause for

apprehension. At any other time she might have been privy
to the council, for when she helped Cattail and the other
women serve, it was not difficult to eavesdrop, to sense
moods and tensions. But that summer she was pregnant, a
fact that had manifested itself to her with much surprise,
and she had not been asked to serve. Her stomach rounded
before her like the rising moon and Yellow Fawn could do
nothing but wait. When the soldiers left, and neither Spotted
Turtle nor Walking Bird revealed what had been discussed,
Yellow Fawn's anxiety grew.

The soldiers returned two more times that summer, focus-
ing their attention on Walking Bird, presenting him with
such splendid gifts that his status seemed almost to rival that
of Spotted Turtle's. That was when she sensed the leadership
of the tribe was shifting, passing from the hands of Spotted
Turtle into the control of Walking Bird and his group. The
thought made her shiver despite the heat and she laid her
hand across her stomach. If Spotted Turtle were no longer to
lead them. . . .

Finally, from Walking Bird's wife, Sweet Meadow Grass,
Yellow Fawn learned all she was to know of the matter.
Spotted Turtle was silent on the matter, a silence that was
rapidly becoming characteristic of him.

"The soldiers want our trade only," Sweet Meadow
Grass assured her. "And they have promised that no more
whites will come into the land."

But the very word *promise* worried Yellow Fawn, for
promises were never kept and the short period of their
duration was bound to be purchased at high and irredeem-
able cost. Although not alone in this presentiment, she was
part of a small but powerful minority, a minority that
included Spotted Turtle, Gray Coat, and other remnants of
the old leadership. Others meanwhile, Walking Bird and his
friends, welcomed trade with the Mexicans, feeling they
had at last found an ally against the powerful whites. There
was even talk of relocating south, to some point more
accessible and amenable to trade.

And so, with tensions growing in the village, Yellow
Fawn had counted days on a stick, waiting for Chase's
return and for the birth of his child.

It was the birth that came first, a wrenching experience that passed her from one portal of being into another, that at once elevated her and reduced her to a crouching animal, chewing willowbark to ease the pain and pulling on the hands of Cattail and Sweet Meadow Grass as if she were a child herself.

Her thoughts were interrupted as the baby cried and she rose to still it. When Chase came this time, he would come to both of them; and when he left he would leave both of them. That would change things too, she thought.

It wasn't Hutch but Rip Paxton who eased tensions in the village for a time. Hutch, whom they always referred to simply as Chase, had been coming among them for four years now. In that time he had taken up their ways and earned their respect as few white men ever had. But he had not captured their imagination; he was too much like them to stand apart.

Rip Paxton, a year younger than Hutch, short and wiry, full of Tennessee talk and daring, burst among them with the effect of a traveling circus. He pitted himself against young men in contests of strength, gambled and lost generously, and filled the nights with tales of exploits whose fantastic proportions in no way diminished their value. He even boasted of knowing Sam Houston, that enigmatic figure who had lived with the Cherokee in the east and earned the name Raven. Houston had recently come to Texas, Paxton told them, though they believed this no more than they believed his other claims.

It was a winter season like none they had yet seen, with driving storms that crowded one upon the other. In Yellow Fawn's lodge, wrapped in wind and rain, Hutch congratulated himself again on having taken Rip on, for Rip could make his own way among the Cherokee, leaving him free to play with his infant daughter.

Her fingernails gleamed like tiny seashells in his hand.

Her cries were full of meaning.

Her eyes were as gray as quartz, starred with black pupils that drank in the world with comprehending gaze.

The first time he saw her, he counted backward in his

mind to the last time he'd been in the village. "Why didn't you tell me then? You must have known and I could have stayed to be with you."

But Yellow Fawn shook her head. "Cattail and Sweet Meadow Grass were with me. And Chase, I didn't know then, truly. I thought I was just at the age where things begin to change, where the moon time disappears, then comes back again. After all these years . . . I didn't know until Cattail asked me questions. Embarrassing, like a young girl."

"And when you knew?"

She brought her hands together, fingers curled in fists, a gesture she often had when explaining herself. "I was so angry, Chase. I felt tricked . . . do you understand? I should be feasting at a daughter's wedding now or living in a son's lodge. I'm thirty-four summers, after all."

Hutch studied her face, a smooth oval that showed no trace of the anger she described, only tenderness and a slightly rueful smile. "Such a great age," he teased. Then, growing serious, he asked, "Still mad about the way things worked out?"

Yellow Fawn shook her head, looking as young as a girl. "No. All my feelings," she uncurled her fingers suddenly, "changed. Another trick, I think."

Hutch touched the baby's cheek. "Lodgesmoke," he said. It was a long and tangled road that brought a man from Caney Fork, Tennessee, to a place in life where he had a black-haired daughter named Lodgesmoke. "Why'd you settle on that name?"

Yellow Fawn came up behind him. "Her eyes." She scooped up the baby. "They're the same color as yours. Like smoke rising from a lodge."

A week later two Mexican officers rode into the village, putting an end to the relaxed mood that had reigned since the arrival of Hutch and Rip Paxton. From Yellow Fawn Hutch learned all that had happened during the summer and observed, with dismay, the struggle for leadership that was taking place between Spotted Turtle and Walking Bird. The officers had come again to press for the tribe's relocation to a more convenient site near Nacogdoches. Walking Bird was in favor of the move, but Spotted Turtle and Gray Coat, his old friend from childhood, successfully argued against it.

When the Mexicans had gone, Hutch sat alone to smoke with Spotted Turtle. He saw the look of sadness on the chief's face and, for the first time, the shadow of doubt.

"I do not trust the Mexicans," Spotted Turtle said, using his old pipe rather than the elaborate one given him by the officers, "and I do not think it is good to move. But when I look at my people, can I say I have done well?"

Hutch didn't reply. In the east the Cherokee had owned spinning wheels and sawmills, farms and fields. They had lived in an organized and prosperous way. But in the few years of their exile, Spotted Turtle had seen his people slip into disarray. The quarreling for leadership was one mark of it, but there were other marks as well. Young ones no longer learned the written language, cotton clothes grew faded, threadbare, and ragged, and were replaced with roughly fashioned buckskin. The women's looms sat idle because cotton and sheep did not prosper in the thick forests and there was nothing to weave. Separated from their people and their land, Spotted Turtle's Cherokee lost the essence of their power.

Yellow Fawn was infinitely concerned about what was taking place in the inner circle of the tribe, a concern Hutch noted with some surprise. Never before had she voiced alarm about the future but drifted, calm as a leaf on the water, certain she could endure any fluctuation of the current. Now Lodgesmoke had knit her to the future and she was alarmed at the rising influence of Walking Bird.

"When the Mexican officers tell Walking Bird they will defend us against the whites, he believes them. I do not trust the Mexicans any more than I trust your people, Chase." Hutch tried to set her mind at rest but she continued in her brooding worry. "We have lived in this land seven years," she said. "Why have they come to us this year and never before?"

"They've come everywhere this year," he said. "All over Texas. Makin' themselves about as popular as ticks in a dog's ear. Folks're getting mad enough to fight back, Rip says."

Yellow Fawn saw it then in a flash of illumination: the Mexicans needed them as allies. That was why their officers had come courting Spotted Turtle and Walking Bird. Perhaps her uncle saw that; Walking Bird, she was certain, did not.

Yellow Fawn turned to Hutch forcefully. "If the village divides in two factions, I will stay with my uncle. Always look for me where he is."

"I been thinking about that," Hutch said. "I been thinking to take you with me this time, you and Lodgesmoke."

For a moment Yellow Fawn allowed herself to drift along with the thought. *To have a man, never to worry . . .* It was like standing on a mountain and breathing in the scent of damp spring blossoms. Then she shook her head. "No. No, Chase, we will stay here." He was hurt, she saw, and it came to her with a jolt how young he was. She stretched out her hand and stroked his cheek as if he were a child. "We will stay here, where we can make a home for you."

"But Lodgesmoke . . . she's part . . . part of my people too."

"And would we live with your people? With your brother perhaps, and his wife? Or would we follow you along the trail? No, Chase. It is better for Lodgesmoke to have one people than no people at all."

After that winter, Cutfoot Creek became a nearer and sweeter place to Hutch. He returned to Spotted Turtle's village more often and stayed longer each time, making such frequent and extended trips that his partnership with Rip Paxton wore thin over it. They parted with no hard feelings, Rip restless and eager and saying, as he left, that he had half a mind to explore the Rio Grande trade, that commerce of mustangs, tobacco, and other contraband that flowed back and forth across the brave river of the south.

That year Hutch appeared along the Brazos only twice, the existence of Yellow Fawn and his daughter still a close-held secret, even from Sarah, who grew more and more convinced that, openhanded though Hutch might seem, his heart beat on a wilder shore.

Chapter Seven

Nacogdoches was not the only town awash in Mexican soldiers. As Rip Paxton had seen for himself, the country bristled with garrisons. It was all part of Mexico's belated, unsuccessful, and unpopular attempt to stamp its own character upon the singularly Anglo frontier.

The Mexican officers, refined and wellborn, saw it as their duty to impose order where there was none and to exact a measure of gratitude from the Anglos sprawling across their land. The garrisons' influence rippled outward, to little settlements like Victoria, San Patricio, and Refugio, to Bastrop in the north and Columbia in the south. It reached into the heart of the *empressario*'s colonies, touching the lives of people like Creath and Sarah and gathering the scattered colonists together in tough knots of resistance.

The summer Lodgesmoke was learning to walk in the north, the half-settled bottomlands of the Brazos River, where Creath and Sarah lived, were in an uproar. The Mexican government had placed vast tracts of coastal lands under martial law; local governments had been abolished and citizens thrown in jail to await, sometimes for months on end, the bringing of formal charges. News of these outrages was carried through the colonies by riders who whipped up feelings of resentment against the Mexicans as effectively as Paul Revere had whipped up feelings against the British.

"It's that durned Colonel Bradburn. Worst spawn ever turned outta the States and that's a fact."

"Who'd a thought a Kentucky feller could turn so dead set 'gainst his own kind? Born with a Mescan heart he was, say his ma called him little pepper belly right from the start.

"An' now he's colonel over us. Boils my blood right smart to think on't."

Sarah heard the voices as she passed the blacksmith's shed, voices she identified as belonging to Amos and Lem Robey, Tom Driscoll, and their other neighbors. She did not hear Creath's voice, for he was always the last to speak in such matters and she passed out of earshot too soon. She smiled to herself as she moved along, a water bucket in either hand and her step sure and firm. The men would rage and talk and hammer out their views in quick, hot spurts, but they would feel unfinished until Creath had spoken his mind to them.

His blacksmith shed, the half-faced camp they'd first lived in, had become a gathering point for the men of the neighborhood and Creath had become their spokesman. His skill was in high demand, just as Jack Ogden had once predicted, and as season followed season, the planting, growing, and harvesting of cotton, their cash crop, fell more and more to Sarah, Nell, and Jonah. Difficult and back-breaking work it was, but Sarah didn't mind: she knew Creath hated cotton. To him it was a rich man's crop, a crop that spelled slaves and slaveholders, large growers against small, all the things he'd disliked about the east. It was a helpless child of a crop that needed constant attention from human hands, and that was how Sarah took it on, for in her days as a Kincaid she'd cleaned and fed and toted many a young brother and sister.

In the two years they'd lived here changes had taken place faster than at the creation. Lowland forests had been converted into fields, other families had come, and the place had acquired a name of sorts: Chase's Clearing, a broad region that stretched across the Brazos and extended miles in either direction. *Chase's Clearing.* It lifted Sarah's heart just to think the words.

"They'd have named it Fool's Clearing if a fella named Fool had been the first to take up land here," Creath pointed out, but Sarah didn't think so. She was sure it was because of him, because he drew men's confidence as surely as his blacksmithing drew their business. She'd seen it come about little by little, the way their neighbors listened to him, the way they looked to him for advice, the way they came to him with every scrap of news. Young as he was, Creath gave them a sense of sureness, for he didn't fret and toss at every gusting wind. He had a steadier way than that; which was why, she supposed, the men chose him as their representative whenever there was a meeting to attend.

Creath was always reluctant to leave her, certain the Indians would sniff out his absence, but Sarah insisted he go, saying she would get Nell or Jonah to come up and stay with her while he was gone. She didn't, and was only frightened once, when Indians thumped and clattered around outside the cabin, annoyed because she'd put the horses in chain hobbles to keep them from being stolen. Her heart had beat in wild alarm at the sounds, but she soothed herself with the thought that if she were going to be scalped they would already have burst through the door at her. Refusing to put out the lamp and cower in darkness, she dragged her spinning wheel out, seated herself, calmed the wild-eyed dog at her side, and began pumping the treadle. The whir of the wheel drowned out the thumpings outside the cabin, though looking up from time to time, thread poised in her hands, she was certain she saw black eyes peering at her through the cracks between the logs.

Creath never learned of the incident. Sarah was afraid that if she told him he'd stop attending the meetings, conventions that were held almost every spring and fall now to discuss and petition against the constraints and injustices of the Mexican government.

That summer, especially, the Mexicans found many ways of chastising the colonists, all with an eye to subduing whatever aim the Anglos had of setting up against Mexico City and joining themselves to the United States. When Creath learned that each family was to be required to pay tax on the slaves they owned, he bolted over the hill past Sarah's wild young peach trees, down to the cabin in the lowlands half a mile distant where Nell and Jonah lived.

Creath had no intention of having his name put down as a slave owner, and figured that Jonah had come near enough to working his way out of debt to be free. "You and me are square now, Jonah. You and Nell can be on your way."

But Jonah had turned down his sudden freedom. "I can't do that," he said. "Nossuh. I got my crops in on that little plot you give me. I got my cabin all fixed up. An' Nell, she makin' a big rag rug for d' floor. You goin' t' turn us outta that, Marse Chase?''

"Maybe you just as soon we take off with the Kronks, get ourselves scalped," put in Nell, whose impression of Indians had undergone certain alterations since the time she'd thought of living with them. "Missy Sarah, she know you're here tryin' to turn us out?''

"I'm not trying to turn you out," Creath said, his gaze shifting from Jonah's light-skinned face to Nell's dark-skinned one. "I just don't want to be a slave man. I told you that a long time ago, and since you've nearly worked free of debt . . .''

Nell, making batter bread, turned to him with spoon aloft. It glistened rich yellow in the firelight. "We can't've come near close to that, Marse Chase," she said. "Why, I figure it'd take us five, six years to work clear an'—''

Creath interrupted her with a sharp sigh. Like Sarah, the woman had a head for figures. Now Jonah spoke up. He was quieter than his wife, more thoughtful, and he steepled his fingers as he spoke. "You don't want to be a slave man, Marse Chase. But you see, I *got* to be a slave. At least look like one. How many free black men you know in Texas?'' His point was clear. Only one of every ten Texans was black, and none of them free. He would be an oddity, an outcast, wherever he went. "You want to call me a free man, you call me a free man. Let Nell an' me rent this land an' go on workin' for you. You pay that tax, I'll pay you back by workin' for you some more."

"I'll still be a registered slave man."

Nell stepped forward. "Missy Sarah hear you turn us off our land, she's not goin' t' feel too pleased 'bout it.''

An understatement, Creath thought, as Nell well knew. "All right," he said at last, standing. "Sure was a pleasure talking to you.''

The irony of his words was lost on Jonah. "An' you too, Marse Chase.''

So it came about that Creath and Sarah Chase were set down as slaveholders and taxed as such, an event that more than anything turned Creath against the Mexican government. In November a new ally was enlisted in the struggle to assert control: the clergy. Technically, colonists had always been required to be not only loyal Mexican citizens but also Catholics; as a practical matter, the issue of religion had scarcely been mentioned.

One day Sarah looked up as she was washing clothes in the yard and saw two figures riding toward her, one of them cloaked in the flowing woolen robes of the church, the other in the dark cloth of an *alcalde*, or governor. When she stepped toward them, hand shading her eyes, they reined in and dismounted.

Sarah was eighteen now, still slender and fine-boned but taller than she had been the day she stood on the deck of the *Talent* and looked out at Galveston Island. Her hair, lightened by the sun, was looped back with a twist of yarn. She hated sunbonnets and never wore them, though the prevalence of snakes and scorpions had inspired her to keep shoes on her feet. Her skin, which didn't tan, took on the permanent glow of a just-ripening peach and Creath loved to kiss the places where warm peach turned suddenly to milk white, saying it was like moving from sunlight into shadow.

"I'm looking for the Chases," the *alcalde* said, looking down at her.

"Creath's away," Sarah said. "Lem Robey's wagon axle busted and he went out to fix it."

"You're his wife?" She nodded. The *alcalde's* name was Burton—she remembered Creath talking of his election— and he looked apologetic. "Father Delgado has come up from Saltillo." The *alcalde* paused again, cleared his throat, and went on. "Do you have a wedding license?"

Sarah stiffened. This was the moment she'd been dreading, the moment so long in coming. It seemed as though the scum that was in the boiling wash pot rose suddenly in her throat. "All our goods were put overboard in a storm," she said, taking care not to lie lest she be caught not once but twice.

It was hot for so late in the year, yet in spite of his nearness to the wash fire and the sun sinking into his dark robes, Father Delgado's skin was dry and white. His hand cut the air like a wing as he spoke. "What church were you married in, child?"

When Sarah didn't answer, Burton rephrased the question. "Was it a Catholic wedding, Mrs. Chase?"

"No. No, we had no Catholic wedding."

Father Delgado frowned, lines deepening from mouth to nose. A sigh of disapproval escaped his lips, reminding Sarah of the gasp of smoke that came from a puffball when you stepped on it.

"I'm afraid your marriage has no validity then," said Burton, not meeting her eye. A silly business this was and he knew it, making sinners and bastards for the sake of the government.

"No validity?"

"Contracts made in any but the true church shall not be honored in Texas," said Father Delgado as if quoting from rote, which Sarah was sure he was. Like the church he represented, he was quick to forgive her sins, real or imagined. "Do you have any objection to the Catholic church? Do you have any presentiment against marrying again according to its doctrines?"

Sarah shook her head; she had no objection to religion of any sort. "There's to be a mass marriage on Saturday next at Parley's Landing," Burton told her. "Father Delgado will perform the services. Will your husband agree?"

"I'm sure of it," Sarah replied.

The weather turned windy and wet at week's end, forcing the ceremony and its participants inside the big room of Matthew Parley's trading store. The ferry, which plied its way back and forth across the Brazos, kept washing up new couples, until at last it seemed that every family between Brazoria and San Felipe had been crowded into this single room. Children fussed at the ado of their parents' marrying, babies were laid under puncheon benches to keep them safe from feet. Of all those Father Delgado remarried that day, some were disgruntled over the loss of a day's work, some angered by the government's new show of arrogance, and some, stronger in their Protestant beliefs, blood-mad over the affront to their own religion. Only Creath and Sarah were lighthearted over the matter, their lips compressed as the vow was pronounced over them, their hearts full of the knowledge that Arden Bell had been defeated at last.

That night when they got home Sarah opened the food safe on the wall and put the folded parchment up high, jamming it into a crack in the wood. Then she reached for a small blue bottle.

"Sarah, what's that?" Creath asked, coming up behind her and catching her in the fold of his arms.

She moved away from him to empty the bottle's contents into the slop bucket. "Tick medicine. It's old and time to be thrown out." She set the bottle down on the corner of the table and turned back to him, hair loose and framing her face. "I guess Arden can't touch us now, no matter what." Lifting her hand, her eyes holding his, she undid the top button of her blouse. Never again would she have need for Nell's baby-stopping remedy, whatever it had been made of.

The next spring cholera boats put in to shore, bringing an epidemic that spread from town to town, leaving one city, Brazoria, so depopulated that it was never to recover. The disease was abetted by damp and windless weather that left pools of stagnant water everywhere and, to the west, caused the Colorado River to flood, washing away cabins and fields and livestock.

Creath and Sarah were untouched by these misfortunes, though heavy rains soaked their fields more than they desired and caused the stream they took their water from to overflow its banks. Sarah had to strain and boil every bucketful to take twigs and mud from it. A half mile distant, Nell complained that the lowland water was even worse. "Jumpin' with toads it is," she said, "an' I got so much work t' do I can hardly get it boiled 'fore we're a drinkin' it."

The hogs enjoyed the mud, rooting in it for drowned rattlers that they ate with gusto, impervious to the poison, but the cats kept to the smith's shed, staring out at the weather with owl-eyed indignation.

In March Lem Robey's son died of the cholera, and two children of a new family farther upriver. Sarah and Creath went to both funerals feeling strong and youthful amid the sorrow, though Creath watched lest Sarah taste the food or drink the water.

Two weeks later Creath put out again for San Felipe,

where a convention of colonists was being held. With certain misgivings he signed a petition asking for the formal separation of Texas from Mexico. The two regions were different in geography, interests, and, more and more, in language and culture as well, and to try to govern them as one could only end in further bitterness. Even Stephen Austin, the greatest of the *empressarios* and the most sympathetic to the Mexican government, realized this.

With no misgivings at all, Creath signed another petition, one requesting the repeal of the decree against colonization. He had not forgotten his dream of settling his family in Texas, though by their letters he knew that the dream was growing dim. Jane, Sarah's age, had married Ly Owen and moved onto a small piece of land twenty miles from Caney Fork. Samuel still worked on the home place, but Johnny had apprenticed himself to a wheelwright in Clearfield and Joseph looked to do the same; Ellen and Alice, mere babes in Creath's mind, were of an age to have flirtations.

His folks were scattering like tufts of down blown from a milkweed pod, he thought, and took hope in the fact that this year there was some chance for the petition's success. Austin had decided to go to Mexico City himself and set off the same day the convention was struck, riding south with Creath and several others, losing them one by one as they made for home, and finally continuing alone, along the main road where no cabin lights reached out to welcome him.

For the first time Sarah was restless at Creath's absence and idled many hours wondering how long it would be until he came back. She could have said something to him before he left but then she wasn't sure. Now she was, and fretted with anxiousness to tell him the news that she was pregnant.

She'd awakened this morning, a Sunday, with the certainty inside her. She felt different in a way she couldn't explain, and for her that was the surest way of knowing anything. She thought of going down to Nell's to share the news but no, she would wait until tomorrow, when Nell came striding up the hill to help her with the wash, when Jonah rubbed himself with oil against mosquitoes and took to the fields. Sunday was their one day of rest, hers as well as theirs, and Nell was likely chin-deep in singing and strange cooking. After thinking it over, Sarah decided to keep to her own nest.

The next morning she was up early. It was a day that promised no rain; the sky showed only fleece clouds, tufts of rabbit fur-trim on a baby's blanket.

Where was Nell? Sarah became impatient, then worried. Leaving her chores, she set off over the graduated hills that led down to the little cabin. With a growing tightness in her throat, she tried to remember if she had seen puffs of chimney smoke in that direction yesterday. Surely she had, she told herself. Surely.

Nell's cabin was still as she approached, as the land itself was sweet and still in the gathering breeze, a warbler's notes sifting down on her. She knew as her hand touched the portal what she would find, for the smell of sickness and diarrhea curled out to her, a smell that marked the lightning quick path of cholera.

A bucket of water stood by the door, dipper still in place. A bowl of cornmeal on the table gleamed up at her like sunlight. On the bench Jonah's shirt waited for mending. Their bodies lay on the bed and all she could think of was how still they were, now that they weren't quarreling.

Sarah bolted from the cabin before the vomit escaped her lips and felt a small satisfaction that she had not fouled Nell's clean dirt floor. She wanted to clear her mouth, remembered the bucket inside the door, then thought better of it. For a long time she leaned against the side of the cabin, eyes closed, the sunlight making strange patterns against her lids.

She knew what she had to do but let the thought spin slowly in her mind, arguing it out at each step. A funeral for them, she thought. But who would come to mourn these friends of hers? A burial then. But she couldn't manage it alone. Nell weighed nearly twice as much as she did and Jonah the same. By the time she could ride for help and come back again . . . and then there was the contagion to think of too.

She went inside once more, come out with rags and flint and steel, and crouched by the cabin door to start the fire. A spark flew out, caught the rag, and acrid orange flame warmed her face. She touched the burning rag to the logs of the cabin and watched shreds of bark begin to burn. But wherever the fire caught it smoldered and went out, for the rainy weather had dampened the outside of the logs.

Sarah tried again and again before she gathered the flint and steel and the remaining rags and went back into the cabin. There she lit the bed clothes beneath Nell and Jonah, lit the hem of Nell's skirt, lit their clothes on pegs along the wall and the length of fabric Nell had set aside to make a curtain of. She pushed the window shutter open on its leather hinges so air would take the flame.

The next day she came back among the cooled ashes, gathered their bones, and buried them herself. It was no work—she was healthy and strong, and Nell and Jonah were as light as angels now.

Chapter Eight

The cabin ashes in the lowlands became a place Sarah and Creath didn't speak of often and when the Brazos rose above its banks a month later, covering the site, it seemed as if an abscess had been cleaned away.

As soon as the waters receded, Creath went out to clear the debris left in the flood's wake. Sarah followed him into the fields that were scattered with branches and planks and the forlorn carcasses of animals.

"What are you doing here?" Creath questioned when he saw her coming down the sloping hill toward him.

"I'm going to help you," she answered, settling her eyes on him.

"It's heavy work, Sarah."

"I know."

He paused for a long moment. "Won't it hurt the baby?"

Her mouth opened in surprise. Anxious as she'd been to

tell him a month ago, that eagerness had long since burned away. Without Nell and Jonah nearby, he'd never leave her side if he knew she was pregnant. And then too there was another worry. What if something had gone wrong inside her the day she went to Nell and Jonah's? Maybe their disease had crept inside her; maybe all she'd done that day had shaken the baby loose. If she lost it, she meant to spare Creath from knowing. She had worked to hide her condition from him and, for the last two weeks, had crept outside in the middle of the night to be sick, always certain he was sleeping when she got back into bed beside him.

"How did you find out?"

"I can count days, Sarah." He smiled, a shy smile that flashed at her like summer lightning. "Besides, I'm a light sleeper."

Despite her worry, the baby was born healthy and sound and for a time their joy pushed aside all the rest of the world. Talk of rebellion against Mexico was constant now, sweeping Texas like a restless wind, but Creath turned a deaf ear to it, preferring to lose himself in the magic of watching his son learn to crawl.

"Keep him away from the lye pot," he would say, and Sarah would leave her soap making, pick Austin up, turn him, and watch him head in a different direction, like a windup toy, until Creath spied some new danger.

She'd long ago accustomed herself to her husband's overcautious nature. Rather than rail she chose to humor him, a wry smile lurking at the corners of her mouth. It was his one fault in her eyes, but that did not mar the overflowing love she felt for him. Sometimes when she looked at him she thought of her girlhood liking for his brother or of her marriage to Arden Bell. Chance had landed her in Creath's arms, but chance had chosen better for her than she had chosen herself. She loved Creath in a way that always surprised her, a way that waxed and waned and came back stronger, stretching to accommodate each new challenge.

Creath and Sarah had never said they'd loved each other, not in words for that wasn't their way, but the certainty of it carried them forward, tied them together, and opened their minds to each other. In a handful of years they had made a little world at the edge of the Brazos. On Austin's first birthday Sarah discovered wild mimosa growing in the woods and dug a clump to climb against the cabin door. Next spring her peach trees, now spreading in an orchard behind the house, would bear fruit for the first time.

In Mexico City Antonio Lopez de Santa Anna was thinking long and hard about people like Creath and Sarah, settlers who thought of themselves not as *Mexicanos*, as he ardently wished, or even as *Americanos*, but as Texans, a breed apart. Firmness was what was needed with them, he thought, firmness and consistency. Else all of Texas would erupt in a bloody rebellion.

Even Stephen Austin, mild and meek, had come to Santa Anna to plead the Texan cause and the Mexican dictator, anxious to rid himself of a persistent Austin, had at last lifted the long-standing ban against Anglo colonization. Yet before Austin could return to Texas with the news, Santa Anna had him arrested and jailed in Orcodado, the prison of the Inquisition, at Saltillo.

Word of Austin's arrest soon swept the colonies, firing talk of rebellion. As Santa Anna sought to tighten his grip on the frontier, the Texans struggled all the harder to shake themselves free. With the repeal of the colonization ban, a new tide of settlers came surging into Texas, strengthening the Anglo presence and making the Mexican garrisons little more than foreign outposts in their own country. Open fighting flared between the Texans and the Mexicans and one day Asa Crocker told Creath that a hothead named Rip Paxton had led a charge against a garrison. Creath remembered hearing the name from Hutch and, on his brother's next visit, he told him about the incident.

"Rip a wanted man?" Hutch questioned. "For what?" The cabin door opened and Sarah stood outlined against the late afternoon sun, a load of firewood in her arms. Hutch glanced up at her. "Wait, I'll take that," he offered.

"Don't stir yourself," she answered lightly, crossing the threshold before he could reach her. She unclasped her arms and let the wood fall into the kindling box. A gust of wind kicked through the doorway behind her, fanning her hair and skirts. She had to step across the long, outstretched legs of her husband and brother-in-law as they talked. So tall they were, it was like stepping across logs jamming a river. But she liked having Hutch with them again, even for a short time.

"Theft or murder for old Rip?" Hutch asked, a grin in his voice as he picked up the thread of the conversation.

Creath shifted Austin from one knee to the other, soothing the child's fussiness so Sarah might have a moment's peace. "Treason, the Mexicans say. As far as I can figure out, Hutch, that friend of yours must be a damned hothead."

"And wanted for treason, you say?"

Creath nodded. "General Cos has got a whole army just below the Rio Bravo, guns pointed north, and he won't negotiate until we turn Paxton over to him." Martin Perfecto de Cos, Santa Anna's brother-in-law, was one of the most powerful generals in Mexico.

"Old Rip," Hutch said quietly. "They'll put him up against a wall and shoot him if we hand him over. The only reason they haven't shot Stephen Austin yet is because he's Stephen Austin. But Rip is nobody."

"I know," Creath said. The eyes of the two brothers met. "Hotheaded, maybe, but he's a Texan—we can't give him up to get shot."

"No," Hutch replied thoughtfully. Standing off to the side, Sarah felt a new worry in the air.

A week later Hutch and Creath were working in the bottomland fields along with the three slaves Creath had reluctantly hired from Lem Robey. He disliked doing it, Sarah knew, for slave labor was slave labor, whether he owned outright or hired from his neighbor. But without Nell and Jonah, and with Austin making so many demands on her own time, there was no choice.

In the cabin, Sarah opened the doors and windows to catch the breeze. The worst of the mosquito season was over and now came that sweet time when you could move through the outdoors without the nuisance of insects. This must have been what that woman cousin of Stephen Austin's, Mrs. Holley, had had in mind when she wrote glowingly of the healthful, near Eden-like climate of the land. Her book, a series of letters east, had brought scores of new settlers into the country. Once arrived, the emigrants found reality somewhat at odds with Mrs. Holley's promises, for she mentioned nothing of the racking fevers of acclimatization, nothing of the sweltering summers, nothing of the alligators that snatched dogs, chickens and children from river banks.

Sarah had met one family who'd packed wheat and rye seed all the way from the east, intent on cultivating it as Mrs. Holley had proposed. They'd stopped off the main road for water and Sarah made them stay to dinner, for the woman was thin and tired and the children's mouths watered at the sight of the blackberries on her table. When the husband told them of his plan to plant acres of wheat and build a mill on the Trinity River, Creath had gently put him to rights. "You must have been readin' Mrs. Holley's book," he said. "But truth is, most all of Texas is too hot for wheat."

The thin woman's eyes rounded with disappointment. "We'll settle for rye," she said, but Creath shook his head.

"Soil stifles it," he replied.

"I haven't had a piece of wheat bread in near four years," Sarah put in as she set the venison roast on the table.

"No bread? Oh, *ma*," the oldest boy cried, as if his mother were to blame for this catastrophe.

"What do you eat then?" the woman asked, and after supper Sarah showed her the metate bequeathed to her by Elva Roberts. So much cornmeal she had ground on it that it now had a slight depression across the surface, like a dip in the earth.

"Spoon bread, it's near as good as anything," Sarah answered confidently, thinking that she was her own kind of Mrs. Holley. How often she'd hungered after light bread and biscuits herself, especially when she'd been pregnant. She didn't tell the woman how deep that craving could be, though. Poor woman, she'd find out for herself soon enough. So it is, Sarah thought; people write of making a grand civilization in the wilderness, as if we were Gabriel's angels. But what it is each day is slapping mosquitoes and wanting bread.

She felt a twinge of parting when the family left in the morning. She always did, for she loved company. Since Nell had died there'd been no woman nearby. There was Maddie Robey just nine miles distant, but Maddie was a brusque, scuttling soul who never slowed to talk. There was Maddie's sister-in-law Jane, softer than Maddie and closer to Sarah in age but so frail in health all her energy was spent on chores. The other women in Chase's Clearing lived farther away, and children and mending, soap making and meal making left little time for long rides. So Sarah loved her visitors, and blessed the fact that the San Felipe road skirted their lands. She'd even made Creath nail a sign to a tree, pointing the direction to their cabin.

Going about the making of dinner, with Creath and Hutch in the fields, she was happy. Sun splashed in through the open door making Austin, nearly a year old now, gurgle with delight as he tried to catch it in his fists. "Oh Aussie," she said, " 'ee cannot catch the sunlight."

Whippoorwills piped above her voice and below it came the hammering of a woodpecker. Butterflies tumbled through the air and Sarah shooed them away whenever they strayed inside, anxious lest they lose their way as they headed south for the winter.

She'd examined it over and over inside her head, why she was so happy when Hutch was with them. It wasn't her long-ago feelings for him, she was sure of that. Nor was it any lack between her and Creath. Nor was it Hutch's need for them, for his absences were still long and frequent and she was as certain as ever that somewhere he had a woman he'd never named to them. But together the three of them formed a unit no two of them could form alone, giving and lending and making new bonds. When Creath and Hutch sat together and talked, as they did in the evenings, Sarah was free to observe them. She was free to drift into still backwaters of thought, watching Creath, letting her feelings play across her heart like sunlight falling through leaves.

She was thinking of the way he looked, calm and thoughtful, when she became aware of someone moving through the woods. It was someone mounted on horseback, it could be any traveler from the road, but she took caution just the same. Catching Austin up, she lowered him into the vegetable bin in the corner and handed him the little man doll Hutch had whittled.

"You stay quiet now, Aussie," she said. Then she took the extra gun from its place on the wall and waited.

In a few minutes she laid the gun aside in relief as a sharp-ribbed, broken-down mare came into view, carrying a slender man whose hunched shoulders hid his silhouette. He dismounted stiffly, as one unused to riding long distances, and came up to her doorway.

"I saw your sign," he said with a gesture, his voice raspy in the smoothness of the afternoon. "My horse needs water and I . . . might you spare some food?" Sarah stared at him as if staring at an apparition. His cheeks were hollow and papery but his dark eyes blazed with a familiar fire. "You've done well here," he added, glancing about the room.

It was then Sarah realized who was standing in her doorway. Rumor had gone round a week ago that Stephen Austin was out of prison, but she had not believed it, not until this moment. He must have come all the way up from Saltillo alone, must have seen their sign posted to a tree as he followed the road home to San Felipe.

"Come in," she said. "Men'll be back soon, then we'll have supper."

He moved through the cabin as an invalid might move, cautious, silent, looking at simple objects as if they conveyed the deepest sense of wonder. Sarah retrieved her son from the vegetable bin and set him on the floor. "What's the little fellow's name?"

"Austin."

At this his eyes grew suddenly watery, as if a wind were tearing at them. "Ah," he said, managing a thin smile. A deep cough racked his chest and when his hand came away from his mouth Sarah saw blood on it. She dampened a rag in water and handed it to him, watching from the corner of her eye as he cleaned the blood from his fingers; fastidious, a gentleman.

He seemed older by a decade than when she'd first met him in San Felipe four years ago. Well, small wonder; he'd been kept in Orcodado for the last nineteen months, a year

and three months of that time in solitary confinement, fed
on rancid food and poor water and confined within dank,
infested walls.

When voices sounded in the yard Sarah rushed out to
meet Creath and Hutch. Creath was already looking quizzically
at the broken-down mare.

"It's Stephen Austin," Sarah explained in a hushed
voice. "They've let him out of prison. But oh, Creath, how
changed he is!"

Hutch rode with Creath to the convention at San Felipe
that year. There Stephen Austin, his cheeks blazed with
fever, endorsed secession and hope for a peaceful and
gradual separation. This, he quickly realized, was not possible. Santa Anna was massing troops in Saltillo in prepara-
tion for invasion. At Goliad, Texans had been conscripted
into the Mexican army and citizens forced to quarter troops
in their homes. Across the frontier word went out that guns
would soon be confiscated, leaving settlers open to Indian
attack.

In the midst of the convention a rider came storming
along the western road, raising clouds of dust. It was Dan
Wheeler, the patriarch whose numerous offspring accounted
for half the population of the little settlement of Unity.

"It's Cos," he cried. "He's marched to Bexar an' made
headquarters there." Wild-eyed, breathless, a patch of gray
hair standing stiff with sweat and dust, he stared at them.
"An' that's not all. Son Johnny, he was there. Cos is tellin'
everyone he has eight hundred pair of iron hobbles with
him. Eight hundred pair, and he plans to use 'em on us!
Plans to march us right to prison in 'em, he says."

"Not me," someone grumbled.

"Nor me," came the echo from several corners of the
room.

The messenger sucked in his breath and looked at the
roomful of colonists. "Well then, who will come and fight
with me?"

The old man's voice boomed across the room and the
grumbling suddenly ceased. The hot anger that had flowed
among them a second before evaporated. All were thinking

of their crops, that this was harvest time, that wives and children would be alone and unprotected. Then Hutch felt his brother rise from the bench beside him.

"I'll go," Creath said. Tall as a tree, it was easy for other men to stand beneath his shadow.

"Me too."

"I'll fight Cos."

"Let 'em come."

"Let 'em take us."

Soon the whole room was standing. Not long afterward, Stephen Austin issued an official call to arms.

Chapter Nine

Hutch and Creath fought together under Stephen Austin and though it had been Creath who'd volunteered first, it was Hutch who took the lead on the field. He could move across the plains as silent as an Indian, slipping from one oak tree to the next without leaving a ripple in the grass behind him. One night he ambushed two sentries, slit their throats, and stole back to camp with their dinner before Creath had gathered wood for a fire.

With no supply lines, food became a prize worth killing for. It was catch-as-catch-can for the Texas volunteers and Hutch's experience on the frontier proved invaluable. Men drew near their campfire, lured by the smell of beans or hoecake or, on rarer occasions, meat. Whether bellies were full or empty, talk kept them hunkered by the glowing embers into the night, talking of which way the fighting was going. It was difficult to assess their situation, difficult to know whether they were engaged in a real war or simply a series of skirmishes that would amount to nothing.

In October, with a force that never numbered above 350, they managed to surround General Cos and a thousand troops at San Antonio de Bexar. The Texans were eager to attack but Stephen Austin, lacking both the troop strength and the will for such a move, tried to negotiate a peace. As the possibility of mounting an attack slipped away, his army scattered like tent pegs across the plains, digging themselves into the sandy soil. For more than a month they camped, and as October turned to November, the Mexican-held city found itself in a true state of siege.

Creath huddled under a coat Hutch had taken from one of Cos's dead sentries. It didn't fit him, had already split across his heavily muscled shoulders, but it was better than nothing. This was the hour he'd come to dislike most, the hour before dawn when men slumbered like corpses in the cold mist, when he alone lay awake, thinking of home and Sarah. If he were with her this was the hour he'd first wake, rising to relieve himself outside the cabin, his feet chilly in the dew, his breath hanging in the sweet air. How he enjoyed that moment, standing in the circle of his own land, and how he enjoyed plunging back inside, into bed beside her, relishing her warmth as he waited for her to stir toward him.

Beside him on the harsh ground Hutch twitched in his sleep. Not coming awake, Creath knew, nor sinking into a deeper sleep: Hutch neither slept fully nor lay in fretful wakefulness as Creath himself did. Instead he hovered someplace between, resting yet alert, like a catfish sculling at the bottom of a stream. Yet a few moments later when hooves sounded along the road, it was Hutch took first notice of them.

They were a ragged contingent coming to join Austin's troops, less than a hundred men who scarcely lived up to their grand title, the Patriot Army of Texas. Most of them were shabbily dressed, few of them were mounted, and all of them were hungry. But they carried before them a white flag showing a cannon and a lone star, edged at the bottom with the words *Come and Take It*. Austin's men adopted the flag, the slogan, and the lone star as their own and set about sharing their meager supplies with the starved newcomers.

The arrival of new men lifted spirits in the camp; there was renewed enthusiasm for an attack but again Austin refused to give the order. He had good reason: the Texans had no artillery and Cos's troops, outnumbering his four to one, were quartered behind thick walls of stone and adobe. But his prudence was wasted on his troops: they had come to fight, not to sit out the winter on the bare plains. Even Hutch's seemingly inexhaustible patience began to fray. Hope for a change came in late November when Austin was relieved of his command and sent east to seek support from the United States. "Now maybe we'll get ourselves a fight," everyone said. But Edward Burleson, Austin's successor, proved as reluctant to attack as his predecessor had been.

For the men who'd been so long encamped, this new frustration was too much to bear. The surrounding plains had been hunted clean, the remaining game frightened off, and firewood was growing scarce. Temperatures dipped near freezing at night and only one man in ten had a blanket. In December the first troops began to desert, returning to the warmth of their wives and children. Hutch and Creath hung on and saw a phenomenon occur: as the settlers trickled away, Americans came to take their place. Not Texan-Americans, but Americans fresh arrived from the States. The Texan cause was hugely popular in the States and when Austin called for assistance, men poured out of the hills of Kentucky and Tennessee to take their places.

These new arrivals were even more restless than the Texans. When Burleson gave up the siege and ordered a retreat, their hoots of protest ripped through the camp. Spurred by their catcalls, Dan Wheeler, who'd rallied the colonists in the fall, echoed his old cry. "Who will come and fight with me?" he roared. Within minutes Texans and Americans fell into line behind him, long-barreled rifles gleaming in the winter sun.

They charged at 3 A.M. the next morning and soon found themselves locked in a bitter struggle. Creath lost track of his brother as the volunteers scattered and the fighting ranged over the plazas and missions of the city of San Antonio. Hand to hand and house to house the fighting went, with Dan Wheeler leading the advance. When a Mexican bullet felled him on the third afternoon, his death

galvanized the furious resolve of the men. In this new surge
of fighting, Hutch and Creath were reunited inside the thick
walls of the Alamo.

It struck Hutch as hugely ironic that the structure, erected
by the Spanish missionaries more than a century before and
converted into a fortress in 1793, should now become a site
for Mexican entrapment and defeat. Fierce, hand-to-hand
fighting ranged across the cobbled plazas and in rooms once
set aside for worship; by the close of the third day, the
Mexicans were forced to surrender.

The shame of having been defeated by a force one-fourth
the size blazed a deep and everlasting hatred into Cos's
mind. The Texans danced around him in a joyous hullaba-
loo, taunting him as they plundered his military stores.

In the melee Hutch salvaged a beautifully worked Mexican
saddle, smaller than an American saddle and just the right
size for Yellow Fawn. For Lodgesmoke he retrieved a
mirror, no bigger than his hand and backed with ornamental
silver. Creath stood apart from the celebration with one
thought in his mind. The fighting was over, the Mexicans
had been defeated. Now he could go back to Sarah and to
Austin. He could return to his smithwork, to spring planting,
to making a lattice for Sarah's mimosa to climb. He had no
notion that, far to the south, Santa Anna was gathering a
force of six thousand, determined to subjugate the Texans
once and for all.

Sam Chase, now twenty and nearly as tall as his older
brothers, was with the tide of Americans drawn west by the
bonfire of the Texas cause. Splashing across the Brazos in
January, he was more than disappointed to hear from Creath
that the fighting was over.

"Over?" he railed, flicking his black hair back with an
impatient hand. "How can it be over? You're still part of
Mexico, aren't you? There's your fight right there, then, for
independence. You haven't given up, have you?"

"No," Creath answered. It was difficult to explain to his
wild-eyed young brother the deep peace he felt at being
home again.

"What about Hutch then?" Sam demanded. "Did he just hobble off too?"

"Went back to trading, should be coming down here the end of this month maybe."

"Damn." Sam's fist smacked against his palm and Sarah couldn't help but smile. She held a soft spot for Samuel, perhaps because he'd been in the mill shanty the day Arden had gambled her away to Creath.

"Don't worry, Sam," she told him. "Trouble of some sort's bound to break out sooner or later. 'Til then, we're real glad to have you."

He was the wildest-hearted of the brothers, she saw, without Creath's rocklike strength or Hutch's quiet patience. Sam, just her age, turned the cabin upside down with his presence, singing and tale-spinning, swinging Austin in the air until he shrieked with delight, making a jumble of her household goods whenever he went near them. To others it might have been a burden but to Sarah, who always craved company, Sam was a welcome addition. When Hutch received news of his arrival on a pass through Nacogdoches, he hurried south to see him.

"I would never've knowed you," he said in disbelief. When he'd left home, Sam had been a youngster of twelve. Sam's presence made him realize how far he'd drifted from his family. Somewhere, across the rivers and over the mountains, he had kin he wouldn't recognize if he came face to face with them; the thought chilled him a little. "What brings you this way, Sam? You figurin' on bein' a farmer too?"

Sam tossed his head. "Hell, I came to fight but Creath says the fightin's over."

"Don't you believe it," Hutch assured him. "Texans never quit fightin' for long. If the Mexicans and Indians don't pan out, we'll start fighting each other soon enough."

With Hutch's arrival, Sam's spirits lifted. "Know what I'd like to do?" he asked one evening. "I'd like to go hunting. Woods are full hereabouts. When I was a youngin', Hutch, you an' pa and Creath always went out and left me back, sayin' I was too young. I damned you to hell for it, too." He laughed, blue eyes flashing. "You never knew that, did you?"

Hutch shook his head. "Never did." He ran his fingers along the barrel of his rifle. "Well, let's see what kind of shot you are. Pa teach you that trick of sighting along your thumbnail?"

"Taught me," Sam said, "and told me I was the only one of his sons to get the information on account of being the most promising shot."

Now Creath's laugh rippled through the room. "I reckon he told us all the same."

"Except for me," Hutch put in. "He told me he was instructing me special because I was the poorest shot he'd ever come across."

It was a brief period of peace, though no one in Chase's Clearing knew it. While Sam, Creath, and Hutch whooped through the woods, scattering white-tailed deer before them and sending game birds whirring overhead, changes took shape around them. Stephen Austin sank into the background, unwanted as a peacekeeper, and the reins of leadership were seized by hotspurs like Sam Houston, Buck Travis, Rip Paxton, and Davy Crockett.

Couriers recruited by Houston told him that Santa Anna's vast army had begun to move north, marching from Saltillo toward Laredo. Houston, who could see into men's minds the way some women could see into their hearts, knew that once across the Rio Bravo the Mexican dictator would continue to sweep north, most probably to San Antonio, bent on avenging Cos's defeat. Two other Mexican generals, Sesma and Urrea, were also massing troops south of the Bravo. The three forces would strike Anglo Texas simultaneously, sweeping through the colonies with the force of a rolling wave, overwhelming whatever hastily organized pockets of resistance they found there. Houston wasn't about to let it happen. He planned to stop the Mexicans at the Colorado River and ordered General Fannin to do the same. His biggest threat, by his own estimation, came from his own troops; peppery as rattlesnakes, they might prove more than he could handle.

One hard-raining night in February Rip Paxton swam his

horse across a bend in the Brazos to Chase's Clearing. He
pounded on the door to be let in and stood with his back to
the fire, water streaming from his buckskins. "You got to
come north with me right away, Hutch," he said. "Santa
Anna's crossed the Bravo at Laredo with near a thousand
men."

Sam's shout, half a man's war whoop and half a boy's cry
of glee, broke the air behind them but Hutch paid no
attention. "Why north?" he asked.

"Houston says we got to get the Cherokee on our side if
we're going to fight and I told him you were the best Indian
talker in Texas. I got a treaty with me."

Hutch was already reaching for his gun, lifting his pow-
der case off a wall peg and wrapping it in a double layer of
deerskin against the rain. The firelight made hollows on his
cheeks. He heard a rustle behind him as Sarah slipped from
Creath's side to pack spoonbread and cold venison for them.
But his eyes, deeper gray than the dawn that was beginning
to steal through the slits between the logs, never left Rip
Paxton's face. "What can I offer them?" he asked.

"Land title," Paxton replied. "If Spotted Turtle agrees to
fight on our side, or even stay neutral, he'll get permanent
title to his people's land."

"It's not Spotted Turtle I'm worried about," Hutch said,
remembering Walking Bird. Between each visit, the young
brave's resentment only seemed to deepen; he felt it each
time he came back, as if Walking Bird had begun to look on
him as a personal enemy. "Who authorized the treaty? Is it
valid? I won't offer them meat that'll be jerked out of their
mouths the minute the fighting ends."

"It was authorized by the whole convention at Washington-
on-the-Brazos. Houston signed it himself. If any man's
word is good where Injuns are concerned, it's Houston's.
You know that, Hutch." Hutch nodded. Like himself, Houston
had lived among the Cherokee until he was almost one of
them. He wouldn't betray his word where they were concerned.

Dressed and ready, Hutch took the leather pouch from
Sarah. She looked fragile in the flickering light, but her
head was steady and her eyes held his, as if she knew
something none of the rest of them guessed at. "You take

care, Hutch," she said, passing her hand lightly over his arm. "You take care of all that's yours."

He looked at her, startled. Sarah *knew*. Somehow she'd guessed that his ties to the Cherokee ran deep below the surface. Her knowledge didn't trouble him but gave a sense of peace. "Thank you for the thought, Sarah," he said, his eyes meeting hers. "I will. And you, Creath, take care of Sarah."

Then he turned to Sam, whose face was flushed with excitement.

"I suppose this is what you've been waiting for. Well, don't go and get your tail shot off. I expect to see you when I get back."

The last he remembered as Rip opened the door was Sam's laugh spilling out against the slanting rain.

Chapter Ten

Whenever she walked through the village, Yellow Fawn felt Walking Bird's eyes on her. It had begun a few seasons ago, when the Mexican soldiers came seeking Spotted Turtle's support, and had grown steadily stronger. She avoided crossing his path whenever she could, kept Lodgesmoke close to her side, and was careful of the words she spoke to Sweet Meadow Grass, his wife, lest they be repeated. Spotted Turtle had prevailed in keeping the Cherokee neutral but Walking Bird and his supporters had neither given up their objections nor their bitterness toward whites.

Hutch's visits, longer and more frequent since Lodgesmoke's birth, provided a respite for Yellow Fawn. She dropped her guard, relaxed, allowed herself to feel protected. She never mentioned Walking Bird's disquieting behavior to Hutch and often wondered if he noticed it. If not, she wouldn't point it out to him. It was her problem, a problem with one of her own people, and in choosing Hutch she had chosen someone whose protection extended only to the borders of the village.

That year, Spotted Turtle achieved the great age of seventy. Although his mind was keen, the vessel that carried it had begun to falter. The dampness of the new land had seeped steadily into his bones, stiffening his joints so that Cattail had to knead his legs to assuage the pain; his hair was growing thin and large dark blotches covered his hands; more and more often, he closed his eyes and drifted in his recollections to a better time, a time when he and Cattail had been young and when the powerful United States did not exist.

"Eh, old man," Cattail was saying gently, shaking his shoulder.

"What?" Spotted Turtle jerked himself back to wakefulness, memories scattering.

"Visitors."

The old man licked his tongue over his teeth, his mouth sour from sleep, and smoothed his hair into place. Not the Mexicans, he hoped. He hadn't the strength to fend off an appeal from them today or to turn aside calls for allegiance from Walking Bird, Black Elbow, and their faction. But when he saw Hutch stooping to enter his lodge, with Rip Paxton just behind him, he smiled broadly. "I am pleased to see you, Chase, and your friend." He turned to Cattail and made a simple gesture. "Call Yellow Fawn and the little one."

But something in Hutch's face stopped the old woman. "They know I'm here," he said in a quiet voice. "I'll see them later." He sat down and Paxton did the same. "We must talk, Spotted Turtle."

The old leader listened as Hutch laid out the terms of the treaty. It was coming at last, a war between the whites and the Mexicans, and it was delivering an unexpected gift to him: title to his people's lands. But his enthusiasm for the treaty didn't show in his face. "If fighting is necessary, it will be young men who go. I do not have the power to sign their lives to you. You must go to them with your treaty, Chase."

Hutch nodded, for he'd expected as much; still, he did not relish pitting himself against Walking Bird at the council. He could speak well enough to one or two men, could convey his feelings to an old friend like Spotted Turtle, but

he disliked speaking to so many, particularly if he felt the
current running against him. Yellow Fawn sensed his
nervousness and, before the meeting that night, passed her
hands over his shoulders. For a moment she stood with her
head pressed against his chest. "Walking Bird does have a
weakness," she murmured.

"What's that?"

"He is very proud." She paused, letting the words sink
in. In a corner of the room she saw Lodgesmoke playing
with the doll Hutch had brought her, a white child's doll
with yellow cornsilk hair and blue eyes painted on a cornhusk
face. "Pretty," Lodgesmoke had said when she saw it,
casting her Cherokee doll aside for the figure dressed in a
scrap of calico. For a moment, Yellow Fawn had felt
inexplicably sad, as if she herself had been cast aside. She
felt Hutch's arms tighten slightly around her.

"Proud how?"

"Proud in a foolish way. He wishes always to be right, to
cling to whatever decision he has made. Sometimes, because of this, he has made grave mistakes. The time he
wished to hunt in a certain place, even when signs showed
raiders nearby. He led the hunting party there and two men
were killed. Everyone knows about this fault and if you
remind them of it, it may seem as if Walking Bird's
opposition comes from pride."

"Maybe he won't oppose me," Hutch said.

"Maybe not." Yellow Fawn's voice was unconvinced.

The council began with Spotted Turtle laying out the
terms of the treaty and inviting the comment of any who
listened. Hutch was not surprised when Walking Bird rose.
Only a few years younger than Yellow Fawn, his face was
hard and handsome, one eyebrow broken by a swooping scar.
From a white man's bayonet, the story went, and though
Hutch had no proof of this he was willing to believe it, for
Walking Bird's eyes, focused on him now, bore a malice so
deep it seemed part of his elemental being. "Sam Houston,
where is he from?" Walking Bird asked.

Hutch tensed at the rhetorical question. Walking Bird was
leading him somewhere, though he couldn't yet tell where.

He forced the nervousness out of his voice. "Virginia and Tennessee mostly."

"And Stephen Austin?"

"Virginia."

"And you, Chase?"

Hutch smiled slightly. "Well now, I'm as guilty as the rest of 'em."

Walking Bird was persistent, unsmiling. "Where are you from, Chase?"

"Tennessee, if they'll claim me."

Walking Bird turned toward the men, young and old, gathered on the floor of Spotted Turtle's cabin. "These men who come to us, who ask our help against the Mexicans, are from the same nest. They have crawled far away from it, have chosen a new flag and a new name for themselves, but they are the same men who pushed us from our lands in the east.

"Now they say they will not forget our help, but what will they say tomorrow? Now they say they will give us our land for all time, but what will they do tomorrow? Now they say we must trust them but if we do, where will we live tomorrow? We know these words well, for we have heard them before. And we know what will happen if we believe them. Houston, their chief, is a friend of Jackson, who sent us here along the long road."

There was a murmur of approval that stirred and swelled like a wave. Hutch hurried to stop it. "Sam Houston is a friend of yours as well," he said. "Didn't he live among your people? Is there any one of you that hasn't heard stories of *Coloneh*, the Raven?"

"Is there any one of us that hasn't heard stories of *Ootsetee Ardeetahskee*, the Big Drunk?" Walking Bird retorted, referring to the other name Houston had earned. A rumble of laughter passed through the crowd and Walking Bird permitted himself a smile. Then the smile vanished. "No, Chase. I say a man who is bitten by the same snake twice deserves to die."

"I agree with you there," Hutch said affably. Yellow Fawn, with her impeccable sense of timing, handed the pipe to him. She'd been passing it among the men, permitted to touch it because, although female, she was a blood relative of

Spotted Turtle, and now she gave it to Hutch, allowing him time to gather his thoughts. Walking Bird saw this and grunted inwardly. The woman was a threat to him. Her double allegiance—to Spotted Turtle and to Chase—made her a powerful force, a force that was always pitted against him.

"A man who is bitten twice does deserve to die," Hutch continued, handing the pipe back to Yellow Fawn. "But what about the man who cannot change his course, even when a new road opens before him?" He waited until he was certain he'd recaptured the attention of the Cherokee. "Doesn't that man risk losing something too?" He paused again, knowing their minds were astute enough to grasp his meaning.

"If we break free of Mexico, Houston will be our chief. Now old Sam may have a few warts on him, but lying's not one of them. Can any of you name a time when he broke his word?" There was silence in the room; even Walking Bird lowered his eyes. Both as an adopted son among them and as a trader on the Neosho River, Houston had always been fair and generous. The only man he'd cheated was himself, standing his clients to lavish celebrations each time they bought from him. Spotted Turtle's voice, thin as smoke, rose through the silence. "We can trust Houston's word, just as we trust Chase's."

"Who has said we trust Chase?" Black Elbow questioned sharply and earned an evil look from Walking Bird, who knew this show of rudeness would turn the tide against them.

In the stinging silence, Chase felt Spotted Turtle's anger ricochet through the room like a bullet. Aged as he was, the old chief was on his feet in a second. "Any man who does not trust Chase goes from this lodge," he said. "Has he not brought the best goods, the best traders, to us? Did he not lead us to this place when the Comanche attacked? Has he not, in all ways, been a brother and friend to us?" Spotted Turtle's eyes bored into Black Elbow. No one spoke and in the silence Spotted Turtle seized a quill and signed the treaty with a flourish.

For Walking Bird, the humiliation was total. He shouldered past Black Elbow, ignoring his apologetic glance, and strode out into the moonlight, past the huddle of lodges and into the fields beyond them. He needed to be alone, to think of some new strategy that would unite his people and turn them in a new direction.

The day before Hutch left with the signed treaty, he delighted Lodgesmoke by allowing her to ride his handsome black horse. Mounted on the Mexican saddle that was her mother's, the little girl glowed with happiness and pride. Such moments were rare in her life and the breathless joy she felt sent a pang of guilt racing through Hutch. Even Yellow Fawn had mentioned that his comings and goings were hard on the girl, who cried for hours after he left and hung back in shyness when her friends discussed their own fathers.

From a gray-eyed, moon-faced baby, Lodgesmoke had grown into a beautiful child. Her eyes still resembled Hutch's but now they were an even deeper gray, illuminated with flecks of silver and fringed with dark lashes. Her hair was her mother's, black and shining and as straight as silk thread. She was taller and slimmer than the other children and even boys two years older could not beat her in a footrace. She owned a pet rabbit, was the apple of Spotted Turtle's eye, and made up stories about the magical friend who lived in the glass mirror her father had brought her from the battle of Bexar. In the spaces between his visits, she was becoming a person, Hutch realized.

One night he dreamed of coming to the village and finding her suddenly grown up, a stranger who told him that Yellow Fawn was dead. Pointing to the shriveled leaves on the trees, Lodgesmoke showed him that the whole world had grown old, leaving him alone to wander like a ghost. Her face, beautiful and elusive, had been bright as she closed the door of the lodge against him. He'd awakened in a sweat and reached out to touch Yellow Fawn, seeking the reassurance of her presence beside him.

"Will you fight too, Chase?" Yellow Fawn asked as he prepared to go. The Mexican saddle had been returned to its place in her lodge and his own saddle placed on the horse's back. A line of worry creased her forehead as she reached out to touch him, laying her hand along his arm just as Sarah had done, an unusual public gesture among the Cherokee.

"Don't worry about me," he answered. "I'm too tall for

the Mexicans to get a direct hit on." His hand stole up to
caress her hair. "I'll be back."

As she watched him go, Yellow Fawn remembered the
day that her husband, White Fox, had ridden against the
Creeks. She could not drive the recollection from her mind.
How strong and confident White Fox had been that day and
how Hutch resembled him now. She shivered and pulled her
hand away from Lodgesmoke before the child felt her fear.

Signing the treaty did not escalate Walking Bird's discontent as Yellow Fawn thought it might. He accepted defeat or
seemed to, conferring with Spotted Turtle and deferring to
him in a way that won back the old chief's confidence. All
of this made Yellow Fawn wary, for Walking Bird's eyes
still followed her about the village, more boldly now than
before, and when she glanced at him he did not look away
but returned her gaze.

Less than a week after Hutch left, she was called to her
uncle's lodge. When she saw Walking Bird sitting to the old
man's left, and when she saw that Cattail was nowhere in
sight, her chest tightened. "Walking Bird would talk of
something with you," Spotted Turtle began, arm outstretched
as he gestured for her to sit. Yellow Fawn was silent, her
face closed, and Spotted Turtle spoke again. "How many
summers will Lodgesmoke be this year?"

"Five."

"She is growing; she needs a father."

"She has a father."

Spotted Turtle chose his words carefully. "It is not good
for a child to be without a father, any more than it is good
for a woman to be alone."

"I have been alone for many years now," Yellow Fawn
replied swiftly. "I do not find it difficult." From the corners
of her eyes she saw Walking Bird stir and heard his grunt of
impatience. Spotted Turtle stilled him with a glance.

"It is not just you I am thinking of. It is the village also."

Yellow Fawn flinched inwardly. She cared for herself and
Lodgesmoke as well as she could, hunting small game with
a slingshot, bartering vegetables and tobacco for bolts of
calico. But for large game, for meat to eat and hides to tan

into skins she was dependent on the men of the village. Even the gentleness of her uncle's voice could not soften the meaning of his words. She was a burden, and it was Walking Bird who had made that fact clear to him. She lifted her chin. "Then I will go with Chase next time he comes," she said. "He has offered before. Sweet Meadow Grass may have my lodge if she likes—it is better than hers." She could not resist this last comment, and saw Walking Bird's eyes dilate with indignation.

"That will not be necessary, niece."

"What do you mean?"

"Walking Bird has offered to take you as second wife."

Yellow Fawn's cheeks stung and for a moment she was left gasping, a fish lifted from the water. "But—Sweet Meadow Grass—"

Now Walking Bird spoke. "There is no law against taking two wives," he said. It was true: polygamy was a long-standing custom among her people, though it had grown less and less common. "I would welcome you into my family, and your child too."

Yellow Fawn refused to look at him. "You cannot take this seriously, uncle," she said. "You cannot think I would marry this man."

Spotted Turtle closed his eyes for a moment, as if sinking deep into himself. "So many summers have I that I can no longer count them. Soon I will be here no longer. What will become of you then?"

"Chase. He will protect me, always."

Spotted Turtle shook his head. "Chase comes and goes like the wind. He is a good man, but that is how it is with him."

Yellow Fawn felt trapped, as if a net were being woven around her. "Don't you see what he's doing, uncle? If he marries me, Chase will come among us no more; there will be no more white men and no more treaties."

"Even so, even so," Spotted Turtle said wearily. He looked at her, his old eyes commanding. "Walking Bird will be a good father for Lodgesmoke. And if fighting comes, he will protect you."

"He will also take your place as leader, once he becomes your relative. It will be difficult for you to oppose him."

"Perhaps that too is for the best."

Yellow Fawn could scarcely believe her ears. In one elastic movement she was on her feet, unable to listen to more. "No," she said firmly. "No, I will not marry this man."

Then she was out of the lodge, her heart pumping wildly. No one, not even her uncle, could force her to marry against her will. But Walking Bird would never forget her rejection. Wherever she walked now, she would have to be careful of her footing.

Chapter Eleven

Sarah stood by as the men were pulled from her one by one. A few days after Hutch vanished into the rainy dawn with Rip Paxton, Sam joined James Fannin's Brazos Guards, one of several volunteer companies. Fannin's five hundred troops at least had the look of a regular army, having purchased tight-fitting jackets and pantaloons at discount from the United States.

Sam's uniform was too small for him and Sarah spent the day before his leaving opening seams and adding bands of cloth. "The material stands out a bit, I'm afraid," she said, biting the thread off and returning the needle to a safe place. "No help for it, though; it's all I have."

But Sam grinned at the bright red stripes running down his legs and circling his wrists. "Hell, Sarah, you turned me into an officer. Men'll get me mixed up with Fannin himself. What do you think, Creath? Want to change your mind and come along?"

Before Creath could answer, Sarah put her hand lightly on his shoulder. "I won't let him go, Sam," Sarah said. "Not after he and Hutch had such a good time cavorting at San Antonio."

But two weeks later she did let him go. There was no choice, not when news reached them that Santa Anna had

crossed the Colorado River and was marching into the heart
of Anglo Texas. All over the frontier cannons boomed with
new calls to arms. At Lem Robey's the men held a meeting
and organized a militia. Sarah clung to Creath before he
left, cheek pressed to his chest.

"If anything happens to me, Sarah, you find Hutch. He'll
get you and Aus to some safe place."

Her head jerked up. "Nothing's going to happen to you.
No need to scare me, just because you and Hutch have got
the end of the world mapped out."

"If you say so. You're the one with all the knowing.
Anyway, I'd best be going." He kissed her and ruffled his
son's hair. "Watch after your mama, Aus."

Sarah closed the cabin door behind him and leaned
against it, trapping herself inside so that she couldn't go
racing after him. "Now, Aussie," she said, "shall we spin
or shall we weave?"

Her glance chanced to fall on the far wall, where Creath's
hat dangled from a peg. It was the sight of the forgotten hat
that finally brought tears to her eyes.

The Texas forces were no match for the well-organized
armies of Mexico. As the volunteer lines collapsed and
scattered, refugees spilled into Chase's Clearing. Now Sarah
had all the company she'd ever longed for. They filled her
table at each meal and unrolled their blankets on her floor at
night. There were more of them than she could handle yet it
never occurred to her to turn them away. They were mirror
images of herself, women whose men had hurried off to
fight, women who'd left their homes so abruptly that the
Mexicans found pans of milk in the dairies and food
standing on the tables.

The rain that had been falling the night Hutch rode north
with Rip Paxton had continued, day in and day out, forcing
the settlers across swollen rivers and ankle-deep mud. Children arrived with measles and whooping cough and Sarah
fed them and dosed them while their anxious mothers
snatched a few hours' sleep. Please keep Aussie well, she
would think, scrubbing her own hands and arms red with lye
soap before picking him up. But one night he pressed into

bed beside her, his face swollen and hot, scarlet splotches covering his chest. She laid him down and pasted him with buttermilk, the only salve she had, quelling the lump of panic that rose in her throat.

She'd never seen before how like Creath her son was, for in looks it was her he resembled, with russet eyes and hair that curled around his face. But the deep silence and long patience woven through him, those fibers came from Creath. Not once did he cry or protest, even when she held his hands still in hers so he couldn't pick the scabs.

"Mrs. Chase?" A scarecrow of a woman, one of those camped on her floor, was shaking her awake. It was light out, dim light that might mean either day or night.

"Aussie," she cried in alarm, reaching out to him. But his forehead was no hotter than before and his breathing satisfied her.

"Mrs. Chase, there's a rider on the road. He says the Mexicans are coming and we have to run."

Sarah pushed her tangled hair back with one hand. Her mouth was dry. "Run?"

"Right away. They're burning every settlement they find and the Indians are right behind them taking what's left."

It took her less than an hour to get ready. She drove the pigs and cattle deep into the woods and freed the chickens from their coop. Her marriage certificate and the deed to their land she rolled into a cylinder and placed inside the coffeepot, hiding the pot in the branches of a cedar tree bordering their cabin. She changed Austin and herself into their best clothes and found a quilt to wrap Austin in. Sam had ridden one horse into the Brazos Guards, Creath had taken the other. She would have to walk away from the Mexicans, and she would have to carry Austin with her. He was not well yet, but she thanked luck that he could travel at all. Her cabin floor was scattered with folks too sick to move. As a last thought she grabbed Creath's hat off the wall and jammed it down on her own head.

She stood for a moment in her yard, Austin already heavy in her arms. In the drizzle the scent of peach blossoms came over her and she remembered that this was the year they were to bear. She shifted Austin to her back, wrapping the quilt around him like a sling. "Hold on to mama's neck," she said.

She was one of them now, a scarecrow woman driven from her home, a scarecrow woman whose man might be anywhere, if he was still alive at all.

In the rainy twilight, mud sucking at her feet, she searched along the San Felipe road for neighbors. Earlier she had spied Lem Robey's wife Jane and walked with her a while, but the woman moved so slowly that Sarah soon left her behind. There was Austin to think of; surely somewhere ahead there was a settler woman who'd take them in.

People moved like ghosts around her, chins turned down, shoulders hunched against the rain. Each new group she found herself among Sarah plied for news, though there was scanty news to be had. The army seemed to have vanished, Creath and Sam and Hutch among them.

There were two routes open to her. She could turn due east in hopes of getting to the States and waiting there until the fighting was over or she could go northeast to the prairies. With little hesitation she chose the second route. The prairies, on higher ground and easier to get to, would be drier for Austin, whose breathing had begun to whistle in her ears.

She crossed the Brazos at a place called Cocknell's Fort, clinging to the upright mast of a raft as Ben Cocknell ferried her and a handful of others across. On the other side she was taken into the fort, given dry clothes, and a bowl of venison stew. Austin's throat was sore and swollen and she had to chew each piece of venison to mush in her own mouth before giving it to him. A kind woman whose name she didn't know pointed to a place where quilts were spread on the puncheon floor and Sarah nodded gratefully. It would be the first sleep she'd had in nearly forty-eight hours. Before laying down she caught the woman's hand.

"Is there any news of the army? Of the Brazos Guards or the men from Chase's Clearing?"

The woman shook her head. "There's a place called the Alamo where the fighting is. Have you heard of it?" Sarah nodded. "They say Santa Anna's trapped our men there but likely that's just talk." The woman didn't tell Sarah all she

knew, that people were saying Santa Anna had slaughtered
the Texans, that the bodies of Davy Crockett, Buck Travis,
and Rip Paxton had been burned in rubbled heaps. She
knew nothing of Sarah but that she was young and tired and
had welts on her neck from her child's clinging to her. She
deserved a fair night's sleep. For all the woman of Cocknell's
Fort knew, she might have a man there herself; tomorrow
would be time enough for the news.

In the middle of the night Sarah was roused by cries
around her. Mexican troops were directly across the river
from them and preparing to cross. Men rustled through the
stockade distributing guns and ammunition. There were
plenty of long rifles to go around but not enough arms to
hold them all, for most of the men had gone off to fight.
Sarah grabbed Ben Cocknell's sleeve as he went by. "Give
me a gun," she said. "I can shoot."

"It's dangerous up on the wall," he said, meaning the
catwalk where the sharpshooters crouched. "The Mexicans
are heavily armed." But she reached out for the gun and
Cocknell handed it to her.

Shapes moved toward her across the water, Mexicans
crowding the raft she'd ridden herself earlier that afternoon. "Wait 'til they're in range, now," someone cautioned
behind her. Sarah did not look at the shapes directly but
watched from the corners of her eyes, the way Creath had
taught her. It was a hunter's way of seeing at night, of keeping
targets from dissolving in the shadows. When the raft touched
shore and the shapes scattered, she lifted the rifle to her
shoulder. Many a thing had she killed in her life, possums and
squirrels, rattlesnakes and hogs, but never a man. Her heart
pummeled against her ribs at the realization. She forced herself
to think of Austin sleeping below, of Creath torn away from
her, of her peach trees blooming in a grove without her. Even
so, her heart caught as she squeezed the trigger.

It was Palm Sunday, someone told Sam. He'd never been
religious, it didn't run in the Chase strain, but still he
paused to mark the day. For nearly a week now they'd been
prisoners of the Mexicans, 350 men and General Fannin
himself, taken at a place called Coleto. Funny, Sam thought,

he had no exact idea where Coleto was. In the south, he supposed, for they'd been in retreat after a failed attempt to reach the Alamo.

The Mexicans had marched them to Goliad and now the captives hunkered across the muddy ground in clumps, some grim-faced and silent, some swapping tales with each other. Sam, at the edge of the cluster, watched the guards that circled them. Snatches of their conversation drifted back to him, a peppery lingo he did not understand. He wished he could fathom what they were saying and his wish intensified as an officer rode up to them, mouth pulled in a taut line beneath his mustache.

Francisco Mortiz Carillo had received his orders the previous morning but delayed acting on them until now. "Who issued these?" he'd asked the messenger in disbelief, though the signature was clear.

"Santa Anna. He signed them in my presence." A vein in Carillo's temple throbbed. "There must be some mistake. Fannin surrendered these troops at discretion."

"I only carry orders, señor. I do not give them."

Carillo had listened for the sound of hooves for more than twenty-four hours, hoping Santa Anna would reverse his decision. But no further messenger appeared and now he could delay no longer. He looked down at the guards. "Santa Anna has ordered the execution of all captured prisoners," he said.

The guards drew back from him instinctively. "And Fannin?" someone asked at last.

"*All* captured prisoners."

A young man with the smooth copper face of a *mestizo*, looked up at him. "When, señor?"

Carillo felt profoundly sorry for the young *mestizo*, for himself, and for the men squatting in clusters on the ground. "At once." His glance fell on a tall young Anglo with red stripes running up his legs and he leaned forward to offer the *mestizo* a word of advice. "Shoot those highest in rank first, then the rest will be easier to deal with."

The *mestizo* nodded and followed his glance to where Sam was sitting.

* * *

The rivers of Texas reached across the land like fingers on an outstretched hand, Sarah thought; the palm was the gulf, the far-spread fingertips the headwaters buried deep in Indian lands.

Sarah had stood on the catwalk at Cocknell's Fort as long as the ammunition supply had held up, firing at the soldiers who poured toward her, at the soldiers who threatened to rip Austin away from her forever. But when ammunition had run low and Mexican reinforcements had arrived, she had abandoned the fort with the rest of the settlers, joining the tide of refugees flowing north and east, winding like a stream toward the next finger on the hand, the Trinity River.

People swarmed on the road around her. It seemed that all of Texas was in flight: people from settlements along the Colorado, the Brazos, and the Navasota; people who told her that San Felipe itself, the capital of Austin's colony, had been burned.

"Can you walk a little while, Aus?" she asked. The quilt she'd used as a sling had been left behind in the flight from Cocknell's fort. Carrying him in her arms, her bones ached as if they were coming apart. "Just for a little while."

She was told they could cross the Trinity at a place called Mattock's Landing, but even before she got within sight of the water she saw more than a hundred people waiting to cross. Pushing through the crowd she discovered why: the river, swollen by rain, stretched two miles wide before her eyes. It was a lake whipped by stiff and treacherous winds. Two days ago, someone had told her, a man had been killed by an alligator when the boat overturned. Now they were taking no chances, using eight men to manage the boat.

"They're taking those with sick children first," someone said kindly. But more than half the women waiting had sick children, most worse off than Austin, and some families had been waiting for two days to cross.

"Isn't there another landing?" Sarah asked everyone she met, holding Austin firmly by the hand. She'd never been in such a large crowd before and was terrified of losing him. Finally she heard of a bridge seven miles upriver.

"People were crossing there last week, though it might be under water by now."

Sarah gathered Austin swiftly in her arms and set out, reaching the bridge a few hours later. The river was much narrower here, though the current was swift and the floor of the bridge was covered with water. Sarah left Austin on the bank and tested the water. The logs of the bridge were rounded and slippery under her feet, exactly the way an alligator might feel if she stepped on it, she thought. There were no railings on the bridge and at its midpoint the water rose as high as her waist. If she lost her footing against the current with Austin in her arms, nothing would keep them from being swept out into the channel.

She made her way back to the bank. There was no way to avoid crossing. She had no food, no blankets, not even dry clothing. Only across the river, where refugees had made camps and were helping other refugees, were those things to be had. She picked Austin up and was about to start across when a miracle appeared before her: a man driving an oxcart.

As it rumbled out of the brush the driver, a man her father's age, smiled. "Ride across with me, little lady," he offered, and Sarah scrambled up onto the seat beside him, clutching Austin on her lap.

The water rose around the wheels of the cart and up to the chests of the oxen. They were midway across when she felt a sudden shudder. A second later she was falling sideways, the bridge buckling beneath them and the wagon turning on its side as it plunged into the water. Sarah resisted the urge to push Austin free and clutched him to her, taking him with her into the depth of the water, trying to cover his mouth and nose with her free hand.

The river current pushed her back against the wagon. She felt a hand circling her ankle and realized it was the driver, pinned beneath the wagon side. When she pushed toward the surface his arm pulled taut. He was lodged tight, tethering her in his desperate grip. She tried again and this time he gave up his hold, allowing her to escape. She broke the surface with lungs bursting and Austin sputtering in her arms. Hooking her feet under the wagon seat to keep from being swept away, she paused to get her bearings. The wagon shook as the oxen bucked beneath the water, trapped and drowning.

For a moment she bobbed there, deciding what to do.

Then she reached down with one hand, caught her skirt, and
wadded it around her waist. Kicking free of her shoes she
said, "Hold on to mama's neck, Aus." She'd swum Caney
Fork many times, but never with a child in her arms and
never against a flood current. Austin was round-eyed with
fright and his grip so strong he sometimes dragged her head
below the surface. But she made land at last, carried far
downstream before her feet touched the muddy bottom.
"Well, Aus, this is something we'll remember, isn't it?"

The muscles in her arms and legs quivered with exhaustion. If she had no child, she'd lay down on the bank. But
there was Austin to think of, and so she picked him up and
found her way to the thread of road on the other side of the
collapsed bridge.

It was past nightfall when she saw the first fires flickering
through the trees. The voices of women floated out to her,
along with the smell of woodsmoke and food. "We're safe
now, Aus," she said, but she was so weary the words were
merely a gurgle in her throat.

Sarah's feet were torn and bleeding from the day's walk
and she was so tired the fires floated dizzily in front of her.
Someone lifted Austin from her arms, someone else showed
her a place where quilts were spread before the warmth of a
fire. For the first time in days, the rain had ceased.

In the gray morning light she saw the place she'd come
to, a quilt city that looked as if a whole nation of Elva
Robertses had created it. But these quilts were damp,
perpetually so, and the faces beneath them strained and
gray. Austin stretched at her side and she noticed with relief
that someone had dosed his raspy chest with a poultice.

Feet brushed by her, new feet coming into camp, and
from her resting place she saw her neighbors crowd around
a piece of paper nailed to a tree. The look on their faces as
they read triggered a wave of fear in her and she pushed
herself up. It cannot be another Alamo, Sarah thought as
she started toward the tree. She caught at a woman's wrist.
"Can you tell me what it says?" She paused and added in a
shamed whisper, "Please. I can't read."

The woman was dour-faced, her eyelids red and translucent as if they'd been rubbed with raw sand. "It's Fannin.

Fannin and his men. Killed by the Mexicans. All of them, after they surrendered.''

Sarah leaned back against the tree. It had occurred to her long ago that Creath might have tried to join his brother, and the men of Chase's Clearing with him.

At first Hutch had been relieved not to find either of his brothers among the sick and wounded hidden in the woods at Buffalo Bayou. He'd spent the last month looking for them, fighting where scattered forces rallied against the Mexicans, helping evacuate women and children to points of safety. But there was no sign of either Creath or Sam, though he knew both of them would have joined the fighting by now. He prayed neither of them had been with Rip Paxton at the Alamo or with Jim Fannin at Goliad. And Sarah . . . from what he could gather, she must have fled Chase's Clearing weeks ago; he looked for her face in the stream of refugees but never saw her.

Pushed east by the Mexicans, Hutch finally struck Sam Houston's forces. "Chase. Aren't you the one that treatied with the Cherokee? Friend of Rip Paxton's?" Hutch nodded in response to both of Houston's questions. "Goddamn, I'm going to miss Rip. But you stay with us, you'll get a chance to even the score for him."

That was all Houston said. He was notoriously secret about his battle plans, usually because he had none, Hutch believed, but that didn't lessen his account in Hutch's book. He unsaddled his horse, unfurled his bedroll, and became one of Houston's nine hundred troops.

Two days later, he was grilling meat over a mesquite fire when Houston plunged through camp on his huge white horse, calling, "Get up, you devils! Get up and remember the Alamo!" They were camped on an arrowhead of land with Cos and Santa Anna and twelve hundred Mexican troops in front of them and Buffalo Bayou behind them. Except for a minor skirmish the day before, all had been quiet. Now Hutch scuffed dirt over the fire and grabbed his rifle. Ten minutes later, he was advancing on the Mexicans.

They advanced quickly through the brush, the undergrowth hiding them until they were almost within rifle range of the Mexican lines. Hutch was in the first wave of men to crash through the flimsy barricades and what he saw before him brought him to an abrupt halt. Santa Anna, who'd never overcome his contempt for the Texans, had seen no reason to deprive his troops of their customary siesta. They were stretched loosely beneath the afternoon sky, rifles nested in upright tripods, officers far behind the lines.

Hutch hesitated, disliking the thought of killing men fresh from slumber, but he was shouldered aside by those who swarmed behind him. Some of the Mexicans were shot, more were gouged with Bowie knives or clubbed to death with rifle butts, the cry of "Alamo! Alamo!" fueling the slaughter. Hutch bypassed the killing and gave chase to those who fled. In less than twenty minutes the line of fighting fell all the way back to the San Jacinto River, where the surviving half of Santa Anna's army was surrounded and captured.

Hutch searched for something heroic to remember from the battle and almost gave up hope of finding it. He stood grim-faced in the cluster of troops around the place where Houston lay, his leg bone shattered by a rifle ball. Someone shouted out that Santa Anna was being brought into camp and Houston glanced up at Hutch. "You're a tall one," he said with a grin. "Figure you can haul me to my feet so we do this right?"

Blood running into his boot, Houston stood just long enough to receive Santa Anna's surrender.

Sarah didn't know that the war was over; she knew only that, because something had happened at a place called San Jacinto, she could go home. She got herself out on the road in short order, her feet so fast and eager she was out of breath as she walked. Someone had given her a pair of shoes and Austin was dressed in the clothes of a camp child who'd died of whooping cough. She'd been reluctant to take the clothes, afraid of what they carried, but had finally accepted, boiling and airing them for hours before she let them touch his skin.

Going home was no easier than her flight had been—the rain still fell, the rivers were still swollen. But this time she knew her destination and this time those she traveled with were buoyed by hope. They had already given a name to what had happened to them, calling it the *runaway scrape*, making it seem a thing over and done with.

After she crossed the Brazos she saw the Robey women. They had gotten hold of a wagon and mule and offered her a ride. "They say every house in the Clearing was burned," Maddie Robey said. "Maybe you'd best stay with us until you've word of Creath."

Sarah clutched Austin tighter to her. "No. No, I have to see my place again. If there were Mexicans or Indians about, there aren't anymore."

But she wasn't prepared for the effect her ruined house had on her, the remains of her pigs and chickens scattered about the yard, the charred frame of logs, the sodden scraps of all their belongings. It would have been easier if it had been swept away, she thought. To see a scrap of deerskin shirt, the burned runner of Austin's cradle, the andirons of her fireplace—that was a cruelty to her. She remembered her coffeepot, saw with relief that it was still where she'd hidden it, and scrambled to retrieve it from the tree branches. Her marriage certificate was safe inside, as was the title to their land. Tomorrow she would see if any of their cattle were browsing in the lowlands.

She was glad things happened the way they did, glad she had time to sort through her sadness and store it away before Creath arrived to see it. She never doubted that he was coming back to her. She would feel it in the air if he were dead, she'd told Jane Robey. One corner of the cabin still stood and she roofed it with branches to make a shelter. Certain house goods had survived—knives and graters, a metal spoon and a cup made of tin. She sifted through the rubble for them, bringing them up like buried treasure and boiling them clean over an open fire. Austin toddled after her, smearing himself with ashes and burbling with delight whenever he pulled some shiny object from the debris. Sarah wondered if he knew it was their own home they were sifting through.

One day she snared a rabbit in a noose made of shoelaces and set it on a spit above the fire. Its juices were just starting to scent the air when she heard a horse's hooves along the road. Instinctively she reached for the hatchet, the only weapon she had, and looked toward Austin. "You come over to mama now," she said calmly.

A moment later she cast the hatchet aside, caught Austin up in her arms, and went running toward the road, the sound of the hooves too familiar to be mistaken.

"Creath!" His shape materialized in the twilight, thinner than when he'd left and with a weary sag to his shoulders, but whole and sound. When she reached him he held her without speaking for a long moment, until Austin fussed and squirmed between them. He swung the little boy up on the horse's back and gave him the reins to play with. Sarah's hand he still held in his, afraid to let go of her.

"I stopped at the Robeys' and they told me you were here. They're burned out and getting ready to move. Lem Robey said we got burned out too."

Sarah nodded briskly. "We'll build again, Creath. Aus and I have already started."

His eyebrows contracted suddenly and she felt his grip tighten on her hand. "Sam—"

"I know."

"And I haven't heard a word of Hutch."

"He'll be back."

He looked at her in the twilight and found her russet eyes steady on his. "How do you know?"

"I feel it."

It had been a long time since he'd felt her presence around him, wrapping him like silk; he moved closer and turned his face down, burying his lips in her tangled hair.

"I love you, Sarah." He wondered if anyone in his family had ever said such words before.

She drew back from him in the dim light. "I feel that too." Her face was as bright as moonlight. "I always have."

PART
II

Chapter Twelve

Sarah and Creath clung to their land until the year's end, giving up only when it became apparent that Chase's Clearing would never thrive again. It was one of a cluster of places to pass out of existence, for the Republic of Texas was sharply different from the wild, struggling state that had wrestled to be free of Mexico. Western settlements like San Patricio, Goliad, and Refugio became forgotten names. Activity now centered in the east, along the banks of Buffalo Bayou where the newly mapped city of Houston was drawing settlers to it.

Creath proved impervious to Houston fever, as the phenomenon was called, and Sarah with him. Neither had any desire to become townsfolk, preferring to scrimp out a living on land of their own. But when Stephen Austin died that December, both felt as if they'd been loosed from their moorings. It was Sarah who suggested moving first, choosing her words carefully to make it sound as if they were seizing a new opportunity rather than giving up an old one. For his service in the Revolution Creath was entitled to bounty lands; Sam Houston had declared as much when he was elected president, and this was where Sarah directed her husband's thoughts.

"Why not stake a claim on the Trinity River?" she asked one night. They were still as poor as snakes, worse off than when they'd first come to the Clearing, and she spoke the words over an open campfire. "The place Aus and I camped during the fighting, it'd make good pastureland. It's a might high and dry for cotton, of course." She smiled. "And I know you'd hate to give up on cotton."

By the turn of the new year, 1837, they'd sold their land to a speculator who, Creath later learned, sold it to a wealthy Louisianan for three times the price. Their claim along the Brazos became a cotton plantation, and it galled both Creath and Sarah that a slaveholder should own the place where Nell and Jonah were buried.

They stayed on the land through the winter, squatting with the speculator's permission until Hutch arrived in the spring to help them move. It wasn't that they were burdened by earthly goods, they had barely enough to fill the saddle bags, but Indians were harrying settlers across the frontier and Creath was reluctant to start north without an extra rifle. They didn't head for the Trinity, as Sarah suggested, for moving east seemed like a retreat to Creath. Instead they followed the Brazos as it forked northwest, climbing up into gentle hill country.

Away from the ruins of their old life, Creath's spirits began to lift. They stopped for three days at a settlement called Industry where he did enough smith work to buy a cow and calf, and when they struck the place where the Bosque River joined the Brazos he lifted Sarah in his arms and set her down with her toes pointing north. "Our cabin will face this way," he said. "Cattle barn over there."

She turned to him with raised eyebrows. "Cattle barn?"

"Well, maybe not right away. Maybe we'll see about the house first. But we'll need a barn. Winters are bound to be colder here."

Once started, Creath and Sarah took root quickly. Hutch spent the summer with Yellow Fawn and came to the Brazos that autumn to find smoke puffing from Sarah's chimney and cornfields spreading away from the cabin like an apron. There were still things they lacked, tools and cloth and niceties like sugar, but they built their nest with speed. There was even a hired boy, a tough and wiry youth named Ben Bonham who'd plunged into Texas when the United States recognized the fledgling Republic. He worked for room, board, and a small share of the profits and was a comfort to Creath on those dark and rainy nights when Indians haunted the edges of the cornfields.

"Not as many mosquitoes here," Creath told his brother that fall, "but the Injuns are twice as thick. If you chain hobble a horse so they can't steal it, they'll hack its feet off and let it bleed to death. Have you heard of a Mexican called El Oso?" Hutch shook his head. "He got the Indians to kill two dozen settlers west of here. Says he's going to liberate Texas and give it back to Mexico. Any Injun that fights with him he promises the moon and stars. You're headed south, aren't you? Can't you put in a word with Houston? Tell him we need some kind of armed relief."

"I'll see what I can do." Hutch's smile was thin for he had Indian troubles of his own. The treaty he'd negotiated with the Cherokee had yet to be honored, and now that more and more eastern tribes were being pushed along the Trail of Tears, Spotted Turtle's people were growing anxious to secure their lands.

When Yellow Fawn discovered that her old enemies, the Creeks, had settled on a stream near Cutfoot Creek she urged Hutch to seek another appointment with Houston. "We did all that was asked of us," she argued, "and Houston is an honorable man. We must know that our lands are ours, Chase."

So he had packed his horse and turned south, pausing at the new homestead on the Brazos to see how Sarah and Creath were doing. "I wouldn't hold my breath on action from old Sam," Hutch cautioned Creath. "He's not exactly what you'd call organized. Have you thought of joining the Rangers?" In Nacogdoches, he'd heard of the new militia companies spanning the frontier.

Creath shook his head. "I couldn't leave Sarah alone."

"Ben Bonham'd be here with her. He's a crack shot, I've seen him. Besides, Sarah can take care of herself."

Hutch's confidence in Sarah grew each time he saw her and two days later something happened that he would never forget. It would stay with him forever, tucked in his mind beside his

first image of the Texas wilderness and the sight of Sam
Houston standing with his shattered leg at San Jacinto.

Sarah was down in the cane breaks along the river,
cutting fodder for the cattle with a thick-bladed knife.
Austin played near her, hiding among the waving fronds,
pushing to her through the undergrowth with a bubbling laugh.
It was still early enough in the year to be warm and she had no
fear that he would take cold from the water. He'd proven such
a hardy little soul during the runaway scrape that she took his
health for granted, believing that he'd inherited the indestruct-
ibility flowing through her own veins.

Sarah sang as she cut at the cane, knowing full well how
awful her voice was, but letting it fill the clear air anyway.
Creath was far beyond her hearing, off with Ben spading up
a new field, but Hutch was nearby, felling logs for a
corncrib, and he smiled at the off-key notes and dour words
that drifted to him.

> Get down, get down, my Pretty Polly,
> And rein your horse to a tree;
> For I have killed six old Virginny girls
> And the seventh one you shall be,
> The seventh one you shall—

Something slapped the water near her, sending drops up
in a shimmering spray. "If you dive in, Aus, you've no dry
clothes to change to."

The cane stalks rippled before her eyes and bent suddenly,
just as her son's cry exploded in her ears. She waded
forward, parting the cane with her hands. *'Aus?!'*

The water churned around her knees and she was nearly
knocked backward by the lashing tail that thrust up before
her. She kept her footing and saw Austin's terrified face.
One of his arms stretched awkwardly, caught in the grip of
the gator's jaws. Sarah remembered hearing once that alligators were helpless under water. Still gripping her cane knife,
she plunged forward and threw herself along the length of
the animal's back, hoping that her weight was enough to carry
him down. Her face landed near his domed head and for one
piercing moment she stared into his eye. Then she got her

hand up and stabbed the knife down into that eye, pushing with all her strength until the blade was buried to the hilt.

The gator's jaws snapped open and Austin bobbed free. Sarah flailed for him in the water, caught hold, and dragged him toward the bank. Hutch was running toward them now. He'd come at the sound of her scream and crested the hill in time to see her knife blade slashing down through the sunlight. "Are you all right?" he gasped.

Sarah was on her knees, feeling Austin's arm with her fingers. The skin was broken, blood splashed across her hands, but the bone was sound. "Fine," she said, glancing up. "I lost my knife."

The alligator rolled and churned in the water, tail lashing the cane flat. Then its pale belly showed above the crumpled fronds. "I think you got him, Sarah," Hutch said. The sight of her pitched across the gator's back was burned into his mind forever. "Just a minute to make sure, then I'll see about getting your knife back." He stretched out his hand and helped her to her feet. She wobbled against him, knees quivering. "Scared?"

She shook her head. "It's the baby," she explained. "The new one."

Hutch looked at her a long moment, at all the mysteries contained within her small frame. "Does Creath know?"

"Not yet, and don't tell him. I couldn't bear his worrying over me."

Hutch nodded. It was their secret, a secret that was still theirs a week later when he rode off to find Sam Houston.

Spotted Turtle lit the pipe his wife handed him, pointed it in the four directions of the universe, and puffed deeply. "It is still good to smoke with friends," he said as he handed the pipe to Chase.

Hutch nodded, his eyes meeting Yellow Fawn's through the smoke. She was standing in the shadows against the wall, firelight glowing along the curve of her cheek. She'd known, even before he told her, the disappointing news he'd brought to the village. It was still early evening and children played outside. Hutch thought he heard Lodgesmoke's cry

among the others as they shrieked back and forth through
the village like a flock of starlings.

Walking Bird took the pipe from Hutch, hands careful not
to touch the hand of the white man. "I do not see any
papers, Chase."

"No."

Smoke hung in the silence of the lodge. Cattail, who'd
been ill all winter, coughed, muffling the cough with her hand.

"Perhaps Chase did not see Houston," Grey Coat suggested
mildly.

"I saw him."

"What did he say?"

The pipe had come to Black Elbow, Walking Bird's
sharp-tongued ally, and he gestured with it. "We do not need
Chase to tell us that. Wait. Be patient. The white men must
council. The papers are not ready. Isn't that what was said?"

Hutch hesitated. That was exactly what had been said,
more or less. He looked at the old chief, his friend.
"President Houston has not forgotten the promises that were
made."

Spotted Turtle nodded. He was growing old and weary of
words. A good night's sleep meant much to him now;
waking without pain, hearing Cattail's cough subside, seeing
Lodgesmoke at his door with a basket of blackberries—
those were the threads that held life together. Why had he
never understood it before? But if he had, he would not
have been chief. And if he had not been chief, one like
Walking Bird would have. "What did Houston say, Chase?"

Hutch looked carefully into the eyes of all the men in the
lodge. "He would like a man of the Cherokee to come to
Nacogdoches, to meet with a representative there, and sign
a new treaty." A rumble of discontent filled the room and he
continued quickly. "The lands promised you will still be
yours, to live on and hunt on as you wish."

"Why a new treaty then?"

"Since Texas became a country, whites from America
wish to come here to settle." Hutch's words were punctuat-
ed by a snort from Black Elbow. "Not on your lands," he
added quickly, "but on lands along this same river, to the
west. To get to these new lands, they must pass across lands

given to you. President Houston wishes to build a road for the whites to use. A road for them to pass along, as a stream passes unnoticed through a forest.''

''Streams widen into rivers when there is enough rain,'' Black Elbow said curtly. ''We have heard all this before, Chase. The whites will take our land no matter what they agree to. Once a white man sets his foot on something, he does not rest until he owns it.''

To Hutch's surprise, Walking Bird had remained silent through the exchange. Now he leaned forward, eyes burning intensely. ''Black Elbow is right: the whites *will* take our land. They will take it because it is there, because they desire it, and because when they pour across the land there are too many of them to resist. It will make no difference what we say; it will make no difference whether we sign a treaty or not.'' Walking Bird paused to catch the murmur of agreement that swept through the room. ''Perhaps it is better to take what is offered than to end with nothing at all. What does Houston propose to give us?''

''What do the Cherokee need?''

From her watching place in the shadows, Yellow Fawn felt a spasm of anxiety. Without realizing it, Chase had shifted his attention from Spotted Turtle to Walking Bird, treating him as if he, and not her uncle, were chief.

''What do we need?'' Walking Bird echoed, lips curling in a bitter smile. ''Look around, Chase. Do you see great plenty? Our ammunition was used up fighting with you in the soldier's town. Many of our weapons were damaged. Since the Comanche came to steal our horses and slaughter our cattle, we have been poor people. And you ask us what we need? We need everything.''

Hutch nodded, understanding why Walking Bird's position had shifted so abruptly: the young brave was prepared to cooperate because he saw no alternatives. It was the same conclusion Spotted Turtle had reached years ago, but Spotted Turtle had sought true peace with the whites. Hidden in Walking Bird's eyes was a hard and ill-concealed hatred, a hatred Hutch felt all through the rest of the meeting.

Later, alone with Yellow Fawn in her lodge, he became aware of her brooding silence. ''What's wrong?'' he asked, catching her around the waist and rubbing his chin against her shoulder. Lodgesmoke had been allowed to stay the night at Spotted Turtle's, to give them privacy. Yellow Fawn slipped away from him and busied herself with his gear, unpacking it, arranging it, setting aside whatever needed mending. "Yellow Fawn?"

"I wish you had not spoken with Walking Bird that way, as if he were equal with my uncle."

Hutch frowned, knowing she would not object over a mere lapse of courtesy. "Why? Walking Bird's always been against us before, splitting things down the middle. If he goes along with the treaty—"

Yellow Fawn turned to him. "Walking Bird is a dangerous man, Chase. Don't you see that?"

"Of course I see it. But Spotted Turtle's old, too old to go to Nacogdoches. Don't *you* see *that*?"

They stood for a moment in silence, gazing at each other over an impasse. Then Yellow Fawn came over to him and slid into his arms. She'd never told him about Walking Bird's proposal, nor would she. "Sometimes it is difficult to see anything at all," she said.

It was the closest she'd ever come to voicing despair and Hutch was quick to tighten his arms around her. "Maybe this isn't a good place for you anymore," he said. "You or Lodgesmoke either. Remember once I said I'd take you with me? The land is changing, Yellow Fawn, filling up with people. There's a settlement west of here that's just begging for a trading house of some kind. It's white mostly but Indians'd come there too and I've been thinking of opening a store there. You and Lodgesmoke could come with me. What do you think?" He put a hand on each of her shoulders and looked into her eyes. "There's a preacher that comes through every year or so. If you want, we could get him to marry us."

She didn't answer right away, torn between conflicting thoughts. She'd seen trader's women and children before, shadow people who never became part of the white towns they lived in. But if anyone could make that different, she believed Chase could. Was it better to go with him or better to stay with her own people, to stay within reach of Walking

Bird's resentment? "I'll think about it, Chase," she answered, but he could already see her beginning to accept the plan.

Suddenly the door burst open and Lodgesmoke hung in the entryway. Her cheeks were flushed and around her neck was the possession she was proudest of, a bead necklace Hutch had brought her.

"What is it?" Yellow Fawn asked, reading her daughter's alarm before Hutch did.

"It's grandmother," Lodgesmoke said. "She can't breathe, she holds her chest like this—"

Yellow Fawn was swiftly out of the lodge, not bothering with her sacred bag because any medicine she had would be found at Cattail's lodge as well. Word that something was amiss with Spotted Turtle's wife had already spread through the village, Hutch noted, for as he followed Yellow Fawn into the lodge he had to step through a fringe of curious women.

Cattail lay stretched on her bed and Hutch caught his breath to see Spotted Turtle kneeling beside her, kneading her hands with his worn and withered fingers. Her eyes were closed, her breathing labored, and a fine film of sweat beaded her forehead.

"What's wrong, Mother?" Lodgesmoke asked.

"I don't know yet. Stay back." And Lodgesmoke slipped to the far side of the lodge where Hutch was, leaning against his long legs as if against a familiar tree trunk.

Yellow Fawn felt Cattail's pulse and found it thrumming like bird's wings, a bad sign; her aunt's mouth was stiff and dry, braced open like the mouth of a fish. She got the old woman's medicine bag and sorted through it until she found a packet of dried leaves. It was the plant the whites called heartsease and because there was no time to make a tea, Yellow Fawn chewed the leaves to a pulp in her own mouth, then transferred the mash with her finger to the mouth of her aunt. Cattail coughed and swallowed reflexively; Spotted Turtle stroked her forehead. When his eyes met Yellow Fawn's, he understood that there was little hope.

Cattail neither spoke nor opened her eyes again. For a long time her fingers clutched Spotted Turtle's hand, then her hold slowly relaxed, her wrinkled hands growing strangely smooth. Hutch wasn't sure how long they'd been gathered in the lodge when Spotted Turtle laid his head against his wife's chest, listened, and looked helplessly up at them. Soon his mourning chant filled the silence and women were rushing in to wash Cattail's body. Lodgesmoke was crying and Hutch carried her home in his arms. It was an unusually cool night and the stars glittered above them.

Yellow Fawn waited until Lodgesmoke was asleep and Hutch lay stretched beside her. Then she turned to him and said softly, "Lodgesmoke and I will live with my uncle now."

For a moment her words didn't sink in. When they did, Hutch felt as if a patch of skin had been torn open. "But what about our trading place? You said you'd think about it?"

He felt the sweep of her hair as she shook her head in the darkness. "Not now, Chase. Spotted Turtle cannot live alone. We will live with him, Lodgesmoke and I. We must. He has no one else."

Sarah's baby was a boy, born with the black hair of Creath's mother and blue eyes that refused to darken to gray. "We ought to name him for Sam," Creath said, but that was a name still painful for them, so they settled on Fannin instead.

Fan was an early walker and gave Sarah fits by wandering out of the cabin whenever she wasn't looking. One day she found him headed off across the yard, diapers dusting the earth, a scrap of branch clutched in one hand. He looked like a bandy-legged farmer taking stock of his holdings and another time she might have laughed at the sight, but not now. Last December Mirabeau Lamar had succeeded Sam Houston as president of the Republic and his harsh Indian policy sent the scattered tribes crashing against white settlements in retaliation. After spending six months in a San Antonio jail, El Oso slipped out of custody, drew a new band of marauders to him and now, in the summer of 1839, was once again raiding freely across the plains. Women, children, and horses were considered prime booty, for all could be traded to the Comanche who controlled the vast, empty lands west of the Republic.

Sarah scooped Fan up in her arms. "I asked you to watch him, Aus," she said reproachfully as she reentered the cabin.

Her son glanced up from the little chair Creath had made for him. "I'm sorry, Mama."

Sarah hadn't the heart to scold him. In his lap was the picture book Hutch had brought him from Nacogdoches. It was the only book he had, worn gray and limp from his attentions; at five and a half, he could lose himself in it for hours at a time and his moments of chief delight came when Creath took him on his lap at night and pointed out the words one by one.

"What's this word again?" Sarah asked, leaning down over his shoulder.

"Wagon."

She nodded thoughtfully. She was determined to master the words in the little book, though they didn't come to her as easily as they came to her son. "Turn the page, Aus," she said, putting her arm around his neck. They hovered together before the magic of the book, breathing in the excitement of the printed words, and for a moment nothing else seemed to exist.

In the fields farthest from the cabin, Creath worked with Ben Bonham, potato leaves curling around his fingers and ankles as he thinned the plants. It was back breaking work, hot and thirsty, with the blue enameled sky hard above them. Creath straightened, wiped his beaded forehead, and gazed off toward the horizon.

"What's that, Ben?" he asked, squinting toward the bleached rim of land as he pointed.

Ben jerked up. "Riders."

A moment later Creath could see them clearly, shapes that slid across the prairie with frightening speed, their yips and cries already filling the air. *El Oso*, he thought, whirling fast and pushing Ben before him. "Run!" he shouted, relieved to see that Ben was already flying away from him.

They'd left their guns at the edge of the field and paused just long enough to snatch them up before dashing toward the fringe of cottonwoods where their horses were tethered. Creath's heart was pumping by the time he reached cover and sweat dripped from his forehead. Ben got down beside him and laid the rifle across the crook of his arm. Hutch had

been right, Creath realized. In a pinch, Ben Bonham was as
steady as they came.

Creath raised his own gun, ready for a fight, but El Oso
and his raiders galloped by without so much as a glance
toward the cottonwoods. For a moment Creath felt profound
relief. For some reason beyond his knowing he'd been
spared. The potato plants glittered before him like emeralds;
he thought of Sarah and his sons, wrapped in the sleepy
cocoon of the afternoon, safe until he returned to them.
Then he saw the band veering to the west as they rode.

He scrambled for his horse and was half-mounted before
Ben caught up with him. "What're you doing?" Ben
shouted in alarm. "You can't go after them!"

"Look at their direction—they've headed for the cabin!
Sarah!" The last word burst from his throat, a cry that tried
to warn her over an impossible distance. Creath wheeled his
horse in a circle, burst from the copse of cottonwoods, and
pounded off across the rolling sweep of prairie.

Chapter Thirteen

Creath urged his horse forward across the dry ground,
keeping El Oso and his raiders in sight. There was no
chance of outrunning them and reaching Sarah first, he
knew, but by swinging west he could put himself between
her and the raiders. He thanked God that he had taken the
trouble to build this cabin as he had built the other one,
with doors front and back. She ought to have enough time to
escape with the boys into the fringe of trees and brush
behind the cabin.

His heart pounded as the cabin came into view and he
dug his heels deep into his mount's sides. But the raiders
didn't veer toward the place as he expected them to. Instead
they streaked straight across the prairie, bent on some other

goal. For the second time that day Creath had the sense of being delivered, saved by some special providence.

He slowed the horse, uncertain whether to ride ahead to Sarah or go back to assure Ben Bonham he'd come to no harm. Suddenly the thrum of hooves cut through his thoughts. Creath jerked his head up. Two of the raiders, riding at the rear, had caught sight of him and broken away from the group. He saw the flex of their horses' chest muscles as they galloped toward him. Sun glinted along their rifle barrels, held aloft and parallel to the ground.

He was caught in the open in an area where the land rolled so gently it seemed almost flat. He slid from his horse and got behind a tree stump. He remembered felling the tree, a big oak, with Ben last spring. Now he wished he'd let the trunk lie instead of chopping it up for firewood. It was hot and sweat trickled down his neck. He took his hat off and set it on the grass behind him, where it wouldn't get ruined.

There were two raiders, both of them Indians he was sure now, though from what tribe he couldn't tell because they wore Mexican clothes. Their braids were wrapped in strips of blue cloth. Creath took aim and fired and the braids of the Indian on the left whipped forward as he fell.

The second raider dropped from his horse and took cover behind a clump of mesquite. They were even now, Creath thought. His double bore Kentucky rifle had one shot left; the Indian squatting fifty yards away had a single bore weapon. The mesquite bush made good cover, its branches moving in the wind. When Creath fired the second shot he caught the Indian's shoulder, causing pain but no real damage. He swore softly to himself, knowing he was alone now and in the open.

To Sarah in the house the two shots seemed to come in rapid succession. They sent her flying for the spare rifle on the wall. "Aus, you watch Fannin, will you?" She looked down at him. Something was wrong, something was draining away inside her. It was as if all the air in the room were funneling away from them. She stooped and kissed him, kissed both of them. "You wait here until someone comes, do you understand, Aus?"

She closed the cabin door behind her and made her way

through the fringe of trees that hugged the cabin. Then she saw the prairie spread before her, saw the dead Indian and the live one, saw the three scattered horses, saw her husband pinned behind the ragged oak stump. His legs must be falling asleep, she thought, cramped and crumpled as they were.

Sarah's mind worked quickly. She wasn't in range of the Indian yet. She would run forward, take aim, and fire so quickly that the Indian wouldn't notice her until it was too late. Preoccupied with Creath and his torn shoulder, he hadn't even seen her yet. She took a deep breath, thought once of Austin and Fannin, and sprang forward.

Creath caught movement out of the corner of his eye and turned to see the flash and billow of Sarah's skirts as she ran. Instinctively, he shot up to turn her back. *"Sarah!"*

Her name ripped through the air, shattered by the shot that caught Creath squarely in the chest. The Indian was up and running, reaching for the reins of the horse nearest him as Sarah's shot brought him down. Casting the rifle aside, Sarah ran to Creath.

He was lying where he'd fallen, facedown, arms flung wide. She could see the rise and fall of his shoulders and knew he was still alive. But when she turned him over the earth beneath his chest was wet and black and blood trickled from his mouth, etching a line across his cheek. She knelt beside him, knowing he couldn't be moved, and brushed the dirt from his face with her fingertips.

"Sarah." Her face floated above him, beautiful and young and scared, the way it had been that first day in Arden Bell's mill. He reached up to her, but his hand fell away. The wind that had been blowing all afternoon seemed suddenly cold around him. "Sarah?"

"Hush now," she said, taking his hand. "Hush now, I'm here."

Her hair fanned around her shoulders, sunlight shooting through the tangled wisps at the ends. She never wore bonnets and suddenly it seemed important to him to tell her how he loved that about her, loved the sight of her hair framing her face. The words were wet and garbled in his throat.

"Hush," she said again, bending closer to him, stretching one arm across his shattered chest.

That was how Ben Bonham found them a few minutes later, Creath's hand growing cold in hers, the two of them fused together by the blood soaking his shirtfront and staining her arm. It was all he could do to pry her loose so he could sled the body home.

"El Oso?" Hutch's face was hard and bitten in a way Sarah had never seen before. He had heard of the raids along the Brazos, heard his brother's name in the list of casualties, and ridden for two days and nights to reach her. Dust had worked its way into the lines of his forehead and his gray eyes were as dark as lead. He looked forty years old, Sarah thought, not thirty.

"That's who they're saying it was. Oh, Hutch, if he'd only stayed down!"

Sarah was sitting at the table, Fannin on her lap, the lamp making halos on her hair. Hutch had expected her to look different somehow, pinched and bitter the way you expected a widow to look, but that wasn't the case. It seemed to him that she grew more beautiful by the year, like some slow-blooming plant. He drew up a chair and sat down across from her.

"Have you thought of what you're going to do?" he asked, lowering his voice automatically because Austin was asleep in the corner bed. The way he dropped his voice made Sarah think again that he was used to being around children, around a child anyway, and that there was much of his life he'd never told them. "You won't be staying on here, I reckon."

She looked at him with startled eyes. "I hadn't thought to go elsewhere. No, I'll be staying." She stretched her hand across the table to him. "You see, I couldn't leave him, Hutch."

The burying had been the worst: she'd wanted to climb down into the earth with him, take the last warmth in his body. Sometimes she thought she hadn't only because of the two boys who would be left behind. Fan might be all right on his own but not Aus. Aus couldn't make his way without her.

Hutch was looking at her. "How will you manage, Sarah?"

"Ben will stay on with us. I already asked him. And I

can do Creath's part, some of it, if I take the boys into the field with me. We'll manage somehow."

"I reckon you will," he answered, embarrassed to have suggested otherwise. "Aus is near big enough to help."

To his surprise Sarah shook her head firmly. "I want Austin to go to school. I haven't figured out how yet, but he has the mind for it, Hutch. You should see him with that book you brought him." She paused. "There is one thing I need to ask of you."

"What?"

"Help me write a letter to your folks. Aus and I have been learning our letters together—I meant to surprise Creath—but I don't know enough yet. If I tell you what I mean to say will you set it down so I can copy the words myself?"

It was important to her, he saw that. "Of course, Sarah. We can do it in the morning before I leave."

"You're going so soon?"

Hutch scratched a thumb along his jaw and nodded. "They're calling for volunteers to go after El Oso. Maybe you haven't heard. Anyway, I mean to join up."

"No, I didn't know." She could see Creath in him, just a little, around the eyes. "Take care Hutch. Will you promise?"

"Don't worry about me, Sarah."

The next morning he helped her with the letter, waiting while she copied it out so he could take it with him to post. While she scratched at the paper, ink staining her fingers, he wandered down to the place where Creath was buried. But it was too painful and too lonely and soon he went back to the cabin, finding comfort in Sarah's presence.

From the Brazos River El Oso turned his band west and south, heading for the safety of Mexico. It was a pattern of raiding he'd established over the last few years, sweeping out across the prairies always to melt back into the country west of San Antonio. Once in the sanctuary of Mexico he was safe. The Mexicans viewed him as a freedom fighter, an image he carefully built and fostered; they believed that one day he would return Texas to Mexico.

The son of an escaped Louisiana slave and a Karankawa

Indian woman, El Oso, whose name meant The Bear, was a squat and grizzled man. In his youth he had been powerfully built but now he'd grown heavy, so heavy he had difficulty finding mounts to carry him. As he drew near the border he was prone to grow lazy, prone to linger for a night at his favorite cantina, prone to believe that no Anglo Ranger would pursue him so far west.

All of this was known to Morris T. Ogg, whose network of information gatherers stretched wide across the Republic of Texas. To Hutch, Ogg was a new type of man, neither a frontiersman nor a farmer but a professional fighter; whenever he could raise a company of volunteer Rangers he'd dash off to fight the Indians, the Mexicans, or whoever else was disturbing peace on the frontier. By no means a big man, Ogg gave the impression of one, mostly by keeping quiet and avoiding wasted motion, and on the whole Hutch liked him. Now Ogg had led them to the hilly, thin soil country west of San Antonio where, concealed behind a limestone ridge, they looked down on a cluster of adobe buildings, blown beige by drifting dust.

"That's the cantina," Ogg said with an abbreviated nod. "No tracks, no extra horses, so they ain't been here yet. But they will be. There's a senorita there El Oso can't do without, so we'll just wait a spell. I plan to ambush them when they get right about there," he pointed with the tip of his pistol. "Anyone's got any problems with that plan, this here's the turn around point."

Like Hutch, the other twelve men in the group had volunteered because they'd lost someone to El Oso's marauders. "I reckon ambush'd be a might kinder than what they did to my pa," a young man said, and there was a murmur of agreement as the men fanned out and hunkered down along the ridge. To amuse himself, Hutch pictured the senorita inside the cantina, someone with dark flowing hair and swinging hips, maybe a little like Yellow Fawn. But when a squat, big-chinned woman with dull hair came out to feed the chickens, he lost interest. There were few women like Yellow Fawn in Texas, he realized. His sister-in-law was one, but other than that he couldn't think of any.

They waited all through the dusty afternoon and Ogg

began to worry that the band would ride through after dark, when they'd be harder to hit. But they came along just as the sun was beginning to set, El Oso in the lead and his men strung out behind him. They were running stolen horses and Ogg quickly adjusted his strategy. "They'll pen the herd in that empty corral there. Wait 'til the horses are in and I give the signal, then fire. Hit the ones on horseback first, you'll have as much time as you need with those on foot."

Hutch waited, his finger near the trigger of his rifle. He knew the men who killed his brother weren't here, they were long dead. Sarah had showed him where she'd buried them, without markers, just deep enough to keep wolves away. But he was anxious to be through with this business of killing, anxious to get back to Cutfoot Creek. His brother's death had left an ache in him, an ache that Yellow Fawn and Lodgesmoke could ease. Ogg gave the signal and he picked up a man in his sights.

At the first shots the band tried to scatter for cover. Ogg had picked his location well, however. Across from the limestone ridge rose a steep, rocky hill; the men who tried to climb it to safety were slowed by the rocks and easily picked off. The road they'd come down offered no protection, for it was wide and open and led back into Texas. Hemmed in, El Oso jogged to the cantina and tried to enter, only to find the door barred.

The fight was over in a few minutes, with no Ranger casualties and a total loss for El Oso. Before the leader's body was dumped into a hastily dug trench, Ogg took a satchel of papers from him. Curious, Hutch took the satchel when Ogg handed it to him and read its contents in the fading light. It was those papers, he thought later, that caused all the grief that followed.

Chapter Fourteen

The next time Hutch saw the papers, they were spread across the desk of President Lamar in Austin. He'd followed Ogg to the capital with them, knowing what they said and what the result was likely to be. Now Ogg was gone, off on another raid, and Hutch stood in Lamar's office.

"It says here," Lamar frowned, "that your Cherokee were about to make a deal with El Oso, a deal to steal horses from settlers and sell them to him."

The room was sweltering and sweat trickled down Hutch's neck. He removed his hat and sat down, though he'd been asked to do neither. "I read those papers myself and that's not what they say. What they say is that *some* Indians *somewhere* on the Cutfoot were talking to El Oso. That could be the Creeks or it could be the Kickapoo."

"Or it could be the Cherokee."

Hutch had the sinking feeling that Lamar might be right. It was all too likely that Walking Bird and Black Elbow, tired of waiting for the whites to make good on their promises, had begun skinning the buffalo at both ends, though it wouldn't do to say so. "Maybe if the government'd get around to titling their lands for them, they'd be a lot quieter."

Lamar looked at Hutch with constrained surprise. "You propose ceding land to enemies of Texas? Why not invite the devil in to dinner? I don't think the people would find that popular at all." Lamar, in his early forties, had been elected on a firebrand platform; he had no intention of changing his policy.

Hutch felt the back of his neck grow warmer by degrees. "The Cherokee aren't enemies of Texas," he replied angrily. "They fought with us against the Mexicans, they signed another treaty in thirty-eight. All they want is their land."

"Their land? They don't even belong here. Let them go back over the Red if they want land."

"Sam Houston promised them land here, along the Cutfoot."

"Houston's a reckless fellow, not above bending a rule or two. He had no authority to offer them land." Lamar paused. "You're a friend of that old chief up there, I know. If your word carries any weight, tell him to move north. Texas isn't a wild frontier anymore. Things like this," he gestured to the papers spread across his desk, "won't be tolerated. Not without bloodshed. Best if you can make them understand that."

Hutch stood up, furious. "I can make them understand that. What I can't make them understand is why their treaties aren't being honored." Grabbing his hat, he slammed out of the office, swinging the door so hard behind him that a crack shot up in the fine-grained wood, ruining the best door in Texas.

"Your brother's woman, how is she?" Yellow Fawn's hair swung forward as she handed the bowl of venison stew to Hutch. It was November, chilly even inside the lodge, and steam drifted up from the bowl.

"Sarah's fine," Hutch answered as he speared a chunk of meat with the tip of his knife. "Got herself some neighbors now and she's bent on getting a teacher for the kids."

Yellow Fawn smiled softly. She had a broad, deep-reaching sympathy for Sarah, for she knew herself how it was to be a woman alone, without a man. "And the Comanche?"

Hutch had gone to visit Sarah because he'd heard the Comanche were raiding as far east as the Trinity River. He finished chewing and shook his head. "She said she saw three of 'em once, at night, but she and Ben scared them off." Although Hutch grinned at Sarah's pluck, he knew the call had been a close one, whether Sarah said so or not. Lamar's Indian policy had fanned sparks all along the frontier, even here in the north. More than once that summer had the Cherokee been ambushed by whites who did not distinguish between one tribe and another, and now whenever the men went hunting they armed themselves for possible skirmishing.

To Hutch it seemed strange to take up arms against other

whites, but he was reluctant to leave Yellow Fawn and Lodgesmoke at such a dangerous time. The same band of Comanche that harassed white settlements to the south might just as easily turn north and thread its way into the camps of the Caddo and Creek, the Cherokee and the Kickapoo. The Cherokee had many enemies, the whites pushing from the south and east, other displaced tribes crowding down from the north, and the most formidable of all enemies, the Comanche, striking from the west.

Despite the unrest, Hutch and Yellow Fawn discovered a tranquility and a closeness they hadn't known before. Spotted Turtle's lodge became a home now, richer for the contributions Hutch made. With a regular supply of meat and hides, Yellow Fawn was able to replace long worn out clothes and footwear; with more of her own time free, she was able to raise more vegetables to trade for small luxuries. There were deerskin robes on the beds and new moccasins each season; when Hutch got up in the morning, there was coffee scenting the air.

To Yellow Fawn it felt as if her life had been a broken stream, a stream she'd followed patiently, even when it disappeared from sight. And now the stream had opened into a crystal pool, still and sweet, deep as her own heart.

Suddenly the door opened and Lodgesmoke burst into the room. "Grandfather said you were home," she cried, running to Hutch. She was nearly ten years old now, leggy as a colt, with eyes that changed, in certain lights, from gray to smoky blue.

Hutch stopped eating. " 'Course I'm home. Got a present for you too." He reached into his shirt pocket and pulled out a bracelet just large enough to fit her wrist. It was carved from a single slice of cherry wood and intricately adorned with forest animals: rabbits and deer, bears and foxes. Lodgesmoke had never seen anything so wonderful and her eyes sparkled as she held her wrist up to admire it. She raced outside to show off her new possession, her yellow puppy at her heels. After she'd gone Hutch reached for his saddle pack. "I brought something for you, too," he said, glancing at Yellow Fawn as he pulled a folded length of cloth out and handed it to her.

The material settled like a cloud in Yellow Fawn's hands. It was cotton, fine-spun and dyed in shades of gray-green and blue, with little specks of peach scattered through the pattern. She hadn't seen such fine material in years, not since she'd left her home in the east. "Where did you get these things?" she asked. "Lodgesmoke's bracelet and this cloth?"

"Soldier at Bird's Fort carved the bracelet for me."

She nodded. Bird's Fort, on the northern end of the Trinity, had become the new link between north and south, closer and more convenient than Nacogdoches. "And the cloth?" She was thinking that surely there couldn't be women at the fort, and who else would want blue material dotted with peach.

"Oh that," Hutch said. "That's from a place that's flung itself up next to the fort. Trading town called Dallas."

"Funny name," Yellow Fawn said thoughtfully, stroking the material with her hand. Hutch didn't hear her; he was rustling in his pack for Spotted Turtle's present, a fire-starting flint shaped like an eagle, also traded for in the new settlement.

Throughout the fall, Hutch kept a wary eye on Walking Bird, and when two Caddo Indians came to visit at the outset of December, he took care to be at the council.

Since the outbreak of renewed hostilities with the whites, Walking Bird had fallen strangely silent, as if this new, open acknowledgment of hatreds appeased him. He no longer spoke of getting title to the land—that was a hope long laid to rest—and sometimes he even treated Hutch as a friend. Yet Hutch had not forgotten the papers found on El Oso's body, or his suspicion that Walking Bird might have been involved. Spotted Turtle had grown old since his wife's death, truly old, and Hutch now found himself taking the old chief's part at meetings, sitting near him and speaking his thoughts for him.

The Caddo had been sent by Lamar to propose a new settlement policy: that the Caddo, decimated in numbers and harried by the Comanche, combine with the Cherokee along Cutfoot Creek.

The proposal was distasteful, yet Spotted Turtle would have a difficult time turning it down. Once the Caddo had moved aside for them, now it was up to them to move aside for the Caddo, for if they didn't no one else would and the remnants of the tribe would be left for the Comanche to pick over.

The two visiting Caddo were treated well, and Yellow Fawn made room for them in Spotted Turtle's lodge. So crowded did the small space become that Hutch and Yellow Fawn had to steal outside, to the edge of the village, to be alone. Not that either of them minded, wrapped in an elk robe with the wind licking high above them. Afterward they hurried back through the chill air to the smoky warmth of the lodge and curled around each other with peaceful sleepiness.

The second time they did this, after the Caddo had been with them for several days, they came back to a lit lamp and Lodgesmoke hovering over one of the visitors with frightened eyes. "He's sick," she said. "I heard him making noises and got up, but I didn't know what to do."

Yellow Fawn soothed her and sent her back to bed. From her place in the corner Lodgesmoke could hear her mother and father murmuring to each other over the sick man. There was no moment of relief, no moment when the light was snuffed out, telling her that all was well. She turned her back at last, curling into a ball and watching the line of her silhouette against the wall.

By morning it was clear to Yellow Fawn that the Caddo had smallpox. "You must take Lodgesmoke and Spotted Turtle away," she told Hutch, "and the other Caddo too. My old lodge is empty, go there with some food and blankets. And don't—" her voice caught—"don't let Lodgesmoke play with the other children."

Hutch's glance shot to his daughter, sleeping in the corner. "You don't think—"

"I don't know, Chase. But smallpox can wipe out a village."

Spotted Turtle refused to leave his lodge, pointing out that as he'd already shared a pipe with the Caddo, he saw no harm in sharing the same air with him. Yellow Fawn shivered as she remembered that pipe at the council meeting, how it had passed from hand to hand and mouth to mouth. Was that how smallpox traveled? she wondered. Through the mouth or the nose? Or was it simply that after a time of living, the time for living was over?

Whatever the mysteries of the universe, time in the lodge came to a halt for Yellow Fawn. She knew that the light paled each morning and grew dim each evening, that food was left at her door, but how many times each of these happened she lost track of. She knew only that the same day Spotted Turtle grew ill Hutch came to wake her in the middle of the night.

"What?" she asked through the closed door.

"Open it," he cried, pounding with such anguish that the logs shook.

Yellow Fawn held up the light and was relieved to see him whole and sound before her; she'd half feared she'd find him sweated and shivering, his face running with sores.

"What is it, Chase?"

"Lodgesmoke."

Yellow Fawn's knees wavered beneath her. She saw Hutch step forward and put up her hand to keep him back. "I'm all right, don't come in. How bad is she, Chase?"

"Sick, I can't tell. But she isn't the only one. All over the village—" His voice trailed off.

Yellow Fawn grasped the door frame. Once, when she was very young, smallpox had come among them in the east, striking every lodge. "You must find a doctor, Chase."

"Where?"

"At the soldiers' town, at Fort Bird. You must get him to come here."

"But that's two days' ride from here. Two days there and two days back. I can't go off and leave you."

Her eyes were fierce, a look he couldn't have summoned if his life depended on it. "You *must* go, there's no other way."

"What about Lodgesmoke? And the other Caddo, he's sick too."

"I know. Someone will bring them to me. Please go, Chase."

As he rode away from the village he remembered the last night they'd spent together, the wind whispering above them.

Hutch reached Bird's Fort thirty-six hours later, having ridden hard and slept in the saddle. The fort was a low, drab place, its logs already weathered gray by sun and wind. A storm was in progress and the blockhouse seemed almost to sink beneath its pelting force. A hundred yards to the west a makeshift Indian village hugged the plain. Hutch felt a chill as he passed, for rising far behind it was a cluster of burial scaffolds.

Inside the blockhouse he located the doctor attached to the fort. "You're Parmer?" he asked, streaming water onto the rough puncheon floor.

It was dark inside the room with lamps lit even in the day. "Yes." Parmer was a young man, with glossy auburn hair and a carefully trimmed mustache.

"There's a smallpox outbreak. You've got to come."

"Where?"

"Up on Cutfoot Creek."

Parmer's brows drew together. "We don't have any settlements up there. I can't ride out, leave these men, just for one farmer and his family."

"It's a whole village," Hutch said quickly, "Spotted Turtle's village."

Parmer looked surprised. "Indian?"

"Cherokee."

"I can't leave my post to treat hostiles."

"They're not hostiles."

"Nevertheless." Parmer lifted his hand, spread his fingers in a gesture of helplessness. "I can't. Do you see? I can't. My first duty is to the men of this fort, then to the people of Texas."

Hutch gritted his teeth. "Who's the commander here?"

"Jeremiah Reeves."

"I want to see him."

"He's out on detail."

"When will he be back?"

"A week, maybe. The Comanche are raising hell west of here." Hutch's desperation filled the room and Parmer seemed truly regretful. "Even if I could go with you, there's very little I could do. Indians have no . . . no tolerance to our diseases. Smallpox and measles run right through them. Look at those Caddo out there."

Hutch tensed, though Parmer didn't notice it. "Caddo?"

Parmer nodded. "The last of them. Epidemic wiped them

out, they're still suffering from it. Now Lamar's trying to get them to migrate north."

Hutch remembered the burial scaffolds he'd seen outside the fort and felt his throat contract with fury. "Did two of them ride out of here last week?"

Realization flashed in the minds of both men at once. With smallpox raging through the camp, the two Caddoes had been sent out anyway, knowingly and perhaps even deliberately. That was one solution to the Indian problem, Hutch thought bitterly.

Parmer swallowed uncomfortably. "There were orders, written orders, from Lamar's office in Austin." A long silence fell across the room, a silence broken only by the rain gusting against the walls of the blockhouse. Hutch looked up to find Parmer pressing a brown medicine bottle into his hand. "It's all I can spare. Dilute it with three parts of water and only give it to those you think have a chance."

Hutch found his way back out into the rain, the bottle small in his hand.

He rode again without sleep and when he saw the silhouette of Spotted Turtle's village rising before him he felt at first a sense of reassurance. The lodges were still there, as they'd been for a hundred of his comings and goings; no fresh burial scaffolds stretched beyond the fields.

But as he drew near, his horse snorted and shied, nostrils flaring. A pack of dogs snarled at him from the shadows along the road and as they melted back into the woods he recognized Lodgesmoke's yellow pup among them. Heart pounding, he looked up and saw no smoke rising from the lodges; they were cold and dark, doors ajar or swung open. A foot protruded from one of them, a woman's foot in a beaded moccasin. He didn't know who she was.

The horse balked now, the smell of death strong in its nostrils, and Hutch dismounted. He ran to Spotted Turtle's lodge, prepared to batter down the door if Yellow Fawn refused to open it for him. But it swung open at his touch and he stepped into the still, silent gloom of the room.

There were sheafs of hides in the lodge, domed sheafs bundled the way mountain men bundled hide for trade. But when his eyes adjusted he saw that they weren't bales of hides but covered bodies, two long ones for the Caddoes, a shorter one that would be Spotted Turtle, and still a shorter one that he couldn't take his eyes from. A small hand escaped beneath the hide covering as if reaching out to him, a hand that was pearly and perfect, nails gleaming faintly, wrist circled by forest animals carved in wood.

"Chase?" His name was chapped and dusty in the room full of death, and in his exhaustion he stood confused. Then he turned and saw Yellow Fawn. Lying in a corner, she'd managed to lift herself on one elbow. He was by her in an instant, cradling her head on his lap, finding a water gourd and dribbling water with his fingertips onto her cracked, bleeding lips. "You must go away from here," she said with effort, eyes fluttering open and closed. "The whole village—"

"I know," Hutch said.

"Then go."

He shook his head. "I have medicine, medicine from the fort." He found the bottle and poured some of the liquid into the water gourd.

"Give it to someone else, Chase," Yellow Fawn said, turning her head away. But he had seen no one else and sat instead with her, moving only to find a lamp and light it when darkness settled over them.

It had begun to grow light again when her eyes opened, clear and bright as they had been the first time he held her. Yellow Fawn squeezed his hand, lighting sparks of hope in him. "It was good, Chase," she said. "You made it good for me." Then the pressure on his hand was gone.

Chapter Fifteen

There were survivors in Spotted Turtle's village, ghost people Hutch found huddled in their lodges. Whether his medicine did any good or not he never knew, but he stayed until the epidemic was over, helping where he could, disposing of the dead. To stop the contagion the bodies were layered in piles and burned and where a whole family had died, as with Walking Bird and Sweetgrass and their child, the lodge was burned down around them.

Before Spotted Turtle's lodge was burned Hutch tried to pull the carved bracelet from Lodgesmoke's wrist, but her hand was swollen and it wouldn't come. Grabbing a large skin bag from the wall he swept through the lodge like a madman, snatching up things that had belonged to them, heedless of possible infection. He could stand to see their bodies burned but not, oddly, these things they had touched and used and loved.

When he finally left the village he took the bag with him, never once looking inside but clinging to it at night, using it as a pillow, letting his tears stain the thin, soft leather. He had no idea where he was going. His old life, the life he'd lived for more than fourteen years, was gone.

He wanted no part of Texas or his own civilization and instinctively turned toward Nacogdoches, his old sanctuary, but the town was full of ghosts for him. He remembered the day he'd met Rip Paxton there, remembered the other traders he'd met and guided north, and the saloon where he and Findley Ware had shared a drink the afternoon he'd learned Creath was in Galveston.

In that same saloon, filled now with different faces, he listened to talk of a new existence. Beyond the border of Texas, along the river that was called the Rio Bravo by some and the Rio Grande by others, men were trading horses and tobacco, doing business with the Comanche and living more or less without constraint of any kind. To Hutch it sounded as appealing as anything and after a few days he traded his big American horse for a hardy Indian pony and headed south.

He didn't take the direct route but jogged his course to see Sarah. She didn't ask questions but knew, in her unfailing way, that some tragedy had overtaken him. "You've always a home here, Hutch," she said, her hand lighting on his arm.

She was twenty-six now, as beautiful as a bramble rose, and seeing her again made Hutch wonder how she'd ever stood losing Creath. But she had, hanging on to the land and the stock with Ben Bonham. There were a half dozen families in the area now, and Sarah's cheeks glowed as she told how she'd gotten them together to coax a teacher up from Houston for the winter.

Hutch felt a sudden desire to reach out, to run his fingers over her crinkly hair, but he didn't. "I aim to go south for a while," he told her. "See what the Mexican trade is like. There is one favor I'd ask of you, though."

"What?"

He handed her the leather bag full of possessions. "Keep this for me?"

"Of course, Hutch. You watch out for yourself now. And take some cornbread, it's fresh made this morning and we've plenty."

After he'd ridden away she opened the bag. The scent of mint reached her, mint dried and crumbled by a woman's hands, the way she herself crumbled fragrant leaves over clothes when she packed them away. There wasn't much inside—a lump of silver, melted and tarnished, that might once have been a gorget; a copper cooking pot, much used and polished; a child's doll, a string of amber beads. The objects tore at Sarah's heart and she sat down, something she rarely did in the middle of a day. Oh, Hutch, she thought, running her fingers around and around the rim of the cooking pot; poor, poor Hutch.

He was gone the better part of two years, losing touch with Texas so completely that the Republic almost seemed to sink and vanish behind him. Houston replaced Lamar as president at the end of the year, though Hutch didn't hear of it until months after the fact, at the same time he heard that the remnants of the Cherokee had withdrawn into lands north of the Red River.

At first the change of scene alone soothed him. He followed the old road of the Spanish empire, El Camino Real, avoiding the Alamo with its memories of Rip Paxton and veering south of the place where Morris Ogg had led him against El Oso. He wanted no more memories rising up before him; only the vast, empty land seemed able to absorb his grief.

He discovered that he could ride for days at a time without seeing another human being, neither settler nor

Indian nor trader, and that suited him. The country was
inhospitable, dry and rocky and so full of brush that he
often had to navigate around dense, impenetrably thorny
thickets. Aside from the brush the chief distinction of the
region was the pecari, the tough-hided pig that fed and
flourished on prickly pear. There were also, to Hutch's
surprise, large numbers of cattle wandering loose, cattle that
seemed neither tame nor truly wild. After passing a few
abandoned homesteads he understood the cattle's origin.
When fighting had heated up between Texas and Mexico,
the Mexicans along the border had found themselves unpopular with their Anglo neighbors. They'd fled south into
Mexico, leaving their cattle to scatter over the plains.

It was too bad, Hutch thought, for the herds were degen-
erating rapidly. The young animals he saw were leggy and
slab-sided, with bones sticking up like boulders beneath
their hides. When he reached the Mexican villa of Piedras
Negras, across the Rio Grande from Eagle Pass, he was
amazed to learn that the animals were the cornerstone of a
thriving business. Rounded up by vaqueros on horseback,
they were added to domestic herds in Mexico or driven east
to New Orleans for sale.

Hutch needed money and worked for a few weeks with
the cow men, but soon restlessness seized him and he
drifted on. For a while he joined in the horse trade along the
Rio Grande, amassing money quickly because he was not
afraid to ride into the *Comancheria* to trade directly with the
Indians. For a time he even hoped to find with them an echo
of the life he'd known with the Cherokee, but the hope was
a naive one. The Comanche were an inscrutable people,
nomadic and, to him, barbaric. Among them he found no
traces of the peaceful life he'd lived with Spotted Turtle's
band; among them he found no woman who drew him as
Yellow Fawn had. The joy the Comanche took in following
the blood trail, in raiding settlements and returning with
captives, was repellent to him and though Hutch was respected
by them because he came without fear and because he
traded fairly, he never became one of them.

One day a captive girl, no older than Lodgesmoke, was
brought into camp after a raid, crying for her father whose

scalp fluttered from a lance. "She'll forget soon enough," said a chief standing near Hutch, speaking in a language Hutch still struggled to understand. "She'll become Comanche soon." But long after he'd ridden away from the camp the girl's sobs echoed in his ears, making him think of Lodgesmoke, alone, her soul drifting in the clouds above him.

Maybe it was the captive girl or maybe it was the novelty of his new life wearing off, he didn't know, but after months of escape memories forced their way back into his mind. Images of Yellow Fawn and Lodgesmoke flickered before him, awake or asleep, torturing him with their nearness. In his dreams he would see them, rounded and alive, moving and laughing and talking around him as if he didn't exist. A sense of loss swirled through his belly, a realization that grew sharper and more difficult to bear with each day that passed.

One sweltering night in Laredo he awoke bathed in sweat, the candle guttered out beside him and unseen insects climbing through his clothes. Through the shuttered window, closed against a horde of flying insects, he caught the spark of a single white star. Suddenly he was thinking of his sister-in-law, of Sarah, and as he fumbled through the dark to pull the shutter open a gentle breeze washed over him. It was the first peace he'd known in weeks.

The next day he sold the string of horses he'd just acquired and, keeping the hardiest one for himself, started north.

"A dark night is what they like best for raiding," Ben Bonham said. "A rainy night or a night without a moon." Sarah's hired man was young, younger than she was, but he'd grown up in Texas and knew Comanche habits. "You've nothing to worry about on a night like this." Ben gestured beyond the cabin walls where stars shone clear and bright in the summer moonlight.

She smiled quickly. "You're a comfort, Ben. I couldn't manage without you."

He said nothing, embarrassed by her praise and by the fact that he'd fallen silently and impossibly in love with her. He finished his dinner, scraping his fork against his plate, and reassured her once more. "This isn't an Indian night, Mrs. Chase, but I'll sleep indoors if it'll set your mind at ease.'' Ben's usual quarters were in the barn loft above the cattle, a clean and comfortable nest that suited him. But during the summer, with the Comanche preying on isolated settlements along the frontier, he'd slept in her cabin more than once, unrolling his bedroll by the door and feeling a deep sense of pride as her protector.

Sarah passed the thought back and forth in her mind, understanding better than Ben himself did the complex welter of his emotions. His mother had died young, leaving him alone with a father and four brothers; from what he said of her, her image had merged with Sarah's in his mind. Sarah would never have let him sleep inside at all, never have fostered the ties between them, except for the Comanche.

Her dread of them was no ordinary fear but cold presentiment, ripping and plucking at her insides. In her mind's eye she saw her sons carried away, saw her own scalp fluttering on a lance, saw her and her kin blotted from the memory of man. That was what had happened to the folks just forty miles east of them in 1836. Parker's Fort was empty now, its logs bleaching in the sun, and the names of the children taken there were ghost names, names that belonged neither to the living nor the dead. Sarah lived in a world where such things could and did happen, and not always to someone else; she'd learned that the day El Oso's men had cut her life in two.

''No, Ben,'' she replied at last, picking up his empty plate. ''As you said, the moon is bright.''

She'd taken to putting Fannin in bed with her, keeping him between her body and the wall, for he was a great sleepwalker and would sometimes unlatch the door. When she awakened in the middle of the night, she thought it was because he'd climbed over her again.

''Fan?'' she whispered. It was as if an internal spring was coiled inside him, propelling him forward even in his sleep. But when she put out her hand, she found him curled beside her, and that was when her heart froze, wondering if this was the night, the Comanche night, she'd been dreading.

Through the darkness she heard the clop of horses' hooves, soft on the powdery earth. There was only one rider but sometimes they did that, sending one warrior to draw attention while others swooped in from behind. She slid her arm out and felt for the rifle. The stock was smooth and solid and reassuring to her touch.

"Mama?" It was Austin, her light sleeper. She found her way to him in the darkness and smoothed his curly auburn hair with her free hand.

"I'm right here, Aus."

"Are the Indians coming, mama?" They were bound as close as twigs in a bundle, and sometimes it seemed he could read her thoughts. She was careful not to let him feel the gun at her side or see the gleam of its barrel.

"No, Aus. You go back to sleep." She stooped by him a minute longer, listening all the while to the hooves that circled nearer in the darkness. The dog was not yipping, as it usually did when strangers approached, and she pictured it lying dead in the woods, throat slashed to silence it.

She took her place near the window, praying that Ben Bonham was awake too. Tree leaves shivered in the moonlight and stars speckled the sky. Her heart was pumping quickly now, her hands steady as she lifted the gun.

Soon the rider came into view. She would have shot at once, a clean shot that would have struck home, but something stopped her. She saw the shadow of her dog dancing beside the horse and hesitated. "Who is it?" she called, her voice sharp and clear.

"Hutchinson." He wasn't sure why he used his full name except that he'd been away a long time and felt, suddenly, like a stranger on her land.

Sarah felt relief sweep through her. She laid the gun against the wall and hurried out to meet him. "Lord, I thought you were Red Bow. I almost shot."

"Glad you didn't." Hutch grinned as he dismounted. Sarah's legs showed beneath the old shirt—one of Creath's, he reckoned—she wore as a nightdress. "Who's Red Bow?"

Ben Bonham came up beside them now, roused from sleep by their voices. His clay-colored hair was sticking up in tufts and he was eyeing Hutch through sleep-narrowed eyes. "Red Bow's a Comanche buck. Been causing trouble up this way all summer."

Hutch looked past Ben to Sarah. "I had a hankering to

see you," he said. "I rode all the way up here from Laredo."

Sarah smiled. "All this way just for a visit? My, my, we'll have to treat him special, won't we, Ben?"

But Ben had gone suddenly glum. "I'll see to the horse," he mumbled, grabbing for the trailing reins.

On the way back to the house Sarah laid her hand along Hutch's arm. "It's good you've come for a visit. We've missed you, Hutch."

He was silent until they'd passed through the door, until she'd lit the lamp that stood on the table. Then he said something he hadn't made up his mind about until that moment, when he saw her eyes resting on him. "I thought I might give you a hand on the place, Sarah, if you're still of a mind to have me."

She felt a spasm clutch at her heart and looked away from him. "Yes, Hutch," she said, rising to swing the coffeepot over the fire. "We'd be glad to have you." Until that moment, she hadn't realized how lonely she'd been.

Hutch stayed on and it touched Sarah to see how he struggled to fit his life to theirs, working with Ben Bonham in the fields and taking over much of the work that had once been Creath's. He was no farmer by nature and sometimes in the evening, as he washed in the basin by the door, she would catch him gazing out across the land and see the restlessness in his eyes. It was a longing he kept to himself, though, and she never mentioned it, realizing that his need for a hearth fire, for familiar faces around him, outweighed everything else.

There were times when the restlessness welled up inside him and then he would disappear for days at a time, hunting and camping on his own, returning exhausted and appeased, always with a haunch of bear or venison for them. It was on one of these wanderings that he came across a piece of land that pleased him more than the others, a place where the scattered trees ceased growing and the great prairies came rolling in from the west. Here he returned again and again, watching the grass turn from green to yellow to tawny red with the seasons, finding in it a peace he'd been unable to find anywhere else.

It was wild and untouched land, of that he was sure, too poorly watered to be of interest to farmers. When he inquired at the land office he found that it was unowned, and that if he purchased an immense swatch of it he could join it to Sarah's holdings.

That autumn the handful of families in the area joined together again to hire a teacher for the winter months. It had been the same the two previous winters, and Sarah was determined that once again Austin would attend. But this year, when she mentioned it, Hutch grinned at her across the table. "Why don't you go with him?" he said.

Ben Bonham's spoon came to a halt in midair and Sarah too, cutting meat for Fannin, stopped to stare at him. "Don't make fun of me, Hutch. You know I've a longing to read, and Aus is so far ahead of me now I can't keep up."

Hutch scratched his thumb along the hard line of his jaw. "I wasn't making fun, Sarah. The school's open to everyone, isn't it?"

Austin, now nine, had begun to develop his own circle of friends, none of whom had their mothers tagging along to school with them. He laid down his fork.

"There's a cost for each pupil," Sarah said, proud that she had fished up the correct word, *pupil*, even if she was illiterate. "We haven't the money." But her hand was plucking excitedly at a loose thread on her apron, Hutch saw.

"There's money," Hutch said. "Money we haven't touched yet, from all the horse trading I did in Mexico."

Now Sarah was thinking seriously, letting her mind escape. "Who'd do the chore work around the house?"

"Ben and I'll manage," Hutch replied, nudging Ben's foot with his under the table. "Won't we, Ben?"

Ben, who'd been in a lovesick sulk since Hutch's arrival, glanced at Sarah and saw the excitement in her eyes. *I'd move heaven and earth for her*, he thought, liking the way the phrase sounded. "Of course we'll manage, Sarah."

"And what about Fan?"

Fannin, who was four, admired Hutch more than anyone

in the world. Hearing his name, he looked up quickly. "Fan
'n me'll get on just fine," Hutch said. "I figured to teach
him to shoot this winter."

"Oh, Hutch, not yet; he's too young, he'd shoot us
all—" She stopped abruptly, realizing that he was joking.

"You go on to school, Sarah."

Austin's stomach contracted in a knot of apprehension.
He imagined what his friend Billy Wilkinson would say.
Sarah laid her palms flat against the table. "I'll go," she
said. "But you needn't pay for it, Hutch. I'll manage to find
the money. Taking care of Fan will be help enough."

Austin's chair scraped back from the table. Hutch, who'd
been watching the shifting expressions on his face, caught
the rung with the toe of his boot. "Something wrong,
Aus?"

"No, it's just that—"

Hutch stood up quickly. "I'm going out to check on that
calf, the one with the swollen eye. Why don't you come
with me, Aus. We'll have ourselves a little talk."

Sarah never knew what Hutch said to her son or what he
might have answered, but a month later when school began,
Aus was up at 4 A.M., saddling her mule as well as his own,
riding by her side all the way to the Wilkinsons', where the
class was held.

The learning caused an excitement in Sarah, an excitement unlike anything she had known before. She came
home through the dark those winter evenings with flushed
cheeks and shining eyes. "I learned to write all of our
names today," she would say, or "Mr. Hobart let me borrow
his reader."

After dinner she would hurry through the dishwashing
and mending to snatch a few minutes before the firelight
with her book. Sometimes Hutch woke in the middle of the
night to find her still awake, sounding out the words to
herself or scratching them in the hard-packed dirt floor of
the cabin. It was the kind of thing Yellow Fawn had often
done—risen in the middle of the night to pursue some
task—and Hutch felt the same sense of peace and comfort
with Sarah that he had felt in Yellow Fawn's lodge. Lying
there in the darkness with her voice murmuring over him, he

would think of his brother and understand how and why he had loved her as he did. It made him feel closer to Creath, somehow.

On Christmas Eve Sarah read the Christmas story to them. Not out of the Bible, for her education was not that advanced, but from her own version, one she'd written painstakingly and in secret during the last month, limiting herself to the words she'd mastered. They made a fuss over her, even Aus and Fan, though both were distracted by the brown paper-wrapped packages with their names on them that sat in torturous nearness on the table, waiting for tomorrow. The packages had come home with Hutch on a trip to town, and Austin's bore the shape and heft of a much longed-for book. He fell asleep with his eyes on the present, counting backward to mark the hours until dawn.

Sarah too spent a restless night, rising when the Big Dipper had swung far around in the sky and slipping outside. Her breath hung in a plume before her and for a long time she simply stood, gazing up at the immense sky above her. The evening had been a happy one, the happiest since Creath's death, with Hutch helping the boys crumble dry cornbread for the wild turkey he'd shot for Christmas dinner and Ben Bonham leading them in Christmas carols. And then there had been her reading to them, the magic of seeing words on a page and knowing what each one meant.

If only Creath were here, she thought, her throat tightening. It seemed, these days, as if he'd been crowded from the cabin, and for that she felt a pang of guilt. At first when Hutch had come back she'd been glad for the company and glad for an extra hand to help her. Since then she'd come to know him differently, come to know him far better than she'd known him before. Sometimes it seemed that bits of Creath came back to her in him, for their looks and gestures, their manner of speaking, were often similar. But Hutch was his own person, too. Buried in his quietness was a sense of humor that caught her unaware, and when she found herself laughing she would feel a twinge to think of Creath. Now she stood on Christmas Eve night, her feelings a welter of confusion, happiness hurting more than pain.

Sarah heard the door pull open and knew without turning that it was Hutch. "Are you all right, Sarah?" he asked.

"Yes. It's just that I miss him, Hutch. More than I can stand sometimes."

"I didn't think there was anything you couldn't bear, Sarah." He laid his hand along the gentle curve of her shoulder, turning her to him. "I miss Creath too."

The name stood between them, drawing them together and keeping them apart at the same time. Sarah drew back. "I forget, you've lost as much as I have. More, I reckon." She was thinking of the things he'd left with her. "That bag you gave me," she said, following her trail of thought, "you've never asked, but it's stored safe away. I'll get it for you whenever you're ready to travel on."

Her face was beautiful in the pale light of the stars. "I hadn't planned on moving on," he said, then he vanished inside the house, leaving her alone with her thoughts.

In the spring, when school ended and planting began and life returned to normal, Hutch hitched the mules to the wagon, put Ben in charge of the place, and took Sarah and the boys on an overnight journey. "Where to?" she questioned, as she swung up onto the seat beside him.

"Where to?" Fannin echoed, twining his arms around Sarah's neck and bracing his legs as the wagon bounced forward.

"Camping," Hutch said with a grin. "Hunting, adventuring. There's something I want to show your ma."

Austin was disappointed that the destination wasn't to be Miller's Raft, the nearest town of size, but Fannin was wild with excitement. "He's a Chase clear through," Hutch was fond of saying of the boy. "He'd go to the moon if there was a way to get there."

They drove all day, eating the food Sarah had packed and stopping to look for the first berries of the season. They were green and hard and Fan, who ate them anyway, was sick for the last part of the ride.

They arrived just before sunset. "What do you think of it?" Hutch asked, looking out at the piece of land he'd seen so often by himself. He was nervous, waiting for her words,

though the boys had already jumped from the wagon bed
and gone racing off through the grass.

Sarah stood up. Grass stretched west as far as she could
see, rolling waves of grass streaked with frothy patches of
wildflowers, purple bluebonnets and fiery Indian paintbrush.
She took a deep breath, exhilarated by the sense of vastness,
of freedom, that the land produced in her.

"Well?" Hutch asked, reaching up to lift her down.

"No," she said. "The view's better up here and I want
to look." She turned in all directions, back toward the
woods that hugged the east, then again to the stretching
grasslands. "It's very special, isn't it Hutch?"

"I thought so," he said. "That's why I bought it." Hutch
grinned at the startled expression on her face. There was no
trouble now in lifting her down from the wagon. "I bought
it for us. I thought it'd make a fine wedding present."

Her hand reached up to touch his cheek and when she felt
his face beneath her fingertips she realized that she'd come
to love him. "Oh, Hutch, you're no farmer. I wouldn't want
you to—to try to be what you're not. Not for our sake."

"I don't mean to farm." He turned her gently toward the
northwest. "See over there where the grass breaks? There's
a fast-footed little stream over there, with just the right
amount of water for stock."

"You're no rancher, either," she answered, wondering if
he felt the nervous desire that sprang inside her at his touch.
It had been so long, nearly three years, since she'd been
touched this way, and now he was taking her firmly in his
arms.

"I hadn't planned on cattle either, Sarah. But I learned a
thing or two about horses in Mexico and I figured I might
raise them. With all the folks coming into these parts,
there'll be a need."

She held herself back a moment longer. "Horses. Well,
horses might work out fine." Then she answered his embrace, her heart widening to meet the prairie. "Oh, Hutch,
I'd be happy to marry you."

Chapter Sixteen

The second year they were married, Hutch bought Sarah a piece of glass the size of a door, freighting it all the way up from Houston where he'd gone to trade horses. He'd been away three weeks and Sarah knew that the tedium of returning by wagon had cost him more dearly than whatever he'd paid for the glass. "You couldn't have brought anything I'd like better," she said, shading her eyes against the brilliance as he and Ben Bonham unwrapped the glass and leaned it against the dark logs of the cabin.

"Are we going to have windows?" Austin asked. At fourteen he was sturdy and square and just a shade shorter than his mother. He'd surpassed any learning a traveling teacher might give him and now rose two hours before dawn to study from whatever books Sarah managed to get for him. The thought of studying by natural light instead of the eye-tiring light of candle or lamp filled him with excitement.

But Hutch squashed his hopes with a shake of his head. "That glass, that's so your ma can have a flower pit. Set her strawberry vines down in there so they don't freeze."

Sarah beamed. Ever since moving to this new country she'd struggled against the weather, weather that was more violent than any she'd known before. More than once ice storms had frozen out her winter garden, just as July droughts had killed off her summer one.

Seeing there were to be no windows Austin lost interest and drifted off to help Ben Bonham. But Hutch caught sight of Fan staring at him with admiring eyes. The little boy was seven now, tall and rangy for his age, and to him Hutch

152

roamed across the prairies with the bold freedom of a god. "Did you see any Indians?" he asked.

Hutch had begun digging a trench the length and breadth of the glass. "No," he said. "Heard about a pretty interesting burial though. Grab a shovel and I'll tell you about it."

Sarah went back to her own work and listened as Hutch spun out the story, a tale about a Texan who died in a blizzard and had to be cremated because the ground was frozen. "But do you know," Hutch told Fan, "when the blaze died down the man stepped out, lively as you please and swearing a blue streak. His kinfolk were mighty surprised but the dead man just brushed the ashes off himself and said, 'Damned changeable weather we're having, even for Texas.' "

Fannin squealed with laughter and Sarah smiled to herself. She wished things were as easy between her husband and Austin, but they weren't. Fan was young enough to think of Hutch as his father, but Austin remembered Creath too well; Hutch would always be his uncle, nothing more. Sarah shook dirt from the spring onions she'd dug. Never mind; she had other plans for Austin, great and secret plans that, as yet, she'd revealed to no one.

Hutch dug the flower pit three feet deep, then fitted the glass with a wooden frame and laid it over the top. Sarah couldn't wait for winter to try it out and experimented with different plants, noting which ones bloomed under the glass and which ones shriveled and died. One morning Fan came running to tell her that a watermelon, months early, was ripening in a nest of leaves at the bottom of the pit.

"I want to tell Hutch," Fan said. "Will he be home tonight?"

"If the wind blows him," Sarah said. "But whenever he comes you can be the one to tell him."

"Make Austin promise," Fan called over his shoulder, streaking off like a lightning bolt.

Sarah leaned her forehead against the nappy red flank of the milk cow, her fingers never losing their rhythm. Hutch had gone off a week ago to look at some horses on an isolated homestead on the Navasota. It was the kind of adventure he loved, and the kind that made her lonely for him.

It hadn't been easy, accustoming herself to his wanderings. Unlike Creath, who'd hovered close, Hutch thought nothing of riding off for days at a time, leaving her alone with the boys and Ben Bonham, trusting that she could manage as well with him as without him. The first time it had happened she'd tossed and fretted all night long. But when he came home she was wise enough to hold her tongue, neither scolding him nor flying into his arms.

"I'm glad to see you safe," she'd said simply, and something in her manner conveyed the fact that she wouldn't hop to fix his dinner. Dinner was past and this was their reading hour, hers and Austin's and Fan's, that's what the set of her chin proclaimed, so Hutch had fixed a plate of venison for himself and settled to listen as they passed the book from hand to hand.

He wondered for a time if she might be mad at him but no, he discovered later when she turned to him in the darkness, she harbored no grudge at all. "I need to go off sometimes," he told her, wanting to explain himself and feeling helpless and clumsy at it. "I need to be by myself. It's nothing to do with you."

"I know," she'd answered, drawing him to her, shedding her nightdress like a snake rippling out of its skin. "I know."

She refused to untie her life for his comings and goings and soon he came to treasure this about her, seeing that it was freedom she gave him. Never did he feel compelled to return simply because she expected him; never did he feel guilty over a meal kept waiting. But it cost her something to accomplish; when he was gone for days on end, as he had been this time, a hollow place rose up in her.

In the space of time she'd been in the cow shed the sky had wheeled and changed overhead. Yellow light fell across the yard, bathing her cabin in eerie sulphur. The air was still and warm where she stood but looking to the northwest she could see grass and trees bending before the wind.

"Fan!" she called sharply, and was relieved when he

skidded into sight. "Get into the house, it's going to storm."

"It's just rain, ma. I want to watch the lightning."

She propelled him into the cabin, her eyes never leaving the northwest horizon. A great bruise was spreading there, a line of clouds tinted gray and green and deep purple. She hurried to gather up the heap of laundry she'd left lying by her wash pot, flinging it back inside the cabin. Austin and Ben Bonham had left for the fields more than an hour ago. There'd be no time for them to come home, she thought, but their position should give them fair warning of the storm's approach. And, thank God, there were no trees to come crashing down on them.

A gust of wind grabbed the hem of her skirt, tossing it up so that she felt cool air against her legs. In a matter of minutes the temperature dropped around her, the warm May morning giving way to the chill spring of the northern plains. Her hair streamed behind her, tugged by fingers of wind. Now everything was in motion around her and the dark bruise on the horizon was spreading, expanding, racing toward her with frightening speed. Looking toward the ragged edge of clouds she saw a thick dark rope dangling down, a coil that bent far to one side like the oxbow in a river.

Tornado. Before her mind had settled on the word her legs were in motion beneath her. The calves had been let out to graze but the four milk cows were still in the cow shed. Across the yard, in the horse barn, two of Hutch's mares were stabled. Sarah hurried to let them all out, slapping their withers and shooing them away from the buildings. Then she ran back to the cabin.

Where could she and Fan go? There was no storm or root cellar, and if the funnel struck they'd be crushed by the logs. Suddenly she thought of the flower pit, three feet deep and long enough to lie flat in. "Fan," she said, taking him by the shoulders, "can you get down in the flower pit by yourself?" He nodded. "You go there right now. Hurry."

"Aren't you coming?"

"In a minute. I'll be there in a minute. You hurry."

She scrambled to gather a few possessions, making a

sling of her apron, tucking their little hoard of cash money
down deep into her bodice. She was on her way out of the
cabin when she remembered the leather bag, the one Hutch
had left with her on his way to Mexico. He hadn't looked at
it once since coming back but she knew it was important to
him. Without hesitating she whirled and darted back inside
the cabin, found the bag, and ran to the flower pit with it
bumping against her side.

Fan was standing in the pit with the glass raised above
him, watching the tornado as it wove back and forth, lifting
and dipping its great black trunk.

"Get down!" she cried, pushing him flat as she jumped
into the pit beside him. She laid her body above her son's
and lowered the glass over them. The air was close and
steamy, but above them it roared with deafening force. She
was seized with the sudden fear that the pit was too shallow,
that they'd be sucked up out of the ground and hurled
through the air. Sarah stretched out with her arms above her
head, digging her fingers into the soft earth wall of the pit,
jamming her toes against the other end.

She felt a jolt as the long glass pane was stripped away.
Wind whipped against her back and for a moment she had
the frightening sensation that the world was being peeled
back, rolled up and carried off by the tornado. Fan squirmed
beneath her and clutched her skirt with his fists. Unable to
shelter him with her arms, she pressed her body against his.
Her back ached and her arms trembled with exhaustion;
then, suddenly, the winds died and sparse, heavy drops of
rain began to fall.

The tail of the tornado had passed over them, Sarah
realized, lifting the roof off the cabin and scattering its
thick, sturdy logs like wisps of hay. The horse and cow
sheds were still standing, but everything they owned, except
what she'd taken into the flower pit with her, had been
lifted, and strewn across the land. Yet when Austin and Ben
Bonham came home that afternoon, safe and unharmed and
driving the mares and milk cows before them, Sarah felt a
ripple of pure joy.

Hutch arrived two days later, and by that time Sarah had
made camp at one end of the horse barn. "I saved this for

you," she told him that night, pushing the leather bag into his hands. She'd waited until they were alone, until the boys were asleep and Ben Bonham had gone off to his loft above the cattle.

Hutch ran his hand over the bag as if it were a living thing. He didn't speak but she saw how much it meant to him, saw how many of his heart's secrets were bundled within it. After a long time he set the bag aside and drew her to him, stroking her hair with his fingers. In response she curled her soft, resilient body around his lean and long-limbed one. "At least we don't have to sneak outside the house," she said and could feel his lips curving in a grin against her neck.

She laughed softly but after a while she rose and went outside, beckoning for him to follow. The boys were old enough now to make sense of the murmurings that came to them through the darkness and Sarah, brazen as she could be by moonlight, was as shy as a girl when her children were near. Hutch followed her out into the darkness.

"I missed you," Sarah said, twining her arms around him, her breath sweet and eager.

Hutch felt a spasm. He could just as easily have come home to find her dead, something he'd never thought about before. "Maybe I shouldn't go away so much."

"Hush," she said, reaching for him.

It was a moonless night, the sky streaked with clouds, and they had wandered into a grove of trees whose branches shut out what little starlight there was. Sarah took his hand and pressed it to her breast. Hutch felt smooth skin and realized that her nightdress was lying in a pool at her feet. A prickle of excitement raced along his spine, raising the hairs on the back of his neck. She was a surprise, Sarah was, and she could always fill him with desire.

But it was more than desire and as she unfolded beneath him, feeling for her welled up inside him, feeling so full and aching it blotted out everything else. Only later, when her head lay still on the crook of his arm and he believed she was asleep, did he dare whisper it aloud to her.

"I need you, Sarah," he said, and to his surprise she turned, burrowed against him, and told him what she'd been waiting to tell him all along, that she was going to have a baby.

Eva Chase was born in February 1846, the same week Texas joined the Union. Sarah said it was the noise of guns and cannons going off throughout the state in celebration that jarred her into labor but Hutch, who found magic in his new daughter, claimed that Eva had timed her arrival on purpose to make her birthday a memorable one.

Because Sarah had no wish to name the baby after her own kin they chose a name from the Chase side, naming her after Hutch's grandmother. Before Eva was a week old, Sarah took up pen and letter paper and wrote the news back to Caney Fork herself, prouder of her writing ability than of the new child.

That same year a new town, Union, sprang up just a day's ride distant, and soon it became a center of commerce for Hutch's horse business. If Eva's memory had stretched back in time, she would have had flickering recollections of being cradled in her father's arms and asked, at the age of six months, to judge the worth of a horse. But her first memories, formed when she was a year old, were of staggering through the tall grass that ran away from their house like an ocean, her older brother Fan pursuing her through the rippling wands.

The double cabin Hutch had built in the wake of the tornado was an elaborate affair, two immense cubes connected by an open passageway, each square with a puncheon floor and a finished loft. He'd located it not on the old site but on the add-on land he'd purchased himself, setting the house so that it looked out toward the rolling tall grass prairie.

Abandoning the old site had caused Sarah a pang. It was the place Creath had built for her and the place where Fan had been born; it was the place where Creath had died and been buried and it seemed almost like abandoning him to go to the add-on land. All of this she kept to herself, for Hutch had his heart set on the new sight, and in the end she allowed herself to be moved.

The new place, as it was called at first, was the only home Eva knew. As a baby she slept in the big corner bed between her parents and soon after in a small bed across the room from them. But one day Hutch carried her up the loft ladder and told her that, as soon as she could climb the ladder by herself, she could sleep there. Eva's pale eyes grew large with excitement. Her two older brothers had the loft in the other half of the cabin to themselves, but it had not occurred to her to expect as much. For the next two weeks she struggled to master the ladder, falling and bruising herself so frequently and severely that Sarah made Hutch take the ladder away.

Hutch did remove the ladder, taking it to the barn and positioning it in a bed of soft hay, where Eva could practice without harm.

Her father and her brother Fan were the two bright constellations in Eva's sky; her mother was someone dimmer, a swift but elusive creature who would fly about the house like a bird and then light, for seemingly endless periods of time, before a book opened on a table. Her oldest brother was dimmer still, a grown man in her mind. When Eva was three he vanished and she scarcely noticed; later she learned that her mother had sent him to Austin to study something called *the law*.

For a long time Eva believed that Austin, the city, had been named for her brother and his great endeavor of studying the law. That, she concluded, was why her mother was so proud of him and why a tough, impenetrable bond existed between the two of them, shutting everyone else out. Early in her life Eva accepted the fact that she would always rank low in her mother's affections, for whatever she did it would not be enough to have a city named after her.

But that was a small seed grain of discontent buried beneath the heaping pleasures of life. It could not diminish the thrill Eva felt when her father swung her before him on the saddle and galloped forward at dizzying speed; it could not tarnish the happiness she felt when Fan climbed a tall and dangerously leaning tree to bring her a speckled bird's egg. She kept the egg in a flannel nest by her bed, warming it with her hands in the hope that it would hatch. It never did and eventually grew light as air, the shell a spectacular bubble that she refused to part with.

One summer morning when Austin had been studying law for over a year, Eva awoke and knew without asking that Fan and her father were about to go off on some great adventure. There was a heavier breakfast than usual being cooked; saddlebags rested on the bench beside the door.

During the night three of Hutch's mares had jumped the fence where they were penned and Fan, tall and wiry at the age of twelve, had talked his way into going with Hutch to round them up. Tight as a bowstring with excitement, he could barely sit down to eat breakfast.

"Save those coals in your pants for later," Hutch said with a grin. "We'll likely need 'em for a campfire."

"What if it was Indians that took the horses?" Fan asked. "Could've been Red Bow's band."

Eva bit her lip, seeing in her mind's eye a bow dripping with gore. The young Comanche who'd risen from daring horse thief to fledgling leader was known to every homestead between the Pecos and the Trinity. As soon as Eva was old enough to know the name, Fan told her a wild story about it coming from the chief's habit of dipping his bow in the blood of his victims. Seeing her fright, Hutch pulled her onto his lap and folded his long arms around her.

"I looked for Indian sign and there wasn't any," he said, "and Ben said he didn't hear so much as a whisper all night long. Likely those mares just took it into their heads to wander."

While Fan waited with ill-concealed eagerness, Hutch lingered to say good-bye to Sarah. "Don't you worry about Red Bow; he's nowhere close to here."

"I know," Sarah said, tamping down the twinge of fear she felt for them. She'd lived so long with her dread of Indians that it had come to seem almost a part of her, like a badly set bone.

Hutch kissed her. "We won't be gone long," he said. "We'll be back—"

"When you're back," she interrupted quickly. If he named a day or a time, her heart would hang on it. Hutch smiled and glossed her hair with his hand.

From the doorway Eva watched her father and brother

ride off. The world seemed a shrunken place without them, the sunlight duller and clouded with the dust of their going.

Chapter Seventeen

He was an *hombre de campo*, a man of the open range, and the only profession he knew was following the wild horses that ran like sweet water through the grassland channels of Texas and Mexico. It was a profession he'd drifted into at an early age, being too restless to farm and too poor to acquire an education. Yet Florencio Prado considered himself fortunate, for the life of a *mestenero*, a mustanger, suited him perfectly; no other circumstances of birth or fate could have produced such contentment with his life.

For more than a week now he'd been trailing this particular *manada*, a herd of two dozen mares and colts led by a dun-colored stallion. *Led* was a misleading word for the dun's activity, for like all competent stallions, this one drove rather than led, taking up the job of rear guard defense, nipping and kicking his charges to keep them in line, relying on a few trusted mares to lead. Prado had seen the *manada* only once, the day he'd decided to follow it. Ever since then he'd kept out of sight, drawing imperceptibly nearer to accustom the fine, nervous animals to his scent, pushing them silently from behind so that now, after a week of hard travel, he knew the band was growing exhausted and ready for capture.

Prado approved of the country he was traveling through, well-watered grasslands broken by draws and thickets of thorny brush, features that made good natural corrals.

He pulled his horse up short when he came within sight of the *manada*, feeling an expansion of pride as he counted noses: harried as he was, the dun stallion had managed to add several mares to the herd. Prado saw the stallion lift his head, scent the air, and gaze toward him with an expression of distrust. A minute later he shot through the *manada*, nipping his lead mares into motion and circling to bring the slower colts into the herd.

Prado allowed himself the momentary joy of watching the animals. Then he set his own horse in motion. This was the final flight of the mustangs. Having shown himself at last, Prado would chase the *manada* until he either captured the horses or lost them on the prairies. Yet that moment of truth stretched far ahead of him, for a stallion like the dun could run twenty miles before he tired, forcing his mares to leave behind colts that could not keep up.

Hutch and Fan had just crested the gentle swell of a hill when they saw the horses surging across the grass floor of the prairie. Fan, who'd never seen mustangs before, felt a jolt of hot excitement flash through him. It was almost a physical thirst, a yearning to hurl himself forward and join the wild run. Hutch saw his hands tense on the reins and smiled, knowing the craving for adventure that could take hold of a youngster and shape his whole life.

"Look there, Fan. There're our mares, right in the middle."

The *manada* streamed before them, earth-colored shapes flowing above the grass like dark water; their own mares, bright mahogany by contrast, were easy to pick out and Fan felt shamed not to have noticed them. Hutch sensed this and said, "I almost didn't see them myself. Look how the others keep them to the center. A *manada* has its own rules, pretty practical ones at that."

Though he didn't show it, Hutch felt the same prickly excitement Fan did. There was nothing more beautiful than a *manada* running in the sun, forelegs stretching, flanks shimmering, manes and tails floating out behind. It brought back to him all the unfettered times of his life, the times he'd ridden through the forests along the Red, the times with Yellow Fawn, the nights he wandered with Sarah to some patch of soft and welcoming grass.

As he watched the racing herd, Hutch caught sight of something else. At first he thought it was a laggard following the band or what the boys along the Rio Grande had called a dog soldier, an outcast stallion too weak to form his

own herd. A moment later he realized it was a rider, a small
wiry Mexican following the *manada* in pursuit.

"He's going to take them," Fan said, his voice a mix of
admiration and aggrieved adolescent envy. Suddenly, he sat
bolt upright in the saddle. "What about our mares?"

Hutch studied his nephew. Fan's eyes were lake blue
beneath the brim of his hat and licks of coal hair spiked over
the back of his collar. He looked just as Sam had the year
Hutch left Caney Creek; Sam, whose adventures had come
to a quick and brutal end. Hutch had a mind now to make
up for that. "We could go after 'em ourselves. You figure
you could hang on for a run like that?"

"Yes, sir," Fan replied and felt self-conscious about the
eagerness that showed in his voice.

Hutch was still watching the mustanger. "All right," he
said, "but you follow that man's lead. He knows what he's
doing." Then with a whoop he spurred his own horse
forward and he and Fan pounded down the slope to join the
chase.

A quick glance showed that the unearthly cry had come
from a white man, a tall Anglo followed by a boy equally
tall, both mounted on big horses. Prado spurred his horse
forward, more eager to break free of the intruders than to
catch up with the galloping *manada*. He had trailed this
herd over five hundred miles of terrain, with no help and no
encouragement, and he resented the arrival of others. He'd
been robbed of his catch in a similar manner before, being
joined at the last moment by Anglo ranchers who, safe on
Anglo territory, rode off with the best horses in the *manada*,
leaving him the scrubs.

Hutch saw Prado surge ahead, realized his fear, and
pressed his own horse ahead until he drew abreast of him.
"*Caballas de campo*," he shouted, his trader's Spanish
coming back to him as he remembered the phrase for tamed
horses. He held up three fingers and pointed. "My mares."

Now Prado nodded and eased a little. With a slight
gesture of his shoulders he indicated that the Anglo should
swing out to one side of the herd. He did this, motioning the
younger rider to the other side, and Prado felt that satisfac-

tion rare in life, of working with men whose skills and understanding matched his own.

They trailed the horses for several miles before the *manada* showed signs of tiring. But even when the mares began to slow, the dun stallion kept them moving. The land they rode through was familiar to Hutch, lying as it did just beyond the fringes of his own holdings. He knew that a few miles to the west lay a deep draw, a streambed with high-cut banks that, at this time of year, should be nearly dry. He caught Prado's eye and motioned to the north. Unable to remember the word for *draw* he held up two fingers in a *V* and brought the forefinger of his other hand down between them.

Whether the Mexican understood or whether he simply trusted him he wasn't certain, but he began working with him to turn the herd. Fan, riding on the outside flank, was doing a good job of keeping the straggling colts from scattering. Hutch saw him waving his hat at them and kicking them in the ribs, rounding them up just as a stallion might and driving them forward.

The mouth of the draw was wide and shallow and Hutch's pulse quickened at the sight of it. They'd pulled near the *manada* now, forcing the stallion to the front of the herd. Prado, whose instincts and eyesight were excellent, saw the mouth of the draw even before Hutch pointed it out and worked his way around to the far side of the herd.

Too late, the stallion saw the trap before him. Hutch saw his muscles strain as he tried to stop, but his effort was useless for the mares surging behind him pushed forward; Hutch saw the rebellious twist of his neck as he jumped down into the dry streambed.

Prado followed the stallion into the draw, placing himself between the *manada* and the opposite bank. Though the banks were sharp and steep and the horses were exhausted, there was still a chance that they might attempt a surge up the other side. Prado turned the *manada*, forcing the horses down the dry streambed, which ran at a sloping incline. By the time they reached the place where water pooled and the horses stopped to drink, the *manada* was enclosed in a natural corral, the walls of the draw rising man-high on either side of them.

Prado lost no time in securing the horses. Taking a knife and a coil of rope from his saddle, he approached the mare nearest him, looped the rope around her body and ran the free end to her front leg, where he tied it securely at the ankle. Then he proceeded to the next horse.

Hutch saw the logic of it at once: so tied, a horse could walk with little difficulty; but any attempt to run would draw the tied leg up short and cause the horse to fall. He had seen many ways of hobbling horses for the trail, but this seemed the gentlest and the most practical. Without comment, he got his own rope out and began to follow suit. Prado noted this out of the corner of his eye, just as he noted that the young Anglo had arrived with the colts, and grunted approvingly.

The horses, exhausted from their long run and logey from the water they'd drunk, offered little resistance. Even the dun stallion was caught and hobbled. But before all of the mares were secured, the supply of rope ran short. Hutch looked to Prado but the little Mexican merely grinned and, with a quick, sharp movement, pulled several long hairs from the tail of one of the mares. He repeated this, moving from horse to horse until he had gathered a handful of bristling horse hairs. Then he set to work, his nimble fingers twisting and dividing the hairs. In no time he'd woven a *cabestro*, a hair rope.

Only when all the animals were secure did Prado turn to Hutch. "My name is Prado," he said in heavily accented English. "Florencio Prado. *¿Habla Español?*"

Hutch squeezed a dab of air between his thumb and forefinger. "*Un poco. Menos que un poco.* I'm Hutch Chase." He pointed to Fan. "My nephew—*sobrino*—Fan." Prado bobbed his head. On his horse, he had been a graceful vaquero, turning and wheeling with the ease of a hawk. On the ground he was awkward and bandy-legged and Hutch, as he studied him, found it difficult to assess his age. "You sure got a way with mustangs," Hutch concluded. "Fan, you take a real good look. This man's a real *mestenero*, best you're likely to see."

An idea was taking shape within Hutch, an idea that had taken root during that first exhilarating surge across the prairies. But he waited to bring it to light until later, when Prado had added his store of jerked beef and brown sugar to the provisions Sarah sent along for supper. Then he voiced the idea, letting it fall like a pebble into the river of stories and tall tales that had been flowing between them.

"I've got a horse raising business of my own a day's ride back. Those're my brood mares, that's why I was so anxious to get 'em back."

"Fine animals," Prado said, running a practiced eye along their backs and legs, taking in the arch of the neck and the set of the eye.

"I've always had it in mind to add a little vigor to my line, take in some wild stock, but I can't manage it alone. If I was to have a partner—well, you'd be welcome on my spread any time, Senor Prado."

The little Mexican stiffened. At first he thought the Anglo, who'd been so amiable all afternoon, was making fun of him. No white man he'd ever known had offered him anything but the short end of the stick. But a moment's silence and a glance at Hutch showed him that the offer had been made in earnest.

"No, senor, I have no wish to settle down. But you," he grinned suddenly, "you would make a good *mestenero* yourself, and the boy too. Out there," he gestured to blue shadows thickening beyond the campfire and Fan, eyes wide, followed the flight of his hand, "out there are thousands of horses, millions of horses, waiting only for the right man to come after them."

"Who's the right man?" Fan asked.

"Someone like this one," Prado said offhandedly, indicating Hutch. "Someone who tastes freedom himself. Only the man who loves freedom can capture the wild horse and tame him without breaking his spirit." He looked at Hutch with raised eyebrows. "What do you say? We could catch a great many horses together, I think."

For a moment Hutch felt a pull so deep and tantalizing that he almost regretted the afternoon and the long chain of events that had led him to such yearning. "No," he said at last. "I have a wife and child."

Prado laughed. "So do I." He reached for his blanket, a multicolored square that served as bed, as protection from the sun, as poncho against driving rains. He handed it to Hutch. "Have you ever touched such a blanket? My wife weaves it for me, to keep me warm while I am away. I think of her each night, and of my daughter too, but still I go away." He looked at Hutch steadily. "A woman accustoms herself."

Hutch handed the blanket back to Prado. "My wife could. I couldn't."

"¿Como no?"

Hutch searched inside himself for an answer. The word that finally came to his lips was one he hadn't heard in many years and one that, until now, he'd never fully understood the meaning of. "Querencia."

"Ah," Prado responded, settling back against his saddle.

There was no exact translation he could think of, no single word that meant, as querencia did, the attachment one felt for a parcel of earth. Wander as Hutch had, he had now sunk his roots deep into these grassy plains. With a start he realized that his true roving days were over, that he could never again pull himself away without a feeling of loss. It was a sign of age, maybe, but he wasn't unhappy over it. His eyes wandered to Fan, who had finally fallen asleep at the edge of the campfire. There was someone who would go adventuring for both of them, he thought.

The next morning they broke camp quickly. Hutch cut out his three mares and accepted when Prado pressed an equal number of mustangs on him. Fan, to his delight, was offered his pick of the colts and showed good judgment in selecting a clean-limbed bay. Before they parted, Hutch repeated his offer of the night before. "My place is on the west side of the Brazos, just above Tyler Creek," he said.

Prado rode off with a wave of his hand, driving the captured *manada* before him.

The infusion of mustang blood gave Hutch's horses a swiftness and spirit that doubled their worth on the open market. Ranchers who were beginning to move into the region, slowly pushing back the ragged frontier, were interested in a different type of stock than the farmers of the lower Brazos. Needing mounts who could withstand bitter winters, work cattle, and compete, when they had to, against swift-footed Indian ponies, the ranchers prized intelligence and endurance far above size and strength. In these qualities Hutch's horses excelled and the Chase brand, as the line began to be called, became the standard of quality throughout the region.

Within three years Hutch doubled his holdings, buying land in the belief that, if he didn't, it would soon be snatched up by others. Sarah smiled at him for this, for the land was to her an endless thing, altogether too abundant and empty. Buying it seemed as foolish as buying the ocean by cupfuls, but she indulged Hutch because she loved him and was content, and because there was nothing else she wanted to do with money. They had few luxuries now and that was all she hungered for, a book now and again, writing paper, the wheat flour that was hoarded up in the cupboard to make Eva's birthday cake.

Sarah was making that cake on the morning of her daughter's eighth birthday when she heard a startled cry and rushed across the passageway that joined the two halves of the double cabin. All her Indian fears surged up inside her, feeling like a blade pressed against her throat.

Eva, who'd long ago mastered the loft ladder, had come down from her room to find a man standing in the open doorway of the cabin. "Who are you?" she'd asked, feeling a streak of fear because strangers were rare in these parts. The man, who seemed scarcely taller than she was, was dressed in a formless, brightly striped blanket that bore a suspicious resemblance to Indian getup; his dark hair and dark eyes, she noted, were another bad sign.

Eva had never seen an Indian herself, but her brother Fan, who saw them almost every time he went to Union with her father, had described them to her in lush and lurid detail. So when the little man stepped forward and said something in a language she didn't understand, she got behind the chair, prepared to use it for self-defense, and cried for her mother at the top of her lungs. It seemed unfair that she should be scalped or carried off without ever tasting her own birthday cake.

Sarah shooed her out of the way with a floury, reassuring hand. "He's no one to fear, Eva," she said, hoping she spoke the truth. Then she focused her gaze on the stranger. "What do you want here?"

"Senor Chase."

"My husband?"

"*Si*. Your husband knows me, senora. Four seasons ago, we chase horses together. He said Prado, you good horse man, you come to my place and we'll work together. So now I come, I bring my family."

Sarah looked past him to the open door. Outside she saw a two-wheeled cart and, perched atop the goods inside, a woman and young girl. Eva watched in amazement as her mother's look of uncertainty vanished.

Sarah swept by Prado and out into the sun-washed yard. She was so glad to see another female face that she might have welcomed Prado even if he'd been the worst outlaw in Texas.

Chapter Eighteen

Eva Chase knew she was plain. She knew it the moment she saw Adelita Prado, four years her senior, descend from the high, two-wheeled *carreta*. Certainly Adelita's beauty did not come from her father; nor could it be seen in her mother, a squat, cone-shaped woman with the broad face and deep-set eyes of the Lipan Apache. Yet somehow these two people had produced Adelita, a butterfly, a girl of delicate limbs and vibrant features.

Eva, aware of her own pale gray eyes and light brown hair, stared at the older girl as if she were an exotic bird who'd veered off course and come to light in their yard.

Adelita's hair was velvet black, springing away from her temples in little wisps, the wisps making lush shadows on her cheeks. Her skin was the warm, supple beige of new buckskin, and when she smiled or laughed one felt as if a flower had suddenly blossomed open. Most entrancing of all to Eva were the two small hoops of gold flashing in her ears.

"Hello," Adelita said, and Eva felt a flood of gratitude.

Unlike her husband and daughter, Therese Prado spoke not a word of English. When Sarah beckoned her to come inside, she turned her back and went about making her own camp beneath a tree twenty yards distant. Sarah was dismayed by this but not defeated. Alien and uncommunicative Therese Prado might be, but she was the only woman within a twenty-mile radius and Sarah was determined to make friends with her. She let her be and by and by was rewarded with the sight of the woman pausing to cast curious glances toward her. It reminded Sarah of the deer that flickered through the woods, alert and curious but poised for flight.

At the hour she usually began preparing supper, Sarah took up her old stone metate, filled a pan with corn, and walked out into the yard. Choosing a spot several yards away from the Prado camp, she sat down and began to grind, as if it were part of her daily routine. When she felt the curious eyes of Prado's wife on her, she looked up and smiled, hiding her disappointment when the woman hastily dropped her gaze.

Eva was witness to these remarkable proceedings, first from the doorway of the house and then, bolder, from her mother's side. After her initial greeting Adelita had retreated to help her mother and Eva had felt a pang of rejection. When Sarah had ground a mound of yellow meal, she swept it into the pan and handed it to Eva with an encouraging smile. "Take this over to them."

Eva walked carefully, full of the importance of her mission, and offered the meal to Therese Prado. She had never been face-to-face with an Indian before, despite all she'd heard about them, and the woman's flat, broad features repulsed her. How could someone as beautiful as Adelita have come from this woman? she wondered, letting her

glance wander to the spot where Adelita was standing. A
gleam of blue caught her eye and she saw that Adelita was
wearing a thong necklace strung with turquoise beads.

Therese Prado moved suddenly and Eva, caught off guard,
jumped backward; it was as if a hump of earth had suddenly
rumbled to life. Reaching into a pottery jar, the woman
withdrew several strips of stiff, dried meat. *"Tasajo,"* she
said, holding the meat near her mouth and making vigorous
chewing motions. *"Tasajo."*

Eva stared at her uncertainly and Adelita's laughter, like
music, tinkled in the air. She thrust a slim brown hand
forward, seized a piece of the jerky, and bit into it with even
white teeth. Feeling compelled to follow suit, Eva did the
same.

Adelita's mother fished up more strips from the jar and,
handing them to Eva, indicated that she should take them to
Sarah. Sarah received them with a smile, drawing just close
enough to the camp to nod her appreciation. Then, with a
sense of solid accomplishment, she went back to her own
house.

Adelita continued to be a source of wonder to Eva. Only
Adelita could balance just so on the high wheel of the cart,
her slim bare feet hugging the iron rim; only Adelita could
smile in a way that lit up everything around her; only
Adelita could hug a battered serape to her and seem as if she
were wrapped in bands of colored silk. Eager to copy the
older girl, Eva coaxed Fan into boring a hole through a
piece of pink quartz, which she tied on a ribbon and wore
around her neck.

Nor was the admiration all one-sided. The first time Eva
invited Adelita up into her bedroom, the older girl came to a
halt on the loft ladder, breathless at the splendor she saw
around her. There was a mirror, a desk, pegs hung with pink
sunbonnets and calico dresses and, lined beneath, pairs of
shoes as black as licorice. Spreading across the bed was a
dazzling mosaic of fabric, a huge eight-pointed star worked
in blues and lavenders and yellows. The room was all Eva's
creation, a carefully tended garden that bore the stamp of
her own personality. Adelita ran her fingers across the

precisely stitched quilt, pausing at the tufts of yarn that tied the layers of fabric together.

"I made it myself," Eva said, sensing that, for the moment at least, she had the upper hand. "It's called the Lone Star pattern."

Adelita continued to move around the room, going from object to object, holding herself so carefully that Eva made a point of flinging herself on the bed with casual ease. "Haven't you ever had a room of your own?" she asked.

Adelita raised her eyebrows, narrow dark wings, in astonishment. "We have never had a house of our own."

Now it was Eva who looked amazed. "Why not?"

"Always, my father is away and we live with my aunts, with my cousins, with any relative not poorer than we are."

From that moment on, Eva kept a close watch on Florencio Prado. Used to living in the open, he showed no sign of replacing his family's makeshift camp with anything more permanent. Worried, Eva took the matter up with her father. Winter would come eventually, she pointed out, her small face serious; chilling northers would sweep down on her friends.

Prado never did get around to building a house for his family, but Hutch and Ben Bonham did—a sturdy square cabin set a half mile away from the Chase cabin. Adelita's father's chief contribution to the venture was to purchase a pig from Hutch, slaughter it, and mix its blood with mud to make a hard and durable floor.

Eva's stomach pitched at the thought of walking on dried blood but resolved to set her feelings aside. She'd worked in secret on a housewarming gift for her friend, a sampler that said *Adelita's House*, and wanted to deliver it the first night the family moved indoors.

"They've just moved in," Sarah said, stopping her. "Give the dust a chance to settle." There was no dust on a pig's blood floor, Eva thought, but she waited anyway.

Two days later when she crossed the narrow stream that lay between the two dwellings, Sarah went with her. They arrived to find Therese Prado stooping by her door, patiently digging at the earth with a knife. Spread around her were flowering vines she'd gathered in the woods, root clumps carefully wrapped in wet cloth.

Soon after the house was built, Prado told Hutch of a large mustang herd running on the grasslands north of Tyler Creek.

"How many?" Hutch asked.

"*Cuarenta*," the little man replied. "Forty. Maybe more."

Fan's eyes were instantly alight and Hutch paused to lean against his shovel. That morning he and Fan had begun fencing in a large stretch of pasture, one they would use to pen mares and foals. "You figure we could take them?"

"Without doubt."

Hutch grinned at Fan. "It'd sure as hell beat digging post holes, wouldn't it?"

They made plans to leave the next morning and even, in high spirits, asked Ben Bonham to go with them. But Ben shook his head and backed away. "No sir, I won't have any part of those wild animals."

"They aren't so bad, Ben," Hutch said with a laugh. "They don't trample but one man in four."

"Well, I don't aim to be that fourth. You get your brains kicked if you want."

Now in his mid-thirties, Ben had settled into life with the attitude of someone far older. Season after season he'd stayed on to tend their fields, keeping to his room in the cattle loft and following Sarah with doglike devotion. More than once she'd felt a pang of guilt over the volume of years he'd spent with them and suggested he stake a claim of his own someplace, find a wife and begin raising a family of his own. But Ben had bluntly rejected her suggestions by saying that there weren't any women in Texas, not marriageable ones anyway, and Sarah had let the matter drop.

Fan was relieved when Ben turned down their invitation to go along. The recollection of that first meeting with Prado had burned a permanent place in his memory and he was anxious to recapture the experience, to feel again the close camaraderie of that day. The next morning when he saw Prado riding toward them, not alone but with Adelita on her own mount, he felt the self-righteous anger of one betrayed. "What's she doing here?" he asked under his breath.

Hutch waited until Prado and Adelita were abreast of them. "Your daughter coming along for the ride?"

"Adelita is a *mestenera*," he replied, drawing himself up in the saddle. "Like me."

Fan snorted audibly but Adelita rode on as if she hadn't heard him, her spirited pony cutting the ground with dainty hooves. Fan was as curious as any sixteen-year-old about the opposite sex and had watched Adelita from a distance since she'd arrived. Now he studied in detail the long lash of velvet braid hanging down her back, the willowy sway of her body as she held her pony in check, the exciting but disturbing stretch of bare thigh that showed against her horse's flank. As if she felt his eyes on her, Adelita turned and smiled, a smile so dazzling it unleashed a welter of confused desires within him. With a profound sense of his own awkwardness, he dropped his eyes and looked away.

After riding all morning they reached a place where the grass thinned and gave way to open ground studded by scrub oaks and yaupon thickets. Following in the direction Prado led them, they soon struck the mustangs' trail, fresh dung laid within the hour, and Fan felt his pulse quicken. When the *manada* came into view, all four plunged their mounts into motion. The stallion, a bay, detected their presence and quickly put the herd to flight.

As they crowded close to the mustangs the stallion quickened the pace. After several minutes of hard chase Fan felt his horse begin to tire and felt a sharp barb of disappointment. There was no draw in sight, no box canyon or circling of brush thicket that might be used as a corral. On level ground like this the mustangs, smaller and swifter than domestic horses, burdened with neither saddle nor rider, would soon outdistance them. He was relieved to see that Hutch, for all his experience, harbored the same fear.

"How're we going to catch them?" Hutch called, the wind whipping his words across to Prado, who'd edged to the far side of the herd.

In reply the Mexican merely turned slightly in his saddle and nodded to his daughter. At this Adelita shot ahead of them, racing until she drew abreast of the bay stallion. Her pony, saddled only with a sheepskin pad fastened with a surcingle, and carrying only the light weight of Adelita, was still fresh and energetic.

Adelita worked her pony close to the stallion and for a few breathless seconds the horses galloped shoulder to shoulder. Then, as Fan watched in astonishment, Adelita reached out, grabbed the stallion's mane, and slipped onto his back. The only thing she took with her was a long *cabestro*, from which she deftly made a loop and, as the horse galloped on at full speed, slipped it over his head. Just before she disappeared from sight Fan saw her toss a second loop around the stallion's nose, creating a makeshift noseband.

With the *manada* galloping out of sight, Fan and Hutch and Prado reined their horses to a halt. "How's she going to stop that stallion?" Fan asked. Even Hutch looked a little alarmed.

But Prado only smiled, dismounted, and began rubbing his lathered horse with handfuls of bunchgrass. "She'll be back pretty soon," he said.

"How do you know?"

"I taught her myself. I used to get horses that way. No more. Too many broken bones." He pointed to his knees, his elbows, his collarbone that sat lower on one side than the other.

Now Fan, who until that moment had been torn with envy, felt alarm. What if Adelita had a similar accident? If she fell with the *manada* following her, she'd be crushed beneath their hooves. He stared at Prado for a long moment, but the man showed not the slightest trace of concern.

"Let your horses rest," Prado advised offhandedly. "When Adelita comes back we'll trail the *manada* home."

Fan rode off to gather up the reins of Adelita's painted pony who, having fallen behind the *manada*, was circling back to them. A half hour later he looked up to see the bay stallion jogging toward them, lathered and winded and content now to let Adelita ride him. Behind them loped the rest of the *manada*, more than three dozen mares and their half-grown young.

It was a striking sight and one that Fan would never

forget. Full of admiration, he hastily mounted his horse, eager to join Adelita. But Prado, sensing his intent, checked him with a glance. "We'll trail," he said swiftly. "Keep your horses to the back, out of the stallion's sight. Adelita knows what to do."

But Prado's words could not diminish Fan's enthusiasm. In his world, Adelita Prado had become a being infused with magic. From that moment on his feelings never altered and he remained hopelessly, deliriously in love with her to the end of his days.

For a year Fan kept his love to himself, nourishing it with glances at Adelita and moments spent in her company. They didn't go mustanging often, for Hutch's main goal was not to sell the horses but to improve his own line through the selective addition of wild blood. But when they did go, Adelita always went with them and those days existed in Fan's mind apart from all the rest.

Then one afternoon when she was thirteen and he was seventeen and they'd gone with Eva to pick wild berries for Sarah, Fan was overcome with a rush of emotion. It happened over a ravine, a dry streambed ten feet deep with a ribbon of clear water running at the bottom. A tree had fallen across the ravine and, just as Fan was about to lead them across, Eva clutched his hand and pulled him back. "Don't," she begged. "I'm scared. I can't do it." Looking down, the ravine seemed a mile deep to her.

Adelita laughed, slipped by them both, and danced out onto the tree, lifting her skirts as she went. She looked back over her shoulder, shot them a teasing smile, and continued across, never once looking down. To Fan it was like watching her skim onto the back of a galloping mustang. He was overcome by her lack of fear, by her flashing smile, by the slim legs and high-arched feet that showed beneath her skirt. He shook free of Eva and followed Adelita. She seemed to be beckoning him, challenging him to follow her. When he gained the other side she reached out to take his hand and he found he could contain his feelings no longer. "Someday I'm going to marry you, Adelita."

He expected the world to stop, expected the woods to fall

suddenly still. But Adelita merely smiled, withdrew her hand, and shook her head good-naturedly. "Oh no," she said. "I will marry a brave man, a *mestenero* like my father."

The words, soft as velvet in her mouth, cut him like a whip; brooding all the way home, he was thinking of ways to prove himself a brave man in her eyes.

To Eva, the moment when she stood on one side of the ravine with Fan and Adelita on the other marked a sharp division in her life. Somehow she had lost her brother, lost the special footing she'd always had in his life.

Though the surface of the relationship between the three didn't change, the threads running beneath it did. Now Fan and Adelita seemed drawn together by an invisible force while Eva floated unattached. She was keenly aware of this and admired Adelita more than ever, feeling no bitterness: in her eyes, Adelita had won Fan's affections because she was a superior being.

One day, having spent an hour in her room trying to braid her hair like Adelita's, she descended the loft ladder and pirouetted carefully in front of Hutch. "Do you think I'm pretty?" she asked.

Hutch saw his own features reflected in hers, the same wide-set gray eyes, the straight nose that was too straight for a girl, the thinness that made her seem more fragile than she was. "I think you're beautiful," he said.

"It doesn't count," she said, frowning. "You're my father."

Hutch felt rejected. "Why shouldn't I be a good judge? I've known you longer than anybody."

Eva laughed, then her face clouded again. "Everybody thinks Adelita's pretty."

"Everybody who?"

"Fan. Fan thinks she's more beautiful than angels."

"Did he say so?"

"Sort of. Anyway, that's how he feels." Suddenly, self-consciously, she touched her earlobes, bare pink crescents of flesh. "When Adelita wears her hair in a braid, you can see her earrings. She's had them since she was a baby and never takes them off."

The next day, a Saturday, Hutch made a trip into Union and a week later made the same trip again, this time returning with a small cedar box that he handed to Eva. "This is for you," he said.

Eva's eyes widened and her cheeks flushed pink. They weren't poor, presents weren't unknown to her, but she could tell by the well-made box, by the dovetailing that joined its corners together, that this gift was unusual. Carefully, she lifted open the lid and found a wad of flannel inside. She moved the flannel and beams of light shot out to meet her. There, nested in the cloth, was a silver bracelet. She lifted the bracelet, turned it, and saw, most wonderful of all, her name traced across the metal. Her eyes darted to her father, then back to the hoop of silver in her hand. Sure of herself now, she slipped the bracelet over her wrist and held it up to the light.

For a moment Hutch saw Lodgesmoke standing before him, admiring her bracelet carved with wooden animals. Then the image fled and it was Eva again, his Eva, flinging her arms around him and pressing against his long legs. "It's the most most beautiful—oh, I'll never take it off, not ever."

The bracelet set Sarah's suspicions running at once. Where else, she asked herself, would he have gotten such a chunk of silver? On Monday morning, when no one else was in the house, she rummaged for the leather Cherokee bag, kept now for many years at the back of a particular cupboard. Her hand trembled slightly as she drew it out for, no matter what memories it held for her husband, it held memories for her as well. Creath's death was bound up in it, as were the seeds of her love for Hutch. It was a bag of life and death, and when she thrust her hand inside she found the melted silver gorget missing.

That night she turned to him in bed and his arm came up automatically to meet her. "I know where you got that silver," she said.

For a moment he lay silent, so silent she began to tense against him. "Well," he said at last, "I figured Yellow Fawn would understand."

Her body relaxed suddenly. Sarah realized she'd been

waiting, waiting all these years, to hear the name. She sat up in bed, drawing the covers over her knees, smoothing them with her hands. "I always knew," she said, "but I did wonder what her name was."

She felt Hutch's hand on her back, caressing, working its way up to the nape of her neck. She felt as if he were holding her up. "Is there anything else you want to know?"

She thought about it for a long time before she shook her head, before she turned back to him, before she lay down and rested her cheek against his chest. "I know I love you, Hutch. I know you love Eva and me and the boys. I reckon that's enough for anyone."

Chapter Nineteen

In 1857 Austin Chase argued the case that was to change his life. He was twenty-four, striking, of medium height and square build, with chestnut hair and piercing russet eyes. He had been away from Sarah and Hutch for nearly eight years, with only brief and spare visits home, and had developed a hardy sense of self-reliance.

Four years ago, finding himself near the end of his studies, he had written to lawyers throughout the state and carefully sorted the replies. He was disappointed that none of promise came from Union or Waco or any other town near home, but he set that disappointment aside. The offer his hopes settled on came from one Carl Grassmeyer, a shrewd and aging German widower who hinted of a partnership down the line. Accepting the offer meant moving to San Antonio, two hundred miles from home, but Austin did not hesitate for long. He packed his bags, bought a stage ticket, and headed south.

For two years he argued lawsuits and land disputes, easy work compared to the greater challenge of dodging the traps Grassmeyer and his daughter were continually setting for him. Lisa Grassmeyer was twenty-three, a white-skinned, dark-haired beauty whom her father had been guarding and keeping for the right man. As a consequence, she'd discovered little of the world beyond the walls of her own home.

One Sunday afternoon soon after his arrival in San Antonio, goaded by Grassmeyer and moved by Lisa's beauty, Austin had rented a buggy and taken her riding. They'd gone just to the edge of town, to a spot favored by those who wished to view the panorama of scrub oak prairie and blue sky lying beyond their city. Austin was no lover of open country, it had been a bane to his family as long as he could remember, but still the sight moved him and when Lisa turned to him, her lovely face devoid of expression, and said "*Ja*, but it is so *empty*, Mr. Chase. Who would bother with such a land?" he'd felt a wave of distaste that tarnished forever her beauty and desirability in his eyes.

The day turned out to be even more trying when the rear left wheel of the buggy worked loose. "We'll have to walk back," Austin said, "and send someone from the livery stable to collect it."

Lisa drew back, eyes wide, hand clinging to one of the shiny black ribs that held the awning aloft. "Walk? I could not do that, I think."

Austin had flagged down the next buggy that passed by, begged a ride for Lisa, and walked back to the livery stable alone. His mother had been Lisa's age during the runaway scrape and she had walked for miles without a word of complaint, often with him in her arms, he thought.

Once the comparison was made in his mind, Austin could not dismiss it. Both Grassmeyer and his daughter failed to notice his flagging interest; or perhaps, practical Germans that they were, they simply thought that interest bore no great weight in the matter. At any rate, Austin was invited to Sunday dinners, included in family holidays, feted on his birthday—all situations that put Lisa's domestic capabilities in the best possible light. Not that she turned a hand in the kitchen herself; she could not have found a butter knife if her life depended on it, but she did an admirable job of directing the cook, the maid, and the hired girl who came three times a week to help with the heavy work.

It occurred to Austin that Lisa had not much to fill her life with and one Sunday evening, after a dinner of sauerbraten and potatoes and pickles, he asked her how she spent her time.

Lisa turned to him, a swoop of dark hair casting indigo shadows on her graceful neck, and replied seriously, "I visit the dressmaker, I take baths to stay cool, and I think of the day we shall be married; also, I raise violets."

The sauerbraten congealed in Austin's stomach and he had spent the remainder of the night in his boardinghouse room, tossing and sweating, wondering how to extricate himself from his dilemma.

He had been with Grassmeyer two years now and had learned more than he would have learned in half a dozen years with anyone else. Grassmeyer was a man of keen intelligence, a man who had mastered not only the peculiarities of German law but also of American jurisprudence as well. "The law is what people make of it," Grassmeyer often told Austin. "It will say what people want it to say, and when they want it to say something else, they will interpret it a different way." As proof he pointed to the laws regarding slavery; slippery statutes that, like a team of horses, responded to whoever's hand held the reins.

Grassmeyer was not an affectionate man, nor was he overly generous: Austin was worked hard for the knowledge he got. Nevertheless, he felt an obligation to his mentor. True enough he'd never purposely misled Lisa or hinted that he intended to marry her; true enough he could continue in the status quo without compromising himself. Yet her comment nibbled at his conscience. Didn't honesty compel him to make his feelings known in plain words?

The next morning he walked into Grassmeyer's office, closed the door behind him, and said, without taking a seat, "Sir, you must know that I can never marry your daughter."

The old German's eyebrows, shaggy as pine branches, twitched slightly. "What did you say?"

"That I can never marry your daughter," Austin repeated, feeling more guilty than he would have if he'd seduced Lisa and gotten her pregnant. "I don't love her and she's too fine a girl for that." The phrase seemed to catch

Grassmeyer's fancy. He saw through the pallid sentiment, of course, but he admired the diplomacy behind it. "I'll understand if you want me to leave."

"Leave? What nonsense." For a moment Grassmeyer looked at Austin as if he felt sorry for him, then he made a gesture with his hand as if sweeping away a minor administrative detail. "You will not mind, then, if you are not the only dinner guest next Sunday?"

"No, no, not at all." Austin fumbled out the reply, unable to believe that a matter that had tortured his conscience and robbed him of seven hours' sleep could be disposed of so easily.

"Well? Why do you stare so? We have work to do, *ja*?"

From that point on, a succession of carefully chosen suitors made their appearance at the Grassmeyer table and within half a year's time one of them, a taciturn bachelor named Carkeet, had elbowed out the competition. The owner of a prosperous freighting company, Carkeet did not propose but simply took Lisa to the house he was having built, pointed to an airy cube defined by raw lumber, and said, "That will be our bedroom. Above that, the maids' rooms."

Misunderstanding, Lisa frowned. "A maid does not need two rooms, I think."

"I meant that you will have two maids," Carkeet corrected.

"*Ja*," Lisa said, beaming. "That will be good." At last she had found a man who understood her.

She harbored no grudge against Austin, went out of her way to ask him to her wedding, and saw no reason not to consider herself his friend. Like her father, Lisa was a practical person; a woman with two maids, she reflected, could afford to be generous.

Austin watched her happiness unfold with mixed emotions. Once married, Lisa spent much of her time in her palatial new home, venturing out only rarely, to her father's office or to his house for Sunday dinner. She continued to live at the center of a country she knew nothing of, to exist behind beautifully embroidered curtains. Beyond her yard, San Antonio swirled with life. It was an international city, its Spanish stamp still visible beneath the tides of Anglos

and Germans who'd come to settle; it was a city that
bordered the *Comancheria*, and more than once, out on the
high, staked plains in parley with other tribes, the Comanche
had boastingly referred to it as their town. Of all this Lisa
was ignorant and yet, Austin had to admit, she was happy,
staying at home and commanding her small empire. It was a
happiness he had never known and sometimes wondered if
he ever would.

In the spring of 1857 something happened that brought
even Lisa out of her habitual reclusiveness. It started out
innocently enough with a retired blacksmith who'd died of a
brain hemorrhage while living with his son and daughter-in-
law in the nearby immigrant town of New Braunfels. The
old man had been buried with such haste that suspicions
were aroused. The body was exhumed, examined, and
within two days the county blazed with the news: old
Herman Tolle had been bludgeoned to death and his daughter-
in-law taken to San Antonio to stand trial for murder.

Tolle was known as a tight-fisted miser, a tyrant who'd
bullied his wife to death and was now doing a fair job on his
daughter-in-law. The consensus in the German community
was that old Tolle deserved to die, the sooner the better. Yet
for Fredericke Tolle to have picked up a heated flatiron and,
striking from behind, carried out the public will herself was
another matter. Once accused, she made no attempt to
conceal her guilt, confessing readily to the crime and flatly
turning down the notion of self-defense.

Just as Lisa, breathless and round-eyed, brought this
news to her father's office, the door opened a second time
and the husband of the accused, Jacob Tolle, came seeking
Grassmeyer's services. A half hour later, Austin and
Grassmeyer were shown into Fredericke's cell.

"Did you kill your father-in-law?" Grassmeyer asked,
settling himself on one of two benches that furnished the
cell. Fredericke nodded. She was a woman in her mid-
twenties, Austin noted, with frizzy strawberry-blond hair
and lusterless blue eyes. "Why did you kill him?"

"Because—" The woman spread her hands before her,
helpless.

"Did he strike you? Were you frightened?"

"I was angry."

"Why?"

"He had just put a bowl of soup in my lap."

"What do you mean?"

"He said it was not fit to eat, dishwater, and I could wash between my legs with it. Then he turned the bowl upside down."

"And it burned you?"

"*Ja*, of course it burned me, a big red mark like a birthmark, and it was not the first time, either."

"Didn't your husband say anything?"

She shook her head, mouth set in a firmly closed line. "Nothing. The old man was his father, you see."

Grassmeyer sighed, leaned forward, and, to Austin's surprise, stroked the young woman's hand. "Suppose you tell me, now, about those other times."

Austin took notes throughout the afternoon as the young woman painted a portrait of her father-in-law. When the interview was over and they left the cell, he asked Grassmeyer whether or not he was going to take the case. The old man answered in the affirmative. "She was provoked," he said. They continued a few steps in silence. Then, "Don't you approve?"

Austin sighed. "It's going to be a hard case. She did kill him, she did strike him from the back with an iron. That's not going to go down well. And with the way she looks, hair all tangled up and that shapeless, stained dress—"

Grassmeyer held up a hand. "We'll get her a dress of Lisa's, put her hair in braids. A little of the wild look we must leave, so the jury can see how the old man made her crazy."

"There's something else," Austin said.

"*Ja?*"

"Fredericke Tolle's German; so are you. To a jury that might look—"

"Like we are trying to sweep things under a rug? *Ja*, it might. So. That is why you are going to argue the case."

Grassmeyer's instincts were exceptional. He kept his defendant in seclusion until the day of the trial, feeding her on milk and meat pies until she looked as round and

innocent as a virgin. From Lisa's ample wardrobe he select-
ed a simple gown of madonna blue, paired it with a white
shawl, and gave his client a pair of white gloves to hold.
"Under no circumstances put them on," he warned. "Let
the jury see your hands. Let the jury ask itself, are those the
hands of a murderess?"

A few days before the trial began he arranged to have
dinner with the editor of the paper and let it slip that his
young partner, Austin Chase, had begged to argue the case
himself. "The truth is," Grassmeyer said with a jovial
wink, "I think he is a little bit in love with her."

The story went straight to the front page, as Grassmeyer
had intended, and the morning the trial opened the court-
house was packed. Half the women of San Antonio had
turned out, anxious to see the accused murderess and the
handsome young lawyer who'd begged to defend her. Much
of the German community had turned out as well, some
having arrived the night before and slept on the steps of the
building to ensure a front-row seat.

Austin was put off by the false newspaper story and by
the thronging crowds, though both, Grassmeyer explained,
would help with an acquittal. He worked through the first
day in the packed, stifling room with sweat dampening his
temples. It was hot, unbearably hot, and he began to
wonder whether he was competent, after all, to defend
Fredericke Tolle.

Then, just after the jury had been sworn in and opening
statements were about to be made, he happened to glance
out at the crowded courtroom. Sitting just beyond the rail, a
food basket balanced on her lap, was a large-boned German
girl with hair the color of ripe corn. She knew he was
looking at her, caught his glance unmistakably, and did not
smile but gazed at him with intelligent gray eyes.

It was as if she were a pillar of fresh white snow, and
Austin found his glance returning to her again and again. He
directed much of his opening statement to her, though he
was careful to look around the room as he'd been taught,
and when he detected her almost imperceptible nod of
approval, his confidence surged.

At the end of the day he skirted through the crowd to the

place where she was sitting, realizing only when he reached
her that he had no notion of what to say. He stood for a
moment, awkwardly silent, but she hurried to rescue him.
"You did such a fine job, I think your voice must be worn
out from talking. My name is Meta Dreiss." They walked
outside and found a still sunlit patch of ground where they
ate bread and cold sausage from her basket. Austin was in a
state of wonder. Meta, Meta of the white skin and gray
eyes, had sailed into his life with the sureness of a schooner
holding to a predetermined course. "You don't live in San
Antonio," he said between bites of bread.

"Yes I do, you have just never seen me before. But I
know who you are."

"You do?"

"Oh yes. My father is a drayman for Mr. Carkeet."

Austin blushed, remembering his long and untidy relationship with Lisa. "And why is this trial so interesting to
you?"

Her eyes flew to his. "Not for the spectacle, if that's
what you think. That story in the paper, it was just to stir up
interest, wasn't it? I thought so." She paused, gazed at him
as if deciding whether or not he was to be trusted, and
decided in his favor. "I'm a third cousin to Fredericke, but
I'd come to stand by the devil himself if he was on trial for
murdering the old man."

Austin was surprised. "You knew Herman Tolle?"

"I was sent to be his hired girl for two years. He was
always after me, grabbing me and trying to cheat me of my
wages on top of it. If I let him touch me, he said, he'd pay
me and there'd be no argument about it. Well, I put a stop
to it, I can tell you. But Fredericke he's never given a
moment's peace. She won't say so, but I know it's true."

"And if you were defending her, what path would you
take?"

Meta thought a minute. "Have you ever seen an animal
tormented over a long, long period of time? At first it
endures everything, waiting for the torment to stop. But all
the while a fury grows within it, until one day it strikes out,
perhaps for a reason but also, perhaps, for no reason at all.
So it was with Fredericke."

Austin was smiling at her. "Can I use those words?"

Meta looked surprised, then she returned his smile. "Of course."

And so he fell into the habit of dining with her each evening and then walking her to her parents' house. Midway through the trial he realized he was in love and told her so.

"*Tch, tch,*" she said, shaking her head and backing away in a way that filled him with alarm.

"Why? What's wrong, Meta?"

"Oh, I knew I loved you so long before this, it makes me ashamed." But she did not look ashamed the next Sunday when, having rented the most expensive buggy the livery stable had, he drove to her house and asked for her hand.

Her father, a broad man with mustaches drooping to his shirt collar, looked thoughtful. "Well, I guess it's good that you're a lawyer—you're not big enough to be a farmer or," he added, "a German." Austin stiffened, then saw the sweeping mustaches trembling with laughter and began to laugh himself. Gustav Dreiss slapped him on the back, a blow that knocked the wind from him. "All right then," he shouted approvingly. "I wouldn't marry her to a man who couldn't laugh at himself, but you, you'll do, I think."

Their second triumph together came a week later, when Fredericke Tolle was acquitted of premeditated murder. Austin's brilliant closing speech, inspired by Meta and coached by Grassmeyer, cemented his reputation throughout the state.

"For those who have looked long and hard for a spokesman of eloquence, compassion, and intelligence, a new star has risen on the horizon: the star's name is Austin Chase . . ."

Austin whooped with delight when he read this, taking Meta in his arms and lifting her off her feet. "That's you that did it for me, Meta. It's your ideas they're writing about."

She took the paper, read for herself, and smoothed it with her hands. "Well, maybe," she said, "but we don't have to tell them, do we?"

The Chases came to San Antonio for the wedding, Sarah and Hutch and Eva and Fan, all dressed in expensive new

clothes and looking to Austin more like strangers than
family. But then, he felt like a stranger himself as he stood
before the Lutheran minister in his stiff new suit and
repeated the words that made Meta his wife. It wasn't until
they'd all gone back to the Dreisses', until the men shed
their coats and dipped their glasses into buckets of cold
beer, that the stiffness fell away and they were all, once
again, themselves.

Meta lost no time in changing from her wedding dress
into a more practical gown. She joined Sarah and her
mother, Gretchen, in the kitchen, turning aside suggestions
that she stay in the parlor. "But I like to help when there's a
party," she reminded her mother. "You won't keep me
away just because it's my wedding day, will you?" Later,
slipping up to Sarah, she said firmly, "You must come stay
with us instead of at the hotel. The house Austin rented is
big enough for everyone."

But Sarah shook her head, adamant. "A new couple
should be alone, no matter how big the house is."

"*Ja,*" Meta's mother put in. "So when you have a fight
no one knows about it."

Meta laughed. "We won't fight."

"So you say now."

Just before sunset Sarah and Gretchen Dreiss went outside to pick hollyhocks for Meta. It was good luck, Gretchen
said, for a bride to take flowers into her new home. "There,
that's enough for a big bouquet. Aren't you coming in?"

Sarah shook her head. "In a minute."

She hadn't been alone all day, hadn't been alone since
yesterday when the stage brought them to town. She looked
up at the sky, where a single blackbird glided. *I never
thought to come to San Antonio, I never thought to see this
place myself.*

Yesterday, as they'd crossed the wide skirts of land
leading up to the city she'd pressed her cheek against the
frame of the stage window and peered through the crack left
by the drawn shade. Hutch and Creath had campaigned
together here; here Creath had shivered in the rainy dawn
and thought of her. A great throb of sadness welled up
inside her. She missed him still. Neither time nor her love

for Hutch had dulled that in her. The longing ache was hers, hers forever, just as Creath was.

She heard a footstep behind her and turned. "Mother?" It was Austin. She'd always thought he looked like her but now as he came toward her she fancied she saw Creath in him. "Are you all right?"

She smiled quickly. "Am I that age already?"

"What age?"

"The age when people start to worry if you slip off by yourself."

He laughed. "You're a girl, Mother. You'll always be. You look as young as Meta."

"Best not say that to Meta," she cautioned, slipping her arm through his. "I do like her, you know."

He squeezed her hand. The blackbird had come to rest somewhere, Sarah thought, looking up to clear the tears from her eyes, or perhaps it had gone back to its nest. At any rate, the sky was empty.

The hotel opened new vistas to Eva. The ground floor was a dining room where, simply by sitting down at one of the tables, you could order whatever you wanted. In one corner of the room a man with red sleeve garters sold newspapers and cigars and, Fan reported, flasks of whiskey on the sly.

These were but a few of the wonders on the list Eva was keeping for Adelita, having pledged herself to write down every new thing she came across. She'd already made notes on the bright gold of her new sister-in-law's hair and the colored glass picture window in the Lutheran church. Yet there was one wonder she didn't write down and that was the happiness of sharing a room with her mother. Her father and Fan were lodged across the hall, and often the doors were left open for frequent comings and goings. But at night when the doors were closed, Eva had her mother all to herself.

In the darkness, in the bed they shared together, Sarah spun out tales that Eva had never heard before; it was as if the jolting stage ride had torn memories loose within her, sent them spinning in her mind like dust devils. Eva

absorbed the stories with wakeful eagerness, learning each
one quickly by heart: how her father had come to Texas first
and lived with the Indians in the north, how her mother,
scarcely older than herself, had become a Chase by being
won in a poker game. The stories made Eva feel closer to
her mother, something she had long and quietly hungered
for. For the first time in her life, she felt as if there weren't
something else or someone else standing between them.

The day after the wedding Eva lay stretched on the bed,
window shades drawn against the intense heat, thinking of
this very miracle when Fan took the stairs two at a time and
rushed in on her without knocking.

"You wouldn't do that if mother were here," Eva accused.

"Well, she isn't here." Fan grinned. "I saw her and
Hutch across the street."

"Stop rocking the bed."

But Fan wouldn't stop, not until she'd given up her
daydream and pulled herself to a sitting position. He threw
down a scrap of newspaper, torn to reveal a quarter-page
advertisement. "Look at this, Eva."

She pushed her hair behind her ears. At the top of the
advertisement was a galloping horse, mane and tail streaming, hooves inches above the ground; hugging the horse's
back was a slim rider in fringed buckskins.

> WANTED: Skinny, wiry young fellows to carry
> the mail through Indian country. Must be expert
> riders and not afraid of death. Orphans preferred.
> Contact Texas Overland Mail Office, San Antonio.

"Well? What do you think?"

A suspicion was growing in Eva's mind. "Oh Fan,
you're not going to sign up, are you?" His silence con-
firmed her suspicion. "But you can't, you're not an orphan."

His eyes were bright, a streak of coral showed over each
cheekbone. "It doesn't say you *have* to be an orphan, Eva.
It just says 'orphans preferred.' There's a difference."

She reached out, her annoyance gone, and grasped his
hand. "You *can't*, Fan. What if the Indians get you?"

"They won't, don't worry." He ruffled her hair with his

fingers. "Anyway, it's too late to think of that now. I already signed up."

Eva's face turned as white as a sheet. She pictured her brother alone on a vast stretch of desert, horse gone and sun beating down, his back quilled with arrows. Why would anyone want to face such dangers? She looked up at him suddenly. "It's for Adelita, isn't it? So she'll see how brave you are."

Fan didn't answer but picked up the advertisement and buttoned it into his shirt pocket. "Don't you say anything to Mother and Hutch. I'll tell them myself when we get home. I've got a whole month before I start."

"Fan? Promise me you won't get hurt."

"I promise. Cross my heart."

The morning they left San Antonio, Hutch and Fan went to the stage office ahead of Sarah and Eva. It was Hutch's idea mostly: town life was making him nervous and he hungered to be on his own land again. A week in civilization, he thought, was enough for any man. The stage wasn't due for another forty-five minutes; Eva and Sarah were still dressing at the hotel, but he was anxious to set his suitcase on the platform, to hold the tickets in his hand, to be on his way home.

Suddenly the plaza stirred to life around them as a troop of riders, pistol handles gleaming in the sun, galloped into view.

"Rangers," Fan said and Hutch nodded. There were twelve of them, booted and uniformed, riding in a loose diamond formation. At the center of the diamond were their prisoners, two Indians, one a bedraggled old man and the other a grim-mouthed buck with two eagle feathers bobbing from the part in his hair.

"That's War Eagle," said someone behind them, for a crowd had already begun to gather.

Fan turned to the stranger. "The young one?"

"No, the other." Fan shook his head in disbelief. War Eagle was famous, more famous than Red Bow and more feared. The deaths of more than two hundred settlers had been laid on his doorstep; it was disappointing to see, now, that he was nothing more than an old man with hairs sprouting from his chin.

Hutch wasn't looking at the Indians but at the face of the Ranger riding at the head of the diamond. It was Morris T. Ogg, Ogg grown older and leaner, Ogg with his cheekbones poking through his tanned skin, but Ogg nevertheless. Hutch put his suitcase down and moved forward, to the spot where the company had come to a halt.

"Morris?" Ogg tugged the end of his mustache and looked down. "I'm Hutch Chase, I rode with you the year we got El Oso."

Ogg twisted in his saddle. "Take charge of those prisoners, get them down on the ground and shackled." He dismounted, turning back to Hutch. "Howdy. I remember you now. You were a good man."

"Still am, accordin' to my wife," Hutch replied and Ogg laughed.

"Sense of humor too. I'd forgotten that part."

Hutch's eyes flicked to the pistol in Ogg's gun belt. "New sidearms, I see."

"Yes sir, Colt-Walker." He drew the pistol from his holster and ran his index finger through the trigger guard. Holding his finger straight, he let the gun swing free. "See that? Perfect balance."

There was a sudden commotion behind them. The Rangers had pulled the young Comanche to the ground and shackled his feet with iron hobbles. But the old chief, War Eagle, had made a sudden lunge for freedom. In one swift move Ogg whirled, cocked the trigger, and fired. A bright bloom of blood showed on the back of War Eagle's shirt and he went down in the dust, face forward, splattering a pile of horse dung.

Ogg's face was as calm as evening sky. "That's the beauty of the Colt-Walker," he said. "If a man's a good aim, he don't need to shoot but once."

Sarah and Eva arrived after the shooting but in time to see War Eagle's body carried off. Eva shuddered, more frightened of the Rangers lingering in the plaza than of the limp, bloody body of the chief. "No need to be scared of them,"

Fan reassured her. "The Rangers, they'll make Texas safe for all of us."

Sarah felt his words prickle against her, hollow as cactus needles. Perhaps it was Hutch's mood she responded to, for he was brooding over the quick-fire way War Eagle had been gunned down. This wasn't going to sit well with the tribes in the north and his face showed it. Maybe that was what she felt, she didn't know. But suddenly she longed to be away on the stage, to be home and safe; when she looked up at the sun it was tipped with orange, as if blood were smeared across it.

Chapter Twenty

On the morning the rider came, Red Bow was preparing to move his people north. It was no great event, for all Comanche were nomadic, moving as easily as wind, and the tribe to which Red Bow's people belonged, the Nokoni, moved even more frequently than most.

Red Bow was much changed from the days when he'd led other youths on horse-stealing raids. In his mid-forties now, he had spent his whole life fighting an enemy whose numbers could not even be estimated. When grass was burned or a forest cut down, he noted, the ground lay bare and empty for many seasons. But when the white man was cut down and his home was burned, other white men came at once to fill the emptiness. It was as if every white man killed split, divided into parts, and became ten new men to fight against. And if the ten new men were killed, a hundred would be found standing in their place.

Red Bow thought to take his people deeper into the country of the Comanche, perhaps as far north as their friends the Kwahadi, who camped deep in the canyons of the Llano Estacado while winter blizzards whirled overhead. He was thinking of this and watching his two wives load the

travois when the rider came, bringing the news of War
Eagle's murder. As soon as he heard the words Red Bow
knew there would be no quiet retreat to the Llano Estacado
that season, or for many seasons ahead.

Fan Chase, riding for the Texas Overland Mail, saw the
frontier unravel before his eyes. The uneasy peace of the
past few years dissolved as hundreds of warriors, mobilized
by War Eagle's death, came sweeping out of the Comancheria.
Fan's route took him along the eastern edge of their territory, from Dallas in the north to San Antonio in the south.

The first time he saw smoke stretching along the horizon
he swerved to investigate, though any detour was strictly
against the rules. All he found was a burned-out cabin, the
bodies of two men, and a blood-soaked scrap of woman's
skirt, the woman herself vanished. Smoke, Fan quickly
learned, meant there was nothing left to rescue, and soon he
had no trouble following Texas Overland's sharp directive:
stop for nothing and no one. He still noted the rising clouds
of smoke, made calculations as to the location, and told the
manager at the next station he reached that a burial team and
a squad of Rangers might want to ride out for a look.

The fighting escalated quickly. In response to the massa-
cre of thirty-two people at Carver's Settlement, a Ranger
named Deek Clayton led a raiding party deep into Indian
country and, on a still spring morning in 1858, attacked a
camp of women and children, taking no prisoners and
leaving few survivors. The Comanche swiftly struck back;
reprisal followed reprisal and soon the whole frontier was
stained red.

It was as if the scab had been torn from a slowly healing
wound, Fan thought, allowing the blood to run free again.
Sometimes he felt Comanche shadowing him from behind
but they never attacked. If they had, he would surely have
been killed. At first, Texas Overland had equipped each
rider with a shotgun and two Colt revolvers. But weight was
of the essence and soon the shotgun and one of the revolvers
were stripped away. Fan rode through hostile country with
one revolver and no extra ammunition. *Save the last bullet
for yourself*, he'd been advised. *You don't ever want to find*

yourself in Comanche hands. What those hands were capable of he'd seen once or twice himself, and thought the advice well given.

For the risks he took and the long hours in the saddle he was well paid, and paid in more than money. Riding for the Mail meant wearing silver-spurred boots and a dashing red shirt topped with a white bandana; it meant walking down the street of any town in Texas and catching glances of admiration as you passed by. Women smiled at you, good ones and bad ones alike, and saloon keepers stood you to free drinks because they were anxious to have you seen in their place.

But the biggest benefit for Fan was the change the Texas Overland Mail worked in Adelita. She was sixteen now, more beautiful than ever, and capable of conveying a great many feelings without the use of words. On one visit home she snatched the white bandana from his neck and tied it around her own throat. "You won't be able to go back if you don't have it," she teased, taking flight across a stretch of meadow. He gave chase in earnest and was almost outdistanced, for she was strong and long-legged, and when he finally caught her they were both breathless from the run.

"Here now, you can't strip an Overland Mail Rider that way. If you do . . ."

"What?" Her eyes, pure black, sparkled above her flushed cheeks. "What?"

Still holding her wrist, he could feel the pulse of her blood flowing like a smoothly contained river. He reached for the bandana with his free hand but found himself touching smooth skin instead. "This," he said, moving forward to kiss her. It was an awkward gesture, he felt as if he'd sprung on her like a snake, but she didn't pull back. Fan was amazed to find her mouth opening, ripe as fruit, to him.

He didn't get his bandana back, for she kept it, and when he appeared at the Overland Mail office the next morning he was docked fifty cents and issued a new one.

"Wild time you had for yourself, Chase?" asked Nate Crowl, the station office manager, with raised eyebrows. He was used to riders giving their outfits away to the ladies, but Fan Chase had seemed steadier than most.

"Sort of," Fan replied with a self-conscious grin. "I got myself engaged."

No words had been exchanged to that effect but nevertheless Fan knew that was what had happened in the meadow; that was what Adelita had meant by seizing the bandana, by returning his kiss, by murmuring, with a little laugh, "You *are* a brave man, Fan Chase."

Like the Indians, Hutch considered a grain-fed horse a liability. On the trail, such a mount meant packing not only your own gear but also hauling corn or oats. A grain-fed horse lost the ability to forage for itself, preferring to wait for its dole of oats, and Hutch had little respect for any animal that couldn't sustain itself on grass or, in hard times, cottonwood bark.

As a consequence of these beliefs, with which Florencio Prado concurred, he'd been able to build a business that required relatively little attention. Even with Fan off riding for the Texas Mail, a wild endeavor that brought a smile to Hutch's lips whenever he thought of it, despite Sarah's worries, he and Prado were able to keep up without outside help. As long as the stallions were kept from the mares, as long as there was plenty of water and grazing land, the horses could see to themselves for days and even weeks at a time. The only animals brought to stable were the sick and those about to foal; the rest were scattered in large grazing corrals where, except for occasional rotations, they could be left for long stretches of time.

This suited Hutch, not because he was a lazy man but because he had no patience for any job that bound him tightly. Unlike Ben Bonham, he took no comfort from work that called for the same activities day after day and season after season. Moreover, it pleased him to raise animals that needed so little interference on his part. It was a mark of pride with him that his mounts were prized for their toughness and self-reliance.

A Chase horse, it was said, was too proud to take sick and too stubborn to die; a Chase horse could run for miles on a moonless night without once striking a gopher hole.

The Texas Rangers in particular valued his animals and the U.S. Army, which looked on Texas as just south of hell, was also starting to use grass-fed mounts. Hutch had standing contracts with both outfits.

One clear-skied morning Hutch and Prado, riding to retrieve some mares from a far-flung pasture, found the mark of an Indian sign. There were tufts of pony hair caught in the bark cracks of a tree and, in a patch of dirt, the print of leather-shod hooves. It galled Hutch that they'd been so brazen about it, not even bothering to disguise their presence on his land. When they reached the pasture, they found fence rails down and the meadow empty. Prado was off his horse first, nudging a pile of dung with the toe of his boot.

"How old?" Hutch's words were hard as kernels of corn and his jaw tight with irritation; the five mares in the corral had been among his favorites, ones he was about to breed to a new stallion.

Prado looked up at him. It was a cool morning, even for late October, and his breath showed white in the air. He nudged the dung again with his boot. "Very fresh. Maybe a day old, no more."

"Comanche?"

"Two." Prado swung back up into the saddle and began to follow the trampled grass. Young bucks full of arrogance, they'd left a trail as broad as El Camino Real. "You stop by my place, tell my wife I won't be home. These lost horses shouldn't be difficult to find."

Hutch drew himself up in the saddle. "You don't think you're going alone."

"*Si.*"

"Forget it. Those bucks might be back to camp by the time you catch up with them."

"I do not plan to fight, only to get our horses back."

"Not alone. I'll go with you."

"*Ah, perdon*, I forget what a great horse thief you are." Prado was grinning. "It is better if I go alone, *amigo.*"

"How so?"

"Haven't you heard the saying, *face an enemy alone or with an army at your back*?"

"No. Don't reckon the Comanche have either."

Now Prado's face grew serious, the smile chased away by a gust of wind. "What about the women?"

Hutch rocked back in his saddle, a sign of surrender. If Prado rode off alone, there'd be no reason to tell Sarah that Indians had struck so close. More important, Comanche had been known to steal stock, leave a bold and tantalizing trail to lure the men away, then swoop down on the house and women.

"Godspeed, *amigo*," Hutch said. Suddenly he grinned, drew his pistol, and offered it to Prado. "And if God isn't speedy enough, use this."

But Prado refused the extra weapon. "I have my own gun, also a knife. Nothing more will be needed. *Adios*. Tell Therese I'll be home tomorrow, maybe the day after." With a quick wave he dashed off. Hutch watched until he was out of sight, then turned toward the Prado cabin.

Prado had little difficulty following the trail. He stopped only when full darkness fell that night and was on his way again well before sunup, as soon as the gray light permitted. In the afternoon, along the North Fork of the Bosque River, he saw smoke hazing the sky in a great circle, still smoke that marked a large encampment. The Comanche bucks had ridden swiftly, driven the mares hard, and returned to their camp several hours earlier, he calculated.

Undisturbed, he unsaddled his horse, staked it in a grove, and prepared to wait for nightfall. He hadn't eaten in more than twenty-four hours and had slept only for five, yet he scarcely noted these inconveniences. What he did notice was the excitement pounding in his veins, the impatient longing to steal into the Indian camp and retrieve his horses. In ordinary times he would have stolen a few of their ponies as well, but with an Indian war flaring he decided against it: he had no wish to start a continuing feud with them.

As soon as it was dark he slipped toward the camp, careful to stay downwind as he approached. He hoped to find the mares together. If they'd already been divided up, given away to friends or potential fathers-in-law, he'd have a difficult time recovering even one of them. But luck, he saw by the light of a slim but brilliantly shining quarter moon, was on his side. The horses were grazing together in a herd outside the village; safe in their own territory, the Comanche had not even bothered to post sentries. The message was clear: *on our land, no one challenges us.*

Prado worked his way into the herd silently, as years of living among horses permitted him to do. He found the five mares, herded them together, and led them away, walking slowly and taking pains to turn back stragglers who wished to follow. He crossed a shallow stream and knew he was nearing the spot where his own horse was picketed. Untying the reins he mounted quickly, circled once through the mares and, with a short, yipping cry, set off at a dead gallop through the moonlight.

His cry and the pounding of hooves set dogs barking, alerting the camp, but Prado knew that no counterattack would come. He was riding fast, his path lying clear in the moonlight. It would take the Comanches several minutes to realize that any horses at all were missing from the herd and when they did it would be too late to mount an effective chase.

Prado rode all night, slowing his pace only to let the winded horses rest. Just before noon, driven by hunger and fatigue, he came to a full stop, killed a jackrabbit, and ate heartily before stretching out to absorb the warmth of the sun's rays. Contented as a rattlesnake, the mares picketed near him on their Comanche lariats, he closed his eyes.

He awoke to find himself staring at the silver-tipped toe of a boot. Looking up, he saw the guns, the uniform, and the hard-bitten face of a Texas Ranger. The rest of the company, he saw as he got to his feet, waited on horseback in a neat row.

"These your horses, José?"

The Ranger, whose name was Jack Hobbs, was more than a head taller than the little Mexican. "My name's Prado. Florencio Prado."

"Whatever. Those your horses?"

"Why?"

"Good number of horses have disappeared 'from these

parts this week. We thought some of Red Bow's bucks had a hand in it, but maybe we were wrong.''

Hobbs stared at him accusingly and Prado replied swiftly, ''Those are Hutch Chase's horses. The Indians took them, I took them back.''

''You Chase's hired man?''

Prado bristled. ''His partner.''

''Anything you say, Prado.'' He hunkered down on the ground, a show of friendliness. Prado hunkered with him. There was a loose branch lying nearby. Hobbs picked it up with a casual gesture, snapped it in half, and handed the freshly pointed end to Prado. ''S'pose you show me where that camp is, José.''

Prado stiffened. The Comanche camp, well-hidden in a the loop of the Bosque, wasn't the kind of place you'd stumble across. To find it you needed a clear fresh trail to follow, as he'd had, or detailed directions, as Hobbs intended him to give.

Once attacked, it wouldn't take the Comanche long to decide who'd given away their location. If any survived, which was more than likely, he'd be fingered as an informer. The Comanche had a sympathetic way of dealing with an informer: they didn't kill him but staked him out, stripped him, and let the women pile live coals on his choicest parts, eyes and genitals first, until he begged to be put out of his suffering and the generous women complied. ''I don't remember,'' Prado said, face blank.

''Sure you do, Mex.''

''No, senor, I don't. Sincerely.''

Now a second Ranger, a box-shouldered man with a nose that had been broken and set unevenly, came up behind Hobbs. ''I don't think he knows a Comanche from a pile of horseshit, Captain. He stole them horses himself.''

Hobbs considered. ''Could be.'' He turned back to the waiting Rangers and nodded. ''One of you boys ride out and find a hanging tree, good stout one.'' A rider galloped off and Hobbs's eyes, pale blue, flicked back to Prado. ''You got anything to tell me, José, you'd better tell me now.''

Reluctantly, Prado jabbed the point of the stick into the ground. ''You ride from here straight northwest, until you come to the North Fork of the Bosque. There will be two streams; after the second stream . . ."

Prado returned with the horses and never told Hutch about the incident. Instead he kept his worry to himself, starting each time he heard an unfamiliar noise outside his door. But as winter settled over the land, driving flakes of snow between stalks of frozen grass, he breathed easier. The Comanche seldom raided when it was cold, preferring to withdraw into the *Comancheria*. By the time spring arrived, Prado no longer watched the horizon with an anxious eye.

Eva knew, long before anyone else, that something significant had occurred between her brother and Adelita. Even during Fan's absences Adelita was different, like a sun that, having passed its zenith, shifted its rays in a different direction. Whatever invisible boundary her friend had crossed, whatever territory she had entered into, Eva felt unable to follow. Adelita became more than ever a being on a higher plane, someone of altered concerns, someone elected to love.

Nevertheless, when Eva went to the outhouse one day and found herself soaked to the petticoats with blood, it was Adelita she went to rather than her own mother. The brief closeness that had flashed between Eva and Sarah in San Antonio had not lasted and presenting such a problem to Sarah seemed, to Eva, tantamount to approaching a stranger with the news. At Adelita's she was given water to wash with and clean clothes, Adelita's, to wear.

"You hurt?" Therese Prado asked, laying her broad, gentle hand across Eva's stomach.

The heat felt good against her cramping insides. Eva hesitated, trying to read in the woman's face how she was supposed to feel. This happened to everyone else, to Sarah and Adelita and to Adelita's mother, every month, but no one ever mentioned it. Maybe hurting was a bad sign, a sign of something terrible going wrong inside her. "A little," she said at last.

Adelita's mother drew her hand away. "I make you something good."

While Therese brewed a cup of hot chocolate, Adelita

settled Eva on her own narrow bed in the corner and told her, in a straightforward but blushing way, why such things happened to women. Eva wasn't surprised, she'd grown up on a horse-breeding farm, but she emerged from the conversation with one misconception: she thought that women, like mares, attracted men with their bleeding. For days on end she avoided Ben Bonham, the old bachelor, fearful lest he be suddenly, uncontrollably taken with her.

Therese told Sarah of Eva's menstruation and if Sarah felt disappointment that it was the Prado woman and not herself that Eva had gone to, she buried that disappointment deep inside herself. Sarah knew that, somehow, she'd failed to forge the bond between herself and her daughter that she had forged with her sons, and often she wondered why that was so.

Perhaps she had no feeling for girls, she thought, or perhaps she was simply tired of the business of mothering; perhaps she somehow resented the affection and attention Hutch lavished on their daughter. But Eva had never seemed to need her as her sons had. From the day she was born, she'd been bounced and dandled and swung and whooped to by Hutch and by Fan, both of them, till there was hardly room for herself in the picture. And Eva, quiet and fragile as she often seemed, was born a fully formed personality. She knew what she wanted, had particular tastes in clothes and in furnishings, had not even let Sarah come into her loft room until she had it just so, just as she wanted it, until it did not even seem a part of Sarah's house. Often Sarah came across a piece of her daughter's needlework, the wrong side as presentable as the right, and felt a sweep of shame: she could not have produced such needlework herself if her life depended on it.

Sometimes she felt that Eva was aware of this, was quietly counting herself superior on a thousand feminine scores: on needlework, on delicacy, on precision of dress and softness of voice and any number of nameless but telling attributes.

One afternoon, when Hutch had taken Eva and Adelita to Union for the day, Sarah climbed the ladder to the loft room. For several minutes she stood on the rag rug without moving, as if fearful that she would leave tracks on the whitewashed floor. She even remembered, later, that she had stifled the impulse to take her shoes off. Then she began to move around the room slowly, thinking *This is not the room of a child and never has been.*

In the carefully lined shoes, in the way the coverlet was turned back just so, there was what seemed to Sarah a terrible tension, as if the least disarray would snap the one continuous invisible wire holding all together. On the desk was a piece of writing paper, its edge parallel with the edge of the desk. Across the top, in Eva's rounded hand, were the words *Ways to be perfect*: and, descending from the words, a numbered list that Sarah did not read. *Ah, Eva.*

While they were in Union, Hutch gave the girls spending money that they used on hair ribbons: red ribbons, blue ribbons, ribbons with tiny flowers woven in them, ribbons checked white and blue like a tablecloth. It was Adelita who struck upon the idea of winding the ribbons through her hair, twining a length of red through her braid in a way that made Fan, on his next visit home, itch to untie the very braid that caught his attention.

Eva looked forward to Fan's homecomings with a mixture of joy and envy. She loved her older brother, loved the fact that he, through some act of magic, could make her feel almost as beautiful as Adelita. Yet the moment would come when he and Adelita would slip away together, trusting her not to follow, and she would recall, always with fresh pain, that he no longer belonged exclusively to her.

One morning Eva appeared at the door of the Prado house very early, a blue ribbon in her hand, for Adelita had promised the day before to braid her hair for her. But Adelita, she learned, had been seized by a sudden desire to go berrying before breakfast and was gone, long gone, without word as to when she'd return. Eva said nothing, knowing Fan had ridden off before breakfast himself on the pretext of seeing a stretch of new fence, but her disappointment must have showed on her face.

"I'm going to the foal meadow this morning," Florencio Prado said offhandedly. "If you want to come along."

Eva's light gray eyes lit up. The foal meadow was her

favorite place, a wide, flower-studded dish of pastureland
where mares were penned with their offspring. "Could I?"
she asked eagerly. "Do you think I could ride Jetta?"

"Adelita took Jetta, but you can have Bocadito."

Eva nodded quickly and followed Prado out of the house,
tying her hair back with the blue ribbon while he saddled
the small paint horse for her. Long ago she had forgiven
Adelita's father for his recalcitrance in house building. They
were on good terms with each other, for it was he who
showed her how to keep her silver bracelet free of tarnish,
giving her a jar of the same sticky gray paste he used to
shine the conchos on his chaps.

The foal meadow lay more than an hour's ride away and
when Eva saw it stretching before her she felt a swift,
exciting leaping of her heart. Wildflowers ran in streams
through the grass, pale moths spun round and round each
other, tracing funnels in the air. The colts and fillies born a
few months earlier kicked their heels and chased each other,
tails as stiff as upraised brushes. *Colitas de ardillas*, Prado
called them, little squirrel tails, and Eva laughed.

Prado went among the horses, checking each carefully
and making mental notes: which mares had abundant milk
and which were going dry, which colts were overly aggres-
sive and would soon need to be separated, which fillies
showed the most spirit and the least shyness toward him.

While Prado went about his work, Eva played with the
young horses. Having been raised with them she had not a
trace of fear, would never think of shrinking back when they
thrust their noses against her and nibbled inquisitively at her
buttons. Feeling a great burst of kinship she would race
across the grass with them until she was breathless and
exhausted, then lean panting against their sides. When she
was smaller Adelita had taught her how to lie, facedown,
head one side, feet on the other, over the back of an
unbroken animal. Light as a saddle and easier to carry
because she was living weight, she'd gentled many a horse
that way. But she had grown too big for that now, and these
animals were far too young. So she simply laid her hand on
their backs, scratching idly, and let them absorb her human
smell.

So occupied, neither she nor Prado saw the Comanche materialize above the crest of the hill. One minute the meadow was still and peaceful, the next minute it churned with brutal life. The band of warriors swarmed forward and Eva was rooted where she stood, legs locked in terror as she saw a hatchet blade slice through the air to catch Prado's shoulder blade. She never saw the hand that held the hatchet, just the bluish gleam of the blade, as if it moved and struck of its own volition.

Reflexively, Prado reached behind him to snatch away the hatchet protruding from his shoulder. That these were Red Bow's warriors he had no doubt; the moment he realized their presence he'd felt a great easing inside himself, almost a relaxation: here at last, no need to wait, to wonder, anymore.

Suddenly he saw Eva, standing as if she were made of marble, eyes wide with terror. He gave up trying to dislodge the hatchet and gestured frantically to her. "Run! *Corre!* Fly away!"

A second hatchet swung down and Prado felt an instant of pain at the back of his skull. Then he was falling forward, his own blood beading the grass. A warrior dropped down on him, knife drawn. Prado struggled free for one final moment, raised his head and saw with satisfaction that Eva, at long last, had taken flight.

The mares had panicked now and were running toward the far end of the meadow. Eva ran with them, never looking back, feeling a strange protection as the horses streaked by her. But they were faster than she. They outran her and soon she was alone, running, hurling herself toward their safe shelter. Suddenly she felt herself grabbed by the back of the neck and jerked to the top of a galloping horse. She was clutched so firmly that she couldn't turn to see the warrior's face but his arm pressed against her ribs, squeezing the breath from her, and his strong Indian smell filled her nostrils.

The Comanche dashed to the end of the meadow, rounding up the mares, then drove them back the way she'd come: the fence was down at the other end and the warriors were gathering all the mares into a herd.

As they galloped, Eva tried to keep her eyes from the

place where Adelita's father had fallen but she couldn't.
One of the braves was standing there, wet scalp already
raised on his lance, and as they rode by Eva saw a white
gleam, a gleam like a bright quartz rock, stained pinkish,
lying in the grass. She couldn't help herself. A tremor
clutched the back of her throat and the Indian was squeezing
her, squeezing her so hard, forcing his Indian smell into her
lungs. She gagged, tried to still herself, failed, and retched
a ribbon of slime that landed on the Indian's arm. His
comrades turned to laugh at him, one offered to take her, but
the Indian simply shifted arms, wiped the slime against her
skirt, and rode on.

The warriors rode away from the pasture, driving the
mares before them and leaving behind the foals. Whenever a
foal tried to follow, causing a mare to pause, to try to turn
back, one of the warriors rode back and shot an arrow
expertly into the young one's throat.

Eva struggled to look back at the meadow as if, holding it
in her line of vision, she could keep herself from being torn
away. The foals were staring after them in confusion,
looking little and lost, cantering a few paces forward only to
stop and stare again. Atop the carpet of grass she saw a
twist of blue, the ribbon torn from her hair, turning peacefully in the breeze.

Chapter Twenty-one

The Comanche rode all afternoon without a break, without
pausing to rest, to eat, to drink, to relieve themselves,
without seeming human in any way and Eva, who felt the
pinch of all these mortal needs, began to wonder if they
might not keep up the pace indefinitely. Her insides were
already strained, for her straddling position and the motion
of the horse rocked her full bladder and only by clenching
her muscles was she able to hold back the rush of urine.

It was past sunset when the band finally halted. Her captor, who'd held her tight before him all day, slid to the ground and pulled her roughly after him. For the first time, Eva saw his face. He was not young, as his firm grip had led her to believe; rather, there were deep wrinkles on his face and his hair showed streaks of silver. His body was short and heavily muscled and his eyes were shot with red, as if perpetually irritated by infection or disease. For want of knowing his name, Eva thought of him simply as Red Eyes.

When Red Eyes indicated that she might relieve herself, Eva thrust her modesty aside and squatted in front of him, her eyes carefully avoiding the stream that ran from beneath her lifted skirts.

The Comanche made no campfire but huddled over their saddle pads, chewing the cold jerked buffalo meat of which Eva was given a small share. She ate hastily lest the food be taken away before she finished, chewing despite the dryness of her mouth and her longing for water.

In the gathering darkness the men were dusky shadows around her, as low and squat as mounds of earth. Their voices rumbled back and forth, speaking a language unknown to her, and when the familiar sound of laughter rang among them she felt a lance-stab of loneliness; if she closed her eyes she might be home again.

Red Eyes felt his way to her in the darkness, pulled her wrists behind her and bound them with a length of rawhide. The other end he looped around his ankle, then lay down and went to sleep.

Eva searched for a comfortable position on the ground, rolling from her back to her stomach to her side without finding one. A bug crawled across her face and she squirmed to shake it off. Other bugs worked their way into her clothes, burrowing until they found naked skin. She'd drifted into a fitful sleep when she awoke abruptly, feeling a cool rush of air as her skirts were jerked aside. In the pale star-gleam she saw a Comanche face above her. It was the brave who'd killed Adelita's father, his expression impassive as his fingers worked to pry open her body. Jerking in terror, she shrieked loudly, a cry that brought gruff, angry words from Red Eyes. The Comanche melted into the darkness, leaving her alone, but all the next day Eva felt his eyes on her, hard and glinting, as if determined to pay her back for the frustration he'd suffered.

The band rode for five days on nothing but dried meat and water. As they passed beyond the grasslands Eva began to lose hope of being rescued. For her, the sea of grass marked the limits of the known world, a world where, conceivably, her father and brother might follow. But now they entered an alien land of gradually escalating plateaus. Here trees and grass twined around sudden upthrustings of rock; here the wind blew with such constant force that the grass withered before it; here the earth was not brown or dun-colored but pale red, as if covered with a thin wash of blood.

Once Fan had brought Eva a game, a small fretted maze domed with glass; beneath the glass a tiny bead rolled, back and forth, always lost. Eva felt akin to that bead, drawn deeper and deeper into a maze of crumbling plateaus. She was far from home and had no idea where settlements, if there were any, lay. Yet settlements there must have been for one morning she was tied and left with the extra horses while the band rode off. They returned hours later, streaked with sweat and dirt and drying blood, fresh scalps tied to their lances.

Despite the high heat of the day the band remounted and rode off at once. Red Eyes did not set her on his pony as usual but motioned for her to get on herself, then mounted behind her. They had ridden scarcely an hour when Eva felt something warm and sticky against her back. With a start she realized that Red Eyes had been wounded on the raid and the streaks of blood on his body were his own. What would become of her if he died? she wondered. Unconsciously, she pushed back against him as if to staunch the flow.

Red Bow had not gone on the raid, had deemed it frivolous to mount a war party to seek out a single man. Yet he had not stopped those who wanted to go and, now, was pleased to see them return with horses and a captive girl in tow. His wife's eyes settled greedily on the captive and she

let Red Bow know, without uttering a single word, that she
wanted the girl appropriated for herself. But this Red Bow
would not do. High Hawk had taken the girl and it was fair
that he should keep her.

So it was that Eva fell into the hands of Red Eyes' wife, a
woman scarcely taller than Eva herself whose thickly rounded shoulders and short neck gave her the squat look of a
mesquite bush. The woman's lips were perpetually chapped,
despite the buffalo grease she glossed them with, and for
this infirmity Eva awarded her the name Split Lip.

The first thing Split Lip did on seeing Eva was to snatch
the silver bracelet from her wrist. Eva screeched in protest
and looked beseechingly at Red Eyes, who was lying on a
pallet nursing his wound, but he stared straight ahead, as if
his thoughts were elsewhere and he could not be bothered to
return them to the present. Split Lip knocked Eva aside to
silence her and then, with a satisfied grin, pushed the
bracelet over her own puffy fingers. But the silver band,
made just to fit Eva's wrist, stuck and would not pass over
Split Lip's thumb. The woman pushed and pushed and even
greased the inside of the band with tallow, but still it would
not fit. With a grunt of disgust, she jerked the bracelet off
and flung it into the fire. Eva leaped to retrieve her possession from the flames, burning her fingers and singeing her
skirt hem in the process.

The smell of scorched cloth was, apparently, repugnant to
Split Lip for, rising swiftly, she stripped Eva's clothes from
her. She didn't bother to unfasten the buttons—perhaps she
didn't know how to use them—but ripped the cloth as if she
were peeling the husk from an ear of corn.

Eva stood naked, thin arms crossed before her, goose
bumps showing on her skin. No male, not even her father,
had ever seen her undressed before, and her terrified glance
went to Red Eyes. To Eva's relief, he was still sealed within
his stare of indifference, gazing at the tipi top. At last Split
Lip handed her a deerskin garment that she pulled on over
her head. The dress, no doubt one of Split Lip's, was too
big but Eva didn't mind; it was at least clean, or seemed so.
At least it would have to do, for the remnants of her own
clothes had already been whisked away by Split Lip.

Now Split Lip handed her a bag that looked, to Eva, like a gigantic distended stomach, and indicated that she should go fill it with water. The Comanche camp bordered a stream and Eva nodded, relieved that she understood what was expected of her. She reached for her pile of clothes, thinking to wash them in the stream, but Split Lip kicked them out of the way. Later, when Eva returned to the tipi they were nowhere in sight; she never saw them again.

It was just dusk and Eva was self-consciously aware of the eyes that followed her through the camp as she walked to the stream. Not the eyes of adults, for they had other things to do; even the warrior who'd killed Adelita's father seemed to have forgotten her, now that they'd reached the camp. But the eyes of the youngsters followed her, sly and narrow, black eyes without the least hint of friendliness in them.

Eva stooped to let water flow into the narrow-necked bag. The stream ran southeast, the way almost all Texas rivers ran. Once Fan had said that the rivers of Texas were like ladders, ladders for settlers to climb. That was always where the first people went, up the river like a ladder, up the streams that made the rungs. Eva straightened. If she walked the length of the stream until it joined a river, then followed the river, she would come upon her own kind, come upon white folks climbing, patient as ants, the ladders of the wilderness.

It was a moment before the word *escape* took shape in her mind and when it did a chill of fear swept her, for her chances of succeeding were slight, even if she managed to get away. Yet once the word was in her mind, it would not be dislodged.

Suddenly, a lump of earth hit squarely between her shoulder blades. Eva turned and saw a young woman, a beautiful young woman, a young woman with blond hair rippling to her waist.

"You mustn't mind her," a voice said. "She isn't right in the head." The sound of her own language rocked Eva backwards. Squinting, she peered into the thickening shadows and saw a girl a few years younger than herself. "My

name is Carol Louise Morgan,'' the girl said, parting from
the shadows. ''My folks called me Callie.''

Eva, dumbstruck, nodded toward the blond woman. ''Who's
she?''

Callie, who, like Eva and the blond woman, was wearing
Comanche dress, shrugged. ''Don't know her Christian
name. She was here when I got here and doesn't speak a
word.''

''Of English?''

''Of anything.''

Eva glanced again at the blond woman, then returned her
gaze to Callie. ''How long have you been here?''

''Two years, a little more.'' She grinned. ''Long enough
to understand their gibberish, that's how I knew you were
here.''

Two years. The time spun out of Callie's mouth like a
long, sticky thread and Eva struggled against it. ''Hasn't
anyone come for you? What about your folks?''

''They killed my folks. The Rangers chased us the first
winter but we went into the Llano Estacado and they
couldn't find us.''

''Llano Estacado?''

''Big canyon in the north, so deep the grass stays green
all winter long.''

From the corner of her eye Eva noticed that the blond
woman had disappeared. The hush of the woods was on
them. Embedded in the spell of twilight, Eva feared that
Callie too would vanish. ''Are there more of us?''

Callie's brown eyes clouded. ''Yes, but . . .''

''But what?''

''You'll see.'' Turning quickly, she dashed back to the
camp, leaving Eva alone by the stream.

It was not long until Eva learned why Callie had been
elusive about the other captives. There were seven of them,
none older than Eva, but the likeness ended there. Taken
when they were young, adopted into individual tipis, they
had long ago forgotten their language and their people.
They spoke and dressed and played as Comanche children;
worst of all, they treated Eva as a thing apart, as a creature

to be prodded and teased and stared at with rude curiosity. Only Callie's intervention made Eva's life bearable and the two girls quickly formed a strong attachment to one another.

Belonging to neither faction of captives was the blond woman. Too old to be considered a child, she wandered idly through the camp all day, snatching bits of food where she could and carrying with her a ragged leather bag into which she stowed bits of refuse from the camp—broken needles, cast-off moccasins, a gourd bowl with a split in its side.

"She had a baby when she came here," Callie told Eva, "but it cried all the time and so they took it away from her. The man who captured her tied it to a rope and pulled it back and forth through a thorn thicket until it died. She cried so much he wouldn't let her live in his tipi anymore and pushed her outside. It was winter then and everyone said she would die because it was so cold. But she never did, only her mind."

"I feel sorry for her," Eva said. They were gathering fire fuel together, flat-dried cakes of buffalo dung. The blond woman had followed them, as she sometimes did, and was staring at them from a distance. "It must be terrible not to be able to talk to anybody." It occurred to Eva that perhaps the woman was German, like Austin's wife Meta, and didn't speak because no one understood her. She wished she'd learned a few words, even if they were only *hello* and *good-bye*.

Suddenly Callie stretched out her arm and displayed a puckered red scar. "See that? She did that. Jumped out at me one morning with a knife in her hand. You be careful of her."

Eva looked swiftly to where the woman had been standing only to find her gone, having taken flight the minute Callie raised her arm and pointed at the scar.

When Eva had been in the camp a little over two weeks, a party of Texas Rangers arrived. Outnumbered and far from their own territory, they had not come to fight but to talk. Split Lip kept Eva inside the day of their visit on the pretext of helping her make a poultice for Red Eyes' wound. That Red Eyes was worse now than he had been Eva could not deny. The hole below his ribs had not healed and now leaked blood and pus continually; whenever he lay down, he coughed up rivulets of blood. Nevertheless, Eva knew that Split Lip's sudden need of her was a ruse. Usually, she was assigned tasks outside the tipi, tasks that gave her a surprising amount of freedom. Today, with the Rangers present, she was kept close inside.

In the late afternoon she heard hooves, iron-shod hooves riding away from camp, and felt as if her lungs were collapsing within her. All day, she had been buoyed by the belief that she would be rescued. She had watched over the boiling poultice pot with bated breath, expecting the Rangers to come into the tipi at any moment. With their going her hopes fled also. *Now I'll never get free*, she thought as she slapped the warm salve on Red Eyes' chest, then stepped back as Split Lip bound the wound with a band of deerskin. *I'll never get free unless I do it myself.*

But two days later, when she met Callie by the stream and snatched a moment of conversation with her, her hopes soared again.

"There's talk of trading us," the younger girl said. "Some friend of Red Bow's, some big chief named Walks All Day, has been captured. That's why the Rangers were here. They want to trade us for him."

Eva's heart began to throb. "Are they going to?"

"Maybe. Or maybe they won't." Her brown eyes touched Eva's. "Rangers have been here before; it's never come to anything."

But Eva's hopes would not be dampened. Each day she expected the Rangers' return; each day she bathed and bound her hair in braids in order to be ready. A week passed and then another and another until it began to seem as if the Rangers had never come at all.

The only thing that changed was Red Eyes' cough, which grew worse, and one night Eva awoke and heard him struggling to breathe. Still pretending to be asleep, she listened as he gasped and labored. From beneath her narrowed lids she saw the bulky form of Split Lip take his head on her lap.

Except for the day with Prado, Eva had never been in the presence of a dying person before, had never even been around someone seriously ill, but the air of death was unmistakable. She lay awake through the long night and felt, she was certain, the exact moment of Red Eyes' passing. It came just as the first stab of sun filtered through the crack where the tipi skins were joined and it filled the room with a lightness she could not have imagined. Split Lip did not cry out but rose, took a knife from its sheath, and carved long, deep mourning gashes on her arms. It was a gesture, at once patient and mysterious, that put Eva strangely in mind of her own mother.

Lark had lived more than twenty summers with High Hawk, whose body lay stiffening on the scaffold. Sixteen she had been when he first caught her eye, and as swift and graceful as her name. Days had had no meaning then and time had stretched before her like a sky blue blanket. The day she married High Hawk she took that blanket into her own hands. It became hers alone, hers to wrap around the two of them or to shake, with a laugh, in the air as she wished.

The years came and went without leaving a mark. In the summer there were buffalo hunts and long racks of drying meat; in the winter there was Palo Duro canyon with its snug carpet of green. Time did not begin for her until the whites first appeared, scudding across the land like clouds before a storm. With their presence Lark became aware of each moon's passing, watching the days drain away like beads spilling from a cup. The world shrank and dwindled around her then: warriors followed the blood trail and did not return, whites took up their old camping grounds, buffalo herds thinned, children did not come quickly enough to take their parents' place. Lark herself had longed for a child, year in and year out, and each time her bleeding came, the passage of the moon seemed especially bitter.

Now her own husband was one of those gone, vanished, dwindling to a bundle of bones atop a burial platform, and she herself, the mischievous-eyed Lark for whom time had seemed so endless, was one of those sad women allowed to keep her tipi only because there were not enough men to take in all the widows. She would make moccasins, perhaps, or stitch an occasional shirt for her food. She would live on thin soup and vegetables and a scant ration of meat and she would do this for the rest of her life, of which nearly half remained.

One night as Lark lay thinking of these things the flap of her tipi moved aside to admit a male form. A strange feeling surged through her, a feeling of anxiety mixed with surging hope. It was true that any woman not protected by a man might be approached, but she had not expected anyone to take an interest in her. She was no longer young and certainly, certainly, she was no longer beautiful. The very fact that a warrior entered her tent filled her with suspicion and yet, at the same time, with a green sprig of hope.

In the flickering light of the fire she saw that it was Spotted Snake who'd entered her tent. Yet he did not come to her but went instead to the place where the captive girl slept. Berating herself for her own vanity, Lark lay still while Spotted Snake roused the girl and pulled her from the tent, his hand barely muffling her cries.

Once they were outside, Lark heard the voice of another man and knew that Spotted Snake had not come alone. Perhaps they would stake the girl out, as men sometimes did with captives, to make her easy to lie with; or perhaps, as they also sometimes did, they would thrust a burning ember between her clenched thighs until she parted them.

Lark said nothing when the girl's cries pierced the night; she said nothing when the excited laughter of men reached her and nothing when the cries came again, faint and pleading. Instead she lay silent, for in her mind the captive was bound up with her husband's death, with the tick of time, with all that would never be hers. And so she said nothing the next night when another man came to drag the girl away, nor the next night, nor still the next.

After they found Prado's body, Hutch and Fan rode around and around the property, around and around in great sweeping circles, lanterns in their hands, shouting Eva's name. Sarah could hear them even when they were out of earshot, their voices calling *Eva Eva Eva* in her mind while she and Therese washed Prado's body.

At dawn Hutch came back to her and said he and Fan were going to follow the trail leading from the foal meadow.

Sarah's heart tightened. "You and Fan alone?" She thought of the brutal gashes in Prado's body. "Oh Hutch, please—" Her husband's look silenced her, a long, firm look that said as clear as day, *You didn't even know she was gone.*

And so she hadn't. She'd thought Eva was off somewhere, with Fan and Adelita maybe, or maybe by herself. Sarah let her hands drop in her lap. She'd always had enough intuitions to build a city of, had feared for Aus, for Fan, for Creath and Hutch, each in their turn. But never a moment's fear had she had for Eva. How could she explain that when she was Eva's age no one had paid her a lick of attention? She had learned by experience that girls of thirteen were capable of living their own lives, of dreaming their own dreams, for hours and days at a time. Now a worm of guilt gnawed her heart, giving words to Hutch's stare.

Later, after Hutch and Fan had set out, Sarah sat alone in the house. I am empty as a gourd, she thought. The silence was unendurable and she fretted her way from task to task, unable to accomplish anything. Well, she would not be alone, she decided. She would go and sit with Therese and Adelita.

Halfway to the little house she noticed that she had snatched up a sunbonnet in her flight. It was Eva's bonnet, pink and white checked, one she had stitched herself. Her hand clenched the cloth tight as she stared at it. A sliver of pain caught in her throat and widened into a stream that choked her lungs, crushing her slowly down against the earth. Legs drawn up tight, she rocked forward and wept against her knees, the bonnet still clutched in her hand.

She was not sure how long she sat that way on the sun-warmed ground. She was only sure that no one saw or heard her—not Therese and Adelita, who had sorrows of their own, nor Hutch and Fan, who had ridden away from her, nor Eva, who had ridden farther still.

Chapter Twenty-two

Now Eva understood what lay behind the blond captive's vacant stare. She felt a morbid kinship with the girl and found herself following her through camp. *We're two together*, she thought, believing that, if only she could draw close enough, she'd pierce the girl's mad silence.

One afternoon she thought she'd succeeded, for the young woman turned to her with a look of sudden recognition. Before Eva could speak, the woman lurched toward her, grabbing the wrist that wore the silver bracelet and jerking sharply. Eva's back hit the ground with a thud as the blond swooped down on her, fingers and knees gouging. Like a predatory bird diving for its prey, the blond woman snatched the bracelet from Eva's wrist, slid it onto her own thin arm, and darted off.

Eva sat for several minutes in the soft dust, a bitter lump swelling her throat. The bracelet was gone. With a tremendous effort of will she sealed off the part of herself that had cared for it. It was difficult but she could do it, just as she sealed off her feelings each night when the men came for her. Yet a wave of fear swept over her and she could not drive it away. What would happen to her if she kept snipping off little parts of herself? Maybe that was what the mad girl had done. Maybe she had snipped away so much of herself that nothing was left.

The incident bathed the world in a cold new light and Eva no longer followed the blond girl. Instead, the next time she and Callie found themselves alone, she said with studied calculation, "The Rangers aren't coming for us, it's been too long."

"I told you," Callie replied matter-of-factly, picking up a flat dried cake of buffalo dung between her thumb and forefinger and dropping it into the bag slung from her shoulder.

Callie was ten, Eva had learned, and not tall for her age. As the bag grew full, it dusted along the ground, pulling Callie's shoulder to one side. Eva stood for some minutes surveying her friend. It was good that she looked younger than her years, good that her monthlies hadn't yet come upon her, for if they had ... she pushed the ugly thought from her mind. "The Rangers aren't coming, Callie, so we have to escape ourselves."

"Escape?"

Eva went on working, aware that, if anyone looked out from camp and saw them gathering fuel on the stretch of prairie, they would see nothing unusual. "Yes, escape. I've thought about it. That stream over there has to join a river someplace, all we have to do is follow it, and when we get to the river we follow that and then, oh, Callie don't you see? We've got to get away, got to escape from here."

But Carol Louise Morgan, not knowing the secret shared by Eva and the ghostly blond woman, shook her head. Her brown eyes clouded over, like the eyes of a deer after it had been shot. "Escape to where?"

"Anywhere," Eva replied. "If we go downriver far enough, down any river, there's bound to be folks, white folks."

Callie shivered and Eva saw, in a swift flash of insight, that for all her spit and dash she was frightened. She'd been taken too young, hadn't the will to fight her way home; if, indeed, *home* was a place that still called to her. Until that moment Eva had hoped to find a strong ally in Callie. Now she gave that hope up and reached out to take the younger girl's hand. "Don't be frightened," she said. "I know just how we'll do it. And when we're away, you can come live with us. Will you come?" *Please, Callie.*

She dropped another buffalo chip in the bag, looked at Eva a long moment, and nodded.

Once as part of her lessons Eva had tried to write a story. Precise as she was, she didn't touch pen to paper until she'd arranged the whole in her mind, until she'd put each incident in place and walked around it several times. When she finally wrote the story, it was as if she were describing something that had already taken place. Now she worked on their escape the same way, choosing what to take, when to go, which way to walk.

It would be on a day they were sent to gather fuel together, she was sure of that. The band had been camped in one spot for several weeks now, and the prairie nearest the site had already been picked clean of buffalo chips. One day Split Lip said as much, making herself understood to Eva in gestures and a few simple words. In the same makeshift way Eva, thinking ahead, replied that Split Lip was not to worry. There was an abandoned buffalo wallow on the other side of the stream, she indicated; it was farther away, but soon she would go over there. By planting the idea in Split Lip's mind, she bought several hours for her future escape. Moreover she began to accustom their captors to longer and longer absences, sometimes keeping herself and Callie out until past dark.

There was also the matter of supplies. Between the crevices of a certain rocky outcropping Eva was slowly gathering provisions: bits of dried meat kept back from her own meager rations, fishhooks found in the refuse between the tents, a length of rawhide rope. One morning getting water she found a prize beyond belief: a knife blade, broken from its handle, glinting up at her through the water. She hurried to grab it up, but before she could carry it to her hiding place Split Lip appeared at the edge of the camp, gesturing for her to come at once. Unwilling to leave the treasure behind, where it might be found by another, Eva slipped it into her moccasin. She walked on it for hours, blade slicing into her skin, blood oozing stickily between her toes. Yet never once did she consider tossing it away.

Red Bow had learned the virtue of waiting without seeming to wait. It was a quality necessary in a chief, especially a chief in time of war. For three moons now he had waited for the Rangers to return with Walks All Day, as they had promised. He had kept his camp here, on a branch of stream so far south he felt vulnerable and exposed, he had watched the fuel and game thin from the long encampment, he had resisted the impulse to move north and west, all because Walks All Day was in bluecoat hands.

Because he was an accomplished chief, Red Bow did not

betray his impatience. Yet when Arrow Tip, a Kiowa, visited him on a hot day in July, he could not refrain from venting his frustration. "By the time Walks All Day is returned," he complained, "there will be snow on the ground."

A look of surprise passed swiftly over Arrow Tip's face and Red Bow leaned forward slightly. "*Hakai*, what?"

Suddenly, Arrow Tip found himself in the uncomfortable position of the messenger of bad tidings. He considered for a moment before speaking. "Perhaps it was only rumor I heard," he said.

But Red Bow would not be put off. "What is it you heard?"

"The bluecoats took Walks All Day to a fort, but there he died. More than a moon ago. His body shook all over with the white man's disease."

Red Bow felt hot anger surge within him, anger he made no attempt to quell. The whites would have let him linger here indefinitely, would have let his people camp beside this stinking stream all summer while the buffalo they should be hunting for the winter roamed far out of reach. With a movement so swift and violent that Arrow Tip drew back, Red Bow bolted to his feet. "Burned Heel!" he shouted, and a young warrior appeared before him. "Have the tents struck at once. We move north! And the captives—"

"Yes?" Burned Heel, of course, knew of the Rangers' proposal and the pending exchange.

Red Bow's fist clenched. "Kill them! Kill them all!"

In the early afternoon, Split Lip had found a hole in one of her favorite baskets and Eva, mindful of the knife in her moccasin, had quickly volunteered to gather willow wands for a new one. On her way out of camp she looked all over for Callie, eager to tell her about the knife, but could not find her and so went on alone, first to the hiding place among the rocks, then to a bend of the stream where willows grew. As usual she ventured as far as possible and took as long as possible, which was not hard to do with the dull iron hatchet Split Lip gave her. Stripping the wands of leaves, she placed them in the stream to keep them pliant. When she had enough, she gathered them up and started back. She knew even before she reached the camp that something of cataclysmic importance was happening. Dust rose from the pony herd and excited voices filled the air. Here and there a tipi rose like a skeleton, one woman peeling off the buffalo hide covering even as another gathered the contents inside. For a moment Eva stood uncertainly at the edge of the clearing. Then she saw Callie running toward her and smiled.

But something in Callie's eyes caused the smile to vanish. Instinctively, Eva shrank back behind a tree. A quick motion of Callie's hand insisted that she stay there. Before Eva could sort her thoughts, a warrior caught Callie from behind, lifting her clear off the ground, something Eva could have done because Callie was so small for her age. Then, with a motion that brought Eva in mind of slaughtering time, the Comanche stuck a knife in Callie's throat and moved it back and forth until he found the big vein.

Bright blood sprayed across the ground and Callie's feet jerked, jerked out a little dance, until they were still and the warrior let her fall. Eva leaned against the tree, slid slowly down, curling in a slow cocoon until her face touched something green and wet and she discovered that she was still holding the willow wands in her arms, holding them as gently as if they were her babies.

Chapter Twenty-three

Hutch and Fan traced the Comanche trail for two days, then lost it at a river crossing. They rode another day in hopes of picking it up again, changed direction, tried upstream and down, but it was as if the band had vanished, had ridden straight up into the fleecy, billowing clouds. Dispiritedly, they went home.

"I'll ride to Union in the morning," Hutch said, "see about getting a Ranger company to go after her."

"No need," Sarah replied. "Ben Bonham already has. I sent him the morning you and Fan left."

That night the bed that held them seemed half a mile wide. Fan, his leave from the Overland Mail exhausted, had gone early in the evening, leaving Sarah and Hutch alone in the house. For the first time in Sarah's memory, her husband lay down with his back to her. When the silence grew so oppressive she could bear it no longer, she said, "You cannot blame me, Hutch, any more than I blame myself."

He made no reply, though she knew full well he was awake, and when she shifted toward him, there was no answering movement from his side of the bed. Eva's absence became an invisible barrier between them. Long ago, Sarah had seen Hutch as someone who moved in a world separate from all others; she had seen his emotions channeled like an underground river, rising above the surface only to dive out of sight. So it was with him again. He took his grief and his sadness away from her, hugging them to him as if they were prizes she did not deserve. With each day that passed Sarah felt him drifting farther and farther away from her. Eva's loss had come swiftly and in one blow; the loss of her husband was slower and more painful, for she was forced to witness it each day. When he finally told her that he was going off to join the Rangers himself, it came as a relief to them both.

Eva crouched behind the tree, face buried in willow wands, until the rays of the setting sun swung around and touched her back. It had been silent around her for a long time; the dust raised by the departing pony herd had settled. And yet she still crouched, afraid to raise her head, afraid to see Callie's body sprawled on the grass, afraid the least movement would bring a Comanche hurtling out of the silence to snatch her up.

At last she laid the wands aside and straightened her body, her legs so stiff she had to pull herself up. There was a rubble where the camp had been: scattered refuse, cast-off cooking utensils, lodgepoles too worn to be used again, the bodies of Callie and the blond woman and the others, tangled in heaps.

It occurred to Eva that perhaps something of value had been left behind and she forced herself forward. Callie's eyes stared up at her, round as doll's eyes. *What happened, Callie? Why did they leave in such a hurry? Why did they kill you all, even the little ones?* But Callie kept her secrets, her husky little voice stilled, and Eva moved on through the camp. Wisps of smoke still rose from the cook fires, ghostly dancers without music.

Eva's foot touched something solid, the blond woman's arm, outstretched, like a pumpkin vine running across her path. Swiftly, Eva stooped and felt for her silver bracelet. But the woman hadn't been wearing it; or, perhaps, someone else had stripped it away from her. She searched through the camp a while longer, hoping to find the bracelet, but no gleam of silver flashed up to greet her. She came away instead with a drinking gourd, a pair of cast-off moccasins, and a ragged trader's blanket. The blanket was her best find, useful not only in warding off the chill of night but also in shutting out the world that swooped too close around her. She clutched the blanket to her as she walked toward the outcropping of rock, determined to retrieve the things she had hoarded there before going on.

Evening was coming on swiftly, a hand heaping up shadows. Eva thought of Callie all alone in the grass, of Callie growing colder and colder. Suddenly she turned back, pulling the blanket from her shoulders. She spread it over Callie's body as if she were putting fresh sheets on a bed, smoothing the folds with her hands, tucking the end around Callie's feet. *Sleep well, Callie; don't forget me.*

At Fort Worth Hutch found the Ranger who'd visited Red Bow's camp earlier in the summer. His name was Wesley Durant, a young and hard-jawed man with eyes so pale blue the irises seemed lighter than the whites surrounding them. "Were there captives there?" Hutch asked. Durant gave a quick, shallow nod, as if calculating each expenditure of energy. Hutch held his hand parallel to the floor, chest high. "A little girl about this size? Light brown hair, gray eyes?"

"Didn't see anyone of that description. The Comanche, they don't trot their prisoners out. Keep you guessing as

long as possible. Have a seat. Coffee?'' Hutch sat but
declined the coffee. Durant, who was used to dealing with
anguished parents, went on by rote. ''We're doing everything we can to get your girl back, Mr. Chase. Working on
a prisoner exchange right now.''

''That's not what I hear.

''And what is it you hear?''

''That Walks All Day died in your stockade more than a
month ago.''

Durant's eyebrows lifted. ''Now how'd you find out
about that?''

''Morris Ogg.''

Durant was surprised again. ''You know Morris?''

''I rode with him once, back in the El Oso days. I reckon
you were just a youngin' then.''

''I was.'' Durant blew on his coffee, took a deep sip.
''But I heard.''

Hutch gave him a long, level look. ''I'd like to ride with
you now, see if I can get my girl back. Morris said you'd be
my best bet.''

Durant hesitated. His usual policy was to refuse volunteers, especially parents, whose emotions made them loose
cannons. But the man sitting across from him was different,
he sensed that. ''Well, I had thought of taking another party
out that way. We don't have any exchange to dangle in front
of 'em anymore and old Red Bow, he can be as mean as
they come.'' Hutch nodded, showing he understood the
risks. ''Just so you know,'' Durant said.

''I know,'' Hutch replied.

''As for Walks All Day, I wouldn't mention that to too
many people. Nobody's supposed to know about the old
chief's death. Least of all the Comanche.''

But the Comanche had found out, that much was clear as
soon as the Rangers reached the abandoned campsite. It had
been two weeks since the slaughter and there was little left
to bury. In the heat of the day, all was clean and silent. The
bodies, torn apart by wild animals, were no longer recogniz-
able: a white ivory arm bone here, a child's skull, small as a
teacup, there. Hutch looked at each scrap as it went into the
hastily dug burial pit. Were Eva's bones so small? Was that

her hand? Her foot? Or was that long thighbone hers? Had she grown taller than he remembered?

Durant tried to comfort him. "Maybe your girl wasn't with them. We never saw for sure."

But Hutch paid no attention to him and searched on through the camp, scuffing up debris with the toe of his boot. By chance he dislodged a small, flat rock, a rock that had been placed deliberately to cover a hand-dug hollow in the earth. There, winking up at him, was Eva's bracelet.

Eva followed the narrow stream winding from the Comanche camp, walking in the water at first because it was the only way she knew to avoid leaving tracks. In the melee of their leaving she had been overlooked; forgotten or, perhaps, deemed too unimportant to ferret out. But once whatever madness had seized them had passed, Eva thought, they might well change their minds. Split Lip might send someone back for her, or the men who used her at night might, as darkness came, think of her again. So she walked in the middle of the stream, trusting the flow of water to cover her footprints.

At first she kept track of the days, tying a knot in a fringe of her dress for each sunrise. But as she traveled downstream time ceased to divide itself into neat, bundled packets for her. Roused by the sound of animals at night she would often take flight down the stream, only to fall asleep, exhausted, on the bank at the first streaks of dawn. At other times she would wake in shadowy half light and be unable to tell whether it was dawn or dusk, whether it was yesterday or today or tomorrow. At one point the hem of her dress caught on thorny brambles and her little calendar was ripped away completely.

The stream, nameless, was her only constant. Even after she left off walking in its center, she followed close beside its banks. When she exhausted her small store of hoarded meat she began to search among the plants growing at the water's edge for something to eat. Taste sharpened by hunger, she discovered a starchy bulb whose flavor resembled wild onions. She ate her fill, fell asleep, and woke in the middle of the night with pains lacerating her stomach.

Retching until she was too weak to move, she fell back in the mire of her own vomit, tears sliding down her cheeks. She lay at the place for two more days, unable to go on, her ankles so puffed and swollen that she had to untie the cords of her moccasins.

When she was finally able to stand again she stripped off her deerskin dress and, with a stick, picked off the dried vomit. Wading into the shallow stream, she cupped her hands and splashed water over her body, parted and smoothed her tangled hair with her fingers.

The effort cost all her remaining strength and, dressed again, she trembled violently. Survival depended now on finding something to eat and this realization propelled her up the bank. Yards from the stream she saw a cluster of mesquite trees, long leaves shimmering in the sun. Quickly, she gathered a handful of fallen bean pods, tore them open, and tried to chew. But the beans were hard in her mouth; even sucking them for a long time did not soften them. Tentatively, she tried one of the empty pods and found it sweet and pliant. Hastily, she slipped off her moccasins and filled them with as many of the fallen pods as she could gather. Tying them together and slinging them over her shoulder, she set off again.

She was still eating from her cache of mesquite pods when, days later, a disaster of immeasurable proportions occurred: the stream vanished. It sank down suddenly, disappearing beneath a shelf of rock to continue its course in secret. Eva stood for a moment in shock. The stream was her life thread and she'd toiled down it, patient as a spider, only to find that it led nowhere, that it cast her up and out onto the immense, trackless land.

But as she watched the water vanish beneath the ledge of rock, she knew that the stream had not stopped moving, simply hidden itself from her. There had to be a way to crawl along its back until it surfaced again. She walked a quarter of a mile, lay down, and pressed her ear to the ground, hoping to hear the stream's gurgle like a distant heart. Hearing only the screech and hum of insects in the grass around her, she sat up.

Suddenly, she recalled an argument her father had had

with Florencio Prado a year ago. The argument centered around mesquite trees choking a certain pasture, mesquite trees that Prado wanted to burn off and that her father wanted to keep.

"They're part of the land," Hutch had said.

"*Si*, but they rob the land. Their roots sink down and drink up the water."

Now the words of Adelita's father came back to Eva. Heedless of the rocks cutting into her feet, she scrambled up a steep hillside and, breathless and panting, squinted off into the distance. There, between dips and slopes, she saw pools of mesquite trees falling away in the distance.

She followed the line of trees across the prairie and came at last to a wide river whose waters moved slowly, like plates of glass sliding over each other.

The unrelieved diet of mesquite pods, so delicious at first, had slowly taken its toll on her. She awoke each morning with queasiness swirling through her body, hand bracing her head against the ache crashing through her skull. Her skin was scorched and swollen from the sun, scored and bleeding from bug bites and thorn scrapes.

Eva pushed on through sheer force of will, her mind consumed by the effort of setting one foot down before the other. One day she rounded a bend in the river and saw green hills stretching in the distance, green hills dotted with animals grazing, heads down. Heart fluttering against her ribs, she ran forward, fell, pulled herself up and started forward again, walking on her bloodied feet until she was close enough to make certain of the spotted flanks, the peacefully swishing tails, the soft tinkle of bells. Tears splashed down her cheeks as she found her way among the cows, reaching out to touch their warm, solid bodies as if they were angels of heaven.

News that a girl answering Eva's description had been found wandering along the Pease River reached Hutch and Sarah a few weeks later.

"I've got to go see," Hutch said, but Sarah put her hands out, as if she could physically stop him. The ride north with the Rangers had nearly broken him. He'd come home in a dark, silent mood from which he had yet to emerge. Sometimes in the night she woke, feeling cool air against her side, and found his half of the bed empty. If she ventured up to look for him she'd find him brooding by the fire, Eva's bracelet in his hands.

"It might not be her. Wouldn't she say her name if it was? And how would she have gotten to the Pease when you found her bracelet so far away?"

Hutch sent her a chilling look. In all this business she'd turned not a hair but looked as beautiful as she had years ago, before Eva existed. "Maybe you'd rather she was dead," he accused.

Sarah shivered. If the girl on the Pease *was* Eva, unable to recall her name or tell what had happened to her, was it such a blessing that she lived? "I just don't want you to get your hopes up," she said weakly. "Why don't you wait until the week's end? Fan will be home then and the two of you could go together."

No, Hutch was resolute. He set out, and that day too, to find his daughter.

The Carver homestead, the last peg of civilization on the Pease River, was a small, rude cabin on a bare, chicken-scratched patch of earth. Drawing him inside, Luleen Carver offered him a place at a rough, hand-hewn table. "She's some better today," Luleen said, pushing wisps of graying hair behind her ears and squaring off across from him, "but if you think you're her pa, there's some things you'd best prepare for."

"What?" Hutch's voice was dry.

"Well, she don't talk for one thing. Not cause she can't, I hear her talking and tossing in her sleep near every night, and it's more than plain she understands what we say to her. Somehow, she just give up on talking, like there's too many things she don't want to say."

"What else?"

"Way she acts. Can't get her to come out of this cabin for love nor money, not even to use the outhouse. Has to pee in a chamber pot even during the day." Luleen saw that Hutch's eyes had wandered to a ragged quilt hung from a line strung across the ceiling. "Hank put that quilt up on account of she was so scared, even of us.'' She stood up abruptly. ''Reckon you're ready?''

Eva, crouched on the other side of the quilt, heard their voices and knew they were discussing her. At the sound of Hutch's voice, something curled up tight within her chest, its iron fingers digging deep into her heart. She couldn't face him; she couldn't let him, as he once had, swing her in his arms and call her his sweet girl.

For weeks she'd struggled to get back to her own people only to discover, the moment Luleen Carver picked her up from among the cows, that she was no longer one of them. She knew things she shouldn't know, things that she could never tell them; deep, disgusting filth had penetrated her skin, filth no lye soap would remove though she rubbed her skin red and scabby in the effort. Lying on Luleen's clean flour-sack sheets she'd kicked restlessly back and forth until, half-asleep, she'd crawled into a corner of the room and found contentment on the dirt floor.

''Eva?'' The quilt drew back and her father, the man who had been her father once long ago, stood before her. Stepping forward he spoke her name again and knelt beside her, his long fingers stroking her head. Unable to meet his eyes, Eva drew up her knees and buried her face in the triangle of darkness there.

Chapter Twenty-four

Sarah held the hairbrush in her hand. ''I'll fix your hair,'' she said, stepping toward her daughter as warily as if she were stepping toward an untamed animal.

Eva shrugged, remained much as she'd been ever since coming home a week ago. But when she saw a blue hair ribbon in her mother's hand, she jerked away violently. *Well, that's something*, Sarah thought; *any emotion is better than none at all. It's none at all that scares me.*

Sarah was the only one Eva allowed up into her room, into the loft room where she'd taken shelter and from which she refused to emerge. The spark of comfort Sarah found in this was quickly extinguished. *Her father and Adelita she can't bear to face, close as they were to her. But I—I come and go like a servant; she pays no mind.*

There were two bad moments in Sarah's days, two bad moments she faced many times each day. The first was when she climbed the loft ladder and found her daughter, sitting or standing, as motionless as marble, eyes on some distant action being played out over and over again in her mind. The second was when she came down the ladder and found Hutch's eyes on her, questioning and full of hope, and she would tell him, with a slight shake of her head, that there was no change.

Nor was it Eva's mental state alone that concerned Sarah. Six months of captivity and flight had drained her health. Her appetite had shrunk to include only a handful of eccentric selections: she would not eat meat of any kind, would chew for hours on a piece of cornbread, would drink only the chocolate mixture Therese Prado showed Sarah how to brew. As a consequence she was thin and pale and suffered frequent bouts of nausea and diarrhea.

After Eva had been back a week, Fan got leave from his job at the Overland Mail. "I don't know if she'll see you," Sarah cautioned. "She won't let Hutch or Adelita up the ladder. Let me tell her you're here."

But Fan held her back. "No, just let me go up."

Eva got behind her bed, jamming herself in the corner with the bed pressed up against her knees. *She looks like an old woman*, Fan thought, fury balling up within him. But he forced the fury aside—it could do her no good now—and sat down on the chair that stood at a little distance from the bed. He said nothing, nor did he challenge her by meeting her eyes. Instead he simply sat, feeling her gaze on him, letting her pry at him and test him with her eyes.

Reaching into his shirt pocket, he drew out a paper sack of roasted peanuts. Shaking one into his hand, he cracked the shell and skinned out the peanuts inside. The aroma jarred something in Eva and she strained forward, curiosity overcoming her fear. Fan extended the peanuts to her. "Want some?"

Eva drew back, paralyzed again, and Fan laid the two peanuts, shiny as pearls, on the bed coverlet. He fished out another peanut, shelled it, and ate the contents himself. Out of the corner of his eye he saw Eva's fingers reach for two peanuts. She popped them hastily in her mouth and swallowed, almost without chewing, as if snatching some stolen treat.

"I brought peanuts," Fan said matter-of-factly, shelling another and laying its contents before her, "because I know you like them." Eyes on him, she snatched up the peanuts as fast as he could shell them, chewing them now before she swallowed. "Of course, you don't like peanuts near as much as the McGregors. No one could. Did I ever tell you about the McGregors? They got a farm just east of Newton Crossing, on my run. Big farm, too, and all they grow is peanuts. Well, once it was storming so I had to hold over there 'til the wind let up, and Mrs. McGregor, she served me up a bowl of peanut stew, with peanut bread to go with it and some kind of peanut pudding for dessert. And then I got to looking at the pattern of the wood on the table I'm sitting at and see it's made of peanut shells, all crushed and packed together, and when I comment on the smell of peanuts roasting in the air Mrs. McGregor says to me, 'Well, of course, boy, peanut shells are the best fuel there is.'

"Pretty soon the little McGregors start trooping in for their dinner and do you know, those youngins have been so brought up on peanuts, so stuffed full with peanuts at each and every meal, that they've got to *look* like peanuts themselves, with lumpy little bodies and I swear, though it was a might hard to see by the light of that peanut-fuel fire, I swear their faces had little dents and dimples, just like peanuts."

Downstairs, moving through her chores, Sarah heard a sound that caused the bowl in her hand to tremble. Setting the bowl aside she stopped, waited, strained every muscle in her body to listen. For a moment all was silence, then it came again, the sound of Eva's laughter.

* * *

Fan managed to come home once each week, riding miles out of his way to do so and rising in the middle of the night to get back on time. Sometimes he would simply sit with Eva, sometimes he would bring her bright, new minted coins or flowers Adelita had picked for her.

"Adelita, she'd sure like to see you," he ventured once, but Eva had turned her head sharply away. The thought of Adelita, beautiful, untouched Adelita, was more than she could bear. Fan let the matter drop but another time, when he handed her a black velvet hair ribbon and told her he'd brought Adelita one just like it, he noticed that she didn't cast it aside but curled it in her hand and held it as gently as a sparrow while they talked.

"There's something else I have that belongs to you," Fan said slowly, watching her face.

"What?" There was the faintest gleam in her eyes and she looked almost herself, almost as if she'd never been taken from them.

"Just this," Fan answered, and drew her silver bracelet out of his pocket. Hutch had given it to him weeks ago to return to her, but he'd waited all this time.

Eva's throat contracted at the sight of the bracelet. All the thoughts she'd sealed from her mind came flooding back to her, memories of the blond woman and Split Lip and Callie. Her carefully bound silence quaked apart and tears, hot as burning brands, slid down her cheeks.

"Here now," Fan said gently, reaching out to stroke her hair. "It's all right. You're home now, Eva." He sat stroking her until her tears were spent, until she lay so motionless on the Lone Star quilt that he was certain she'd cried herself to sleep. Rising softly, he let himself down the ladder.

Alone in the room, the voices of her family murmuring below her, Eva opened her eyes. The bracelet still lay on the coverlet where Fan had placed it. She lay for a long time looking at it, lay until a determined spear of hope thrust forward inside her and, reaching forward, she grasped the bracelet and returned it to her own wrist.

* * *

Fan wasn't sure whether he'd done good or ill with the bracelet, but Adelita assured him. "Crying is good for "To let it all out."

They were lying together in a hammock Florencio Prado had long ago slung up behind his house, a hammock that commanded a view of the starry sky. "Do you think so?"

"Yes," she murmured, caressing him.

She was a prickly pear of a woman, Fan thought. He'd go to the devil trying to understand her. At seventeen, Adelita still bore traces of the girl who'd chased mustangs and snatched away his kerchief in mischievous delight. Yet behind her dancing eyes lay a sweetness that could shine forth with unexpected brilliance, like silver flashing up from the bottom of a stream. Responding to her caress, he buried his face in the hollow of her collarbone. "I love you Adelita." His hand slipped inside her blouse, across the warm curve of beige skin. "Adelita—"

There it was again, the prickly pear side of her: her sharp knee jamming between them like a lever. "Only with the man I marry," she said with a little smile, her voice like honey.

Exasperated, he laid his head against the black silk of her hair. "Then let's marry. I'm a dying man, Adelita, wasted near to the bone from wanting you."

She sat up, swinging her legs over the side of the hammock, scuffing the soles of her bare feet back and forth across the soft dirt. "You really wish to marry me?"

"Yes. Always have. God, Adelita, I thought I was pretty clear about it."

"I thought you were teasing."

"No you didn't."

"Well," she twisted her head and glanced at him over her shoulder, eyes bright, "when?"

"Now, tonight."

She laughed. "No, I don't think so."

"Soon then, any time you want."

Suddenly she turned to him, face serious. "My father, he's only been dead . . ." She began to count, then shook her head. "It wouldn't be right. And not just for him, for your sister too. We can't marry now, while Eva's . . . without Eva," She kissed him. "Do you see, *querida*?"

Fan nodded, puzzled again by the font of sweetness flowing within her.

One morning, on a day when Fan was expected, Eva dressed herself and came down the loft ladder to wait for him. She'd grown thin, too thin for the dress she wore, but no one paused to notice. Her very presence lifted their spirits.

The next day Adelita appeared at the door, an empty basket over her arm. "Fan's taking us to dig flowers," she said casually, as if she'd received no prompting at all from Sarah.

Eva glanced in swift panic at her brother. In all the weeks she'd been back, she hadn't once ventured outside. "Fan, oh—no, I can't."

Sarah, poised in the passage that connected the double cabin, caught her breath. The idea had been hers but now, sensing Eva's terror, she felt a jab of guilt. *You expect too much of her*, Hutch had said. Maybe he was right.

"Just to the fallen log stream," Adelita said, smiling as she stretched her hand out to Eva. "To our place, our secret place. No one could find us there, could they, Fan?"

"Nope."

Adelita held out her hand a moment more and then, slowly, Eva's own hand stretched up to meet it. "We won't go long, will we? Not past dark?"

Sarah stole to the door and watched them move off across the yard. As they passed beneath an oak tree, branches hanging down, Eva reached up and snatched at the green leaves. The sun shone through her cotton dress and for an instant Sarah saw her daughter's body outlined against the sky, caught in a web of light between Fan and Adelita.

Why hadn't she known before? Sarah wondered with a gasp. Why hadn't she put the signs together? The strange appetite, the nausea, the cessation of monthlies, all signs she'd know in herself quick enough. But not until this minute had she realized that Eva was pregnant.

PART
III

Chapter Twenty-five

The Confederate unit waited on the crested redoubt above the Indian camp, their uniforms, in this year of 1863, faded to assorted and disparate shades of gray. They were two hundred miles northwest of Dallas, by Johnny Steele's calculation, and, judging by the pale shimmer of light along the horizon, it was near sunup.

The unit's commander, Tom Ellis, rode up and down before his line. "Artillery hold fire until the command is given. Mounted troops' aim is to scatter the enemy toward the river—Bradshaw's company is grouped on the other side. Women and babes in arms are to be taken prisoner. All males past walking age, considered active enemies, shoot on sight." Ellis's words were as clean-clipped as his mustache. "Any questions?" The line was silent except for the whicker of a horse. "I reckon not. You've all fought Indians before."

Johnny Steele, two days past his twenty-first birthday, felt the usual sour fear-taste at the back of his mouth. He'd been fighting Indians more than half his life, since he was twelve years old and they'd first come hooting around his folks' home place on the Perdenales River. The fear-taste still came into his mouth each time he fought, though he'd long ago learned to set it aside.

Tom Ellis had a flair for timing and at the exact moment

the sun touched the barrel of the cannon, while the camp below them still slumbered in the dusk, he ordered the company forward.

"Hell," said the man next to Johnny, "I wish they was Comanche."

Glancing sideways, Johnny saw that the man was grinning. *No fear in his mouth*, Johnny thought. He himself wasn't particular about one Indian type over another. These before them were Kiowa, Black Quill's band, whose men had massacred twenty-three settlers at Mineral Springs two weeks back. Sorting them out was necessary if the folks of Young County were ever to come out of their stifling, crowded forts. But Johnny had no personal feelings toward the Indians one way or another. To him, *Kiowa* and *Comanche* were interchangeable.

Johnny's aims in battle were simple: to ignore the sour taste in his mouth, to keep his seat on his horse, to do what was necessary where the enemy was concerned, and to ride back with his scalp intact. So far, he'd always succeeded.

Now as they swept forward the man beside him, the tall fearless man Johnny had come to admire, rose in his stirrups and shrieked out a Rebel yell. If any Kiowa were in doubt about their predicament, none were now.

The first volley of shots were fired and soon Johnny lost track of his companion in the battle but later in the day, when they were driving the prisoners they'd taken toward Fort Worth, he looked at him with bemusement. "You fight like a wild man, you know that?"

Fan Chase leaned back in his saddle, the energy of battle still flowing in his veins. "I am a wild man, Johnny, and three years of fighting've just made me wilder."

Johnny had been with Ellis's company less than a year but he was willing to take Fan's word on it. "If Robert E. Lee got you east of the Mississippi, I believe the war'd be over by Christmas."

Fan laughed. He liked Johnny Steele, liked his steady drawl, gloried in the fact that he'd walked into Texas barefoot in '54, having come all the way from Missouri behind his father's mule cart. Before cholera had carried Johnny's folks off they'd been cattle people, and that didn't surprise Fan at all. Johnny was like a steer himself, steady and powerful, unhurried because he could afford to be. Once on foraging detail they'd come across a longhorn and used the last of their ammunition trying to bring it down. The longhorn had stood, wounded and immobilized, until Johnny dismounted, walked up to it, and dispatched it with a single fist-blow to the forehead.

And then, too, Johnny looked up to Fan, which always helped. "If I'd of gone east, Johnny, who'd be here to fire up you cowboys? God, boy, you'd see a good herd of longhorns and turn out after them, let the Indians slip clean through your fingers. No, my brother Aus went east with Hood. Me, I'd rather fight Indians than Yankees."

"How come?"

Fan checked his horse to a slow walk and for a minute Johnny thought the question was going to go unanswered. Then, "Ever hear of Florencio Prado?" Johnny shook his head. "How about Chase horses?"

"Your folks, I bet." Johnny had never made the connection before, and Fan hadn't mentioned it.

"Hutch Chase is my stepfather. Florencio Prado was Hutch's partner. Knew more about mustangs than any ten men I ever met. Red Bow's band of Comanche scalped him, took my sister Eva captive." Johnny's eyebrows lifted and Fan added quickly, "We got Eva back right away, though." He made an almost visible effort to shift his thoughts, away from what Johnny wasn't certain. "These horses we're riding now are Chase horses. Hutch sells 'em to the Confederacy, double the business he did before."

"He's got a new partner then?" Johnny was a man who liked all the details in place.

Fan laughed softly, picked up his horse's pace again. "No, and no hired help either. Every man who can stick his pants to a saddle these days is off fighting somewhere. But my ma, she's turned out to be right good with a lariat, so she helps him while Eva minds the house. And Adelita, she can dance a horse in off the prairie if she's a mind to."

"Adelita? Another sister?"

"When she wants to devil me she is. Adelita's Prado's daughter. We've been engaged . . . let's see, going on six years now.'' Johnny looked astonished and Fan added with a wink, ''She's worth waiting for, you understand.''

Johnny was silent for a moment. Kiowa squaws and their ragtag children trudged ahead of the column and, fleetingly, Johnny wondered what would become of them after they were left at the fort. ''I sure would like to see your outfit sometime,'' he said, his thoughts returning to Fan. It wasn't the outfit that drew him but the notion, which Fan had managed to convey over the last quarter mile, of a bursting, bustling family behind it. Johnny was family hungry, and he knew it; for, over the last five years, he'd had none to call his own.

Less than a month later, Fan nudged Johnny from a dawn slumber after an all-night watch. ''You still want to meet my family?''

Johnny sat up. ''Sure.''

''Wake up then.'' Fan waved a handful of papers at him. ''Ellis says we need fresh mounts. I've got orders here to buy them from Hutch, take any man I want with me as an escort.''

Johnny blinked. ''Let me get this straight. You got orders to buy horses—''

''Right.''

''For the cavalry—''

''Right.''

''From your own stepfather?''

''Right.''

''Isn't that a little cozy? How do they know you'll get the best deal?''

''Hell, Johnny, I can't get anything but. The Confederacy's plumb out of money, we got to get those horses on credit. Naturally, they figured I was the best man for the job. Are you getting up or not?''

''I'm getting up.''

Fan laid a hand on his shoulder. ''Just one thing. You lay an eyelash on my Adelita, I'll whip the hell out of you.''

Johnny nodded.

''We won't go to the house right away,'' Fan explained to Johnny, his eyes flicking up at the blue enamel sky. ''Day like this, only reason anyone but Eva'd be at the house is if they're dead.''

They crossed a series of gently rolling hills and came suddenly upon a herd of horses. At first the herd seemed motionless, a somber patch-quilt wadded in the fold of hills. Squinting against the sun, Johnny saw that the herd was moving, moving slowly, a trio of riders circling behind it.

Johnny's first reaction was not a word or a thought but a jolt of excitement. Grass rippled around the herd, grass as dense and rich as a carpet, tall, heavy-headed, without a single patch of earth showing through. Perfect land for cattle, Johnny thought, if the Chases had had a mind for cattle. He sighed because the horses' hooves were cutting up the fine grass.

With a yip that startled Johnny, Fan took off, galloping in a straight-arrow line toward the herd. For a moment Johnny stuck 'at the top of the hill, wanting to follow Fan but uncertain about breaking up a family reunion. Then, fearing he might be forgotten entirely, he charged after his friend.

Fan didn't pause when he reached the herd but dodged his horse toward a slim, straight-backed rider whose face was hidden beneath a flat-crowned sombrero. In answer to his approach the rider flashed a teasing smile, the white edge of which was just visible beneath her hat brim. Then she shot off, leaving her place behind the herd and streaking away from Fan. Johnny saw that her skirt was pushed up, wadded around her knees to facilitate riding, and he caught a dazzling glimpse of bare leg. *Must be Adelita*, he thought as he watched Fan go after her.

''Spook these horses and I'll tar the both of you!''

And that must be Hutch. Johnny felt foolish. Now that he'd reached the herd, Fan was a half mile distant. But Hutch turned to him with a good-natured smile, his face as lined and weathered as a canyon.

''Howdy,'' Johnny offered and introduced himself, adding, ''I came down with Fan to buy some horses from you.''

Hutch chuckled dryly. ''Steal them, more likely. Confederacy doesn't have a cent that I know of.''

Johnny's eyes wandered to the remaining rider. Hatless, a tumble of red roan hair down her back, she was the only one

who'd kept after the advancing herd. As if sensing his gaze
on her, she turned, nodded, and then shifted her attention
back to the horses.

Sarah gazed out across the moving herd. In the moment
she'd turned, she'd caught the flash of something familiar in
the young stranger, something that echoed down to her
across the long chain of years. Sun striking warm against
her back, she tried to place what it was but couldn't.

They were moving the herd from an old pasture to a new
one. As they neared the fresh site, Sarah caught the smell of
water flowing from a stream. The scent jogged her memory;
water had been all around her the day she went down to the
mill shanty with Sam Chase. Now she knew what it was,
the sense of familiarity in the stranger. It was the same
sense of solidity, of safe harbor, that she'd felt the first time
she saw Creath. She dropped back and asked the stranger
what his name was. Then, with an arresting smile she said,
"We'll go up to the house just as soon as we get the herd
penned."

Eva counted the horses in the yard. Five. Fan had brought
someone with him. Any other time she would have gone
flying out to meet her brother but the stranger made her
hang back, anxiety tightening her throat. She disliked anyone unknown to her.

Hurrying to the passageway, she paused, listened, and
was relieved to hear only silence from the other side of the
cabin. *That*, at least, wouldn't be a problem, and maybe the
stranger would soon be on his way.

The outside door opened and the family swept in, bringing the smell of grass, hot sunshine, and horses with them.
Fan lifted Eva off the ground, swung her in a circle, and set
her down facing the stranger. "This is Eva," he said, his
arm protectively about her waist.

Johnny felt them clustering around her, the whole family,
as if she were a dove in a nest. And so she was, he thought,
a wood dove with large gray eyes and a tender, full-lipped
mouth. At first glance she wasn't beautiful; her subtle colors
were drowned out, overwhelmed, by those around her. But
as Johnny studied her, the rose-on-white of her skin, the soft

antelope color of her hair, he felt a spark of pleasure. When Eva moved to pour coffee for them, he hurried to help her, doing his best to balance cups on saucers as she poured. He wasn't used to such niceties and hoped she didn't notice his awkwardness.

The cups and saucers were changes Eva had made in the house. On her sixteenth birthday a year ago, Hutch had promised to get her anything she wanted, hoping she would ask for new dresses or a trip to New Orleans, as other girls her age would have. But Eva had looked him squarely in the eye and said, without the least hesitation, "China."

Hutch mistook the request, whether in earnest or in jest Eva wasn't certain. "China. Well, I hadn't figured on going that far."

"Not the country, dishes. Plates. Cups. Ones that match each other."

Such things had never been important to Sarah, or to Hutch either, but they were to Eva. To get them she made one of her rare trips from the house, accompanying her father to Union where she ordered, from a catalog, cream white dishes patterned with starlike flowers of blue.

Nor were the plates the only changes Eva brought to the house. Down came Sarah's plain, serviceable curtains and up went her own lacy ones. From the magazines that strayed her way she copied elaborate embroidery patterns; her sewing box, a gift from Fan, bloomed bouquets of multicolored thread. All the care she had once lavished on her loft room Eva now spent on the rest of the house. As if, Sarah often thought, she could make herself safe behind a barricade of china and lace.

For nearly four years, ever since her return from the Comanche, Eva had lived behind that barricade, burrowing deeper and deeper into an invisible cocoon. It was something they never spoke of, but all of them felt it. Eva was sliding away from them, a branch caught in a current that would carry her over the falls. Now for the first time, as she watched Johnny Steele shift his saucer from one knee to another, Sarah saw a way of reaching through that barricade.

"Mighty good coffee," Johnny said and fell silent. What did you say to a girl like Eva Chase? he wondered, and why hadn't Fan made more of her? Or was it that Eva too, like Adelita, was off limits to him?

Eva reached smoothly for the coffee pot, granite blue enamel without a single chip. "More?" she asked, though her eyes didn't meet his.

"Thank you."

Across the room, Adelita flung her bare, bold arms around Fan's neck. "Have you come home to marry me?" she teased, her lips grazing his cheek.

Fan pulled her down on his knee. "Sure have."

"And leave me a widow if you get killed? Wouldn't that bother you at all?"

"Not half as much as lying in my grave thinking of you with somebody else."

Adelita jerked away from him, black hair swinging. "*Que egoista.*" She cocked her head. "Maybe I won't ever marry you."

Adelita's boldness lay in sharp contrast to Eva's silence. Johnny finished his coffee. "I've never seen cups like this before," he said. "Blue inside."

Eva's eyes fastened on him. He was big, not tall and lanky like her father and Fan but square; she caught the motion of muscles bunching beneath his shirt as he lifted the cup. His eyes, the shade of cured tobacco, were wide spaced and a shock of hair, mahogany brown, tumbled between them like a forelock. The china cup looked as fragile as a shell in his hand.

Impulsively, Eva leaned forward. "Do you want to see something?" Johnny nodded and, swiftly, she wiped the cup free of grounds with her napkin. Then she inverted it, holding it up to let the light filter through. "Look."

Now all of them were watching spellbound, as if a moth had suddenly spread its wings to reveal a span of diamonds. Eva, oblivious to them, bent nearer Johnny, making sure he could see up into the shining blue cup. "It's like the sky, isn't it?"

Just then the door to the passageway creaked open. Billy Chase, William Hutchinson Chase, up from his nap early, toddled into the room. "Ah!" he cooed, dark gray eyes alight.

Johnny Steele laughed with surprise. "Well now," he said, "you didn't tell me about this little feller. You didn't tell me there was a little brother."

Eva looked up, eyes wide with alarm, and Sarah saw the teacup tremble in her hand. Swiftly Sarah rose, crossed the room, and picked up Eva's son. "You can tell a Chase anywhere, can't you?" Sarah asked Johnny with a smile. "He doesn't look a might like my side of the family, but that dark hair, that's from Hutch's mother. Fan got it too."

There, she thought, it's an official lie now, told to another person. She waited for lightning to strike but it didn't. Instead the air felt soft around her, soft as a cloud. Over the top of Billy's head, she saw Johnny Steele helping Eva gather up the cups and saucers.

Sarah lay restless and wakeful until finally, fearful of waking Hutch, she rose and slipped outside. It was an old habit of hers, leaning against the walls of her cabin to think, the night sky spread like a hand above her. Tonight the moon slipped in and out among the scudding clouds, a marble appearing and disappearing in a child's fist.

Billy. She'd sat with Eva all night when he was born, all night and part of the next day, waiting while he pushed his way into the world. Lying in the bed, turning and sweating against the sheets, Eva's hips had seemed narrow as the small end of an egg. Yet not once had she cried out. Not once had she asked for water or comfort or any of the familiar things women asked for in childbirth. She'd simply waited, dumb as an animal, teeth sinking into the flesh of her own forearm until the blood ran.

After the baby was born Sarah cleaned the mucus from his nose, incapable, as she'd thought she might be, of simply laying her palm across the tiny face and holding it there. No, she had enough guilt-barbs stinging her already; she couldn't bear another. So she had washed him, bundled him, and put him in the crook of her daughter's arm, an act she later saw as one of incalculable cruelty. Eva looked at her in grieved bewilderment, then turned her face to the wall. When the baby began to cry, it was Sarah who picked him up and, thereafter, Sarah who walked and paced with him at night.

So it had been for the three years since. What Eva did for Billy she did as an older sister might, with a quick distraction that erected a subtle, impenetrable barrier between them. Sarah had hoped this would change when she went to work with Hutch, had hoped her absence would pull Eva closer to the child, but it didn't. At the end of the day it was still Hutch and Sarah that Billy went to for affection. He'd come to think of them as parents and of Eva as a silent, remote being who managed his bodily needs with as little fuss as possible. When he'd begun to talk, Eva had taken his small finger in her hand, pointed firmly at herself, and said, "Eva, *Eva*," until he'd repeated the name. There was no one in his life to learn the word *mother* for.

Until now, Sarah thought, leaning back against her house. Because she hadn't wanted to spoil Eva's chances with Johnny Steele, she'd let the young stranger think Billy was her own child, hers and Hutch's, but was it believable? She counted in her head. She'd been forty-four when Billy was born, not unheard of; and it helped that she looked younger, years younger, than her age. It helped too that Billy's skin was light as dogwood blossoms and that his eyes were no darker than Hutch's.

The door creaked open behind her. "I thought you might be out here," Hutch said.

She couldn't see his face but the shifting moonlight revealed the jutting lines of his cheek and jaw. Even after all this time, in spite of the rift of Eva's capture, she loved him fiercely. A gust of wind fanned her hair back against the house and she lifted her chin, scenting the air. "Rain, I think."

Hutch said nothing but stood there, studying her profile. In his eyes she hadn't changed since the day they'd married, had changed very little since the first time he'd seen her in Galveston, a basket of food in her hand. For some time now he'd held that loveliness against her: *How could things happen and leave no mark on her?* Yet now he saw he'd been mistaken; it was just that the marks ran deep below her surface. He touched her hair. "I think you did the right thing, Sarah."

It had been a long time since he'd touched her hair that way and she looked up at him, a glance so full of loss and yearning that it tore his heart in two. "I guess I'd do just about anything for her, Hutch."

Suddenly he was holding her, wrapping her in his arms as he used to, coaxing her toward the cattle barn. "Come on," he whispered, "let's scandalize Ben Bonham."

"Let's," she answered, and felt her heart shoot up, light as a star, soaring past the homely world around them.

Chapter Twenty-six

Fan brought Johnny Steele home to visit four more times during the next two years and finally, when the war ended, he brought him home for good. "Somebody's got to give this boy a home," he said with a wink. "After all, he's an orphan."

Ben Bonham had died of pneumonia the winter before, telling Sarah on his deathbed that he'd always loved her and considered his life as well spent as any. Now Johnny stepped into his place, moving into the barn loft and taking charge of the cattle. But soon it became clear that Johnny Steele had no intention of remaining a hired hand.

"Your line's gone puny," he told Hutch. "Penned and inbred. I'd like to turn them out to graze, way you do with your horses." Before Hutch could answer, Johnny added, "I'd like to round up some range cattle too, start mixing them in. They'd bring some vitality to the line. I'll go halves with you on owning them. What do you say?"

"I'll think about it."

While Hutch was thinking, Johnny put his plans into action, coaxing Fan out onto the plains with him with the promise that rounding up longhorns was at least as exciting as chasing mustangs. It wasn't, Fan discovered, but it did run a close second. They came back from their first venture stiff and thorn-scratched, driving a dozen slab-sided long-horns before them.

"Made up your mind yet?" Johnny called to Hutch as he herded the cattle past.

"Nope. Still thinking." But Hutch was grinning inwardly. Misgivings he might have about cattle, but none about Johnny Steele.

Sarah, for her part, would have let Johnny herd elephants past her door. She'd watched his relationship with Eva grow from that first visit, had seen the way Eva's cheeks flushed pink with life whenever he was near. All during the war she'd worried that something would happen to him, or that, at the war's end, he'd drift away from them. "If a Comanche takes his scalp," she said to Hutch, "we might just as well lay Eva in the grave beside him."

There'd be no need of that now. For Johnny, Eva would smile and laugh as if she'd never seen a dark day in her life. One day Sarah came into the cabin in time to see Eva's Lone Star quilt swirl down through the loft hole, a cloud of sheets and pillowcases sailing after it. Finally Eva came down the ladder herself. "They're for Johnny," she explained in response to Sarah's startled expression. "He doesn't have anything but a blanket, so I'm giving him these." Scooping the bedding up, she'd moved purposefully off across the yard toward Johnny's loft in the cattle barn.

With Johnny, Eva would venture from the house, not only on foot but also on horseback, often with Fan and Adelita but often just the two of them alone.

"This place of your pa's is about the biggest I ever saw," Johnny said one day. "How far's it go?"

Eva thought a moment, then shook her head. "I don't know." A strand of hair blew free of its pinnings and lashed against her cheek. "I've never thought about it."

She was smiling. Through the parting of her lips Johnny could see the faint gleam of her teeth. He smiled back. He was in love with her. He'd known it for some time now, though he hadn't said anything. "Is the sun too hot for you?"

"No."

"Then maybe we could ride a ways farther?" She smiled again and nodded. "There must be a lot of pretty places on a spread like this," Johnny said. "I'd like to see the prettiest."

Eva drew a sharp breath. That was the foal meadow. She'd been there only once in the years she'd been home, and that was with Fan and Adelita. Even in their company she'd felt the grip of fear, had turned anxiously toward the horizon and paced back and forth across the place where Prado had fallen, as if she still might see blood on the grass. But now Johnny had asked to see the prettiest place and, because she didn't want to disappoint him, she led him to the meadow.

It was a day in late summer with cicadas screaming in the grass and the sun glossing the horses' satiny hides. The sky stretched flat overhead, the pasture stretched flat below it, and for a moment Eva felt dizzy, as if sky and meadow were rocking, swinging up like a huge pendulum, tipping the meadow on its side. She closed her eyes and saw mares being driven by the Comanche, saw a little colt stop in stunned surprise, an arrow in its throat. Then she opened her eyes, saw Johnny Steele before her, and felt the meadow rock gently back into place.

She moved out into the grass, not quick and bare-legged as she'd been that day with Prado but held back, wading against the tide of her skirts.

"There's a stream this way with a willow tree beside it," she said. "The wands are so long they choke the water. The tree's like a woman with long hair, a woman bending over to wash her hair." She smiled, a smile that illuminated her face. "It's the marvel of the county, though no one knows it."

Johnny followed at her side, spellbound by the way she moved through the grass, by the way she held her head, by the soft, mourning-dove quality of her voice. He reminded himself of a tadpole caught in the transparent jelly of an egg. As a boy he'd studied those eggs, discovered that a youngster might, if he looked close, see the beating heart of the tadpole through its translucent skin. That was how he felt now, all thin skin and beating heart. He was going on twenty-three years old but knew no more about women than he had when he was thirteen. Eva, to him, was the repository of all the feminine beauty in the world.

A mare, recognizing Eva, came up and paused beside her, waiting to be scratched. Eva pressed her face against the animal's neck, rubbing beneath the mane with her fingertips.

Johnny watched, eyes drawn to the white crescent of neck that showed between Eva's collar and her upswept hair. Leaning forward, he pressed his lips to that cool white crescent at the nape of her neck.

Eva whirled around, so quickly she came away with strands of horse hair caught between her fingers. "What are you doing?"

Johnny saw grief in her eyes, inexpressible disappointment in him, and saw her chest rise and fall in panic. In the moment his lips had touched her neck, he'd felt her whole body stiffen. "Eva, I'm sorry, I—" But she was walking away from him, arms clutched across her chest. "I'm sorry," he called again, catching up with her.

"It's not your fault." She wouldn't meet his eyes.

"Yes, it was."

"No, it has nothing to do with you." Her profile was iron.

Johnny felt a wave of fear; he'd lost her, frightened her away forever. "Oh God," he mourned, "I've done a terrible thing."

She stopped at the words, arms going limp at her sides. Suddenly she laughed. Not a sharp laugh or a cruel one, not a laugh directed at his anguish or his inexperience. Simply a laugh, gentle as a ripple of wind. "You think you did a terrible thing?"

"Don't you?"

It would always be a mystery to him, the way she waded back to him through the grass, light brown brows drawn together, cutting an arch of bird's wings across her pale forehead. "No. Oh, Johnny, I didn't mean to make you think so."

Johnny wanted to reach out again, wanted to tell her not to

mind what had just happened between them, but he held his hand still at his side. "You going to show me that willow tree?"

Nodding, she took his hand and led him down to the stream, to the place where the willow was. But the pool made by its choking branches no longer existed: Hutch had chopped the tree back a year ago and its wands had just begun to grow again, stiff and yellow as broom straws.

"It's not the same," Eva said with a look of startled revelation. She turned in a circle, came back again to face Johnny and the tree. Then her eyes darted past him, searching the horizon as if it were a face. "It really isn't the same at all."

Thinking he read sadness in her voice, Johnny touched her shoulder. This time she did not tear herself away but let him kiss her, trembling at first but then suddenly, surprisingly, blooming for him, uncurling like a leaf stretching toward the sun.

Chapter Twenty-seven

Fan had lived through the war in the belief that Adelita would marry him as soon as he came home. But now, months after Appomatox, she still refused, putting out objections as easily as a cactus put out thorns.

"What are you going to do?" she questioned. "We don't even have a place to live."

Fan, who hadn't bothered with such considerations, thought aloud. "Tired of soldiering, and the Texas Overland's sold out to the telegraph company. I'll work with Hutch, I guess."

Adelita snorted dramatically. "You sound just like my father used to, no real plans at all. And because of it we lived with relatives. My poor mother. Now I know how she felt."

"Wait a minute, Adelita. You won't have to live with relatives. I'll build us our own house."

"Where?"

Fan scratched his forehead and motioned vaguely. "Over there somewhere. About midway between my folks' and your mother's."

Adelita whirled away from him like a dust devil. "No, I want my own place," she said.

"It'll be your own place."

But Adelita hung firm. "No. All my own." She stretched her arms wide, a wing span. "The land too."

"Oh now, Adelita, be reasonable. Where'd I get money for something like that? You think the army mustered me out with anything but the shirt on my back? You think Texas is a gold mine these days, with Yankee Reconstruction going on?" Adelita wasn't listening. She was marching away from him with a firm, quick step. "Adelita? How'm I going to do it? Tell me that."

She paused in her march and glanced back at him, her smile dazzling. "I don't know, *querida*. But if you love me, you'll think of something."

Fan sought refuge in the cattle barn, where Johnny was greasing the wounds of a calf who'd been attacked by wolves. "Adelita doesn't know what she's asking," he said. Picking up a clean straw, he bit the end cleanly. "I tell you, Johnny, I'm a desperate man."

Johnny dipped his fingers into the bowl of gray-white bacon grease and rubbed the calf's flanks. "How desperate?"

"Somewhere between bank robbing and honest work."

Johnny was thoughtful. "Desperate enough to go in on a cattle farm with me?"

Fan jerked the straw from his mouth. "Ranching? Where'd we get the land?"

"I was thinking of trying to buy some from Hutch."

"Hutch'd rather have gators on his land than cattle. He's never liked them much. Too domestic. Horses, they border on the wild."

"Even so, I was hoping he'd sell me some." Johnny finished with the calf and wiped his fingers on a wad of straw. "I asked Eva to marry me. I'd hate to take her away from here."

Fan's jaw dropped; a grin sparked his blue eyes. "You're going to marry Eva?" Johnny nodded. "You and Eva'll be married and I'll still be courting Adelita. Is there a male word for old maid, do you suppose?" He paused. "Well, say we did go in together, say Hutch would sell us land. Where'd we get the money?"

"Last time I was in Union," Johnny began, his squarely molded face serious, "I saw in a paper that they're paying gold for cattle in Kansas, as much as five, ten dollars a head." Fan snorted in disbelief but Johnny didn't swerve. "I was thinking, Fan, you and me could go north, put together a herd along the way. Texans are so cash starved, we could get beeves dirt cheap, handle maybe three hundred between us." He grinned. "We could handle more, if it wasn't for you being a greenhorn at trailing."

Fan was thinking. *Three hundred head at, better be conservative, three dollars profit a head* . . . He glanced at Johnny. "You've trailed before?"

"Many a time, with my pa."

"What about Indians?"

"We pay them off with a few head, my guess is they'll let us pass."

"And if they don't?"

Johnny grinned. "You're the Comanche fighter. Hell, why do you think I'm taking you with me?"

Fan nodded. "Fair enough."

"One other thing," Johnny said. "There's got to be other men thinking the same way we are, but they won't set out 'til next spring, when the grass is fresh. They'll flood the market all at once and the price'll drop, maybe even go bust. If we start soon and move quick, we'll make Kansas by the end of November, hit the railheads early and maybe even name our own price."

"You've got this all planned out, I see."

"I been thinking some."

"I just got one question, Johnny."

"What?"

"Has this ever been done before? Two men driving through Indian country?"

"Not that I know of."

Fan grinned. He liked that part best of all.

As soon as Fan explained his plan to Adelita, she set the wedding date. The two were married two weeks later, on the day before Fan and Johnny set out for the north. A minister came out from Union and Therese Prado moved to the Chases' temporarily, so the couple could have her small cabin to themselves. It was early September and there were no flowers to gather for a bouquet or wreath, but at the last moment Eva unearthed her old hair ribbons, the ones she and Adelita had bought long ago in Union. She ironed them carefully and, with Adelita's help, wove them into a coronet, letting the ends stream down Adelita's long, graceful neck.

Standing just behind them as they took their vows, Johnny swayed close to Eva and whispered, "You'll have flowers when we're married, I'll see to that." Eva said nothing, didn't turn her eyes to his, but Johnny felt her hand close over his, soft and firm.

After the ceremony the newlyweds set out over the hill to the Prado cabin. "Send up for food if you get hungry," Hutch called after them. "Come to visit if you get bored with each other."

Sarah laughed. "Don't count on it," she said, her hand stealing out to touch her husband's thigh. "Fan's a Chase isn't he?"

"And a Kincaid too." Hutch winked at Johnny. "You'll be lucky to get him on the trail by Friday."

Eva stood up swiftly. She felt alone, cut off from their banter. All the world took delight in this one thing, this one thing that, in her mind, stood for torture and humiliation. She glanced at Johnny. *Will Johnny, Johnny too . . . ?* She pushed the thought from her mind, too paralyzed to think it through.

At dawn the next morning the young men set out, driving before them the few dozen longhorns they'd gathered themselves and bringing behind the extra horses they'd rented from Hutch.

Fan maintained a look of alert wakefulness until they were underway. Then, when the house was out of sight behind them, he slumped in the saddle. "We got to stop, Johnny, so I can get some sleep. Adelita wore me out."

Johnny laughed and looked closely at Fan's face. Beneath the brim of his hat, there were circles under his eyes. "Sleep in the saddle if you want, but we can't stop. We've had these longhorns penned at your place for more'n a week. That's home to them now and if we stop, they'll head back for it."

Fan let out a sigh. Johnny stopped, went to one of the pack horses, and fished up a bottle of the raw peppery whiskey he'd purchased in Union. "Have some of this, you'll feel better."

Johnny took a deep sip, Adam's apple bobbing. Tears leaped to his eyes. "God, what's in this stuff?" He held the bottle to the light. "Look at that. Johnny, I swear those're rattlesnake buttons floating in there."

"Do you feel better or not?"

"I don't know. Burns so that I can't tell."

Johnny grinned. "That's the idea."

Billy stood in the yard, watching the dust cloud raised by the departing cattle. Fan and Johnny stood taller than giants in his six-year-old heart and right up until the last grain of dust settled he hoped that one of them might come dashing back for him, yelling to take him on the journey with them.

Johnny and me got to thinking, who'd mind the horses . . . ?

Each of us thought the other one'd asked you . . .

The truth is, Billy, we'd rather have you with us than any full growed man we might meet along the way . . .

So ran the thoughts in Billy's mind. But in truth Fan and Johnny had barely noticed him, so busy were they with the cattle and the horses, with their good-byes to Eva and Adelita and Hutch and Sarah. Billy had stood in the center of them all, invisible as wind.

It was a feeling he was familiar with, the odd, unspoken

feeling of being both the rim that held their circle together and the stranger who was forever thrust outside it.

His first memory in life was of a soldier in a gray uniform who came to buy a horse from Hutch. The soldier had no money but he paid for the animal with a large, flat piece of glass trimmed with wood. A window, Hutch had called it, and spent the rest of the day fitting it into the wall of the cabin. The next night Billy piled firewood below the window and, climbing up, stood on tiptoe to look in. There like a picture, framed by the smooth glass, were his parents and his sister Eva, perfect and happy as they sat around the table, their faces washed in soft lamplight.

At that moment Eva had chanced to look up. Seeing him, her face stiffened and she stood up abruptly, so abruptly the tablecloth jerked, sending the lamp on its side with a crash. Oil soaked the cloth and a sudden flame shot up.

All the rest of his life Billy remembered that moment, the look of fear and fright on Eva's face as she stared at him through the leaping flame. He got the same feeling, though to a lesser degree, from the rest of the family. Only Sarah was an exception. With her he didn't feel the strain of reticence he felt with the others. Sarah could hold him, rock away his hurts, meet his eyes without looking away. Yet Sarah was eternally busy, her presence in his life so scant it opened, rather than filled, a deep need in him.

Billy grew up spending much of his time alone, much of his time watching, much of his time separated, in one way or another, from those around him. As he watched the dust cloud settle on the horizon, he suddenly realized that there'd be no one to look after the cattle left behind by Fan and Johnny.

"I can mind the cattle," he told Hutch. The thought of sleeping in Johnny's loft room, with Eva's Lone Star quilt still on the bed, caught his imagination. "Please let me."

"We'll see," Hutch answered. But over the next few days Billy begged so hard and so persistently that, in the end, Hutch let him have his way.

Billy felt more comfortable around animals than he did around people and it gave him a fine feeling to rise before dawn and bring in the cows, who'd been grazing all night,

for the day's first milking. In the afternoons he rode out to
where the herd was grazing, though this was unnecessary.
The weather was still reliable, it was neither breeding
season nor calving time, and the animals could just as easily
have minded themselves.

But Billy rode out nevertheless. By no means tall for his
age, he kept his seat on a full-grown horse, riding coming as
naturally to him as breathing. Sometimes, looking out over
the backs of the cattle as they grazed, he pretended they
were buffalo, the wild buffalo Fan had told him of. Other
times he pretended they were longhorns, fractious and
half-wild, and he was driving them, alone, up the trail to
Kansas. Finding a lariat coiled in Johnny's gear, he took it
with him and spent entire afternoons practicing.

One day Hutch crested a hill and came upon the sight of
Billy jogging after a cow. The cow was old, past milking
age, but of a tough and wily nature that sent her dodging
expertly across the pasture. Hutch watched Billy follow her,
lariat coiled in his hands, guiding his horse with his knees.

The Comanche was there in him, in the sturdy legs and
rounded ribcage, in the dark, coffee-colored hair and in the
easy way he sat the horse; but Eva was there also. As Hutch
watched Billy turn and canter, it was the curve of his
daughter's cheek he saw, her light skin and the grace of her
movements. And it was the mingling of the two together,
Comanche and Eva, that jabbed him like a knife.

Even so, he smiled when Billy finally snagged the old
cow. Holding his horse in from habit, always wary of
startling a herd, Hutch started down the hill at a lope. "That
was some roping," he said as he approached.

Billy had been aware of Hutch's presence at the top of the
hill for some time, had ridden better because of it. "Thank
you, sir." Only rarely did he call Hutch *father*, for experience had taught him that the word fell flat as rain on a rock.
More often, he called him by his first name, just as he
called Sarah by her first name. "I was just practicing."

Hutch studied the boy. "You like cattle, do you?

"Sure." Billy paused. Something in Hutch's face prompted
him to continue. "I like horses too. And buffalo, of course.

Fan says Texas is made of buffalo, says it's just so much dirt laid over buffalo bones.''

"Does he now?"

"That's what he told Johnny."

"I see," Hutch responded. "Ever seen a buffalo yourself?"

"No."

"Like to?"

"Yeah, sure."

"Well, I reckon we might arrange something."

Hutch wasn't sure what prompted him to do it, to pack bedrolls and food and take Billy off on a week-long trip. Perhaps it was Eva. Now that Johnny Steele had proposed to her, her happiness curled through the cabin like a vine, sending up shoots and flowers wherever she stepped. Yes, maybe it was that. But it was something within himself as well, pure loneliness he guessed. Since Prado had been killed, he'd had no close companion on the range. There was Sarah, of course, but Sarah was his love and that was different. Soon Fan would be going away from him too; he and Johnny had already approached him about buying land and Hutch had agreed. If anyone was to fill the gap in Hutch's life, it would be Billy and suddenly it had seemed important, more important than anything Hutch could name, for the two of them to ride off together.

They set out on a clear November morning. Winter was coming down from the northern plains, bringing the buffalo with it, and Billy's eyes grew round at the sight of the huge, hump-backed beasts. He and Hutch had entered into wild country, empty country that, for the most part, had yet to be settled.

"Aren't you scared?" Billy asked one night as they settled beside their campfire. They'd seen Indians that day, a band of braves chasing buffalo, and now wolves howled in the darkness around them.

Hutch glanced at him over the rim of a dented coffee cup. "Scared of what?"

"Wolves and such. Indians."

Hutch shook his head. "No, I reckon I'm not."

"Why?"

"I lived with the Cherokee once, didn't I ever tell you? Got to know their ways. That takes some of the fear away."

Billy leaned forward, hugging his knees. Too much like Eva, Hutch thought, looking at his face; too much like her and not enough time between the two of them. In his mind her birth had been one day, Billy's the next. Hutch pushed the thought away.

"What were their names?" Billy asked.

"The Cherokee? Oh, Spotted Turtle and Cattail, they were old people, husband and wife. And Walking Bird and Yellow Fawn and a little girl about your age named Lodgesmoke."

"What happened to them?"

Hutch tipped out the grounds in his coffee cup. "They're gone." He was silent for a moment. Then, reaching out, he smoothed the blanket up over Billy's shoulder. "You go to sleep now, nothing to be scared of."

Billy pretended to sleep but then, after a while, opened his eyes. He felt safe and warm in a way he never had before and, wanting to make the moment last, lay awake a long time. As he watched Hutch through the flame of the campfire he remembered another flame, the flame of the spilled lamp with Eva's horrified face behind it. Stirring himself whenever he began to fall asleep he watched on and on until at last his eyes grew heavy and the two flames burned together in his mind.

Chapter Twenty-eight

Eva would not work on clothes for her wedding. "It's bad luck," she said. "If I do, Johnny might not come back. Something terrible might happen to him."

So Sarah and Adelita and Therese sewed around her, Sarah going to Union herself and coming back with cloth and a pattern for the wedding gown.

"Will you try it on at least?" Sarah asked when the gown was basted together. Eva consented and stood, as motionless as a statue, while the women fitted the dress around her.

It was going to be an extravagant wedding by the standards of the day; Hutch and Sarah had already made up their minds on that score. They were doing it because Eva was their only daughter, they told themselves, but the real reason ran deeper. Eva's wedding was a chance to sever past from present, and they were going to make the most of it.

The gown itself was of pale cream satin, with a scalloped neckline that hugged Eva's shoulders. It was a beautiful dress, more beautiful than any she'd ever owned, but it made her feel vulnerable and exposed. As the women measured and pinned the hem at her ankles, Eva brought her hand up to her collarbone. Like a stem, she thought, like a bird bone; anyone could break it.

"Put your hand down," Sarah said. "I can't measure."

Eva let her hand drop and resumed her statuelike stance. The women stood up to inspect her while Adelita picked up the gossamer net veil and arranged it over Eva's head. As the lace floated down over her daughter's face, Sarah saw tears in Eva's eyes.

"I can finish, I guess," Sarah said, and hurried Adelita and Therese out of the house. Alone, she turned to Eva. She couldn't read her expression, muted behind the veil, but a tear splashed down onto the flawless satin.

"Will it stain?" Eva asked,

"I don't think so," Sarah replied. "It isn't important at any rate. We could pin flowers over the spot." She paused, wanting to say more, wanting to remind Eva that all men weren't like Comanche, Johnny Steele least of all. But the barrier that had always been between them stopped her.

Sarah sighed. She'd done what she could, taken Billy on as her own son, led him to believe that she and not Eva was his mother, and worry over that nagged her still. Had she done enough or had she done too much? Had Eva's chance for happiness been won at Billy's expense? He wasn't an ordinary child, anyone could see that. As if he knew, Sarah sometimes thought, that they had all lied to him. Well, there was no help for it now.

"Can I take the dress off?"

"What?"

"Are you finished pinning, mother?" Eva had removed the veil and was looking at her, her face so dry-eyed that Sarah almost imagined she'd seen the tear splash down. But no, there was its shadow, still damp against the satin.

"Yes. I'm finished." Awkwardly, she patted Eva's arm. "Don't worry so. Johnny loves you."

The words were flat and thin and she didn't blame her daughter for not answering them.

Twice while Fan and Johnny were away marauders, drifters who'd mustered out of the army and into professional outlawry, rustled horses from Hutch. Reluctantly, he set about hiring a dozen hands, experts with guns as well as horseflesh, the first outsiders, except for Ben Bonham, who'd ever come to work for him. It was a decision he'd long put off, for he liked the isolation of his life. Now, with renegades combing Texas and Fan and Johnny moving out of the picture, he had no choice.

"That's the price of being a wealthy man," Sarah teased in bed one night. He did not answer but lay on his back, staring straight up. She raised herself on one elbow. "What's wrong?"

"Makes me feel old, hiring those young men. Seems like just an eye-wink ago it was me getting hired to take traders to the Red River country. I remember one of them, Findley Ware; I thought he was old but he was young, younger than Austin is now. Hell, Sarah, where does it all go?"

His hand found hers and she grasped it quickly. "I don't know, darling. Into the land, I guess, like rain sinking down."

"Good thing I've got you then," he said, turning to her suddenly, burying his face in her neck. "You'd make a dying man feel young."

Sarah had no desire to make love; she was exhausted, tired to the bone from the work she'd done that day, but it was easy to accommodate him and she saw no reason not to. She'd done the same long ago for Arden Bell, a man she didn't love; it took no effort to do as much for Hutch, whom she loved with all her heart.

Afterward, when they lay against each other in the darkness, he said, "One good thing about hiring those men, I can take some time off. Remember how me and you and the boys used to pack up and go off overnight? I was thinking next spring we could do that again, just you and me."

Sarah paused. "Eva'll be married by then."

"Mm."

"I was thinking, Hutch. Billy'd have to stay with us."

Hutch sighed and shifted his arms beneath her. "Hadn't thought of that. Well then, it'll be even more like it used to be, won't it? You and me and a youngin."

Upstairs Eva lay awake, straining to hear her parents' voices. She felt a great surge of relief to know they'd keep Billy, for what would she have done if they wouldn't? She'd thought of it often, her thoughts always leading her to a blank wall. He was her son, she was responsible for him. More responsible, certainly, than her mother or her father. Yet she felt not the least responsible; if she'd given birth on the prairie, she was certain, she'd have left him behind.

At first she'd thought she felt that way because she was young. *Let mother take care of him for now. When I'm older, I'll feel differently. When I'm older and ready for children, I will love him.* But she didn't. She was ready for children now, ready to start a family with Johnny Steele, and still her heart was closed to Billy.

Other things that had happened to her Johnny would soon find out, would discover as soon as he slipped her bridal nightgown from her shoulders. Why not tell him of Billy too? What her mother had said the other day was true: Johnny loved her. He'd accept her son, if she told him. No, it wasn't fear of losing Johnny that kept her silent. It wasn't for his sake that she kept Billy thrust to the back of her mind. It was for her own.

The second week in November, before a blowing wind that withered the grass before it, Fan and Johnny reached the railhead at Sedalia, Missouri. Of the three hundred fifty head of cattle they'd accumulated, they'd given a dozen to the Indians whose lands they crossed and lost another half dozen along the trail. Other than that, they'd weathered the five hundred miles without a scratch. Droving in the winter might have its disadvantages, Johnny said, but at least the heavy, ice-laden rains kept the water holes filled.

While Johnny kept watch over the herd, Fan rode into town in search of a buyer and found not one but several, all willing to compete against each other. No one had expected to see a hide or a hoof before May, and news that two men had battled their way up from Texas alone caught the town's imagination. Fan found himself much in demand at the town's principal saloon, where he was quizzed about the particulars of the trip. A Chicago journalist mapped out the route, wrote a story to accompany it, and sent it home to his editor, titling the piece "The Steele-Chase Road, Avenue of Empire."

The name Steele-Chase Road stuck. It never did become an avenue of empire, for the railroads were already pushing west, to cities like Abilene and Witchita, taking the avenues of empire with them. But long after the trail was fenced and farmed, the name remained. Like the Chisholm Trail that replaced it, the Steele-Chase Road stood for adventure, courage, and daring exploits.

Many of those exploits were invented by Fan himself as he sat in the Empress Saloon. The truth was, the trip had been uneventful and though it took courage to endure eighteen-hour days in the saddle and the misery of icy, wind-driven rains, those weren't the kind of hardships that kindled excitement. By careful dickering and skillful story telling, Fan managed to clear eight dollars a head on the cattle, and by the time he and Johnny left town they were wealthy men.

"You know what the irony of all this is, don't you?" Fan asked Johnny as they packed the money in two sets of saddle bags.

"What?"

"For the first time in six years I'm in a town with money in my pocket and no captain waiting to mark me absent without leave. I could walk into the Empress and buy any fancy gal that caught my eye. But the hell of it is, I'm a married man now.'' Johnny laughed and Fan added, ''You aren't though, not quite. You want to raise a little hell, I'd be the last to tell Eva.''

Johnny shook his head. Though he'd rather die than let on to Fan, the truth was he'd never been with a woman. As a youngster he'd been too honest to lie to good girls and too poor too pay for bad ones. Then the war had come along and he'd met Eva and that had put the matter to rest. He'd wait for her, he decided. It gave him a sweet feeling to think that, of all the men and women on earth, the two of them would only know each other.

Chapter Twenty-nine

Eva and Johnny were married on the first day of March 1866, not at home but in the sanctuary of the First Presbyterian Church of Union. Eva had been very clear about wanting a church wedding. ''I want God there,'' she'd said. ''I want it to be in His house.'' As if, Sarah thought, she could forge a bond so strong that nothing would ever threaten it; well, that was Eva for you.

They arrived in Union the day before the wedding and took rooms in the Claymore House, the city's best hotel and the only one with a dining room capable of producing the sort of wedding breakfast Hutch felt his daughter deserved. She was going to be married at 8 A.M. and, though the celebration wouldn't be large or long-lasting, he intended it to be lavish. He signed the registry book for three adjoining rooms, one for Fan and Adelita, one for Sarah, Eva, and Therese Prado, and one to be shared by himself, Johnny, and Billy.

Austin and his family arrived on the late afternoon stage, having come part of the way from San Antonio by rail. They were the first in the family to experience train travel and Sarah and Hutch, veteran adventurers by nature, were anxious to learn the details.

"Instead of dust there's coal smoke," Meta told them. "You have to shut the windows against it. And all the children running up and down the car screaming. Well, it gave me a headache, I can tell you. So after a while I pretended I didn't know them, wasn't their mama, and went to the back of the car. There's a place where you can stand between the cars and watch the world rush by. Things were lovely then. Only," she leaned closer to them, "don't tell Austin, but I think it's where people go, you know, to meet each other? While I was standing there, a man came out and tried to take up with me."

Sarah laughed and Eva, standing on the other side of the lobby, glanced at her mother. So did Austin, who was standing beside her. "Ma still looks young, doesn't she?" he asked and Eva nodded, thinking all the while, she's never laughed like that with me.

"I'm glad you came, Austin. I didn't expect you to, it's such a long trip, but it means the world to me."

"You didn't think I'd miss your wedding, did you? After all, you came to mine."

That had been ten years ago, the last time she'd seen him, and so much had happened since then. He'd been in the war and she . . . her mind turned away and came back to focus on Austin. He seemed younger than before. Meta had done that, she guessed, Meta and the five children dashing back and forth across the lobby.

"These are your cousins," Hutch said to Billy. The contrast was marked. Eva's child, quiet and sober, had nothing in common with Meta and Austin's boisterous, bright-haired brood.

"You can sleep in our room tonight if you want," the oldest of the bunch said. "Can you run? Let's play tag. Not It!"

"Not It! Not It!" cried all the other children behind him. Billy stared at them, uncomprehending. Then the youngest girl pointed to him and cried, "Billy's It!"

All their eyes were on him and he felt a wave of shame, as if he'd wet his pants or messed himself. Never in his life had he played a game of tag, though he understood it was a contest of some sort. What was *It* supposed to do? He searched frantically for Hutch, for Sarah, but they were on the other side of the lobby, deep in conversation. His cousins were still staring, staring and staring. With a kind of shamed desperation he looked up and said, "I'm It."

At the words the children scattered like marbles. Billy was saved by Meta who, without pausing in her conversation, stretched out one hand and caught the collar of the child nearest her. "There'll be none of that here," she said firmly.

Now the children clumped in self-conscious silence. Joe, the oldest, turned to Billy. "Ma says your pa raises horses. Shoot, I wish my pa did something like that. *We* live in town." He said it as if living in town were the worst fate that could befall a boy.

"Do you like horses?" Billy asked shyly. His mouth was dry but when Joe nodded he began to think, with some hope, of the horses, their own sleek horses, in the livery stable down the street. He walked across the lobby, his cousins following him. "Hutch, they want to see our horses. Can we go?"

Hutch nodded, and Meta too. "Better leave the baby with me," she said. "And mind Tom, Lissa, so he doesn't get kicked." Lissa, a girl of Billy's age with large, cornflower blue eyes, picked up three-year-old Tom and carried him on her hip.

"Why do you call your pa Hutch?" Joe asked.

Billy shrugged. "I just always have, that's all. Come on, let's go."

Billy did sleep with his cousins that night, but he did it with a torn heart. He wanted to be with them, wanted to belong to their little circle, and turning down their invitation, he sensed, would be taken as an offense. Yet as he lay awake between Joe and the next in age, Creath, he felt uncomfortable and out of place. His cousins were noisy, he didn't understand half their jokes, and their quick, abrupt bursts of energy startled him. He wished he were in the room down the hall, with Hutch and Johnny, yet he wouldn't have risen and gone there for a hundred dollars.

The next morning, the wedding morning, Billy rose early, before anyone else was up. He'd long had it in his mind to do something for Eva, to surprise her in some special way, and now he intended to do it. Crawling past Creath, he found his pants and slid into them, feeling in his pocket for the carefully folded ribbon and the folding knife he'd brought from home.

What're you doing?" Joe whispered. The oldest, he was like a watchdog, alert to any unusual stirring among them.

Billy looked at him, dark eyes calculating. "Promise not to tell?" Joe nodded. "I'm going to pick flowers for Eva. You know, kind of a bouquet."

Joe swung his legs over the side of the bed, grinning. "I'll go with you."

Billy had had it in his mind to go alone, to plunder backyard gardens like a blockade runner slipping through enemy waters, but now he saw that Joe clearly meant to go with him. If we get caught, he thought, at least there'll be two of us.

But they didn't get caught. In fact, Joe scaled fences and avoided yards with active dogs so effectively that Billy began to think he'd had previous experience. He didn't know. Maybe that was what city boys did. Or maybe Joe, two years older than he was, already had a girlfriend to give bouquets to. "You steal flowers at home?" he asked.

Joe shook his head. "Apples." And the two boys grinned at each other.

They collected a double armful of flowers and got back to the Claymore House just in time to change their clothes.

"You give her half and I'll give her half," Billy said. It seemed only fair; Joe had taken as many risks as he had.

But Joe refused. "No, she's your sister and it was your idea. You go ahead." So Billy pulled out the ribbon he had brought from home, a blue ribbon he'd found in Sarah's keepsake chest, and tied it around the stems. He had no way of knowing it was the same ribbon, kept all these years, that Hutch had found fluttering in the foal meadow the day Eva was captured.

Eva walked down the aisle of the church, eyes fixed on the altar before her. She'd picked the church for its windows, two bullet-shaped wonders of stained glass, one on either side. As she passed between them the morning sun splashed blocks of crimson and blue and green across her satin skirt and she tried to think of it as a mystic baptism, a baptism of light and color for her new life, washing away all that had ever happened to her.

At the end of the aisle Johnny waited for her. She felt his eyes lifting her up, pulling her forward. If it had been any man but him she might have turned and run away, might have kept all her secrets secrets forever. Because of him, she walked forward.

Later, she remembered very little of the service. She recalled looking down from within the cocoon of her veil, anxious to see whether the spot from the tear shed weeks ago had actually vanished. She recalled Adelita in a dress of deep lavender, transforming the ordinary color into something rich and exotic. She recalled the organ music, though not the song that was played, and the way the ring felt when Johnny slipped it over her finger. They were marrying with silver rings, not gold, for Eva wanted her ring to match the bracelet she'd worn from childhood.

At the wedding breakfast she was unable to eat and slipped away from the table to change into her traveling suit, a dark green skirt and jacket trimmed with bands of velvet so deep green they were almost black. She and Johnny were heading for their own place right away. They'd talked it over and decided that was where they wanted their honeymoon to be, in their own half of the double cabin he and Fan had completed just a week ago. The other half of the cabin would be empty until next week, when Fan and Adelita moved in.

Just before she and Johnny left, while everyone else was growing rosy on the wine Hutch had insisted on ordering, Billy rushed up to her with an armful of flowers. She felt herself reach stiffly for them, her voice an old woman's voice. "Thank you, Billy. My, but they're nice." As she lifted them her eye caught the flash of something blue and shining. The ribbon, she thought, *that ribbon*. No, it couldn't be, couldn't be the same one. Still, the leaves of the flowers trembled in her hands. *As if he knows*, she thought. *Yes, as if he knows exactly . . .*

"Eva?" Johnny had her by the elbow. "The buggy's loaded, why don't you come say good-bye to your folks."

Her kiss to Sarah was dry and mechanical, but she left tear marks on the front of Hutch's shirt. Then she said good-bye to the rest of them and was suddenly in the buggy beside Johnny, heading out of town against a fresh spring wind, a great feeling of freedom lifting her heart.

In the hotel dining room, at the end of the tables that had been pushed together for the party, Billy saw the bouquet of flowers lying. She hadn't thought to take them with her.

Clouds caught them before they reached home and the wind strengthened, carrying the smell of rain with it. It tugged at Eva's bonnet and she reached up to tighten the bow beneath her chin but Johnny stopped her. "Take it off," he said. "You won't get sunburned."

A little self-consciously, Eva removed the bonnet and laid it at her feet in the bottom of the buggy. Now that they were alone, now that they were married, she wasn't certain what to say to him. Being alone with him was different now than being alone with him a week ago had been. In the long furrows of silence she planted seeds of worry.

Had he been with other women? she brooded, studying his profile beside her. Of course he had, he must have been; it was foolish to think otherwise for he was twenty-four, had been on his own, and served in the army. He had been with other women and would compare her to them, women with smooth sleek bodies who had never borne children. Eva gnawed her bottom lip.

"I don't think we'll make it," Johnny said beside her.

Eva was startled. "What?"

Her husband pointed up at the clouds. "Going to rain, I think, and we've still ten miles to go."

"I don't mind getting wet," Eva said, relief in her voice.

"Well, I mind that you do." They were on their own land before the rain began and Johnny tucked into a cluster of trees. "Not afraid, are you?"

As if I'd melt, Eva thought; *as if I'd never been wet*

before. But sitting beside him, rain spattering the canopy of leaves overhead, she enjoyed the feeling his words stirred in her. "No, I'm not afraid."

They sat for a long time but the rain showed no sign of ending. When the day began to fade around them, Eva suggested they drive on.

"Certain?" Johnny asked.

Eva nodded and they set off again, water streaming from the buggy awning, rain blowing in the open front and soaking her skirt. By the time they reached the cabin she was wet to the skin.

She had it in mind to change into dry clothes while Johnny was seeing to the horse and buggy but it took her several minutes just to find the matches she and Adelita had packed and sent up with the household goods. Eva lit a lamp and the room flared into shape around her. Boxes stood against one wall and the open shelves, her kitchen, were still bare. But Johnny, sweet Johnny, had somehow found the box with bedding in it, had made the bed in the corner himself and spread their Lone Star quilt across it.

There was a stand beside the bed and on it a pitcher filled with lilacs. He must have done it the day before yesterday, she thought, bending down to inhale their fragrance.

The door opened at her back. "Your ma said lilacs are your favorite."

"They are." Her fingertips touched the tiny flower buds. "You must have brought these all the way from the house."

"No, they're from our own bushes."

"Our own?"

"Guess you couldn't see them in the rain. Come here a minute." He guided her to the door and showed her the bushes he'd planted, clumps Sarah had given him from her own plantings. Their flowers, cream and deep violet, trembled in the rain and their heart-shaped leaves glistened dark green.

"Oh, Johnny, you couldn't have given me a present I'd like better."

Now it was her husband who seemed ill at ease. "I'll get a fire going," he said. "Fan said he put dry kindling in the box."

Soon the glow of the fire reached out to warm her. She picked up the basket of hotel food Sarah had sent with them. "Are you hungry?" she asked.

Johnny shook his head, took the basket from her hands and set it aside. "You're still wet," he said, "and shaking."

She said nothing but stood while his hands began unhooking the long row of clasps and buttons that ran down her back like a spine. She felt her armor being lifted away from her, the heavy green jacket and velvet trimmed skirt, the tight-woven barricade that hid her so effectively. The clothes dropped in a green pool around her.

Johnny saw, above the lace border and white satin ribbon of her chemise, the raw scar. It cut the pearl white mound of one breast, a welted brand puckered at the edges. When he began to unfasten the chemise, her hand curled over his.

"No, oh, Johnny . . ." Head lowered, her cheeks seemed to have gone bone white.

"Ssh," he said. He opened the chemise and slid it from her shoulders. He was glad she wasn't looking at him, for at that moment his expression contorted in horror. Burn marks he could recognize anywhere and these had been made deliberately, with long heated brands, he thought. Whoever had done it had drawn across the tender skin of her chest as if she were a chalk board. The two longest lines, beginning beneath her arms, vanished into the waistband of her petticoat, the extended arms of a *V* that met at the junction between her legs.

He was silent so long that Eva looked up at him. "Fan must have told you . . . the Comanche . . ." Tears choked her voice.

"Ssh," he said again.

Eva couldn't believe the feeling of being picked up and carried to the bed, of being petted and stroked by Johnny and kissed so tenderly she wanted to weep. Awkwardly, she lifted her arms and drew him down to her.

I don't know what to do with my hands, she thought, her mind wild with panic. The Comanche had held her hands, pinned them to the ground above her head. What did other women, normal women, do?

Johnny was looking down at her, eyes full of tenderness. "Is it wrong? Shall I stop?"

"No. It's just that . . ."

"That—?" he prompted.

"I love you, Johnny." He moved inside her again, a movement that took her along with it. "Love you," she echoed. Her hands found their own way then, gliding over the tops of his shoulders and down the center of his back. She dug her heels into the soft, familiar fabric of the Lone Star quilt and arched herself up to meet him, arched so hard and so fiercely that her back hurt for hours afterward. Tears slid from the corners of her eyes and ran back into her hair, warm as sea brine, full of life.

The trip home was a lonely one for Billy. His cousins had left Union by stage, the return train trip to San Antonio still ahead of them. They'd filled the entire coach with their boisterous presence and it had seemed to him, as they squabbled over seating arrangements, that nothing could be better than being part of such a family. Fan and Adelita were off too, on a stage headed for Dallas where Fan was going to see about acquiring a new bull.

With only Hutch and Sarah in the house, Billy felt restless. "Let's go check the horses," he urged Hutch, yearning for the bond of human closeness.

But Hutch's legs were cramped from the long buggy ride home. "You go if you want, son," he'd answered. "This old hoss is done for tonight." And Billy had felt oddly rejected.

That night Billy lay in his loft room listening to the silence of the house. It wasn't the loft Eva had lived in for so many years but the one on the other side of the cabin, the one called the boys' loft, which Austin and Fan had shared during their growing up years.

Alone, he remembered a story Austin had told at the wedding breakfast, a story about how Fan had snored so as a boy that Austin would roll to the edge of his bed, stretch his leg out, and nudge Fan with his foot until he was silent. "I'd just keep nudging and nudging, pushing him, until he rolled over and shut up. Once he rolled all the way off the bed and hit the floor, still sound asleep and snoring to beat all heck.''

Billy wondered what it would be like to have brothers, even one brother, to share things with. He wouldn't mind, he told himself, if that brother snored; it would be fine with him. But what if he was the brother who snored? He remembered the discomfort he'd felt with his cousins, the anxiety he'd experienced over not knowing how to play tag.

Rising, he fumbled in the darkness until he came upon a wooden box Hutch had given him. He opened the lid and ran his fingers across its contents: marble, whistle, the claw of a pheasant with a tendon still intact so that, when you pulled it, the claw contracted. Then his fingers came to what he was looking for, a strip of cloth as smooth as water. It was the blue ribbon he'd tied around Eva's bouquet. He wasn't sure why he saved it, just as he wasn't sure, now, why he lifted it and pressed it to his cheek.

He sat for a few minutes more in the darkness, a restless and hollow feeling growing within him. Then he slipped down the ladder and out into the moonlight. He walked toward the cattle barn, the barn that had been his domain all the while Fan and Johnny were away. He had felt needed there, had felt, best of all, important.

He lit a lamp and set it on the old stump Sarah used for a milking stool. The barn was empty, the cattle gone. Hutch had given them, with no pretense of the sacrifice he was making, to Eva and Johnny as a wedding present. Glad to get rid of them, he'd said; he'd never liked keeping cattle. But Billy missed them. Without them, it seemed he had no place, nothing to do. His gifts at handling them had been forgotten, just as his bouquet had been.

He held the ribbon up and let it dangle, a blue snake. Eva. He had a sister, he reminded himself, but she hadn't thought enough of him to keep the flowers he gave her.

He remembered the night he'd stared in at her through the window. He remembered the way her expression of happiness had changed to one of horror and the way she'd sent the lamp crashing so that flames had jumped up between them. But now that memory was overlaid with another recollection, the recollection of his trip with Hutch.

Suddenly, he longed to feel the warmth of that bonfire again, the fire that had embraced him and drawn him into its circle of safety. Lifting the glass chimney, he held a dry straw to the flame and watched it flame in his fingers. He gathered two more straws and lit them, but the flame seemed small, smaller than the campfire Hutch had built. So he pushed scraps of hay together to make a mound and, just as Eva had done, tipped the oil lamp over onto it.

Flames shot up in a jet, forcing him backwards and he felt an inexpressible rush of satisfaction. He remembered the ribbon he was still holding and held it to the fire, watching flame devour it from the end up. His fingers were burned before he cast it away, though he didn't notice.

The fire was spreading now, licking across the oil-soaked straw that littered the floor. From the first explosive jet, the rafters had caught. Tatters of flame raced along the old wood, burning splinters dropped into stalls mounded with fresh hay.

Billy watched in fascination. It was like diving deep, he thought, deep into a pond on a hot day and touching the cool slick mud on the bottom. He stood until flames boiled on all sides of him, the wind they made breathing against his face. He found his way easily to the door and walked calmly out into the night. Only then did he begin to tremble, to feel the sting of burns on his hands and arms. Only then did he sink down hugging his knees, the mystery of what he'd done lighting the sky before him.

Chapter Thirty

The cabin Johnny and Fan built was a larger version of Hutch and Sarah's, two square rooms, each with a loft space, connected by a dog-run passageway. The idea was that each couple would have a half to themselves, as privately as if they were in separate cabins, but that privacy was seldom enforced. Doors to passageways were left open, voices called back and forth, meals were taken together.

Marriage had not settled Adelita, who learned to round up longhorns with the men. In her absence, running the house fell to Eva. It was a fair arrangement, for all the couples' spare cash went into building a herd and Adelita's help was sorely needed, but Johnny worried about leaving Eva alone during the day.

"I don't mind," she assured him. "I'd tell you if I did."

He did not for a moment believe her. There were still Comanche raiding Texas, more in the Panhandle than here, but he knew she saw their shadows every time she glanced toward the horizon. She never talked of them, told him nothing of her captivity, but often at night he would come awake abruptly, jolted by her violent shaking beside him. She didn't wake during these dreams and seemed not to remember them, but in the morning there'd be deep shadows, like violet bruises, beneath her eyes. As he came to know her, Johnny discovered that he could still her shaking by stroking her in her sleep. Sometimes then she would wake, clasp his hand in hers, and draw her to him.

Still that didn't solve the problem of leaving her alone during the day. One morning Johnny rode into Union and came back late in the afternoon with a *morral*, a sacklike Mexican saddlebag, dangling from his saddle horn.

"Yours," he told Eva, unhooking the *morral* and setting it on the ground. The *morral* moved and she stepped back but Johnny nudged her forward. "Go on," he said, "he's got to learn your scent." A black nose thrust into view and Eva, kneeling, opened the *morral* to release the Mastiff puppy within. "He's just a newborn but I saw his father, outweighs me by a good twenty pounds. This one'll get just as big." Suddenly, Johnny's brow furrowed. "Not scared of him are you?"

Eva shook her head. "No." She was picking the puppy up, letting him chew the strands of hair that escaped the coil at the nape of her neck. "What's his name?"

"He doesn't have one yet. I got him for you, I figured you'd want to name him yourself."

She rubbed her cheek against the puppy's head. It wasn't

just the need of a watchdog the puppy filled but the need she had to hold something in her arms.

Eva longed for a baby and in her daydreams a little girl with bright eyes filled the cabin with her presence. She already had a name chosen, Callie Lou, though she told it to no one, not even Adelita. Children with Johnny would come, she promised herself; fate wouldn't be so cruel.

Except for the lack of a child, Eva was happy. She'd always found pleasure in caring for a house, but this house of her own creation she found meaning in as well. She was its center, its light, Johnny said; he and Fan and Adelita pressed around her like leaves around a bud, closing out the sadness of the past.

"I want to have Christmas here," she told Johnny that first year. It was to her some internal test, to see how she'd weather having Billy in her house. Johnny did not know this, of course, for Eva had told him nothing more than the scars on her body had, so he'd ridden to Hutch and Sarah's with the invitation. Eva had seen her parents often during the summer, at her place or theirs, and she'd even seen Billy, but never within the walls of her own cabin. She couldn't postpone the moment forever and Christmas seemed as good a time as any.

For two weeks she lost herself in cooking and decorating, patiently unweaving a length of white cotton cloth and using the pulled threads for drifts of snow that she arranged across the fireplace mantel around a manger scene that Hutch had whittled for her, year by year, as a child. She made presents for everyone as well: dried flower sachets for the women, red pepper salve for Hutch's rheumatism, new shirts for Johnny and her brother.

It was Billy's present she drew a blank on. She would have made him a shirt too but realized, when she looked at the cloth, she had no idea what size he was. He was a blur in her mind and in the end it was Johnny who supplied Billy's gift by purchasing a pound of ribbon candy in Union. Eva put the present into his hands herself and received his to her in turn: a pincushion he'd made with Sarah's help. Even so she was unable to weaken, even a little, the wall she'd erected between them.

So it would always be, she thought after Christmas as she gathered the thread snow and fed it to the fire; there would always be that torn place in her life, that place that would go unhealed. Well, she could learn to live with that, she thought; there were so many other things, Johnny and the house, Fan and Adelita and the baby they'd just learned they were expecting. She could work around the torn place. But reconciled or not, her cheeks were wet to think of it.

Whenever supplies were needed the couples took turns going to Union, leaving one day and returning the next. On a late January morning Fan and Adelita set out under a gray sky and by noon snow was ticking against the walls of the cabin. When the wind gusted, ferreting out the unchinked places between the logs, Eva felt its chill spray against her back.

Johnny had expected snow and gone out to shift the herd to the low pastures. Squalls were common, if short-lived, winter nuisances and high-ground pastures always caught the worst of it; hilltop grass might be covered for days, though pastures pocketed in the lowlands usually remained open.

"It's mornings like this I wish the world'd eat buffalo instead of beef," Johnny had said as he dressed. "Buffalo, if we raised them, are at least smart enough to plow the snow aside." Cattle were a different matter altogether, he told Eva. They'd stand hock-deep in snow and go hungry, never thinking to push through to the grass beneath.

Johnny will want a big dinner tonight, Eva reflected. She remembered the roast hanging in the spring house. Worried that it might be frozen if she didn't retrieve it now, she pulled on her coat. It was just after two, the peak of the day, though she had both lamps and a fire going all morning. When she opened the door, wind drove against her face. The snow was coming down thicker than she'd imagined; already the yard was covered, not a straw visible above the rippling white.

Eva stepped back and closed the door. If snow had covered the yard, it had covered the low pastures, too. She had no great knowledge of cattle, wasn't sure how long they might thrive without food. All she knew was that her husband had taken his herd to feed in a pasture that, by now, was drifted over. Eva's mind raced. There was hay in the barn, stacked in bales on the flatbed wagon against just such an event; but if the squall continued at this rate, Johnny might not be able to get the wagon out.

Quickly, she tied a shawl over her head, snuffed out the lamps, and found a pair of Johnny's gloves. As a final thought she wrapped half the cornbread she'd made that morning and took it with her. "You mind the house," she told Duke, her dog, who yipped and whined behind her.

In the barn she found a lantern, checked to see that it was full, and hung it from a prong of the pitchfork that stood upright against the wagon post, held in place by an iron ring. Then she hurried to harness the two mule teams.

She was glad, now, for all the rides Johnny had taken her on during the summer. "It's our land," he'd said, "you ought to know your way on it." At the time she'd resisted, her newfound happiness seeming too precious to risk on the open prairies, but now she was grateful. By going over the terrain in her mind she was able to guess which pasture he was likely shifting the herd to and though the stinging snow blanketed the trails, she could still find her way.

It was dusk by the time she caught sight of the herd and her husband, a lone pinpoint figure moving among them. He was trying to hold them back, she saw, for they were moving steadily with the wind to their backs.

"Johnny!" She was chilled to the bone, her chest tight with the cold, and she had to call three times before he heard her. When he did, he circled up to her. He was smiling, and far too practical to ask what had propelled her out into a snowstorm.

"I sure am glad to see you, Eva," he said, swinging from his horse onto the wagon seat beside her. "Only time I was gladder was the first time we met." He took the reins and guided the wagon down to the herd. His horse, one of Hutch's and well-trained, followed behind.

"I thought the pasture would be snowed over," she said.

"It is."

"Yes, but . . ." Her upper teeth gnawed her lower lip as

she looked across the bunched backs of the cattle. There were hundreds of them, nearly a thousand, she guessed, for Johnny and Fan had been gathering a herd all year. The bales of hay, piled high though they were, would scarcely feed them all. She saw that now. "Oh, Johnny, I thought there'd be enough to feed them. There isn't."

He turned to her, brown eyes warming the cold away. "It doesn't matter. You did exactly right, Eva." He pointed to the herd. "See them moving? When cattle get hungry in a storm like this they start to drift, move with their backs to the wind, looking for food. I've been trying to keep them hemmed all day, keep them from wandering to hell and gone. This hay, this is just enough to keep them interested. Think you can take the reins again?" She nodded. "Good. Go slow now, I'll tell you if it's too fast."

While Eva drove, Johnny pitched hay down to the cattle, spreading a thin line across the snow. When full darkness came he lit the lantern. It jounced against the post as the wagon pulled forward, its pale light swinging back and forth, cutting white strips from the darkness.

"Cold?" Johnny called to Eva.

"No," she answered. Her fingers, inside her husband's large, loose fitting gloves, had been numb for hours.

"Well, we're almost done anyway. Then we can go home."

When they finished they unhitched the mules, left the wagon standing on the prairie, and started home, each riding one mule and leading a second.

"I think the snow's letting up some," Johnny said. "I smell a thaw in the air."

"Do you?" She wished she could see his face in the darkness, the way a sailor longed for the familiar sight of the Pole Star overhead.

She was bone weary by the time they finally reached the cabin. It was chilly inside, for the hearth fire had burned itself to embers hours ago. Johnny quickly built it up while Eva lit the lamp on the table.

"You must be hungry," she said, remembering the cornbread she'd taken with her. It was still sitting in the wagon, forgotten about. "I'll fix something."

But Johnny stopped her. "I'm not hungry," he said, catching her around the waist. Her hair, sleek and tawny, felt like cold satin as he slid his fingers through it. "I'm just hungry for you is all."

The center of the room was covered with a rag rug Eva had made and suddenly Johnny was pulling her down on it. "Here?" Eva gasped, taken aback by his boldness, but she was falling with him, bending like a blade of grass. Her fingers, no longer numb, traced the open *V* at the top of his shirt, curling the silky chest hairs in tufts. Then, moving down, she began to unfasten the buttons.

The rug, when her bare back touched it, was warm from the fireglow and Eva felt as clean as if she'd been washed in snow.

"Eva is beautiful," Johnny murmured. "Eva is white flour bread. Eva is clear sky in the morning." His voice sang in her ear, a nursery rhyme. It was something he'd invented the first weeks of their marriage, a lovemaking song to make her forget what the Comanche had taught her about herself. The pattern was always the same: *Eva is . . .*, but he filled it in with different words, tender words or words that, sometimes, made her laugh. "Eva is the world," he said.

Before he could go on she looked up, touched her fingers to his lips, and answered, "So is Johnny."

Afterward they did not move to the bed, though Johnny did get up to fetch pillows and blankets for them. As he tucked the quilt around her he smiled. "You're a natural born rancher's wife, you know that? I don't think one woman in a hundred would've thought to bring that hay down."

Eva felt a surge of happiness. Here was another thing, then, that she could do. If it ever came to just the two of them against the world, the two of them would not crumble.

The summer Billy was twelve a wonderful thing happened. The Texas Central Railroad, which had built a line to Union the year before, proposed building a spur out to the Steele and Chase holdings. Johnny and Fan had led five drives by now, delivering an average of four thousand head north each year. By seizing the opportunity to freight the cattle, even at a modest sum, the Texas Central saw an opportunity to clear a profit the first year,

Billy watched the rails go down with impatient excitement; those shining lines were the arms of the world, he thought, reaching out to pull him to it. That they were going to his sister's place and not his own did not much bother him. Often he raced through two days' worth of chores, ate a dog-tired dinner, napped, then rolled a bedroll and rode off in the dark so as to be on hand at sunup to watch the track laying crews.

"We hadn't ought to let him roam so," he heard Sarah say to Hutch once when both thought he was out of hearing.

"I roamed," Hutch replied. "I turned out fair enough."

"You were different. You had . . ." There was a pause as she searched for the right word. "*Foundations*. A family."

"Billy has a family. He has us."

Again there was a silence. "I don't know. It isn't the same, Hutch. Often I think he knows it."

"Has he said something? Asked?"

"No, just the same, I think he senses. He has my blood in him, don't forget, and though it's a power long gone from me, I used to have a way of sensing things when I was young. Perhaps I passed it on to Eva and Billy." There was a rustle, she was pressing close to him. "Oh, Hutch, things didn't turn out the way I thought. It seemed all of Eva's happiness rested on it, seemed that I . . . I could reach into time and change things. But I couldn't."

Billy pondered for a long time over Sarah's words but all he got from them was what he'd known before, that he was different, that there was some dark shadow surrounding him that repelled the simplest touch. Why else would he have been left alone after the burning of the barn? They'd wanted to whip the daylights out of him, he saw that in their eyes, but they hadn't. It was a sign, like Eva's look of fright through the window, of how different he was.

Yet in spite of this there were moments of closeness, moments when Hutch took him off with him on some adventure, moments when Sarah, pausing in her work, told him stories of how the Chases had come into Texas and fought to take possession of the land. "You're part of that,

Billy,'' she'd say, ''never forget it.'' He felt as if she was
trying to build him up, the way his father tried to build up
weak and inferior colts.

As he grew, a stocky and quiet boy with a handsome face
and straight, dark brown hair, he found that he felt most
comfortable alone. Then the summer of the railroad spur
came, and when he hovered around the men of the track
crew, men who knew him not at all, he found that he felt
comfortable around strangers as well.

The men of the railroad crew were unlike any Billy had
known before. They worked like devils all week only to
throw their wages to the girls and gamblers of Union every
Saturday night. This made them dashing figures in his eyes,
especially when they invited him down off his horse to help
with such chores as a boy could do. For bringing up cold
water from the stream at noontime he received a penny a
bucket. He kept the pennies tied in a red bandana that he
found one night, left behind by one of the men. The man
missed the bandana the next day and asked about it, but
Billy, as solemn-eyed as an owl, said he hadn't seen it. He
knew that what he was doing was akin to stealing and
promised himself that soon he'd return the bandana. He
never did though, and soon his conscience stopped troubling
him about it.

Inspired by the track-laying crew, Billy conceived of
going into business with his sister. Eva's cabin was but a
half day's ride from the spur now, so far had the rails snaked
across the land. The men spent a good deal of money
buying food in town and bringing it out with them and Billy
thought that he and Eva might just as well have the profits.
If she made up sandwiches, he was prepared to tell her, he
would carry them out to the crew and the two of them
would split the profits.

But when he appeared up in her cabin doorway, he caught
her by surprise. Eva was tending Adelita's children, the
toddler and the new baby, and she gave a yip of surprise at
the sound of the door scraping open behind her.

''What are you doing here?'' she asked sharply, pulse
flailing in her veins at the sight of her son. Her voice woke
the baby, who was teething early. ''Why didn't you knock?''

Billy shrank back. "I . . . I wanted some water."

"Well, come along in then. Johnny and Fan and Adelita are with the cattle, if it's them you're looking for." Her voice sounded coarse, even to her own ears.

Billy sat in silence as he drank the water. She didn't ask again what he was doing so far from home or how he intended to get back before darkness fell. *I ought to ask him to stay,* she thought, *to supper and overnight. I ought to.* But she couldn't and only felt her happiness return when he'd ridden off.

Having failed to put his proposition to Eva and lacking both the initiative and the imagination to carry things further, Billy sank back to his position as water boy and hanger-on. Yet the railroad remained a source of delight and wonder to him, and one day he succeeded in convincing Hutch to ride with him to view the goings on.

Hutch had resisted seeing the railroad, was none too happy that it was even crossing land that had once been his. It was like fencing the land, something else he'd resisted. For Hutch the pleasure in owning a piece of earth came in leaving it be. Often, riding after strays or searching for fresh pastureland, he would come across an abandoned corral and realize, with surprise, that he was still on his own land.

Sixty-one years old, his hair silvered and his joints plagued by the rheumatism he took pains to hide from Sarah, he had survived the lean years of Reconstruction to become, by local reckoning, a wealthy man. Yet wealth didn't much concern him. What gave him happiness was the emptiness of the land around him and the sight of Sarah coming in from the garden, feet bare and skirts hitched up as if she were a girl; it was the glimpse of clouds boiling along the horizon, the whole sky moving, and the wild tossing of trees in the wind; it was coming in from a storm, soaking wet and knowing Sarah had dry clothes waiting.

As he rode along with Billy to the railhead, it was Sarah his thoughts drifted to. He was lucky to have married her, as he'd always been lucky with the women in his life. Yellow Fawn and Lodgesmoke, Sarah and Eva; he'd wandered away from all of them at times, his mind on other things, but they'd always been waiting when he came back. And Sarah,

Sarah seemed able to wait without changing or growing older. Her bright hair had begun to fade at last, to gray on the sides, but Hutch never noticed. She always looked the same to him, her eyes as russet as a doe's, her hard, light, body turning soft and sweet at his touch. She could have passed for a woman in her thirties while he was hurtling away from her in time, growing older with each step. Sometimes he felt the distance widening between them and longed to snatch her hand and pull her forward through the years, fearful of leaving her behind.

"There," Billy cried, pointing ahead to where the rail crew toiled.

Hutch looked and saw the built-up grading, a line of earth laid bare, the grass already ragged where feet and pebbles and oozing resin had discouraged it. He mustered enthusiasm for Billy's sake but later, alone with Sarah, he cried to think of that raw scar of land. "Spotted Turtle was wrong, I reckon, saying that only the land never changes. It's changed more than he'd know, more than any of us thought to see."

Sarah didn't answer but wrapped her arms around him. For some reason she remembered a long-ago night when Austin, her favorite, had come crying to her in the middle of the night. "What happens when we die?" he'd asked. Just that moment, lying awake in his bed, he'd realized that his name would sooner or later add itself to the human toll.

"Why, we go up," she'd answered. "We go up to live with God." Half-wakened by the voices, Creath had stirred beside her.

"I don't want to go!" Austin had whispered furiously, his hand gripping hers in panic. "I don't want to!" And so Sarah had slipped from her own bed and gone to his and held him while he cried out his anger at mortality.

So now it was with Hutch, she thought, stroking his hair; except it wasn't his own death that grieved him but the transformation of the land. The two of them would die and go, and the land itself would not remember them. Sarah had thought of this long ago and come to peace with it. If nothing ever changed, what would have been the purpose of it all?

Chapter Thirty-one

With the coming of the Texas Central, Johnny and Fan no longer had a reason to trail their cattle north to market. They stayed home one year but by the next, 1873, both were restless for another drive.

"I don't understand," Eva said to Fan with a slight frown, "why you can't stay home."

"Me either," Fan grinned. "Got a taste for dust, I guess. Can't live without it."

"Don't try to talk sense to him," Adelita cautioned Eva. "He's as thickheaded as his steers."

Laughing, Fan reached out, caught his wife, and pulled her down on his lap. "Hey, who was it said she'd only marry a brave man, huh? You go fishing that way, you can't throw back what you catch."

They were big on horseplay, Fan and Adelita, and when he began tickling her she shrieked and kicked his shins with her bare heels. Her peals of laughter woke the newest baby, her third, and she looked up with a startled, abashed expression.

"Never mind," Eva said, moving swiftly across the floor. "I'll see to her." Therese was Eva's favorite of the children, a sweet, tiny thing who'd come early into the world and was so small her head fit into a china teacup. "Poor little Therese," she crooned, "Poor little life, do your parents keep waking you up?" On the other side of the cabin Fan and Adelita shrieked louder than ever.

In Eva's mind, Therese was the child she herself had longed for, the Callie Lou child that had long ago taken root in her heart. Her body had remained empty, a barren battlefield, she'd sometimes think to herself, running her fingers along the ridged scars; no wonder a child couldn't grow there.

It was God's gift to her that Therese had come along, and

God's gift that her brother and sister-in-law were so generous with their children. For if much of the work of raising the children fell to Eva, so did much of the love, a fact that Adelita, in her fair-minded way, accepted without resentment. Whenever one of the children called Eva *mother*, she didn't bat an eyelash but smiled warmly, delighted by the happiness on Eva's face.

Johnny was as anxious for another drive as Fan, but for different reasons. The markets that lay to the north and east had for several years been receiving a steady stream of cattle and the price of beef was in decline. Yet in the rapidly expanding territories of the west, prices were as high as ever.

"I been thinking," Johnny said one evening in early 1873, "we could split the herd this year, give half to the Texas Central and drive the rest to Colorado ourselves. We'd get a higher price there, though we'd have to cross some mighty tough country."

"I'm for it," Fan said, not stopping to hear the particulars.

"He lives to make me a widow," Adelita said with a heavenward glance.

"What do you think?" Johnny was looking at Eva. "Live without me a few months?"

Eva returned her husband's gaze. He loved her, she was sure of it, but he would never understand the unquenchable emptiness she suffered in his absence. Johnny's eyes were shining with ill-concealed eagerness. "I'll be fine," she told him, hand curling around the napkin in her lap. "Go."

He did, leaving with Fan, two thousand head of cattle and a dozen hands not many weeks later. The hands were carefully picked, for not every man that trailed cattle was eager to cross the formidable Staked Plains. More than one veteran warned Johnny that he'd lose his cattle in the unforgiving country of the Panhandle. "No grass to eat, no water to drink, only sky, rocks, and Comanche."

Well, the Comanche were more or less taken care of, having been steadily depopulated by a generation of warfare with the Rangers. As for the country itself, Johnny doubted it was as inhospitable as most believed. "The buffalo lived there for a million years," he reasoned to Fan, "and they didn't live on rock."

To shortcut the question of water, the drive left early, as soon as the new growth of grass permitted, when meltwater from the winter might still be found and before summer heat would fire the cattle's thirst. They followed the Brazos River northwest until it was joined by the White, then followed the White as it jutted farther north. Johnny's plan was to leapfrog the herd from river to river, always hoping they'd find water in the next streambed.

By the time they reached the Prairie Dog Town Fork of the Red River the undertaking had acquired all the earmarks of a routine drive. Only the land through which they moved was different, Johnny thought. It was wind-blasted, treeless land that tilted steadily up, a giant table, the shirttail of the Rockies. Johnny was awestruck and Fan, too, took a liking to the land, for it reminded him of the vast, empty stretches he'd covered at top speed in his Texas Overland days.

"I was sort of hoping we'd run into a few Indians," he commented. "Kill me a few, just for old times' sake."

"Cheerful devil," Johnny replied, remembering Fan's bloodlust for Comanche killing but understanding it now that he'd married Eva. "I think you've been out in the sun too long, baked your brains like a lizard's."

Fan grinned. "Nope. I just hate to go home without a story to tell is all."

Two nights later Johnny woke up with cold stinging his face and a dull ache that told him he'd been sleeping with his legs drawn up for warmth. Yet it wasn't discomfort that woke him; nights were cold as a matter of course and he was used to waking with aching bones. It was something else, the rumble of the herd and cries whipping along on the wind.

As Johnny jerked upright, he felt a shower of cold down his back. The freakish spitting snow that had begun at sundown had increased, pocketing itself in the folds of his blanket. He hadn't expected anything more than a dusting so late in the year, but now the air boiled around him, thick with swirling flakes.

On the other side of the campfire, Fan was up too. "What's wrong?"

"The herd," Johnny shouted. He grabbed the horse nearest him and swung himself stiff-legged into the saddle. "Get everybody up." Digging his heels into his mount's sides he shot off. Before he'd gone more than fifty yards, a curtain of snow blotted out the camp behind him.

Johnny guided his horse by the sounds of the herd. They'd drifted already from their night pasture, the two hands assigned to keep watch trying without much luck to keep them in check. Other hands began to appear now, red-eyed with sleep, collars and bandanas turned up against the wind.

"Shall we try and turn them?" Ed Adams called to Johnny.

Johnny shook his head. Lead steers moving out, the herd had picked up speed. Halting them would be as futile as turning aside a river. "Can't. They'll scatter if we try. What we've got to do is follow them, keep them together until the storm spends itself. Mose and Adams, you see if you can catch up to the leaders. Skip, Hank, Shady John, ride over here with me. Rest of you take the other side with Fan. Any man that leaves his saddle other than to answer the call of nature'll have to answer to me, understand?"

They trailed the herd for the next thirty-six hours, snatching minutes of sleep in the saddle and drinking cups of freezing coffee relayed up to them from the chuck wagon. So fiercely did the storm blow that Johnny feared the whole herd might be lost, but by some instinct the lead animals avoided the shallow ravines where snow piled in horn-high drifts. Then on the second morning they came to a great sagging lip of land, a lip broken by a narrow trail that sank out of sight between stunted juniper trees.

Mose Drinkwater came galloping back to Johnny in alarm. "Lead steers is trying to go down," he shouted. "It's either shoot enough of 'em to make a roadblock or let 'em go."

Johnny shifted in his saddle. He tried to peer ahead, but the blizzard cut short his vision. There was no telling what lay ahead and he knew there was every chance in the world that the cattle might be heading into a cul-de-sac. If so, it would be a disaster, for cattle were a tribute to the natural law of inertia. Once moving, they'd keep moving, piling up and crushing each other until not one in ten was left alive. Still, his leaders had been right until now.

Johnny waved his hat at Mose, motioning forward. "Let them go!" he cried. "String them out, don't let them crowd too close. Give the leaders plenty of room."

All the rest of the day the herd funneled down the narrow trail. The descent was gradual and sometimes it seemed almost as if they were moving over level ground, but by midday Johnny realized they'd left the roaring winds above them. Several hours later, the first steers stepped out onto the floor of a canyon that was carpeted with mesquite brush and rich grass.

While the exhausted cattle fed and watered and the men took their first rest in three days, Johnny Steele explored the meandering, broad-bottomed canyon floor. It must have been a riverbed once, he reasoned, the channel of some immense, deep-flowing cataract. Now only sweet streams remained, sweet streams that, protected by the canyon's high walls, neither froze in the winter nor ran dry in the summer.

Fan galloped up to Johnny, a big grin on his face. "Don't this beat all for luck?" he questioned. "Caught in a blizzard one minute and, damn, here we are the next."

Johnny turned to him. In the distance he could see slow-moving black clumps, buffalo that hadn't yet been hunted off. "You know where we are, don't you?" he asked. Fan shook his head. "Comanche heaven, the Palo Duro Canyon. I reckon we're the first white men that've ever found our way here."

Johnny let the herd fatten on canyon grass for two weeks before driving them on to Colorado, where they sold for twice the price the Texas Central steers had gone for.

"You know what this means?" Fan asked on the way home. "We can double the size of our home herd, run twice as many steers west next year. Wooeee! It's a great life, ain't it, Johnny?"

Johnny nodded, for he'd been thinking along the same lines himself. Yet when they reached home a few weeks later they found bad news waiting for them. The spring rains, which had gotten off to a promising start, had vanished the same week the drive left. Scarcely a drop had fallen since and the summer grass was withering in great patches of reddish brown. Spring-dropped calves got a slow start and the cows' milk, Eva told him, had turned thin as whey. Nevertheless, Johnny went about building up the herd as usual, adding even more head than he ordinarily might have because, as the drought progressed through the summer months, he found his neighbors anxious to part with their stock.

The wild, untamed longhorns that hadn't drifted north to escape the drought were in flight south, and Fan, with a crew of vaqueros, rounded up hundreds of them as they crossed the plains. By the end of August, Johnny and Fan had more cattle and less hope of feeding them through the winter than at any point in their eight-year partnership.

"Worried?" Hutch asked Johnny.

It was the first of September, as parched and sweltering a day as any of them had seen. Though she'd dusted herself with cornstarch in the morning to stay cool, Eva's under-arms and the backs of her knees were slippery with sweat. She was glad for the cool, ripe peaches Sarah had sent with Hutch and for the cold water that splashed over her hands as she washed them. Only Adelita, who had the biology of a lizard, loved such weather. She was out in it now, getting the cows in for evening milking.

"Have a peach, Pa," Eva offered, gliding between her husband and father. "Johnny knows what he's doing."

Hutch glanced at Eva. The pinched, angular look was gone from her; Johnny's love, he reckoned. Eva was as beautiful as the peach she handed him. "Oh, I figure Johnny knows," Hutch replied. "I was just wondering is all. My horses, they can get through a bad winter on nothing but cottonwood bark. But cattle . . . well, you couldn't make a bale an acre out of what's out there."

"We'll be all right," Eva insisted. "Johnny's always taken care of me."

"You figuring to keep your herd through the winter?" Hutch asked, biting into the peach.

Johnny's gaze met Hutch's. "I am."

Hutch smiled. He liked Johnny, always had. "I'll say one thing for you, you got nerves of iron."

"Not really. But the drought's likely to bust by the end of the month. That's usually the way. Dry spring, wet fall, unless it's the other way around. Things even out."

But they didn't, not that year, and the air began to cool without more than a sprinkling of rain having fallen. They were moving toward winter now, moving out of grass growing time, and ranchers all over Texas began to panic. No one wanted to utter the dread words *die up*, but soon that was what was underway, a mass selling and slaughtering of herds because they could not be kept through the winter.

Those who sold first got the best prices for their stock, but as the market was flooded, prices dropped; whole herds were sold for their horns and hides and their carcasses left to rot. Some mornings Eva woke to the smell of death on the wind, though Johnny told her it was a trick of her mind.

Johnny and Fan hung on to their stock as floor after floor dropped out of the market. When a meat packer from Kansas offered to build a tallow factory on their land, right by the railroad spur, Johnny sent him packing in short order, using words he hadn't used since his army days.

"You've got another plan, of course," Fan said as the meat packer rode off. He'd thrown in his lot with Johnny, trusting his judgment, but now even he was beginning to worry.

"Of course I've got a plan," Johnny replied. "You remember how we found the Palo Duro last year?" Fan nodded. "Plenty of grass there, wasn't there? Water too. Hell, Fan, we could run a herd twice, three times this size there."

"You mean you're thinking of wintering the herd there?" Fan began to smile, his enthusiasm growing. "It'd work. Sure, it'd work."

"I'm not just thinking of wintering," Johnny said. "We could start a ranch there, Fan. Indians are all scared off except for a few beggars, and we could sell our cattle from there as easily as from here. Land's dirt cheap too, I've looked into it. General consensus is, it isn't worth much. Of course, it'd mean leaving here.''

Fan's blue eyes suddenly sobered. "Have you talked to Eva about this?"

Johnny shook his head. "I wanted to talk to you first. The thing is, Fan, as long as we're here, we're at the mercy of the weather. Droughts, die-ups, blizzards, they'll always be nipping our tail. But Palo Duro, that's a slice of paradise. We could stake out the biggest ranch in the state before anyone else even finds out about it." He paused, brown eyes glistening, head thrust forward. "What do you reckon Adelita'll think?"

"Adelita?" Fan tossed his head as he laughed. "Adelita'll be half-packed before I've finished explaining it to her."

Approaching Eva wasn't so easy and Johnny had put it off for days on end. He'd figured out long ago that the Staked Plains country, which the canyon bisected, was where the Comanche must have taken her, the place where things so terrible had happened that she still kept them clenched deep in her mind. He had no idea how she would greet the notion of going back there, even if it was with him.

He could put it in terms of saving the herd, he thought, but that seemed unfair somehow. So he simply began by describing the canyon to her, letting its beauty come to her through his words. "We could build a fine ranch there," he finished.

She did not look at him at first but continued to gaze at the needlework in her hands. It was pink and white checked gingham, gingham she was smocking into a dress for Therese, who was just learning to walk. "And Fan and Adelita?"

"They come too, of course. And the children."

Eva took a stitch, left the needle in the fabric, and lay the work aside. Looking up, she saw burning eagerness in her husband's eyes. "My folks," she said, "I suppose it's too far for them to visit often."

It was almost as if she were talking to herself, Johnny thought, letting her thoughts run free.

And she was, but only half her thoughts. The other half

she kept to herself. If Hutch and Sarah couldn't see her often, then neither could Billy. There'd be no moments of surprise, no turning to find him framed in her doorway, staring at her with accusing eyes. Still, wrenching herself from this sheltered place would cost her dear, as Johnny well knew by the look in his eyes.

"I'll not lie to you, Eva," he said. "There's no other folks there yet and might not be for quite a while. It'll be a lonely world. I won't take you if you don't want to go."

Eva stretched her hand out to him, her white as a dove hand. "Oh Johnny, you make my world, don't you know that? I'll be happy enough wherever you are." She even managed a smile for him, though her heart was quivering beneath the lavender-striped cloth of her bodice.

Eva's mastiff, Duke, was to be left behind. Johnny worried that the trail would be too much for him, that he'd stray off and tangle with wolves or wander into the camp of starving Indians who'd look on him as a fine meal.

On the morning the two couples were to set out, Hutch and Sarah, Billy and Therese Prado stood in the yard, watching as the last belongings were loaded into three canvas-topped wagons.

"Isn't it a wonder," said Eva, "that all a body owns in the world can come down to such a little parcel?"

She felt uncomfortable, Sarah saw, as they all did, anxious to be finished with the ripping and tearing of this parting. Behind them, the double cabin stood empty except for items deemed not worth taking. The land had been sold back to Hutch, who hadn't wanted it to go to strangers, and the cattle given over to cowhands who would set out later, after the heat of the day had passed. Duke, who'd sensed for days that something was amiss, paced and quivered at the end of a chain driven into the ground with an iron stake.

Eva was dry-eyed as she worded a good-bye to Sarah. "Johnny says Fort Bascom isn't too far off, just a hundred miles or so, so we'll be able to get mail through that way. I'll write."

But there were no words for her good-bye to Hutch, who she clung to and who cried along with her. When at last she pulled free of him and started to climb into the wagon, she caught sight of Billy standing at Sarah's side. Almost as an afterthought, she hurried to say good-bye to him, stiff as a board with fear he would fling his arms around her.

Good-byes finished, Johnny helped her into the wagon while, ahead of them, Adelita bounded up beside Fan with the same grace she'd displayed so long ago on the two-wheeled *carreta*.

Sarah and Therese Prado stood next to each other while their children vanished from sight. What thoughts glided and took shape behind Therese's calm moon of a face Sarah had no idea. She only knew that she herself felt a great, sticky web of sadness within her. She'd had Eva to herself all these years, so many years when she stopped to look back at them. How could it be that they'd never grown closer? Yet they hadn't, and now the hope that they would was sailing away, a white wagon top tacking across the dry, burnished grassland.

Suddenly something dark moved in the corner of her eye. With a great lunge, Eva's mastiff tore the stake from the ground and plunged forward, running toward the retreating wagons.

Hutch started, as if he meant to go after the dog, but Sarah caught his hand in hers. "Leave him go," she said, soft-voiced. "Ah, leave him go after her." And Hutch did, as if the dog was all their hearts.

Chapter Thirty-two

Eva did write, especially during those months of 1874 and 1875 when fighting flared suddenly between government troops and ragged bands of Comanche who refused to come to the reservations.

The newspapers make much of what they call the Red River War Eva wrote, *but we haven't seen a single hostile.*

*All the fighting is to the north and west of us and I am not
the least afraid . . .*

More often, though, her letters were filled with commonplace events.

The house is finished and we have moved into it . . .

*Yesterday, Adelita brought home an antelope fawn whose
mother was killed by buffalo hunters . . .*

Little Therese talks quite a lot now . . .

*It is so warm there are berries growing in the canyon
even in December . . .*

*Indians came begging this morning. I gave them bread
and coffee, which even the little ones seemed grateful of . . .*

We have named our place Antelope Run . . .

*August 1875: At last we have a fort nearby and oh, you
cannot imagine how many people are coming in . . .*

Sarah smoothed the letters with her palm. She had been
scanning them all morning, trying, as she often did, to read
between the lines. But their smooth tranquility was as
impenetrable as canyon rock. If Antelope Run were not so
far away she would go see for herself how Eva was doing.
And not just how she was doing, Sarah admitted to herself
as her hands played over the letters; she wanted to see Eva
just, she thought, to *see* her.

There was movement in the doorway, and Sarah looked
up. Billy had come in. "I'm going to Union," he said. "Be
back tomorrow or Sunday. Do you want anything from
town?"

Sarah frowned involuntarily. "Hutch might need a hand
before you go."

Billy shook his head. "No."

"Did you ask?" She disliked the question but couldn't
help asking, for Billy had more than once gone off with
chores undone.

"He said I could go on."

Even after he told her this he continued to stand awkwardly
in the room, a soft-faced boy of sixteen. Hutch had been
sixteen, less than sixteen, when he first caught Sarah's eye,
yet he'd seemed a man to her. Sarah wondered if a girl
could look on Billy as such.

Billy cleared his throat. "Hutch said . . ."

"Yes?"

"That you should give me money, five dollars, for mowing in the meadow this week."

Sarah sucked in her cheeks as she went about getting the money. That was Hutch for you, overgenerous wherever Billy was concerned. Now the boy had formed the habit of going into town on the weekends, where ranch hands and hired men whooped and hollered away their wages and where Billy, Sarah assumed, whooped and hollered with them. Knowing Billy liked to go, Hutch found reasons to put money in his pocket.

"Did you say you needed anything?" Billy asked almost sheepishly, feeling Sarah's disapproval as he pocketed the money.

"No, nothing."

After he'd gone she saw Eva's letters, still lying on the table where she'd left them. White-winged, precisely lettered, folded into neat envelopes, they were scattered there like so many years, years she could gather and shuffle in her hands. *The year Nell and Jonah died . . . The year Eva was born . . . The year we came here . . . Creath's year . . . Eva's fourteenth birthday and the year Billy was born.* Shuffle she might, but the results were always the same.

She had them out of sight and the table clear by the time Hutch came in a few hours later. "Billy left for town already," she said, taking from the cupboard but two plates and cups for dinner.

Hutch sat down and began pulling his boots off. "I figured as much."

The plates came down on the table with a metallic crash; Eva had taken her china pieces with her years ago. "Five dollars, Hutch? Five *dollars*?"

Sarah was staring at him, eyes burnished with distress. Hutch had the sense of looking at a high-strung mare. "Well now, Sarah, it isn't going to break us."

"No," she said, "it might break *him* though. When did you ever see five whole dollars at his age?"

Hutch's smile was benign. "I didn't, not that I can remember." He paused. "But if he works like the men, Sarah, he ought to get paid."

She shook her head vehemently. "Creath, when I met him, wasn't drawing salary from your pa. Just the opposite. Billy ought to work because this is *his* place."

Hutch stood up and walked around to her. "But he doesn't feel that way, Sarah." His voice was soft, his horse-gentling voice. "Do you see that? He doesn't."

Even at sixty-five, even without his boots on, Hutch was the tallest man she'd ever known, a tree to lean against. She held close to him for a moment, then looked up, mouth stubborn. "Even so, Hutch, we've got to stop this."

"Stop what?" Hutch was startled; he'd thought the conversation closed.

Sarah chose her words carefully. "We'd never have let Aus or Fan do as he does."

"Times are different, Sarah. And Billy doesn't get into any real trouble in town. I'd hear about it if he did."

"That's not what I mean. It isn't just town or chores or the money. It's everything. It's like we're paying him, Hutch, paying him because we've kept silent all these years." Her brow furrowed. "Sometimes I think we ought to tell him the truth."

Her husband's body went tight as a bowstring and his hands closed over her shoulders. "We can't. Don't even think it, Sarah. It would kill Eva."

"She's stronger than you think."

"So you always say. But she isn't like you, Sarah. You've never seen that."

He was wrong, she thought, though she didn't say so. "I was reading her letters today, reading each one over and over." The mood between them changed. Suddenly Sarah was all softness, leaning against him, looking up into his eyes for an answer. "Do you think she's happy, Hutch? Truly happy?"

"Of course. Why wouldn't she be?"

"She wants a baby. It's clear enough when you read her letters. Motherless animals, little Therese, talk of a town and a school coming. When I was her age I was having my last already."

"Well, you started young."

Sarah bit her lip. "I keep thinking, what if Billy's to be

her only child? Shouldn't he *know*? Wouldn't it be better for both of them? I know children can come anytime, but it's been so long for her and Johnny.''

Suddenly, Hutch's own youth came echoing back to him, knitting a link between past and present. ''Yellow Fawn was older than Eva when we had Lodgesmoke, and it was her first.''

For a moment Sarah didn't move. After all these years Yellow Fawn was still alive for him, so alive she crowded into their private conversation. Then Sarah's mind fastened on the other thing he'd said, Lodgesmoke's name. It was his last secret, the last thing he had to himself, and he had shared it with her.

The drought that had driven Johnny and Fan to Palo Duro Canyon was made up for over the next few years, especially in 1876, which arrived with a spring so wet and muddy it reminded Sarah of the Runaway Scrape spring forty years earlier. She woke each morning to the sound of rain beating the sides of the cabin and more than once crawled up onto the roof herself to nail fresh shakes over some leaky spot.

The rain was bad for Hutch, whose rheumatism bothered him and who worried continuously about the weather's effect on his horses, but other than that it promised to be a good year. They came to their peace over Billy, not because he'd changed but because, at seventeen, he was rapidly moving beyond their control. Even so, Sarah made it a point to expect certain chores from him. As long as he was under her roof it would be so.

Like Billy, Hutch's hired hands, of which there were now more than a dozen, expected the weekends off. Usually a few remained behind to look after things but on a Friday in March when Nina Nash, the voluptuous nightingale of the plains, was slated to perform in Union, Hutch let them all off early. Slickers hiked against the morning drizzle they set off, even Chris Walker, the foreman.

''Sure you won't be needing us now?'' he asked, a pang of conscience crashing head-on with his desire to see Nina's expansive, alpine-white bosom quivering with song.

''Nope, you go on,'' Hutch answered. ''Weather looks to

be clearing. Nothing's going to happen here that I can't handle myself.''

So the men rode out, closing the cookhouse and bunkhouse behind them. They would have been halfway to town, Sarah calculated later, when the weather changed. In the early afternoon the half-cleared skies turned dark as a new storm front came racing across the horizon. The crack and flash of lightning flickered in the distance and Hutch began to worry about a certain tree-crowded pasture. ''There's more than three dozen horses there,'' he said, brow puckering, ''and if they start huddling under the trees, lightning's bound to get some of them.''

''It's still a ways away,'' Sarah said, watching the cloud roll on the horizon. On the high plains you could track a storm for half a day before it reached you. ''Maybe it'll blow itself off before it gets to us.''

But Hutch remained restless and, an hour later, told Sarah he was going to move the horses to a safer place.

''Billy'll help you then,'' she replied.

Billy, who was slicking his dark hair back before the mirror, turned in protest. ''I've got a ticket to see Nina Nash tonight,'' he said. ''If I don't leave now, I'll miss everything.''

Sarah wanted to hit him. God help her, he was her own flesh, but she wanted to swing her open palm against his face for letting Hutch go alone to bring in the horses. ''You ride fast, you'll get there in time,'' she replied.

''But I'm already dressed.''

Hutch came between them. ''It's all right, Sarah. He can go.'' He grinned at her. ''You think I can't handle forty of my own horses?''

''I'll go with you then.''

''You, little thing? No, stay put, make me a good dinner and I'll be back before dark maybe.''

Sarah was angry, though not at him. ''It's dark already,'' she answered, ''and getting darker.''

Hutch laughed, looking, for a moment, like the daredevil guide who'd been the first to trace the reaches of the Red River. ''Well then, I reckon you won't worry if I'm late or not, will you?''

He leaned forward to kiss her. When Sarah looked up

Billy was gone, having seized the opportunity to slip away before more was said of his staying home. Through the sound of the advancing storm, she heard the retreating beat of a horse's hooves.

By the time Hutch reached the horses rain was falling heavily, so heavily that he paused to watch. It was a favorite sight of his, one he had no words for. He knew only that he loved to follow with his eye a single sheet of rain as it swept across the prairie, loved the way the grass bent and swayed, loved the damp wet smell of life that came up to him from the earth.

The horses were beginning to bunch beneath the trees and as the lightning forked closer he hurried to roust them out. There was a low meadow he could move them to, a meadow sheltered from the winds and devoid of dangerous trees. As he drove the herd before him he thought of Florencio Prado and imagined, in the thick-falling rain, that he could almost see his shadow moving among the horses.

There was talk of fencing in the prairie these days and, now that the Indians were gone, call for bigger, slower horses. Even Hutch himself, over the past few years, had begun to ration oats to his mounts. So much had changed since the days he and Prado had gone streaking after wild horses. The railroad spur on the land had remained, too expensive to tear up, and sometimes horses were shipped from there to the army's northern forts. The double cabin Eva and Johnny and Fan and Adelita had shared had been turned into a bunkhouse, used when the men were working far-flung reaches of the land. Hutch sighed. For a moment it almost seemed that Prado had been the lucky one, never growing older, never seeing changes. Yet for all those changes there was still the rain and the smell of fresh spring grass, the wet satin of horses' rumps, and the peace of crossing his own land. When a man died, those things were no more.

To reach the meadow he had to drive the horses into the wind. Unnerved by the storm, they were difficult to manage but Hutch found himself enjoying the work, grinning as rain sloughed down his back. He hadn't had such a good time in months, he thought.

As he neared the low meadow he urged his horse to a gallop. It was one of the new oat-fed breed, big and impressive but not so responsive as the smaller, grass-fed horses of the past. Suddenly he felt a jolt as the horse stumbled. In the near darkness, the gelding's hoof had struck a gopher hole.

There was a clean snap as Hutch hit the ground, though he didn't register it at the moment. His thoughts were busy elsewhere. That was a grain-fed mount for you, he thought. No wits whatsoever. Grain clogged the senses of a horse and made him stupid.

Shifting himself, Hutch tried to sit up and found he couldn't. Pain shot through his leg and now, as if in echo, he remembered the snapping sound. Reaching down he felt, through the cloth of his pants, where the break was, splinters of bone pushing through skin. He reached for the trailing reins of his mount, thinking that somehow he could drag himself up, but the horse stood out of reach and no amount of calling would bring him nearer.

Swearing to himself, Hutch managed to roll onto his stomach. Elbow by elbow, he dragged himself toward the horse. He'd almost reached him when a bright fork of lightning cracked the sky above them and the horse, spooked by the noise, shot off. Well then, Hutch thought, collapsing against the wet earth, I'm pinned.

But he wasn't worried. Sarah would come looking for him eventually. He had no doubt of that.

In the house Sarah put in a worrisome afternoon. Anger raced through her whenever she thought of Hutch going off after the horses. Whether he admitted it or not, he was sixty-six and too old for such high jinks. Her anger wasn't directed at him but at Billy, at Chris Walker, at all the sounder and younger men who, in her mind, had abandoned him to the task. Thinking these thoughts, she attacked her house chores with a fury that would not spend itself. By nightfall, when he did not come home, her anger had turned to brooding worry. She did not hesitate but set out in search of him, thinking that if nothing was amiss and he beat her home, laughing when she returned sodden and foolish, then so much the better.

Why hadn't she thought earlier that day that something was amiss? Where had it gone, she wondered, all the knowing that had been in her bones when she was young? She would have to get it back, she thought as she saddled a horse; just for this one night, just long enough to find, on the oceanic acres of land, the one spot where Hutch was. If that power no longer came easily to the surface of her being, then she would reach inside herself and wrench it back by force of will.

Sarah's knowledge of the land helped her, as well as her knowledge of the workings of her husband's mind, and, as she drew nearer, her knowledge of the horses themselves. Thinking she was their evening ration of oats, they came out to surround her and she let them lead her on to the meadow.

"Hutch?" she called, circling around and around in the rain, eyes devouring the land at every flash of lightning. "Hutch?"

And at last she found him. "Don't let the horse step on me," he said calmly through the darkness. "I knew you'd come, Sarah."

She stooped beside him and felt for herself the shattered bone. He was in shock, she guessed, for though he didn't know it he was shaking, shaking so that he almost pulled her down when she tried to lift him. He'd been lying in the rain for hours, chest flat against the chilly, sodden ground, and his skin was death-cool to her touch. She got him onto her horse, pulled off her shawl and wrapped it around his shoulders.

"Don't do that, Sarah," he said. "Folks'll take me for a woman."

"Who's to see you?" she retorted. "Now wait here, don't go galloping off without me."

By pretending to have an apron full of oats she caught a mare from the herd and got herself up onto its wet bare back. Digging her fingers into the mare's mane, catching up the reins of Hutch's horse with her other hand, she started home.

Behind her, Hutch grinned. He wasn't so dazed or in so

much pain that he couldn't admire the straight set of her back. "You know something, Sarah?" he called through the rain.

"What?"

"For two old folks, we can still raise some hell, can't we?"

She turned. A flash of lightning took him back ten years, twenty years, farther than that even, to when he'd first married her. She was smiling at him and the world, once again, was wild and young and sweet.

It wasn't the broken leg that killed Hutch, for Therese Prado sat with him while Sarah rode, hell for leather, into town to get a doctor to come set it properly. No, the bone showed every sign of healing nicely. It would be stiff, the doctor warned, but Sarah deemed that a blessing. A game leg was just what Hutch needed to save him from his reckless ways. Except that, Sarah thought as she pulled on her stiff black mourning dress, those ways were gone for good.

It was lying in the rain that did Hutch in, lying in the rain that gave him pneumonia. She'd done everything she could, tried to keep him in bed, tried to smear his chest with the hot-pepper poultice Therese had concocted, tried even to warm him with her own body. He would have none of it except for the last, of course, for he was always glad to have her body near him. But as for the rest there was nothing she could do. He was not an invalid, he told her, not an old man. And that, she saw, meant more to him than living on, even living on with her.

It hurt. Watching him go, letting him go, hurt. And now on the day of the funeral she was angry at him for leaving her behind. When she tried to clasp a strand of jet beads around her neck, her fingers broke the strand and the beads scattered across the floor.

"Are you ready?" Billy asked. He didn't look like himself for he was wearing a suit, one hastily purchased in Union for the occasion, and there was a hangdog expression on his face, as if he'd had a hand in Hutch's death.

And so he had, Sarah thought, though perhaps no more a

hand than Hutch himself. That was how the world worked;
they were all helpless machinery within a clock whose face
was eternally hidden from them.

"I'm ready," she said, lowering the veil over her face.

The funeral was for form's sake, the hands and the
minister and Billy and Therese grouped around the patch of
land Sarah had chosen.

As if to make sure I'd really bury him, she thought; *oh,
Hutch, how could you leave me?*

To Sarah it was as if the two of them weren't there,
neither she nor Hutch, but were off together somewhere
carrying on their own conversation.

*I'm going to tell Billy the truth now, Hutch. It can't wait
any longer, or what's to become of him?*

It seemed to Sarah, as she looked off across the spring-
time prairie, that Hutch had moved at last beyond his mortal
love for Eva, at last was in a position to see the larger shape
of things; it seemed he told her, in a whisper of wind, to do
as she thought best. And so after the service, after they were
left alone in the house, Sarah sat down and told Billy that
Eva was his mother.

Billy bolted from her presence, as she'd known he would,
and soon she heard the furious rustle, from his loft room on
the other side of the cabin, of a life being swept up and
packed away. By the end of the day he had set off, clothes
rolled in a careless bedroll behind his saddle, riding one of
Hutch's best horses and carrying in his pocket what little
money he had.

Well now, Sarah thought, *he'll make his own way in the
world at least; for good or ill, his own way.*

A colossal silence filled the room and Sarah realized that,
for the first time in her life, she was completely alone.
Strange she didn't mind it more but felt, instead, a sense of
peace.

Chapter Thirty-three

For Eva Johnny built a jewel box of a house nestled just below the eastern rim of the canyon. Antelope Run, protected from winter winds and plentifully supplied with grass and water, prospered by its unique location. Soon other ranchers were hurrying into the Panhandle to stake out ranches in other canyons. There was only one Palo Duro, however, and no other ranch in Texas could support as many cattle as the compact, densely carpeted grasslands of Antelope Run.

No longer bound to raise animals that could survive long drives and the rigors of the open range, Johnny and Fan were free to experiment with meatier domestic breeds. They tried Herefords and shorthorns and finally settled on the newly imported Aberdeen Angus.

The Angus were stocky and hornless animals whose glossy black backs glistened in the sun. Often Eva would pause in her work, step onto her porch, and look down on the distant, blurred patches as they moved, slow as hour hands, across the canyon floor. Hills falling sharply away before her, she had the exhilarated sense of being suspended in midair. And yet, at the same time, she felt wrapped in security, for the sight of cattle would be forever linked, in her mind, with happiness and Johnny.

Fifty hands from Eva's porch lay the house Fan had built for Adelita. In outward appearance the two dwellings were nearly identical: both faced west, both had extended porches, both sat with their backs snugly to the canyon wall. From a distance, coming up the trail that led from the canyon floor, they looked like two stolid old maids gossiping on a green porch of land.

But in Adelita's house visitors were likely to trip over children's toys or saddles brought in for mending; eyes might throb, after awhile, from the wild, not necessarily harmonious mix of furnishings and colors. Eva's house was different, with patterned carpets and rosewood chairs and windows curtained with lace.

A well-worn path connected the two houses, a path worn by small feet, for wherever Eva went Adelita's children quickly followed. She kept them during the day just as she had before, making games of such commonplace tasks as egg gathering and milking and churning. Recently Hutch, turning nine, had begun to work with his parents and Johnny every day, but he still came to Eva and Johnny's in the evenings, often bringing his parents along with him.

Here below the rim of the canyon, in the last place she expected it, Eva at last found the meaning of her life. She was the center of the two families, the still center around which the rest of them revolved. This she knew, and felt, and gloried in.

Removed from civilization, living in a region whose population was less than one person to the square mile, Eva made her house extraordinary, so extraordinary that the first settler women into the country, pausing at Antelope Run on their way across the Staked Plains, saw it once and never forgot it. Eva's house was noted in journals, in letters, in conversations wherever two tired, company-starved pioneer wives came together for a moment of rest.

In talk and legend the house at Antelope Run became palatial, and men coming over the rim of the canyon were often disappointed not to find a huge ranch house sprawling below. Their wives knew better, though; it was the elegance of Eva's house that drew them and from their first glimpse of the white-painted lattices at either end of the porch, they were satisfied.

As the country opened up, so many emigrants passed by the canyon that Eva soon learned to keep simple food, coffee, and lemonade constantly ready. To women who had lived in canvas tents and rented rooms as their men pulled them west, the house at Antelope Run was everything they dreamed of. It was the East they'd left behind or, more likely, never seen. It was the home they yearned to have, the home none of them, least of all Eva herself, had ever had before.

In furnishing Antelope Run Johnny was Eva's co-conspirator, for it was he who freighted crates home from Fort Elliot and he who ordered catalogs for Eva to peruse. It was extravagant, she knew, and she might have felt guilty if she were doing it for herself. But she wasn't doing it for herself. She was doing it for Johnny and Fan and Adelita and, most of all, for the children. For, living on the edge of nowhere, how were Hutch and Florencio and Therese to know anything of the world, unless she brought it to them?

The newest splendor, arrived on Eva's thirtieth birthday, was a spinet piano that stood against the inside wall of the front room. The spinet had been a surprise, ordered by Johnny to encourage his wife's singing. For Eva's voice, when she wasn't too shy to use it, was astonishingly beautiful, a pure and clear contralto that contained, in Johnny's mind, all the lovely sounds in the world.

Eva knew nothing about music but Johnny had ordered books and sheet music as well. With the quiet zeal that was peculiarly her own, Eva had set about teaching herself clefts and notes and fingerings. Within a month she knew enough to find her way through familiar songs, striking chords with her left hand and picking out the melody with her right.

Coming home unexpectedly one afternoon Johnny heard her singing and thought, for a moment, he'd ridden above the canyon into the fields of heaven. So he told her, anyway, as he came through the door.

His compliment brought a blush to Eva's cheeks. She would have closed the polished lid over the keys and hurried to get whatever it was he'd come home for, except that he asked her to play on. She did for a while, then pulled Therese onto her lap and guided her small, eager hands through "Skip To My Lou."

Johnny watched his wife's beige-blond head bobbing beside Therese's dark one, both of them intent on the black-and-white keys. Like Sarah, Eva was slow to age. There were no fine lines at her eyes, no slackening of the firm skin of her body. Touching her breasts, Johnny always felt as if he were reaching for just-ripened peaches; her stomach was smooth, as flat as a pan of milk. Not having children, he thought, that probably made as much difference as anything. He didn't miss having children of his own, though he knew she did. She never said so, never spoke of it, but he knew.

"I could listen all day," he said, smiling. "Wish I could stay."

Eva swivelled to him on the piano stool, Therese still on her lap. A rope of tawny curls came down the left side of her neck, the newest fashion, and her head tilted to the side as if weighed down. "I have great hopes for Therese. We'll work up to Chopin yet, won't we?" She had encountered the name, *Chopin*, in the bundle of sheet music and had guessed, by the welter of black notes across the page, that he was someone to be dealt with.

She was only half joking about her hopes for Therese. Eva sat down at the spinet every afternoon and, though Florencio couldn't be coaxed to such a girlish pastime, Therese soon learned to pick out the nursery rhyme tunes Eva taught her.

That was why the two of them, woman and child, were sitting together at the spinet two days later when hooves pounded into the yard. There was no reason to be afraid, Eva thought; Duke would bark at anyone he found suspicious.

Eva registered the hooves and noted that they had come down from the canyon rim, not up from below. It wasn't one of her own, then, but a stranger alone. Possibly a soldier from Fort Elliot. They often made excuses to stop, hungry for a woman's smile and a cup of coffee. Good, Eva thought; if he was headed back to the Fort, she had letters he could post for her.

She heard the scrape of boots on the porch and, closing the spinet, called out, "Come in."

In the moment before she turned around, Billy's eyes took in the scene, the shining wood of the spinet, his mother's arm clasping Therese on her lap, the soft happiness of her voice. A flame of envy seared through him. All this love and care and never a drop for him, never a drop. She'd cast him away, he thought bitterly, yet everyone believed she was good and he was bad. He knew that now; knew that, even in their moments of closeness, Hutch had held back from him. The truth that should have been his had been willed to Eva; given away, as if he had no claim on it.

A soft, dry cry came from Eva's throat at the sight of her son. For a moment she felt as if the walls of the canyon were closing over her. To the rest of them he might resemble her or even Hutch, with his wide-spaced gray eyes and full-lipped mouth. But she alone had known the Comanche and saw, in the instant she stood up, an apparition that carried her back in time.

"What are you doing here?" she questioned.

Billy didn't answer but seemed, almost, to smile. Eva felt Therese tug impatiently at her hand. With a rustle of stiff skirts she led the child out onto the porch and called for Florencio. When he skidded around the corner of the house, she told him to mind his sister. Then, turning back to Billy, she closed the door behind her.

It didn't make a noise, Billy noticed; that was how perfectly the door fitted the frame of Eva's house. He saw now that there was wallpaper on one wall, sprigged floral bouquets tied with wafting blue ribbons. The wallpaper made him think of the bouquet he'd gathered on her wedding day, the bouquet she'd discarded and left behind.

"What are you doing here?" Eva asked again to break the silence. Billy sat down on an armless chair whose back was a rose oval banded with carved wood. Stepping over his legs, Eva took the chair opposite him. "You've grown, Billy."

It was her calm, her elusive, sisterly calm, that broke through his smile. Trembling with anger and hurt, he thrust his head forward. "Why didn't you tell me? Ever, *ever*? Why didn't you?"

Had she known, before that moment, what had brought him? Had the look in his eyes warned her? Eva wasn't sure. She only knew that, looking at her son, something rose up inside her. She hated him, this child of hers, and her hatred furled itself around her like a cloak, protecting her from his piercing look. "I couldn't," she answered, voice taut, fingers smoothing the lilac gray fabric of her skirt.

"But you *should* have. You were my mother, you should have told me, not left me alone all those years."

"Left you alone?" Her voice lifted with her eyebrows.

"Mother was better for you than I could have been. Mother and Father both."

"But you were my mother. *You*, not them."

Eva felt bitterness curl inside her. Why was he doing this to her? "Do you think I could have wanted you? I was scarce fourteen, a baby with a baby. Or maybe you think," she went on, brittle-voiced, "maybe you think that I kept you from your father, that I should have told you about him."

Slowly one of Eva's hands reached up, unpinned the brooch at her neck, and began unfastening the buttons of her bodice. The hand and body seemed detached from each other, part of separate beings. Billy watched in fascination, unable to look away. Methodically, the moving hand finished with the buttons and began laying aside clothing, layer after layer, as if husking an ear of corn. Blouse and stays and chemise parted to reveal the bare flesh. Above the lacing of red scars, Eva's eyes met her son's.

"Your father did this, you see, though I can't say which of them was your father, there were so many of them. They would drag me out of the tent at night, drag me out right under the nose of Red Eyes' wife, who never said a word, and stake me out on the ground the way Pa used to stake hides for fleshing. They all took their turns, though when they were through they didn't let me up. No, they'd go off and sleep for a while and come back again, or sometimes, in between, they'd heat brands and make these marks."

She paused, two fingers poised on one of the scars. "I have them on my legs too. My yes, you don't think they'd miss an opportunity like that, do you? One goes all the way up, inside of me." Suddenly, her voice quieted. Modest again, she began fastening her clothes. "I know what you're thinking. You're wondering how Johnny can stand it, can stand to be with me. Well, I wonder myself sometimes. But he does, that's the miracle of it. I'm sure he figured out long ago who you are, though we've never discussed it. Sometimes, I think happiness rests more on what isn't said between two people than what is." She paused. "I'll tell him now if you want."

Eva stood before him, perfect again. She'd even managed, he noticed, to get the brooch straight, as if she'd spent long years practicing for just such an event. She turned to the mirror, smoothed her hair, then turned back to him. "Why did they tell you now? Ma and Pa, I thought they'd never say a word."

He realized then that he had beaten Sarah's letter. Eva had no idea that Hutch was dead. In one clear moment Billy saw the way laid open to repay her, to wound her as she'd wounded him.

"I guess you haven't heard yet," he said. "Hutch died. Pneumonia, some days back. After he went, Sarah told me, seemed to think it was the fair thing to do." Billy could almost see his mother collapse before him, see the moorings of her world tremble and shake.

"Pa?" Eva sank down onto the chair, eyes looking helplessly up at him. "Why didn't anyone send for me? Didn't he ask, say anything?"

"Not a word." Lips compressed, Billy felt a river of satisfaction. He grabbed his hat and started off. He was mounted and in the saddle by the time Eva reached the porch.

"Billy, wait," she called. "*Wait!*"

But he didn't lift a shoulder or turn back to look at her, just kicked the horse's ribs and galloped off, up the steep road that led to the canyon rim and the dry, arid plains beyond.

Chapter Thirty-four

From Antelope Run, Billy turned east. He had it in the back of his mind to do as Hutch had once done, to trace out the winding course of the Red River, to what purpose he had no idea. But there was something else in his mind too, an urge just as strong, to go and see for himself the people of the Comanche, living now on reservations hugging the southern edge of Indian Territory.

What he expected to do once arrived he didn't know, for Billy didn't think that far in advance. There was a garbled expectation of proud warriors and a noble, defeated race, people who would sense he was one of them and welcome him to them. The vision of a Comanche princess lit the corners of his mind as well, dark eyes seductive above a fringed and beaded dress, hips graceful as she drew him into a dance whose steps would come as naturally to him as breathing.

To find the Comanche, Billy had to cross the Red River. After their final bid for freedom a year before, the last tribes had been removed from Texas and relocated to lands stretching between the Red and Washita rivers. Clusters of villages spread out from Fort Sill, where annuities were regularly dispensed, and as Billy wove his way from camp to ragged camp, he saw nothing and no one that induced him to stop.

Far from enticing him with their way of life, the squalor

of the Comanche repelled him. Cut off from their rich supply of buffalo robes, they made their tipis of inexpensive, quick-to-rot government canvas. No sloe-eyed maiden in a fringed dress approached him, only squat and grubby girls in grease-splotched calico. The men regarded him with wary, watchful eyes and those who befriended him did so, it seemed, in order to best him at an infinite variety of gambling games.

Bedded for a night in the squalor of a camp, dogs sniffing at his feet, gambling cronies snoring noisily across the fire from him, with nothing more to look forward to than a breakfast of horse meat stew, Billy would wonder what on earth had brought him here and where on earth he was going. Brooding over his precarious future, he would become aware of the fierce spinning of the earth and the weakness of his ties to it. What kept him, he wondered, from simply sliding off into space? Soon he would be lying with fingers dug into the earth, seeking a hold on the planet. Sometimes, too, he thought of his mother, of Eva lying amid such squalor. But the instant the image rose up inside him he pushed the thought aside, saving his sympathy for himself.

Billy drifted from camp to camp and by the time he reached Fort Sill he was nearly broke, having lost to the Comanche the meager store of money he'd arrived with. For a few days he considered joining the army but the blast of reveille in the morning darkness, the prospect of long days on scant rations, and the absolute curtailment of personal freedom closed that path to him, and instead he hired on as a civilian drayman.

Hauling government goods to various camps around the Fort, Billy came to observe at even closer hand the people who'd once been the lords of the plains. Deprived of the horse and the buffalo, most had tumbled into thralldom. But not all, and that was what galled Billy most: the very Comanche he came to admire would have nothing to do with him. Proud and aloof, men who'd been chiefs but a few years ago kept disdainfully away from him and kept their wives and children away as well. To them Billy was simply a white man, a light eye, without even the redeeming dash of a blue uniform.

The one exception in all this was the remarkable Quanah
Parker, the mixed-blood chief who treated Billy as nearly
human. Offspring of a Comanche warrior and the captive
Cynthia Ann Parker, Quanah Parker gave both races something to be proud of. As long as he'd resisted the whites,
Quanah Parker had fought with intelligence and courage,
but once reconciled to the fact that the days of buffalo were
gone forever, he'd begun, with a redirection of intelligence
and courage, to show his people how to prosper on the
reservation.

Unique among the Comanche, Quanah Parker was quick
to take advantage of the good things of white life. On his
first trip to Quanah Parker's camp, Billy found the chief
sitting on his front porch reading a newspaper. Quanah
Parker's people did not live in sagging canvas tipis but in
neat log houses lit with kerosene; they did not slaughter all
the cattle allotted to them by the government but kept back
enough to start their own herd.

Billy was taken with the tall, broad-faced chief. Like
everyone in Texas he knew the story of the captive Cynthia
Ann, and this gave him the feeling that there was between
the two of them some special tie. He and the chief were
both of mixed blood, with warrior fathers and white world
mothers. If things had been but a little different, Billy
fancied, he could have been a Quanah Parker himself.

Suffering a severe case of hero worship, Billy began
trading favors with other draymen to get the routes that led
to Quanah Parker's camp, even giving up part of his own
salary to do so. In all probability he could have traded
routes at no cost at all, for Quanah kept his people farther
from the Fort than other camps and most draymen hated the
overnight trip. Billy gloried in it, though, and by the time
he'd worked at the Fort a year, had come near his goal of
striking up a first-name relationship with the chief.

"You Billy Chase, you come up on my porch and rest?"
It wasn't a question so much as a command, and Billy
hurried to comply. The day was exceptionally hot, even for
August, and his mules rested in the sparse shade while
several young men unloaded the wagon.

"Damn little breeze," Billy said, glancing at Quanah

Parker and hoping the *damn* made him sound like a man of the world.

The chief smiled gently. He was wearing white man's clothes as he always did, to set an example, but his long, thick braids were wrapped with fur and a gold hoop gleamed in one ear. "Yes," he said, "little breeze."

After awhile the door opened and a Comanche woman appeared, a wooden tray in her hands. It was one of Quanah Parker's wives, Billy knew, one of the five wives the commissioner of Indian affairs had told him he must choose among. Rather than choose, Quanah had nodded at the commissioner and said mildly, "You tell them." Unable to face the women, the commissioner had ridden off.

Now the squaw, the youngest of the wives, offered the tray to Billy, whose eyebrows lifted in surprise. "Beer?" he questioned, reaching for one of the foam-topped mugs.

"Beer," Quanah responded contentedly, lifting his own mug to his lips. "Good medicine."

More beer came to replenish their mugs and Billy drank far more than his host. The wife who carried the tray onto the porch grew younger and more comely with each serving and soon, as the afternoon spun on, Billy's tongue loosened. He told Quanah Parker the story of his birth and the secret of his half-Comanche heritage.

"You're Comanche?" the chief asked. He looked astonished, Billy thought, as if a bedbug had just proclaimed itself his relative.

"Yes."

Quanah Parker settled back in his chair. "Well then, you ought to try to make something of yourself."

Billy thought about the chief's words all the next morning as he drove back to the Fort. Until Quanah Parker had pointed it out to him, he'd thought he *was* making something of himself. But now he looked at his life with a new, coldly critical eye. Most of his fellow draymen were old, their vigor and passion spent, many of them lamed in the war. The pay was poor, the work fierce, the prospects for advancement nil. Quanah Parker was right, Billy thought; this was no beginning for a life.

Within another month he gave his notice, rolled his

clothes and blankets into a bedroll, and buttoned his last pay envelope into his shirt pocket. On his way out of reservation lands he stopped to say good-bye to Quanah Parker, telling him, in a vague way, that he was off to do great things. The chief smiled slightly, though whether in encouragement or amusement Billy was never certain.

For the next four years Billy wandered back and forth across the plains, getting work regularly enough but always, for one reason or another, moving on. Making something of himself wasn't nearly as easy as he'd expected it to be. Life, he thought with a pang of self-sympathy, was a lot like mustang-breaking.

Growing up with Hutch's horses he'd seen for himself how, season in and season out, fresh hands turned up to try their luck with mustangs. Some of them learned to break horses easily and well, for the horses seemed to allow it, to sense something special in the men. Other hands, just as determined, just as hardworking and well-meaning, belonged to that group of men whom the horses hated. There was no reason for it, at least none that Billy could ever see and, worse yet, no cure. After a few seasons and a lot of broken bones, the men would drift off into other, less glamorous careers.

Life, Billy thought, was the same way, a capricious mustang, inviting some men and throwing and trampling others. He himself was one of the thrown. Looking back at the pattern of his life he could see it clearly; the realization, somehow, comforted him.

In the autumn of 1879, Billy signed on as a cowhand at the Circle S Ranch near Jacksboro, intending to stay put for the winter. He needed the job, for a recent bout of gambling had left him horseless, coatless, and all but shoeless. Yet as soon as the winter rains set in and he found himself slogging through hoof-deep mud, he began to think of escape. Tascosa was the place that beckoned him, that rough and lively boomtown that drew bad boys from all over the Panhandle. His wanderings had never taken him there but now, suddenly, it loomed large in his mind. Tascosa was the place for him, not here, chasing steers through dung-clotted mud.

Billy left the Circle S at night, sneaking out of the bunkhouse and taking, with little difficulty, a horse from his employer's *remuda*. It wasn't like stealing, he told himself. He was leaving before payday, so his wages would offset the horse. The trade wasn't exactly a fair one, for the cow pony was easily worth a hundred dollars and Billy was owed only twelve dollars and change. He didn't scruple over details, though; the horse was necessary for his escape.

The one thought that occupied Billy on his ride west was the dilemma of whether or not to change his name. He was young, he reasoned, and dashing, and likely to make a name for himself in the bars and saloons of Hog Town, the lively section of town. But there was already one young Billy making his presence known there, Billy the Kid, and he didn't want the two of them to be confused. Maybe he ought to think up another handle, he brooded, and for several miles the idea of living under an alias appealed to him. Then he thought of his family, whom he hadn't seen or been in contact with for three and a half years. What if he died, shot down in some duel, and none of them would know? No, he decided, he would keep his name, so his kinfolk could read from afar what had become of him.

Tascosa in the February drizzle was smaller and tamer than Billy hoped to find it but, undaunted, he tied his horse to the rail of Mike Peck's saloon and entered into its smoky recesses.

Women with low-shouldered gowns of stained and crumpled taffeta eyed him as he approached the bar, jet feathers or celluloid tiaras jammed onto their heads. They were beautiful to Billy, the first available women he'd seen in months. They became even more beautiful after he began to drink, buying shots with money from his last Circle S pay envelope.

Aside from the fancy women and the bartender who served him, no one took notice of his arrival. The patrons of the saloon were crowded at one end of the room, one end where the smoke hung thicker and where, on a gilded perch swung from the ceiling, an immense green and yellow parrot sat. Curious, Billy elbowed his way through the crowd.

Behind the green felt table, cards flashing through her hands as she shuffled, stood the most beautiful woman Billy had ever seen. Black-eyed and cream-skinned, dainty red shoes showing beneath the hem of her skirt, she looked up at Billy with a warmhearted smile. Remembering the stories he had heard, Billy knew that the woman before him was Creole Nan, the tenderly loved wife of the saloon's owner and the shrewdest monte dealer west of the Mississippi.

Nan was beyond Billy's reach, literally and figuratively. The green felt table stood between Nan and her customers and it was common knowledge that Mike Peck, half-Irish and half-Karankawa Indian, would fell anyone who so much as rearranged a spangle on his wife's blouse. Yet so seductive was Nan's smile that Billy found himself moving forward, his money already out of his pocket. Nan's slender, delicate fingers began to deal the cards.

So long as he played, the liquor was free and Billy felt cheerful as he stood before Nan's green felt table, the green and yellow parrot squawking and swearing above them. Nan herself never said a word, letting her smile and her parrot speak for her, and even after Billy had lost most of his money he still thought her the most beautiful woman he'd ever seen. His only goal, as he staggered away from the table, was to find a job that would give him enough money to allow him to return and stand, for a few golden moments, in Nan's presence.

At the bar Billy struck up the acquaintance of a woman who introduced herself as Midnight Rose. How he and Rose passed the next few hours Billy wasn't sure. He had a vague memory of more liquor, of a perfume-fogged room, of Rose's swift slippery flesh against him. Then he was at the bar again and Midnight Rose was gone. It was late and the saloon was considerably emptier than it had been earlier in the evening. Suddenly Billy became aware of a big man sitting next to him, a man as broad and hump-shouldered as a buffalo. "My God," Billy said, "who're you?"

The big man laughed, pushing back his hat to reveal a

gleam of white hair. "I'm Big Bob Speaker," he said, blue eyes alight. "Who're you?"

"Nobody," Billy replied, the glow left by the whiskey and the exertions of Midnight Rose fading fast.

"Well, Nobody," boomed Big Bob, "I'd like to buy you a drink anyhow."

He reached for the bottle in front of him and drew the cork out with his teeth. Showing off, Billy thought sullenly. Then, looking down, he noticed that Big Bob's right arm was missing. It took him several drinks to work up to asking about it. "Did it happen in the war?"

"What? My arm? Nope, I was born that way. Had a little bitty hand at the shoulder, my ma told me, but it dropped off before I was a year old."

Billy didn't know whether to believe Big Bob or not. "Are you left-handed?"

Big Bob roared with laughter. "I sure am now."

They killed the bottle and after awhile Billy realized that he liked Big Bob, who spun out tales faster than a spider spun out thread. Some of them, to Billy's ears, sounded almost believable.

"You'd think a man with one arm'd have trouble with the ladies," Big Bob confided, "but not me. I felt my way into more corsets with one arm than most men did with two. Married the prettiest girl in Falling Rock."

Falling Rock. It had a nice, romantic sound to it, but not a Panhandle sound. "Are you from Texas?" Billy asked.

Bob's glass came down on the bar with a crash. Drops of whiskey flew in the air. "Son, never ask a man if he's from Texas. If he is, he'll tell you. If not, no need to embarrass him."

The bottle was drained. "Another soldier," Billy mumbled, reaching into his own pocket, ready to stand Big Bob to another round of good cheer. "This one's on me." But a few moments of probing left him white and shaking. "Good God," he said, pulling himself to a standing position. "Call the sheriff, I been robbed!"

"I am the sheriff," Big Bob said. "Who robbed you?"

Billy cast back over the long evening, over the parrot and Creole Nan and the gaming table, over rounds of whiskey and Midnight Rose. "I don't know," he said at last. "But I came in here with a week's pay, and it's gone now."

"Son, that's the story of all Tascosa. Didn't you leave yourself something? Keep back a little grub stake in your boot?"

Billy shook his head, certain that he could hear his brain rattle as it pulled loose from its moorings. "I got nothing left at all," he said.

"Well, I guess you'll have to come along with me then."

The last thing Billy remembered was Big Bob hoisting him onto his back, lifting him like a sack of flour, and carrying him out of Mike Peck's Saloon.

Chapter Thirty-five

Oh God, he'd been thrown into solitary. That was Billy's thought when he opened his eyes some hours later, for he was in a pitch dark recess that gave off the odor of damp earth. Putting out his hand he touched the wall. Just as he thought, dirt.

His hand glided down over his body. He was still wearing his clothes, even his boots, but someone had thought to throw a quilt over him, a patch quilt whose yarn tufts he could feel with his fingers. Leastways folks have some humanity, Billy thought; *wonder what all I did, wonder if I killed anyone*. Probing his aching mind for details, he fished up the image of Creole Nan and her parrot. *God, maybe I tried to shoot the parrot*, he thought, pushing himself up.

A door opened and blinding light split the darkness. Billy's eyes throbbed, pain that reached to the back of his skull. "Jesus!" he cried.

The door closed, bringing darkness back. "Sorry about that." A match sparked against a lamp wick and the room was bathed in mellow light, light that illuminated the dusky, mountainous form of Big Bob Speaker. Billy's mind cleared a little. Big Bob pulled a chair alongside Billy's cot and sat down with a mighty creak. "Feeling pretty punk this morning, are you?"

"Like a road crew's laying track through my head," Billy replied, trying again, unsuccessfully, to sort through his thoughts. "Did I get arrested?"

"Tascosa's got too many serious lawbreakers to worry about. Now what's your name, son? You remember it this morning?"

"Billy. Billy Chase."

"Good." Big Bob stood and Billy saw that the shirt-sleeve, on his missing arm side, was neatly folded and stitched down. "Sorry about sticking you back here in the dugout, but it's the only place I have. Reckon you can stand?" Reaching down, he grabbed Billy's collar and hauled him to his feet. Billy wavered but remained erect and Big Bob smiled approvingly. "Let's see about some grub then."

The thought of food sent Billy's stomach pitching. "Oh no, sir. I'm not hungry. Besides, I don't have any money to pay you back."

"That's right, you're plumb broke, ain't you?" In the soft yellow light of the lamp, white stubble stood out on Big Bob's face. When he scratched a thumb along his jaw it made a sandpapery sound. Billy felt better suddenly; the same gesture had been Hutch's.

"Yes sir. Except for my horse I reckon I am plumb broke."

"Better work for me then. I been needing help of some sort for a while now." Big Bob paused, raising an eyebrow. "You're not wanted anywhere, are you? Tell me the truth now."

"No sir, I'm not wanted at all."

Big Bob nodded as he opened the door and led Billy into a sunlit room. The room was heaped high with paraphernalia, not the usual house and horse stuff Billy was familiar with but odd bits of metal and screws and tools, sheets of paper with figures and diagrams that ran off one page and onto the next. Shoved into the room almost as an afterthought were a table, chairs, a stove, and two bed pallets, quilts drawn up and smoothed in an incongruous show of domesticity. Billy, eyeing the pallets, remembered Big Bob's saying something about marrying a pretty girl. "You live here with your wife?" he asked.

Big Bob had a pan smoking atop the stove. He cracked two eggs into it. "Nope, wife's dead," he said, sprinkling the eggs liberally with hot sauce, "I live here with Georgie."

Billy continued his inspection of the room; it took his mind off his pounding temples. The dugout room where he'd slept was at the back of the structure, while the front was made of clean, light logs. The house, he realized, was set into a low-domed hill, part cabin and part sod shanty. Light poured into the room through high, fruit crate-sized windows. Looking out, Billy saw a stretch of bare prairie. "What happened to Tascosa?" he asked in alarm.

Big Bob gave the eggs another shot of hot sauce. "Oh, it's still back there I reckon. Lest it's burned down since last night."

Billy's suspicions were aroused. Maybe he'd been kidnapped by this one-armed man. "I thought you were the sheriff."

Big Bob nodded. "Still am."

"Then why don't you live in town?"

"Tascosa ain't no place to live. 'Specially for Georgie."

Georgie, Billy had gathered by now, was Big Bob's son. Peering out the window again, he saw a curiosity he hadn't noticed before: a tall, pyramid-shaped framework topped with a bladed wheel that spun like a pinwheel in the morning breeze. "What's that?"

"Windmill," Big Bob replied, sliding the eggs onto a metal plate. "Brings water right up from the ground. Take a good look, son. They'll be all over Texas someday, then you can say you saw the first."

Billy saw a slight form perched high in the latticework of the pyramid, boots dangling, a kind of captain's spyglass held up to one eye. "How high is that thing?"

"About a hundred feet." Big Bob came up behind him and peered out the window. "Georgie likes heights. Me, I'm too heavy to climb. Here're your eggs, eat them before they get cold."

Billy took the plate and sat down at the table, where Big Bob had cleared a space by moving aside a book whose cover, when Billy read it, said *U.S. Geographical Survey*. He tasted the eggs. They were hotter than hellfire and he found himself choking for water at the first bite.

"What do you need?" Big Bob asked cheerfully. "More hot?"

"Water," Billy gasped.

Big Bob handed him a big tumblerful. "Drink as much as you want, just make sure you eat all them eggs." He hovered like a gigantic, shaggy owl while Billy ate and asked, when the plate was finally clear, "How do you feel now, son?"

Billy touched his head gingerly. "Better." He shook his head, waited for the surge of nausea, and grinned when it didn't come. "Yeow! Really better."

"Eggs and hot, best hangover cure I ever come across."

Suddenly the door opened behind them. "Blue haze hanging on the ridge this morning, Pa. I marked it down." Georgie's voice was high and adolescent and Billy turned around to see, in the doorway, a freckled, feminine face glowing beneath the brim of a battered hat. He hadn't figured Big Bob's Georgie for a girl but here she was, with light blue eyes and wisps of wavy, strawberry-blond hair escaping from the confining brim of her hat. When she pulled that hat off, he saw that her hair was cropped short, chin-length and wavy.

"Billy Chase," Big Bob said, "this here's my daughter Georgiana."

"Morning," Georgie said, laying down her spyglass and compass and a piece of paper covered with notations and coordinates. "Having a good day, are you?"

Billy nodded numbly. Never in his life had he seen a girl wearing britches, much less looking so good in them.

Nothing more was said about work that day, because it was Sunday, Billy supposed. But on Monday morning Big Bob rousted him out of his bed in the dugout room at 4 A.M.

"Time to rise and shine," Big Bob bellowed. Billy grunted, clutched the blanket to him, and rolled back toward the wall. A minute later he was naked and shivering. Big Bob had stripped the blanket from him and sent it flying across the room. "Rise and shine, I said, if you mean to sleep here tonight."

Billy sat up, fingers clutching the edge of the cot. "If I'd of wanted to get up this early," he grumbled, "I could've joined the army."

"Still a possibility," Big Bob replied. "Door's right to the front of the house, you shouldn't have any trouble finding it."

The cabin was lamplit because it was still dark out, but by the time Billy staggered into the main room, Big Bob was drinking coffee and Georgie was flipping pancakes on a griddle. She was wearing man's pants, as she'd been yesterday, and a billowing shirt that looked like a castoff of Big Bob's: he could see the place where the sleeve had been stitched down. As she worked, her back to the men, Billy watched the slender column of her neck, visible below her cropped hair.

"Were you sick?" he asked.

Georgie turned around, not at all pleased. "What?"

"Were you sick? Is that why your hair's cut off?"

The pancakes were done now and she began dividing them on three tin plates, the burned ones going to Billy. "I've never been sick a day," she said. "My hair's the way I like it." She set the pancakes down in front of him and glanced across the table at her father. "I told you he'd be trouble, Pa."

But Big Bob was lost in the pages of a geographical survey. "Leave him be, Georgie," he replied, then went back to his reading.

Billy poured molasses over the burned pancakes and ate heartily. "Good flapjacks," he told Georgie, trying to make amends.

But Georgie was having none of it. She'd pulled her own book onto her lap and was reading. Geological abstracts, Billy saw, when he got a chance to peek at the spine, just like Big Bob. Ignored by both father and daughter, Billy finished his breakfast in silence. It seemed an eternity before Big Bob laid the volume aside, stood up, and asked, "Well, boy, you ready to start work?"

Work. Billy's pulse quickened with excitement. For a while, he'd feared that Big Bob had forgotten or, worse yet, changed his mind. But Big Bob Speaker, sheriff of Tascosa, still wanted him to help in the important business of upholding the law.

"I sure am," Billy answered. "Just one thing. I parted with my gun somewhere along the line. Lost it to Creole Nan, I think. Anyway, I'll need something to borrow 'til I can afford a new one."

"You won't be needing a gun, I don't think," Big Bob said.

"But what if I get in a fix, come across some cuss that gets the drop on me? How'll I bring him in without a gun?"

"Bring him in? What are you talking about?"

Billy was confused. "Didn't you say you'd been needing help? Help keeping law and order?"

Big Bob's face contorted with laughter. "God, boy, did you think I was hiring you on as a deputy? Doesn't that beat all, Georgie? No, I already got a deputy, leastways this month. I usually lose about one a month."

Billy felt his cheeks burn red with embarrassment. "But—"

"Tell you what. If there's an opening, I'll let you know." Big Bob grabbed his hat and jabbed his sheriff's badge into his shirtfront. "Mule work around here is what I had in mind for you. You can earn your bed and grub that way. Georgie'll tell you what to do, won't you, Georgie?"

Billy stood for several minutes after Big Bob had gone. Georgie was younger than he was, seventeen if she was a day, and, moreover, she was a girl. He expected to turn around and see her light blue eyes sparkling with mirth.

Instead he heard her voice, calm and friendly as she began to gather the tin plates. "You mustn't mind Big Bob," she said. "He has his ways, that's all."

Billy felt a flicker of liking for her. Perhaps this wasn't going to be so bad after all. "What're we going to do?" he asked.

The sun was up now and Georgie, looking out the

window, seemed to be calculating its angle. "I've got to get up on the windmill and make my sightings before the light changes."

"Sightings for what?"

Georgie smiled. "Oil. Big Bob thinks there's lakes of it floating around."

"I haven't seen any."

"Underground," Georgie emphasized. She picked up the notebook, spyglass, and compass he'd seen her with yesterday. "While I'm gone, you do the dishes.'

Billy's jaw dropped. "Dishes?"

Georgie nodded vigorously. "That's right. Somebody's got to do them, you're the one."

"I can't do dishes," Billy protested.

"You know anything about surveying?" Georgie asked. Billy shook his head. "Get to it then," she said, "if you want to eat tonight."

Billy waited until she was gone, then kicked the wall of the cabin as hard as he could. *Get to it then, if you want to eat tonight.* She was just like her father, Big Bob. Prettier and younger though, that was for certain. And what was this about lakes of oil? There was enough oil in Pennsylvania already to light every lamp in America for the next hundred years. The only other use for it was as medicine, and how much of that could a nation drink, anyhow?

Picking up the dishes, Billy began to wonder what he'd gotten into. It was the times, he told himself; the times were just plain bad. Hutch been the the lucky one, born fifty years earlier and coming along just in time to open the frontier. Why, if he'd been born back then, he would have been just like Hutch himself, carving the name *Billy Chase* across the wilderness. But not now. Now all the chances for greatness were gone.

Mowed down by history, that's what I been, Billy told himself. Mowed down by history and doing dishes, woman's work, while Big Bob's daughter sits up in that windmill looking for oil.

Chapter Thirty-six

Life at Big Bob Speaker's wasn't the glamorous, hell-and-high-water life Billy had come to Tascosa to lead. In fact, weeks went by and Billy never once found an opportunity to return to the town of Creole Nan and Mike Peck.

At Big Bob's he worked for room, board, and a modest wage. *Modest*, Billy thought, wasn't the word. Looking inside his first pay envelope, he felt a wave of bitter disappointment. "This isn't much," he protested.

"Neither is the work you do around here," Big Bob replied. "Georgie did a better job keeping house when she was eight years old."

Billy was insulted. All the dishes he'd done! "I earned four times this much when I was hauling for the army, and didn't end up with scalded hands, either."

Big Bob bit the end off a fresh cigar and looked up at him. "You're free to go, son, anytime you want."

Feeling much abused, Billy turned away. It was always the same. Anytime he complained, anytime he voiced dissent, Big Bob had just one answer: *You're free to go, son.* And though he often thought it would serve Big Bob right if he did go, he stayed put. The truth, though he hadn't yet admitted it to himself, was that he was happy at Big Bob's.

With Billy's arrival, Georgie turned many of her house chores over to him, devoting her time to the spyglass, her grid maps, and the massive geological surveys published by the government. Billy saw that, however menial, his work was needed; his coming had made a difference in the household. Under Georgie's instruction he learned to make bread and became quite an expert at it, kneading the dough with a fierceness Georgie herself had never managed.

"That's good," she said, observing him. "It's the kneading that makes it rise." To herself she wondered what hidden anger made him attack the bread so. That Billy had many secrets she was certain but, like Big Bob, she didn't ask what they were. Asking a man's past wasn't the custom in Tascosa. If Billy wanted to tell her what was inside him, he would. One day, in his own time, he would come around to it, she reckoned.

As Georgie worked, papers and calculations spread across a table, she could feel Billy's eyes on her. Growing up in the Panhandle, where there were few women and even fewer young and pretty ones, it was a feeling she'd long been accustomed to. That was the real reason Big Bob kept house out here instead of in Tascosa, she knew, to keep her safe.

Big Bob's fears weren't unfounded. Two years ago, when Georgie was fifteen, she'd run off with a handsome cowboy named Chris Walsh. She'd had no idea what marriage meant, had no idea that she and Chris were off on anything but a lark. She was in a hotel room in the little town of Lipan, fending off Chris as he tried to feel his way under her shirt, when Big Bob caught up with them.

"It's not that men are bad, Georgie," Big Bob explained, "just that they're men. So you'd best learn to handle them." Then Big Bob showed her how she could have stopped Chris Walsh in his tracks. Not long after the escapade Chris drifted out of the Panhandle country, but Big Bob kept a sharp eye on Georgie nonetheless.

Georgie looked like her mother, the spitting image, and Big Bob worried that his wife might have passed more than looks along to her daughter. Though Georgie had grown up thinking her mother was dead, the truth was somewhat different. The truth was that Libbie Wheeler, the beauty of Falling Rock, Pennsylvania, had run off with a Union soldier six months after Georgie was born. Big Bob, who was known as Big Bob even then, and had served in the army despite his one-armed status, had come home from the war to find his infant daughter living with relatives. For a time he toyed with the notion of revenge but decided against it. For a year he worked in the Pennsylvania oil fields, as he

had before the war. Then, on the advice of an old-timer who
believed that oil lay west of the Mississippi, he took his
daughter and moved to Texas. Georgie had known no other
home and she had no recollection of her mother at all. Still,
Big Bob brooded from time to time, there might be streaks
of Libbie Wheeler in her. The incident with Chris Walsh
had put the thought foremost in his mind.

Billy knew none of this. He only knew that, as the weeks
passed, he was more and more drawn to Georgie. For her
sake he learned to bake bread and endure the humiliation of
housework. For her sake he climbed the windmill one
afternoon when a storm was blowing up to retrieve the
sheet of figures she'd left there. Her smile of approval
filled him with something he'd never known before, not
even with Hutch. For the first time in his life Billy felt
needed, a heady drug even if he didn't recognize it as
such.

By the time spring arrived Billy knew that he was in love
with Georgie, so deeply in love that he could scarcely sleep
for thinking of her. Even during the day his thoughts
wandered with visions of what might happen between them:
he and Georgie stretched out on Big Bob's bed, Georgie
telling him, with adoring eyes, that he was the only man in
the world for her.

None of these things happened, of course. The little
household was rooted in firm routine, and nothing seemed
likely to disturb it. Big Bob set out for Tascosa early each
morning and often didn't return until after sunset. Something should happen in those hours, Billy often told himself,
but nothing ever did. He had his tasks and Georgie had
hers, and in the time left over Georgie dove deep into her
studies, perfecting her knowledge of surveying and retriev-
ing, with great delight, obscure bits of geological information that she passed along to Big Bob. Billy was left out of
these goings on, just as he was left alone on Big Bob's days
off, when Georgie and her father went roving off across the
prairie in search of oil.

How did men and women get together? Billy wondered.
Hutch and Sarah had managed it, and Fan and Adelita and
Johnny and Eva, and it had all seemed natural enough. A

woman set her cap for a man and went after him, wasn't that the way? But Georgie was different, unlike any woman he'd ever seen before. She might best him at checkers or show him how to scrub the collar of Big Bob's shirts clean, but that was the end of it. He would have to take things into his own hands, Billy finally decided; he would have to let Georgie know that, if her cap was set for him, she could come on.

He bided his time a few more weeks until, one scorching morning in early June, Georgie came into the cabin with bare, muddy feet. She'd been off exploring a place she and Big Bob called the Gas Crack, a ten-foot deep fissure that, when surveyed from atop the windmill, gave off a bluish haze. Cheeks glowing, Georgie held a screw-top can up before him. "Know what's in here, Billy?" she asked. "Gas. Gas leaked by oil down underground. Unscrew the lid, hold a match to it, and you'll have light for hours. I can't wait to show Big Bob."

Billy looked at her, then at the can. "How'd you get it in there?" he asked.

Georgie grinned. "I sucked the air out of the can, jumped down into the crack, unscrewed the lid, and let it fill up. Oil is coming right up through the floor of the world there, Billy."

She crossed the room and set the can down on the table. "Here now," Billy said, "you're getting my floor all dirty. Stop, let me get a rag."

Georgie's pants were rolled up, cuffed above the knee, and she balanced on one leg at a time, her hand on Billy's shoulder, as he wiped the mud and oil from her feet and legs.

The feel of Georgie's leg, smooth and firm and enticing, triggered a fire in Billy. Somewhere between cleaning her left calf and her right knee, he lost all pride and patience.

"Oh, Georgie," he gasped, standing up. His arms went around her in a lunge, the momentum of his body propelling them, by luck, toward Big Bob's bed.

Georgie fell first, on her back, and Billy on top of her. In the second that separated them she got her knee up. Later, looking back, Billy was certain there'd been a crunching sound as her kneecap mashed against his groin. Howling, he rolled away from her. Curled in a fetal position, Billy lay gasping and helpless on the bed.

"Are you all right?" he heard Georgie ask. Billy choked and gasped, unable to answer. The deep nausea, along with his wish to die, was slowly passing. Georgie waited a few minutes, then hauled him up to a sitting position. "Yes, I guess you're all right. Here, have some water." She handed him a dipper. "I'm sorry I had to do that, Billy."

Billy said nothing but continued to sit on the edge of Big Bob's bed, hands pressed between his legs.

"I guess you haven't known very many girls, have you? But you ought to understand, Billy, that's not the way to do things." Her face, with its spattering of freckles and large, cornflower eyes, showed a kind of embarrassed concern for his ineptitude.

Billy felt humiliated, rebuffed and rejected. As soon as he could he got to his feet, went back into his dugout room, and rummaged for his money. "Reckon I got a day off coming," he told Georgie. Then he added, with what he hoped was a manly air, "Reckon what just happened between us was because I been without a woman too long. So I'm going into Tascosa for a spell."

He expected her to look hurt or remorseful, or maybe even jealous. But Georgie just nodded and said, calmly, "You'll have to take one of the mules, though. Pa's got your horse."

Steal a man's horse, Billy thought furiously as he saddled up the mule, quite forgetting that the horse was his only because he'd stolen it from his employers at the Circle S Ranch.

In town Billy made a beeline for Mike Peck's saloon where, after a brief reconnoitering to make sure that Big Bob wasn't around, he shouldered his way to the bar and bought a bottle.

His groin still ached but not half so much as his pride; it was his pride, torn and bleeding, that took a second bottle of whiskey to repair. Billy wondered how it had happened that he, with both Chase blood and Comanche blood flowing through his veins, had been not only rebuffed but damned near emasculated by a weed sprig of a girl who, from a distance, might well be mistaken for a boy.

Holding the bottle by the neck and finding his legs a bit shaky when he tested the floor, Billy staggered back to Creole Nan's gaming table. As dark-haired and black-eyed as Georgie was fair, Nan looked up at him with the silent, seductive smile she bestowed on all comers. *There* was a woman for you, Billy thought; there was a woman who'd know better than to knee a man's balls halfway to his throat. Taking another swig from the bottle, he fished in his pocket and put his money on the table.

He lost, of course. Oh, he won some hands now and then for encouragement, but Creole Nan had swift fingers and a way of distracting men with her smile while she dealt. It was her table, not the food or girls or whiskey, that kept her husband in good cigars and silk shirts.

A shadowy suspicion of this dawned in Billy's drink-befuddled mind as he neared the bottom dollar of the pay he'd been hoarding for weeks. Seeing that her client was drunk Nan grew careless, cutting back on the dazzle of her smile and letting her mind wander. Billy noticed that there was a pattern to his winning and losing, with him taking every third hand and the house getting the two in between.

Well, he'd catch her, he thought. He'd keep a sharp eye out, see where she was cheating, and make a fuss about getting his money back. He wasn't sober enough for that, however. In fact, it was doubtful he could have caught Nan even if he hadn't had a drop, she was that fast. Other men with keener eyes had tried and failed and learned, as a consequence, not to bet so much.

Billy reached in his pocket for another dollar but felt only cloth. No, it couldn't be . . . he couldn't be broke so quick. But he was. Wiped out. Seeing the expression on his face and guessing his predicament, Nan gave him a farewell nod and turned her smile elsewhere.

"You cheated me!" Billy cried out in protest, lifting the

bottle and taking a final sip for courage. "You layered the deck!"

Nan was silent but the parrot above her began a high-pitched screeching. The bird had squawked, on cue, because of a certain gesture Nan made with her hand. Hearing the squawk, Mike Peck came rumbling out of his office like a freight train. "What's the trouble here?"

"Your wife cheated me," Billy replied.

Mike's eyes darkened. He was half a foot taller than Billy and a good eighty pounds heavier. "Suppose you tell me how she did it," he said, jaw muscles taut.

"I don't know how she did it, exactly, but—"

"Then you'd best take them words back," Mike warned.

All the whiskey he'd drunk had made Billy stubborn. And stupid. "She cheated me," he repeated.

Suddenly, the crowd cleared around them and, across a wide, bare stretch of saloon floor, Billy saw Mike bearing down on him, huge and angry as a bull. Oh God, now he was going to get killed. Billy grabbed the empty whiskey bottle, broke it against a table, and pointed its jagged neck edge at Mike Peck. The saloon owner slowed his charge and, for a moment, the two stared angrily at each other.

"Get the sheriff," somebody whispered and Midnight Rose, standing near the door, hurried out.

"Well son, it looks like you're about back where you started, don't it?" Big Bob asked the next morning. He'd let Billy stay the night in jail, despite his wails of protest.

"Let me out of here," Billy said, fists clutching the bars of his cell. "What kind of friend are you, anyhow?"

"Best one you've ever had, from the looks of the way you've turned out. You'd best get a handle on that."

"Are you going to let me out or not?" Billy demanded.

Big Bob didn't answer but set about straightening his office. He sorted through papers, made coffee, and tacked up the latest *Wanteds* while Billy sat in agony, head throbbing. When the coffee boiled, Big Bob poured himself a cup and pulled a chair up by Billy's cell.

"Georgie told me what happened," he said. "Hellfire, son, there ain't a man alive that ain't been kicked in the balls once or twice, by a woman if he's lucky and a mule if he's not. But that ain't a reason to go off lickering up. Mike was fixing to kill you when I walked in."

Billy remained silent. He remembered almost nothing of the evening before. The squawking of Creole Nan's parrot was his dim recollection.

Big Bob stood up and reached for the keys. "You figure you're ready to join society again?" he asked, and Billy nodded. "Just one thing, son. Don't be mad at Georgie. She was just showing good sense. If I'd have caught the two of you together, and I would have, sooner or later, I'd have skinned the hides off you both." Big Bob's blue eyes, frosty as a January sky, met Billy's. "I'm not saying this to hurt your feelings, son, just to make things clear. You are about the sorriest figure of a man I ever did see, and I want you to keep away from my Georgie."

Billy felt hot color stand out over his cheekbones. "I said I was sorry about the drinking sir," he protested, though he'd yet to make apologies of any sort.

Big Bob turned the key and swung open the door. "It isn't just the drinking," he said. "Look at you. Do you have a nickel left in your pocket?"

"No."

"Got any skills to get yourself a job? A *good* job, I mean?"

"No. You're not firing me, are you?"

Big Bob told him he wasn't, then continued, "Got any thoughts about your future?"

"No, sir. I haven't gotten around to that yet."

"How old are you, son?"

"Twenty-two."

Big Bob looked truly grieved. "Why, that's just pitiful. I don't know what happened to you, son. You seem to have all the right parts in the right places, but somehow you just never caught hold of life the way you ought to. Georgie has, you see. That's why I couldn't let her take up with you. It'd be a pure waste."

Billy left the sheriff's office, a streak of shame burning in him. Big Bob's words stayed in his mind all during the long ride out of town. *Son, you are a sorry figure of a man.*

It was the same thing, more or less, that Quanah Parker had told him.

Well, if it was a sense of direction Big Bob wanted to see, it was a sense of and direction Billy would show him, for now that he'd seen behind Creole Nan's seductive smile, Billy was more set on having Georgie than ever before. If neither she nor Big Bob would give him a nod in his present condition, he would raise himself in their sights.

Once Billy had made up his mind to that, the path before him was clear: he could think of no swifter, surer way to win the Speakers' approval, father and daughter alike, than to feign an interest in their own hare-brained hobby, oil.

Chapter Thirty-seven

"Oil," Big Bob said, "is the key."

"Key to what?" Billy panted. The dome was a steep fifteen-foot rise, a hill that rose from the ground like the crown of a hat. Too tiring for the mules, Big Bob had said, so Billy had been elected to haul the gear while Georgie and her father frisked ahead of him. "Key to what?" Billy asked again, watching the curve of Georgie's rump in her trousers.

Big Bob, having reached the top of the summit, looked back at him. "Why, the future."

It was that kind of grandiose, sweeping statement, Billy thought, that made him doubt Big Bob's grasp of reality.

"You don't believe that but it's true," Big Bob went on, frosty blue eyes fixed on Billy. "Ain't my fault if you haven't the sense enough to know it. Hand me that cane pole, now."

Sweating, Billy dropped the gear. He'd reached the top of the dome and, looking off across the brush-speckled flatlands, he could see other domes rising in the distance. He hoped he wasn't going to have to climb all of them.

Big Bob drove the cane into the ground, using his doubled fist as a hammer. There was a hiss as gas escaped through the hollow tube and Big Bob smiled. "Georgie?"

It was the custom, Billy had learned, always to let Georgie strike the match. It would have been bad luck to do it any other way. Georgie held the match over the tube and a flame, nearly transparent in the fierce sunlight but flickering blue at the bottom, appeared. When Georgie took the match away, the flame held its own.

"I knew it," Big Bob said, contentedly, though he'd known no such thing; not for sure, anyway. The common wisdom on oil-hunting revolved around creekology, the study of streams and cracks and fissures in the earth where oil was likely to be found oozing. But recently Big Bob had formed the notion that certain rises in the land might consist of more than dirt and rocks and buffalo skeletons.

If Big Bob was right about the hill, Billy thought, he might be right on other counts as well. Like his preposterously confident belief that huge reservoirs of oil lay beneath the floor of Texas when everyone else, even the authors of the geological surveys, agreed that oil east of the Alleghenies was a long shot at best.

Georgie was laughing, cupping her hands protectively around the flame as a sudden gust of wind fanned her hair back from her face. For the first time in the months since he'd decided to ingratiate himself to Big Bob, Billy felt a kindling of excitement. Damn, maybe Big Bob was right and everybody else was wrong.

The wind dried the sweat on the back of Billy's neck and, standing at the top of the dome, he felt cooler. "Tell me about this hill," he said, turning to Big Bob. "Why'd you think it'd be a good one?"

Big Bob glanced at Billy, saw that he was serious, and began a long, rambling and jargon-laced monologue that Billy tried passionately to follow.

It wasn't Big Bob who proved Billy's best teacher but Georgie. Over the next weeks she proved invaluable to him at unravelling her father's roundabout explanations. "You mustn't mind Big Bob," she explained. "He isn't trying to confuse you, not purposely."

"You certain of that?" Billy asked. Since his moment of revelation on the gas dome, it had more than once occurred to him that Big Bob was deliberately befuddling him.

"I'm certain," Georgie answered. "He likes you, Billy."

"Now there, I know you're wrong." Billy had potatoes in a pan of water in front of him and was scrubbing the dirt off, using his thumbnail to pick out the eyes. The clean potatoes went to Georgie, who peeled them so expertly that the scraps, paper thin, weren't going to make more than a mouthful of dinner for the sow penned outside. Since Billy had taken an interest in oil, Georgie had begun to help him with the chores.

"No, he does like you Billy. It's just his way to be hard on a person in what he says." She paused, head cocked to one side. "Hasn't he ever said anything about me?"

"You? Hell, Georgie, you're as perfect as God made." Billy wondered if she knew he was expressing his own opinion, not just echoing Big Bob's. Apparently not, because she laughed.

"Big Bob and I have had our go-arounds, no mistake. That's just an example of what I mean. Big Bob might tell me I'm a headstrong mule, but he'd never tell anyone else I am. That's his way. And I've heard him say, more than once, that he thought you had grit."

"He did?"

Georgie nodded vigorously. "Surely." She'd heard Big Bob say no such thing, but thought the lie was in order. "The important thing about Big Bob," she went on, "is to follow his feet, not his words."

"Huh?"

"Look at the way he treats you. Has he ever turned you out of here? Ever told you outright that he doesn't want you around?"

"Nope."

"That's what he thinks, then." She shifted her gaze, momentarily, from the potato in her hand to Billy. "There's few men Big Bob would have into his home to live like family," she said, and Billy felt a wave of guilt for the lustful thoughts he was thinking about her.

After that he tried hard to see the high regard Georgie claimed Big Bob had for him, but it remained elusive, as elliptical as Big Bob's discourses on oil.

"Something happens to his mind when he tries to explain things," Georgie told Billy a few days later, acting again as intermediary.

"You believe Big Bob's right about the oil?" Billy asked.

"I don't believe," Georgie answered, "I *know*."

"How long has Big Bob been looking?"

Georgie shrugged, memories of her early life dim. "Since we've been in Texas, I guess."

"Then why hasn't he ever found any? If it's all just floating beneath our feet, it seems he ought to have tapped into it by now."

"But he did," Georgie answered, unfurling a map. "Look here."

Billy drew close. The map, handmade by Georgie, was of Texas, with crusts of Indian Territory to the north, and Louisiana, to the east, added on. There were no cities on the map but shaded concentric rings, jagged lines, and crosshatchings to indicate the features of the land. Some places, Billy saw, were colored over with a wash of colored ink. "What's the red mean?" he asked.

"That's where oil's likeliest."

Billy didn't reply. One of the eccentric red patches flowed across the land where he'd grown up, across Hutch's land. That, he thought, disproved the whole thing, for never had a horse come in from the range with oil on its hooves. Other red patches, sparse in the Panhandle, piled up along the eastern coast. Georgie's finger plunged down into the midst of them. "Right there," she said, pointing to a place just north of Galveston. "That's where Big Bob founded the Daisy City Oil Company. It was going to be our big chance, our winning ticket. Big Bob had backers and equipment."

"What happened?"

"The contract called for the backers to go at least a thousand feet deep. But there was a hurricane on the coast and the backlash winds tipped over our rig. The backers lost their nerve at five hundred feet, even though there were oil indications all along. They ended up suing Big Bob.''

''But you had a contract,'' Billy protested.

''We had a contract,'' Georgie said without bitterness, ''but they had money, lots of it. And being that one of them was a county judge, it looked like Big Bob just might end up in jail.''

''But how? He didn't do anything illegal.''

Georgie smiled. ''Oh, I expect he did somewhere along the line. He usually does, though generally nothing big enough to hang for. Anyway, we didn't wait to find out. Big Bob heard a sheriff was needed up here and we lit out. No one's going to arrest a sheriff now, are they?''

''What happened to the company?''

''The rig was sold, shaft sealed over.''

''And nobody ever found oil?''

''No.''

''Why'd you say he did, then?''

''As good as,'' Georgie replied. ''It wasn't our fault they lost heart.''

Billy looked down. Georgie's finger was tapping the Daisy City spot on the map impatiently, as if she'd like to thump sense into the men who lived there. He noticed that here, around Tascosa, there were almost no red spots at all. ''If Big Bob knows where the oil is,'' he asked, his gaze sweeping down and across the map, ''why doesn't he go dig there?''

Whisking the map away from him, she began rolling it up. ''All that land's taken,'' she answered briskly. ''Ask a cow man if you can dig his range up and see what he says. No, this is the land that's open, so this is the land we look on.''

Georgie could tell him more about oil in one sentence, Billy discovered, than Big Bob could in an hour. Her instructions were simple and direct. ''Look for gas first,'' she told him. ''It's easiest to spot because it gets into everything, air, water, everything.''

This was the distillation, more or less, of Big Bob's discourse of the night before. To Billy, it made perfect sense.

"Cold?" he asked.

Georgie, intent on her work, didn't answer. It was a rainy November afternoon and the two of them had climbed to the top of the windmill, where gusts of wind drove the rain against their faces. Taking up Big Bob's canvas coat, which he'd brought along, Billy held it like a tent over Georgie's head. Later, when the rain increased and he ducked under the coat with her, she did not protest. It was maddening, standing so near her that he could smell her damp skin and the peppermint soap she used while all the while her attention was focused elsewhere. But a minute later she was turning to him, handing him the spyglass.

"Look over there," she said, pointing. "You'll see a haze."

"Gas?"

"Maybe, or maybe just mist. We'll have to go look."

Billy took the spyglass while Georgie tried to manage Big Bob's coat. She wasn't tall enough and the garment flapped wetly around them.

"Sorry," she said when a wet sleeve swung around and slapped Billy's chest.

Billy could stand her nearness no longer. Taking the coat back from her he wrapped it around both of them and kissed her. To his surprise she didn't squirm; nor did she knee his groin, which was a relief in itself. Instead her mouth opened, a peppermint-tasting flower. He leaned toward her in desire, moving both of them closer to the edge of the railed platform.

"Be careful," Georgie said. "Big Bob and I built this rig ourselves. It's never been tested this way. It might tip over."

The idea of hurtling through the air with Georgie in his arms excited him. Something like that *might* be worth dying for, he thought. But while he was thinking this, she slipped out of his arms, gathered up her equipment, and began climbing down. There was nothing to do but follow her.

Billy thought that the kiss would change everything between himself and Georgie. It seemed logical that life would now become a series of escalating thrills made all the more exciting by the necessity of hiding their doings from Big Bob.

But that wasn't what happened. Georgie managed to keep him at a distance, though how she did it was something of a mystery to Billy, who kept a hawk's eye out for any opportunity to slip up on her. Her elusiveness baffled him, for he'd failed to sense that she was still making her mind up about him.

When Georgie looked at Billy Chase she saw a man in a half-formed state. Unglamorously, she compared him to the aborted litter the sow had once delivered, creatures that were neither tadpole nor piglet. So it was with Billy. He'd grown some since coming to them, had lost his layer of adolescent softness.

But his soul she was still wary of. Her single experience with Chris Walsh had taught her a valuable lesson about men. Namely, that it was a game of let the lady beware. A man might put on any face he wished, paint the scenery the way he wanted you to see it, but it was up to you to look behind his handiwork.

"Georgie," Big Bob had told her on the long and humiliating ride home from Lipan, "any man can be a saint and a savior while he's courting. It's the devil in him you've got to pay attention to."

She didn't aim to end up in the arms of another Chris Walsh. Billy was an unfinished soul, despite the improvement he'd made, and whether he'd come to amount to something or not was still in question. It was a good sign, she thought, that he didn't come rushing after her but read her cues and, however baffled and moon-faced, had the sense to keep his distance. And so, when he asked her to the Christmas dance that was going to be held at the ostentatiously named Tascosa Opera House, she accepted.

From his dugout room, Billy heard Big Bob and his daughter wrangling over the invitation.

"I thought I made myself clear," Big Bob boomed. It was late at night, past 1 A.M., Billy guessed. There'd been a hanging that day and hangings always occasioned fistfights, heavy drinking, and overtime for Big Bob. "I spoke to him

and I spoke to you," Big Bob went on. "I want you two
to keep clear of each other."

"But you like him, Pa. I know you do."

"Not for a son-in-law."

"Hush, Pa, he'll hear you."

"Let him come out and face me then," the sheriff
bellowed and Billy, beneath his blankets, decided to let
discretion pass for the better part of valor.

There was a moment of silence, then a rustle as Georgie
turned back the covers and slid into her bed. "I'm going,
Pa, and not another word about it."

"You do," Big Bob replied from the other side of the
room, "and I'll disown you."

Billy's heart sank. It'd been a long time since he'd felt this
low and he expected to face Georgie's refusal in the morning.
But when he got up she was all smiles. By noon she had an
old trunk open and was scouting a dress to wear to the dance.
"There must be one in here somewhere," she murmured.

Big Bob, Billy noticed, had left for town earlier than usual.

Having found nothing in the clothes trunk to wear, Georgie
bought a dress in Tascosa, a beige, green, and rose plaid
with pleated trim at the cuffs and collar. It was a dress in the
tie-back style, the skirt drawn taut across the front and
brought up in a cascade in the back. A bustle, the sales-
woman informed Georgie, was absolutely essential.

But Georgie drew the line at this added expense. She
was Big Bob's daughter, after all; she should be able to
make her own bustle. Her creativity fell along two lines,
one that involved looping a folded towel over a string tied
around her waist and another that used the same string and a
large tin can. The towel looked more natural but the can,
lighter and more comfortable, won Georgie's vote.

She and Big Bob didn't settle their dispute but remained
at loggerheads, locked like two buffalo. When the night of
the dance arrived, Big Bob wouldn't even look up from his
survey books to say good-bye.

"Maybe we oughtn't to go," Billy said as he held the
reins of Georgie's horse.

"Lord," she snorted, swinging into the saddle, "don't go

soft on me Billy. Big Bob'll live out the night. He'll get over it.''

At the Opera House Billy and Georgie danced and ate gingersnaps and drank lemonade. For a few pennies more they could have drunk lemonade laced with whiskey but Billy, on his best behavior, passed it by. For dance after dance he was the model of a perfect beau, suppressing his jealousy when Georgie was danced off in the arms of someone else, keeping his touch discreetly light on her body. It was almost as if he could feel Big Bob looking over his shoulder. Well, I wish he were, Billy thought with a frown; then he'd see I'm not so bad for her as all that.

He was, in fact, good for Georgie, for although Big Bob had encouraged the flowering of her brains and intellect, he'd never done much to water the garden of her womanhood. With Billy Georgie felt important and wise, the way she imagined women felt with their men, and she felt cared for. If Billy would but buck up a little as a man, instinct told her, things between them would work out fine.

When they walked out of the Opera House after the dance they discovered that a crisp, chill wind had sprung up. When without a word Billy stripped off his jacket and wrapped it around her, Georgie felt a surge of tenderness stronger than any she had ever known before. It was this side of him Big Bob never saw, she thought; this side of him maybe nobody had ever seen.

''Billy?'' she asked. ''Do you have a family?''

''No,'' he answered.

Cold moonlight fell on the road before them, for there wasn't a cloud in the sky. Everyone had a family, Georgie thought; Billy wasn't so old that he could be the last leaf on the tree. But, sinking deeper into the recesses of his jacket, she decided to let the matter go.

They rode on in companionable silence, or what Georgie mistook for companionable silence. Billy was quiet because his mind was busy elsewhere. He was wondering, plotting, whether and how he might kiss her good night. ''Damn,'' Georgie whispered softly as the house came into view. There was no lamp gleaming in the window to welcome them. ''I always leave a light for him.''

"Well," Billy said, "the moon's bright, at least."

"Oh, Billy, it's the idea of it," she answered. "He could at least have left us a light."

They unsaddled the horses and gave them oats. No chance to kiss Georgie there, Billy thought. But his hopes were still high as they headed toward the house. She might be put out about the lack of light, but he certainly wasn't.

Georgie walked swiftly across the yard, skirt whipping around her legs, and reached the door before he did. Billy saw her look of surprise as she pressed the latch. "He's locked us out," she said, glancing at Billy. Then she turned back to the door and threw herself against it.

"You've made your point, Pa!" she shouted. "Now get up and let us in!" Silence. Georgie doubled her fists and pounded. "Pa! I know you're awake! Let us in!" Georgie waited a moment more and when nothing happened she turned sharply, skirts whirling.

The woodpile lay to the side of the yard, ax and hatchet sunk for safety's sake into the stump where the chopping was done. Georgie pulled out the hatchet and marched back toward the house.

"Better give me that, Georgie," Billy said.

She sent him a withering look. "I haven't gone mad," she said, "I'm no Minnie Deevers." Minnie Deevers, a Panhandle celebrity, had gone to the asylum two years ago for hatcheting her husband to death.

Georgie steamed across the yard like a locomotive and, reaching the house, swung the hatchet sharply at the door. It took three strong swings before there was a hole big enough for her to reach inside and undo the latch. "There," she said, pushing the door open.

By the time Billy finished putting the hatchet back for her, Georgie had lit the lamp on the table. His hopes for a kiss vanished. He couldn't do it in front of Big Bob, even if Big Bob *was* pretending to be asleep. "Good night, Georgie," he said.

" 'Night, Billy."

As he undressed in his dugout room he heard the thump of a tin can, her bustle coming off. Then he heard her voice.

"Good night, Pa. And just so we get off on the right foot tomorrow, I'm not going to hold this against you."

Big Bob mulled the thought over in his mind. Georgie seemed happy with her evening, seemed to have come to no discernible harm. Still, the sheriff brooded, there was something lacking in Billy Chase. It should have been him, not Georgie, who hatcheted the door open; it should have been Billy who showed the pluck and backbone. Yet when morning came and Big Bob saw the *leave-it-be* message in his daughter's eyes, he said not a word. Maybe she saw something in Billy Chase that he hadn't yet discovered; it was possible, slim chance though it was.

Chapter Thirty-eight

Whether moved by the spirit of the season or by the warning, leave-it-be look in his daughter's eyes, Big Bob put the matter of the dance behind him. The household had a small but festive Christmas, with Georgie roasting a turkey and Billy punching up an experimental but highly successful yule bread laced with raisins and citron. He had presents for both of them, which he put by their plates expecting none in return. Yet from Georgie he received a wallet that she'd made herself, burning his initials into the buff-colored leather, while Big Bob gave him a leather-bound copy of Gregg's classic, *The Commerce of the Prairies*.

The gifts pleased Billy, though the wallet was as stiff as a dead man's skin and the book had been written nearly forty years earlier, and he put them beside him on his pillow when he went to bed that night. This, then, was what Christmas was about, this warm feeling that, until now, had always eluded him. He remembered the Christmas spent at Eva's the year after she married Johnny Steele and the sad, hollow feeling the holiday had given him. Reaching out, he felt with his fingers in the darkness for the wallet and book. Somehow, the memory of that Christmas pained him less, now. It even pained him less to think of Eva; there were whole long moments when he could remember her without the familiar bitterness tightening his throat.

When January weather set in, Tascosa quieted substantially. "Too cold for one *macho* to call another one out for a shoot-up," Big Bob explained. "Freeze their balls off before either one of them could take aim."

Whatever trouble was likely to break out in town, a runaway wagon or a drunken cowboy, Big Bob felt that his deputy could handle it, and there were whole days when he stayed out of Tascosa. On these days he went tramping around the countryside with Georgie and Billy, and one week, when Georgie came down with a cold after washing her hair in icy water, it was just the sheriff and Billy alone.

That week took on a golden aura for Billy, reminding him of the times when he and Hutch had gone camping together. Since deciding to take up the Speakers' interest in oil, Billy had become a believer. He no longer saw Big Bob as a fool but as an explorer and an adventurer in his own right. The frontier had changed; there were no wilderness roads to carve and no mustangs to round up, but there was oil to be hunted and captured.

"Creekology," Big Bob said as they paused beside an ice-crusted stream, "is the bottom rung of the ladder. You'll never climb high without it. Hand me that jar, will you?" Billy did and Big Bob knelt to scoop thick, half-frozen ooze, managing deftly with his one arm. "You think this oil is just lying here and we just happened to run across it, but that isn't the way of it. I've been scouting this section for half a year, following streams every which way looking for signs."

"What sort of signs?"

Big Bob stood up. "Fizzy water, sour springs. Myself, I go by taste. I reckon I've drunk a little of almost every stream in this part of the world, son. Paid the price for it, too. Oil water's unpredictable, can either bind you up tight as a drum or give you a case of the flying ax handles."

Billy took the jar from Big Bob, screwed the lid on, and

wrote the date and location on the label. Other families canned food, the Speakers collected oil sludge. The samples, after their purity and quality had been assessed and recorded, went to feed Big Bob's refining experiments.

"What's the water taste like?"

Big Bob hefted himself to his feet. "Little slick on the tongue, anywhere from lemonade to kerosene and everything in between. Takes years to develop a reliable oil tongue. Sometimes the taste is faint and sometimes what you take for a good sour tang doesn't mean oil at all but something else."

"Sour, you say?" Billy was thinking of a remote spot on Hutch and Sarah's place, a shallow pool ringed by sparse tufts of bunchgrass. No one had ever tasted the water that he knew of. The horses avoided it of their own accord and the smell kept humans at a distance, no matter how thirsty. The family called it the Stinking Spring and more or less ignored it. "Can you smell oil water?" Billy asked. "Sort of like rotten eggs?"

Big Bob nodded approvingly. "You been studying up some on your own, I see."

For a moment Billy thought of telling him about the Stinking Spring. But then he would have to tell him about Hutch and Sarah and quite possibly about Eva and how he came to find himself drifting through life on his own. No, the Stinking Spring could wait; he would tell him another time.

Despite his enthusiasm for discovering oil, Billy still had doubts about its value once discovered. "What good is it," he brooded, "beyond lamps and medicine?"

"Why, industry, son," Big Bob answered, slamming his fist onto the table for emphasis. "Machines of all sorts."

Billy snorted. "No one's going to give up coal for this putrid-smelling stuff."

Big Bob was unruffled. "Oil can do anything coal can do. More, in fact. It's lighter, take it right along with you. It takes a ton of coal to do what three bitty barrels of oil can."

That winter, quite possibly to convince Billy on the point

Big Bob set out to perfect an invention he'd sketched out some years earlier, an oil-burning stove.

"Not inside, Pa," Georgie said adamantly, and drove Big Bob outside to test his experiments. Soon Billy discovered why. The sheriff blew up two outhouses, killed a goat, and maimed the pig testing his invention. One particularly violent explosion left him with a singed hand.

"Oh, Pa," Georgie said as she poulticed and bandaged the injury. "You've only got one hand, I wish you'd be careful with it."

"You'll say different when I get that stove right. Just think of it, no more wood to chop."

A week later, in spite of his singed hand, the stove was working well enough to be installed. It smoked a little and required that a window be left open, but those were small prices to pay. Seeing that the stove was a success, Big Bob set about making improvements on it. One chilly night Billy came in from milking the cow to find the sheriff nailing narrow lengths of tubing to the wall.

"Need some help?" he asked.

"Nope," Big Bob mumbled over the nails held between his teeth. He used his head to hold the tubing in place while he hammered. When the nail was flush with the wall, he grinned down at Billy. "What you'd say to having heat in that dugout room, son?"

Billy looked up. "Heat?"

Big Bob pointed to the tubing which, Billy now saw, stretched from the wall above the stove back toward his room. "We'll just channel some of it back your way."

Billy smiled, not half so glad over the heat as he was over Big Bob's kindness. He caught Georgie's eye and she nodded vigorously as if to say, *You see, Billy. What did I tell you?*

Bib Bob planned to finish the project the next morning but, just after breakfast, the deputy's son came riding to the door. "My pa's sick," the boy said. "Can't work today so he said to ride for you." Then he was back on the horse and gone, skinny rump bouncing against a saddle so worn you could see the wooden frame through the frayed seams.

"Damn," Big Bob said. "Well, I got to go. No telling

what might happen if word got around there was no one minding the store." Biting through the knotted tie of his bandage, he began to unwrap his hand.

"Stop that, Pa," Georgie protested. "It isn't healed yet."

"Don't matter," her father told her. "I'm not going to have to use it. All I've got to do is be there and look like I'm ready for action."

"I'll come with you if you want," Billy volunteered. "You could deputize me for the day."

Suddenly, having made the offer, Billy was afraid the sheriff might laugh at the idea. He didn't though, just shook his head firmly. "No need, son, but thanks."

In the early afternoon sleet began to fall and, seeing no possibility for outside work, Billy made a double batch of bread. "Do we have any raisins, Georgie?" he asked. "I thought I'd make one of those raisin breads. Here's cinnamon right here but I'll be damned if I can find the raisins."

"What?" she looked up, distracted. She'd been in a glum mood ever since Big Bob rode off, and the sleet ticking against the windows didn't help.

"Raisins," Billy repeated and she got up and found them for him. "You're in a funny mood today," he said, taking the raisins from her. Georgie looked down, mouth puckered. It wasn't like her to pout. "What's wrong?"

"It's my birthday."

"Huh?"

"My birthday. I know it isn't Big Bob's way to remember such things, but still . . ." She looked up at him, eyes a wide and heartbreaking blue.

"He'll remember, Georgie. Of course he will. Why, I bet he comes home from Tascosa with a present for you."

She shook her head. "It's clear you haven't been here for birthdays before. Big Bob doesn't believe in them. Doesn't believe in them for us, anyway. I didn't even know I *had* a birthday until an aunt sent me a card once. Sometimes I think maybe it has something to do with my mother. Maybe she died when I was born, maybe I killed her. I don't remember and Big Bob never talks about her."

Billy thought of telling her about his own mother but didn't. Why bring Eva into all this? Besides, he had a better idea. Georgie settled back down to her books and he went back to his bread baking. A cake. He'd seen Sarah make them before, had stood by and licked the batter bowl with his finger. Flour, eggs, water, something to make it rise, something to make it sweet, and here he was with a jar of raisins in his hand.

He poured the batter into a skillet and spelled out her name, Georgie, with chopped-up raisins. To his disappointment, all but a few of the raisins sank during the baking and he had to explain, when he showed her the cake, why here and there raisins had formed themselves into chains.

"You tried to spell my name out?" she asked.

He felt foolish. But, he decided, a man owned up to his failures in the kitchen. "I didn't think about the raisins sinking."

"Oh, Billy!" She put her arms around him. "Billy, it is the best, the most wonderful . . . nobody's *ever* made me a cake before."

He could have kissed her. He certainly wanted to, with the smell of her peppermint soap around him and her body curling soft and kittenlike in his arms. But something warned him not to spoil the moment. He'd come a long way in the past months, in her eyes as well as her father's, and he didn't want to undo it all.

"I don't know what it'll taste like," he said. "I kind of had to guess as I went along. Want to try it?"

"No," she said. "Let's wait for Pa. I want to show him."

They waited far into the evening, holding dinner until both of them had rumbling stomachs. Finally, dispirited again, Georgie said, "Well, we might as well have the stew at least. No sense starving."

Billy went to the window and looked out. "It's sleeting harder now. I'm sure it's the weather that's keeping him, Georgie. Maybe he decided to stay the night."

"Maybe," she said.

After they ate dinner Billy tried to get her, again, to taste the cake. But Georgie refused. The cake had become a symbol to her, one she wanted to present, intact, to her father.

They did the dishes and finished the evening chores and still there was no sign of Big Bob. "I guess there's no point waiting up," Georgie said at last. "He'll be here when he's here." Quietly, she began getting ready for bed. Billy noticed that she left the cake on the center of the table, a glowing lamp beside it.

It made him feel bad, his cake uneaten and Georgie so forlorn. He wanted to get into bed beside her and hold her, just hold her, but that was a pipe dream. He'd never settle for just holding her, even if she let him get that far. "Good night, Georgie," he said from the door of his dugout room.

" 'Night," she answered.

"I forgot to ask, how old are you?"

"Eighteen."

Eighteen. Billy lay awake for a long time thinking of her. Eighteen was grown up, at least where the law was concerned. If Georgie ran off with him, there wouldn't be a thing Big Bob could do about it. Not legally, at any rate. The only problem was, Georgie wouldn't run off with him. There was no point in even asking her to.

Billy shivered. The room was cold, ice crystals clinging to the moist earth walls. He'd sure be glad when Big Bob finished with the heating tubes.

A few hours later he came awake again, knees cramped and stiff from being drawn up to his chin.

"Damn," he heard Georgie say. "Oh, *damn*!" There was the scrape of a man's boots and at first he thought she and Big Bob were having a row. "Tell me again. Are you sure?"

There were tears in her voice and Billy was up in a flash in the freezing room. He pulled his pants on but didn't bother with shirt, socks, or boots before he raced into the main room.

"What's wrong, Georgie?"

Mike Peck was standing in the lamp glow. Georgie sat on the edge of the bed, hair mussed, face streaked with tears. "Somebody shot pa," she said. "He's dead."

Disbelieving, Billy turned to Mike Peck, who nodded slightly. "Where . . . where is he?" Billy asked, mouth as dry as dust.

"Undertaker's," Peck said, lowering his voice. "You can come around tomorrow and make arrangements." He glanced at Georgie. "Will she be all right?"

"I'll take care of her."

Peck nodded. "I'll go then," he said, "leave you alone to work things out." He retrieved his hat from the table where he had laid it down, beside the birthday cake.

"It was his hand," Georgie said in the silence that followed Peck's departure. "Nobody would ever have got the drop on him if his hand hadn't been banged up that way." Suddenly she rose, went to the table, and mashed her fist into the center of the cake. "Nobody."

Billy was inclined to agree with her.

Chapter Thirty-nine

Georgie moved swiftly through her grieving for Big Bob and went, dry-eyed, to the hanging of the man who'd shot him. Then, as spring rains licked the prairie into life around them, she settled back down to her studies. Even without Big Bob, she meant to find oil in Texas.

Her resilience was a disappointment to Billy, who had harbored visions of solacing her grief. But soon it became a worry to him as well. Georgie grew more and more absorbed in her father's pursuit, as if by proving his oil claims she could bring him back or rescue his image, still tarnished from the Daisy City fiasco. It was a hopeless task to Billy's way of thinking, for even if they found clear promise of oil they'd be hard-pressed to build a rig or rally backers.

Nevertheless, Billy went with Georgie on all her oil hikes and one day, standing by a greasy, foam-flecked streambed, he thought again of the place on Hutch and Sarah's land. That thought and Georgie's nearness unlocked a chain of feelings in him, a yearning for the home he had left behind and a sudden longing, surprising to himself, to put down roots.

"Georgie?" Kneeling beside the stream, she looked up, giving him her whole attention. "I lied to you. About my family, I mean. I do have folks."

She rocked back on her heels, set the can she'd been skimming with aside. "I reckoned you did."

He came around and sat down beside her. At first he meant only to tell her about Hutch and Sarah, to pass both of them off as his parents. But soon he found himself unweaving the whole story for her, telling her about Eva and the Comanche and how, after Hutch had died, he'd gone off on his own and ended up in Tascosa.

"Oh, Billy," she said lightly, stroking his cheek with her fingertips. "Poor Billy."

He warmed to her sympathy. "So I'm kind of like you," he told her, "I never had a mother, either."

"No, I think you have. Sarah, she sounds like a good mother. Lots have had a worse one." Georgie paused. "Does she know where you are?"

"No."

"You mean you haven't written her in all this time?" He shook his head. "Oh Billy, Billy," she murmured, "what's to become of you?" But even as she grieved for him her arms were slipping up around his neck and her mouth was pressing, like a cool flower, against his cheek.

Struck by the wonder of what had happened between them that afternoon, Billy stole up behind Georgie that evening while she was making corn cakes and wrapped his arms around her, breathing in the clean peppermint scent of her skin. To his surprise, she pulled away from him. "Leave me be, Billy, so I can get supper."

"But—"

She swept him with a blue-eyed glance. "You're thinking of this afternoon?" He nodded. "So am I. I'm thinking I shouldn't have done that, maybe."

He stepped forward again, ready to reassure her. "But I love you, Georgie. It wasn't just . . . well, you know."

She spooned out a small cake and slid it into the oven.

Unpredictable as the stove was, it was always best to make a trial run first. Straightening, she turned to him. "You love me, you say?"

"Yes."

"Then you're asking to marry me?"

Billy drew a sharp breath. Marry. The thought hadn't even crossed his mind. "Couldn't we just sort of live here together?"

"No, we couldn't."

"Why not?"

She cracked the oven door to look at the smoking griddle. "Well, for one thing, what would we do with the children?" He was silent; he hadn't considered that possibility. "No," she went on, "I've been thinking all afternoon, Billy. We either have to get married or you have to leave. It won't work any other way."

He felt anger flare up in him. Marry or leave, just like that. Who did she think she was? Big Bob's daughter, that was clear. "Are those my only choices?" he asked sharply.

"They're *our* only choices," she replied. He missed the meaning of her words because, temper seizing him, he was already slamming out of the house.

Billy found solace in his old remedy for frustration, alcohol. Riding into Tascosa, he sold his saddle to the first cowboy he met and spent the rest of the night drinking at Mike Peck's saloon. When his money ran out he reeled into the darkness, found his horse and, after several failed attempts, got himself up on the barebacked animal.

The glow of Mike Peck's whiskey had diminished considerably by the time he neared home. The cabin loomed ahead of him, perfectly dark. He knew that by not lighting a lamp Georgie was showing her anger toward him just as Big Bob had shown his on the night of the Christmas dance. Then another thought struck Billy. Sliding down off the horse, he bumped through the darkness, feeling for the door. It had long ago been repaired and now, trying it, he found it firmly locked to him.

"Damn," he whispered, moving off across the yard to the woodpile. He put out his hand, feeling for the handle of the ax or hatchet. Cold awareness dawned on him as he groped. "Damn and hellfire," he whispered again. She'd hidden them, both the hatchet and the ax. Probably had them indoors with her right now, he thought, or stowed someplace where he'd never think to look.

He though of calling out to her, of pounding on the door and demanding to be let in. But that would lead to nothing and he didn't want to face the humiliation. So, taking the saddle blanket from the horse and making a mattress of it, he lay down and went to sleep in front of the cabin door.

Georgie found him there in the morning, almost stepping on him on her way to the outhouse. He looked up at her, his head throbbing as he squinted against the blazing sun overhead.

"Georgie," he said, grabbing the hem of her skirt because he was afraid she'd sweep by him without stopping. He shifted himself to a sitting position. "I've been thinking."

She looked down at him. "Thinking of what?"

"Thinking you're right about getting married."

"Get up, Billy. I can't talk to you way down there."

He scrambled to his feet, unmistakable relief flowing through him. "You'll marry me, then?"

She shook her head. "I won't marry a drinking man."

"I won't ever do it again. Ever. I promise, Georgie."

"Promising isn't doing. You make good on your word, then we'll see."

"I thought you said we couldn't stay here together without getting married."

"I changed my mind," she said. "You can stay, if you don't cause trouble."

Billy stayed because he loved her and because, whether she realized it or not, she needed him. The money that had been collected by a pass of the hat at Mike Peck's saloon and given to Georgie at Big Bob's funeral was running out and, though Georgie didn't seem concerned, Billy began to brood over it. Not long after the drinking episode he rode into Tascosa and got a job dressing beef and hog carcasses for the town butcher. It wasn't the best of jobs but it was honest work, work that brought pay in the form of money and fresh meat.

Still, Billy would often find himself riding home, the

stink of meat on him, and wonder how someone who'd been raised by a man like Hutch Chase had come to settle for so little in life. It was at these moments that he would think of going back, of living again on the wild majestic land he'd grown up on, of taking Georgie back there with him. Once started on such a track, his mind would circle to the Stinking Spring and to Georgie's map with the red patches streaking across his family's holdings. But what would Sarah say if he asked to punch holes in her land? Here his thoughts always stopped and he became aware again of the bleached landscape around him and of the flies buzzing around his blood-caked work clothes.

It was late summer now, the weather warm, and Georgie always had a washcloth and a basin of water waiting for him on a plank at the side of the house, fresh clothes beside it. "You clean up and relax," she would say. "Supper's almost ready." Billy would strip down and wash while, inside, she put out plates for their meal. It made him feel important, this small and simple routine. When he was dressed and she came around to gather up his soiled clothes, he felt as if her world turned around him, as his turned around her.

No, his job might not be the most rewarding, but it put behind him forever his days of keeping house and peeling potatoes. Georgie did those things now while, in the evenings, he followed the path Big Bob had blazed through the geological surveys. He was thinking, more and more consciously, of the Stinking Spring on Sarah's land.

One night while he was reading Georgie paused in her chores, staring at him so intently that he looked up at her. "What?" he asked.

"I wish Big Bob were here," she said, "to see you." She came around and sat down across from him, eyes as intense as sapphires. "You've changed for the best, Billy."

He smiled. "Glory be, you noticed."

"Of course."

He closed the survey book with a snap. "Does that mean you'll marry me now?"

He thought he saw a slight nod of her head but her hands were clenched in her lap. "There's one other thing I want you to do, Billy."

He felt a pin prick of irritation. "Haven't I done enough already, Georgie? I got a job, I stopped drinking. There's no satisfying you. I do one thing, then you want me to do something else."

"Certainly," she replied with a firm dip of her chin. "That's what makes progress, isn't it? Men satisfying women." She let things quiet between them, waited until the annoyance was gone from his eyes. "I want you to write to Sarah, Billy. Set things right with her, at least." She didn't, he noticed, mention Eva's name.

Billy didn't say anything and after awhile Georgie rose and went back to her chores. Glancing at him as she swept the floor, she knew he was thinking it over. That was his way, bristle, sulk, then go ahead and do it. It just took some getting used to. Big Bob had never quite understood that about Billy. He was too impatient, Georgie guessed. But she wasn't; she could give Billy all the time he needed.

By the end of the week he'd written the letter, making a deliberate show of writing and addressing it while Georgie watched. "What did you say?" she inquired, realizing that he wanted her to ask.

"Told Sarah what I've been up to these years, told her about you and Big Bob and Quanah Parker. Told her too I might be coming home, bringing my wife with me. What do you think?"

Georgie smiled, feeling a great lightness wash over her. "Yes," she said, letting him see her happiness.

He picked her up, swinging her feet off the floor. "Do you love me now, Georgie?" He gave her a little shake. "Do you?"

"Yes." She was free to say it now. "I love you, Billy."

Chapter Forty

Billy's letter reached Sarah one warm evening in early autumn. She'd found it under her door when she came home, put there by the foreman, Hank Andrews, who must have been in Union that day.

Sarah smiled to herself as she lit a lamp. Her house door hadn't been locked; it never was. Hank could have walked in and laid the letter on the table, but that wasn't his way. He was a sober, polite young man who had strict ideas about limits and boundaries. That was why, she supposed, he'd argued so fiercely and convincingly about the need to fence the land. It seemed that all the young men who worked for her these days were sober and polite. There wasn't one of them, she thought with a rueful smile, that Hutch would have gotten along with.

Laying her shawl on the table, she turned the letter over. The handwriting wasn't Eva's, as she'd expected. Pulse quickening, she ripped open the envelope and hurried to the end of the letter. Billy. *Well now*, she thought, *what would you think of this, Hutch?* Then, sitting down, she read the letter carefully, read it twice through, relieved to discover he'd come to no harm in the world.

She'd always known that Billy would come back to them sometime, but she hadn't realized until now how she'd waited, *waited*, for the moment. And bringing a wife with him at that.

"Well," she said aloud. "I suppose I've everything I want now. I suppose now I can get old." She wouldn't do that, of course, she'd worked too long in the opposite direction and it went against her grain.

After Hutch had died, Sarah had kept up the horse breeding business, hiring more hands and turning more of the work over to them but still, when the spirit moved her, taking an active role herself.

At first her life had been a quiet one but soon, after a calculated lapse of time, suitors began to make themselves known, men who had known and respected Hutch for years and didn't like the idea of his widow going it alone. They were good men, marrying men, and if she'd had a mind to marry again, any of them would have made a fine match. But Sarah was a Chase woman; she would not change her name for anyone.

"Don't it get awful lonely out here sometimes?" Lew

Claire asked her one night, driving her home after a Fourth of July picnic.

She shook her head. Lonely. She'd never even thought of it. For a man, a widower like Lew, it was different, maybe; but for a woman like herself, there was something to being unmarried that she enjoyed. It had taken her a long time to admit this, for doing so seemed almost a betrayal, yet it was true. All her life, her time had been used up by others: by brothers and sisters back on Caney Fork, by Arden Bell, by Creath and their children, by Hutch, by Eva, by Billy. Sharing herself had been the making of her, she knew that, but now that she held time in her own hands she would not let it go.

A few years ago a bookseller had opened in Union, and there were months when Sarah's purchases singlehandedly supported the store. She made her way through Dickens and Thackeray and Elliot and Austen, preferring their chattiness to the oddly impersonal writing of her own countrymen. Of the Americans, only the recently come along Mark Twain gained her liking. James Fenimore Cooper, she thought, must have been writing about the settling of some other continent.

Without a husband and children depending on her, Sarah was freed from an endless round of cooking and feeding and washing up. It was surprising, she often thought, how little time and effort it took to feed oneself. Often, with a feeling of supreme rebellion, she would carry her dinner plate to the round-topped table beside the sofa, tuck her feet up, and read a book while she ate. If Lew Claire or some other visitor came to interrupt her evening she would entertain him so good-naturedly that he would go away happy, unaware that his visit had redoubled her desire to remain single.

It was to soften her rejection of Lew Claire's pressing, urgent marriage proposal that she went off, in 1880, on a trip she'd long been contemplating. Sarah was by now accustomed to rail travel and had been to San Antonio several times to see Austin and Meta. But there were no rail connections to the Palo Duro frontier, and the only time she'd seen her children there was when they'd come down, in 1878, to bury Adelita's mother.

Therese Prado, suffering a painful cancer of the stomach, had stubbornly clung to life until Adelita arrived with her children. "They are too white," Therese said in Spanish, studying her grandsons' short-cropped hair and her grand-daughter's clean, manicured fingernails. The boys were tall, like the Chases, and so full-grown she didn't recognize them. Young Therese was a princess who wrinkled her nose at the little cabin with its sickroom smell. "They don't even look like us," Therese went on, her last words. "What would your father say?"

Adelita took her mother's bad humor in stride but Eva was distraught at the funeral, the sight of Therese Prado's withered, moon-shaped face carrying her back over the years, over the sharp divide of her captivity to an unscarred time in her life. *I wonder if she'd cry so over me,* Sarah found herself thinking, not at all sure of the answer. But before Eva went back to Palo Duro, she found a moment to be alone with her mother.

"Have you heard from Billy at all?" Eva asked.

Sarah shook her head. Eva had written her, of course, of Billy's trip to Antelope Run. That was the last she knew of her grandson. But she had great faith in anyone who carried Chase blood in him. "Give it time, Eva."

"Time. Time was always what *I* wanted, time to stop hurting, time to have my own children. With enough time, I thought, I would come back for Billy. As if he were a jacket left behind at a picnic." She paused, gray eyes wide with pain. "Well, there won't be any children. I saw a doctor in town last year, quite a good one. He said there are scars inside me. I told him about the Comanche. I had to, of course."

Sarah felt cold sweat start from her armpits, imagining what it must have taken for her daughter to go and lay herself before a doctor, to strip herself and her secrets bare. "Oh, Eva—"

"It doesn't matter anymore. I've gotten used to the idea. Truly. But it's changed me. I want to see Billy. And, now that I do, he's gone."

"He'll come back."

Eva shook her head. "Not to me. He hates me, he's a right to."

Sarah felt helpless, as if she were on one side of a canyon and Eva on the other. "People change, Eva. Even our children."

But Eva's head went down into her hands. Words failing, Sarah reached out and drew her daughter to her. It was the first time, she realized later, the first time in all these years, she had ever done such a thing.

Except for that one visit, Sarah had not seen Eva or Fan or her grandchildren since they'd moved to Palo Duro. Then in 1880, with Lew Claire pressing her for marriage, she bought a stagecoach ticket and posted a letter that said, in effect, that she would be there when she got there. Lew saw her off himself, his brow still furrowed at the idea of her going off by herself.

"Don't worry about me," Sarah told him, leaning from the stage window. "I've money, I've a book to read, I'll be fine."

She didn't go directly to Palo Duro country but took the northeast-bound stage instead. It had long been in her mind to see the Red River country, to explore, even in a tame way, the lands that Hutch had traveled. It was built up now, as she'd expected it to be, with towns and farms and not a trace of the Indians who'd lived there. But Sarah was a woman of imagination and there were still unsettled stretches where she could envision her husband, young and unfettered, moving on horseback through the crowding pines. In so doing, she felt as if she'd forged one last and binding link between herself and Hutch. Though he was dead, though time was rushing on around her, they still held close, hands linked across an invisible abyss. That was the miracle she discovered on the banks of the Red. She would have visited the site of Spotted Turtle's village, too, if she'd known where it was.

From the Red River Sarah traveled on to the ranch at Antelope Run, a shift of at least two hundred years. The luxury of Eva's house disturbed her at first, made her feel once again like the backwoods girl who'd never slept on sheets until her wedding night. But she adjusted after awhile, staying for more than a month before a longing for home suddenly seized her. It was a good visit and, though Billy's name wasn't mentioned, Sarah came away feeling closer to Eva than before.

Once home again, Sarah suffered from the age-old affliction of travelers everywhere: she discovered that, in her absence, the world had grown substantially smaller. She was sixty-five years old in 1880, with abundant energy, enough money to do as she pleased, and the prospect of living another hearty decade or more. She would have to find something to do with herself, she thought; either that or marry Lew Claire, who still had not given up his suit.

That winter the stove exploded in the county schoolhouse, killing the teacher and burning the building to the ground. Bypassing the public process, Sarah donated an acre of her own land, had a building erected, and got Hank Andrews to pack and cart her books to the sight. Classes reopened six weeks after the fire, with Sarah filling in as teacher until a suitable replacement could be found.

No one ever did come to take her place, much to Sarah's delight. From time to time some newcomer to the area would argue the need for a formally educated, properly accredited instructor, but an afternoon with Sarah almost invariably charmed the troublemaker into submission. If not, the county powers stood squarely behind her, for not only was Sarah Chase an adequate teacher in their minds but an economical one as well, charging not a dime for her services.

So it was that from harvest time until planting time Sarah was not at home during the day. Which was why, when Billy and Georgie arrived, the house was still and empty. "It's just like her not to be home," Billy said, picking up the note she'd left on the table for them. Reading over his shoulder, Georgie saw that her husband was smiling.

There was awkwardness in the beginning, not between Sarah and Georgie, who took to one another, but between Sarah and her grandson. Only when Billy saw that Sarah

was willing, at least for the time being, to leave the past
sealed behind them, did he begin to relax.

"I'll let you two have the other side of the cabin," Sarah
said, opening the lid of the linen chest. "That's where I
moved the bed after Hutch died." Her hand hesitated among
the sheets, plain ones she'd stitched herself and ivy-bordered
ones Eva had embroidered long ago; she rose with the plain
ones in her hand.

"Where do you sleep?" Billy asked. The place where the
bed had stood was occupied, now, by a sofa.

"Up in the loft, in Eva's room. I thought the exercise of
going up and down the ladder would be good for me."

She swept past him with the sheets over her arm, across
the walkway and into the other side of the cabin. There, she
thought, Eva's name had been said; Billy would have to get
used to it if he stayed. She would not disown her daughter
for his sake. She unfolded the sheet and cracked it in the air
letting it billow above the bed. When it came to rest, she
saw Georgie's face above it.

"Let me help," Georgie said. As they tucked and smoothed
the sheet around the mattress, her eye caught Sarah's.
"He's told me about Eva, told me everything that happened."

Sarah nodded, unable, suddenly, to meet Georgie's eye.
What must she think of them, a family that raised a boy
without telling him who his parents were? But Georgie went
on talking as she smoothed the top sheet. "He doesn't hold
it against you, not anymore."

Sarah straightened abruptly. "Did he say so?" Georgie
nodded vigorously and Sarah felt, for the first time in years,
a sense of peace.

The loss of bitterness was only one change Sarah saw in
Billy. He wouldn't stay on without lending a hand, he told
her firmly, and so she sent him along to Hank Andrews. He
didn't try to usurp the foreman's position, as he once might
have but did, Hank reported to Sarah, whatever was asked
of him.

Someone had taught Billy to work, and work hard.
Georgie, Sarah supposed at first but later, hearing stories of
Big Bob, she changed her mind. It was clear that Big Bob
Speaker had blazed a trail across Billy's life as certainly as

Hutch had, leaving him the better for it. Bit by bit, from Billy and Georgie, Sarah discovered the personality of Big Bob and, in the process, learned about his oil dreams.

Sarah's first reaction was *Well, isn't that just like a man for you? Now that the land's tame, they have to find something new to wrestle, have to go either up in the air or down under the ground to find it.*

It was Georgie's enthusiasm, even more than Billy's, that drew Sarah, and when Georgie unfurled her handmade map of Texas Sarah traced, just as Billy had done, the path of red ink blotches across the northern crescent of her land.

"How would a body know," she asked, "if there's oil in the ground or not?"

"The only sure way," Georgie said, "is to dig. But there are surface signs to point the way."

It was a February night, Sarah would mark it down in her diary later, and the room seemed warm. Rising, she crossed the room and opened the window an inch, the window Billy had once looked through to see Eva staring back at him. "What kind of signs?" she asked, turning back to them

"Remember the Stinking Spring?" Billy asked, and when she nodded he explained, quickly, unable to keep the excitement from his voice, how the land gave itself away.

Sarah remained silent for some minutes after he finished. "I suppose you came home with an eye to looking into it," she said, "the Stinking Spring place."

Billy felt ashamed suddenly, as if he'd tried to use her, when that wasn't the way of it at all. "No. It's your land, Sarah."

She remained pensive, lost in thought. "It'd be like digging up his bones in a way, wouldn't it? Hutch'd never let me rest, knowing I put a hole in his land."

Georgie glanced across the room at her husband and something in her look kept him from speaking.

"Well, past is past," Sarah murmured. "I never asked to live on without them." She looked up, her russet eyes clear. "I'll think about it, Billy. Lord, but it's warm in here, even with the window open."

Rising, she slipped from the room with a rustle. Billy started toward the door after her.

"Ssh, no," Georgie said, catching him by the arm. "Leave her be."

"But she thinks I came home just for that," Billy replied, his face twisting suddenly, "and I didn't. I didn't!"

"She'll know that, Billy. Just give her time."

Outside, Sarah leaned against the wall of her house and let the chill spring air stream across her she looked up at the moon. Inconstant moon, she thought, the line coming back to her because she'd finished the school year, last week, with a class reading of *Romeo and Juliet*. It wasn't true at all, just poetry. The moon was as constant a thing as she knew, constant in its coming and going, constant in showing its dark face and its full one. Her moon was the same as Shakespeare's, but how everything had changed below; how everything would keep changing, in spite of all of them.

Chapter Forty-one

Nothing more was said about oil although, with the coming of summer, Sarah had more time to think the matter over. The blue-bound geological surveys, brought along by Georgie and Billy, made their way onto the bookshelves beside Dickens and Thackeray. Often at night, after her grandson and his wife had gone to sleep, Sarah would take one of the books onto her lap and read, absorbed, until dawn light broke the window's darkness. Twice Georgie came across a book left open on the sofa and both times she returned it to the shelf without a word. When Sarah was ready, she would say something.

And if Sarah never said? Georgie mulled this very real prospect over in her mind for days. Staying on then would mean the end of Big Bob's oil dreams, something she'd never thought to face. Yet there were real compensations to be enjoyed. There was Billy, for one thing. He'd finished his apprenticeship under Hank Andrews and moved on to equal footing with him. Georgie watched as, day by day, her husband grew more confident, changed in the way she'd always believed he would. He seemed at peace with himself, maybe for the first time, and, oil or no, she would not take that from him.

There was Sarah to think of too. Their coming had made a difference to her, even if she never said so outright, and it was clear to even a newcomer like Georgie that Sarah had missed the lifelong habit of looking after her own. Nor was the consideration all one way. Never having had a mother of her own, Sarah came into Georgie's life like a gift. With the end of school and the coming of summer, the two women spent long hours together, each one starved, in her own way, for the company of the other.

Beyond all these considerations, there was one other consideration Georgie took into account. Something she had, as yet, told no one.

"There," Sarah said, pointing, "is where the railhead used to be." Georgie followed the line of Sarah's outstretched arm to a mound of earth, covered with sparse grass, snaking across the prairie. "Hutch was dead against it," Sarah went on, "and after Johnny and Fan moved their outfit to the Palo Duro, it was just a scar across the land. I had it torn up two years ago, though the money the scrap brought barely paid for the trouble. Still, it's what Hutch would have wanted."

She slapped the reins and horses started forward, wagon wheels creaking, empty pails bouncing in the wagon bed behind them. She and Georgie had come this way in search of blackberries, a number of which, she knew, grew on the stream that ran back from the old abandoned cabin. "Just over the rise," she said, "is Eva's old place. It's still standing; Fan and Johnny built well."

Georgie, busy absorbing the oceanic drift of land around her, became aware of Sarah's glance fixed firmly on her.

"I don't know what Billy's told you about Eva," Sarah said.

The wagon rolled down a yellow-grassed slope. It had been a statement, not a question, but Georgie understood that Sarah was waiting for a reply. "I know about the

Comanche, of course, and about Johnny Steele and the Steele-Chase Road and the Antelope Run ranch.''

Sarah felt a nerve pinching inside her. It seemed so sparse, a scrap collection of facts, scraps with bits of life clinging to them. ''But Eva herself,'' Sarah said, searching Georgie's face, ''did he say anything about *her*?''

''No.'' Georgie was silent for a long moment. ''I don't think he knows anything about Eva, Sarah.''

''He doesn't.'' Sarah bit her lip, thinking of the day when she'd gone up into Eva's room, Eva's complex and impeccable room, and felt shamed by it, thinking of a piece of paper that said, in precise handwriting, *Ways to Be Perfect*. ''There's more to Eva than the things that have happened to her, Georgie. Billy's got to know that, someday.''

Georgie nodded, not understanding the exact meaning of her words but grasping, clearly enough, their implication: someday Billy would have to make his peace with Eva, too. She'd known that herself for some time now.

They reached the low, shrublike tangle of cherry trees and picked until their buckets were full, Georgie moving easily among the brambled undergrowth in her man's pants and tucked-in shirt.

''If I were younger,'' Sarah said, eyeing her, ''I might try pants myself. It looks convenient.'' It was the first time she'd ever commented on Georgie's maverick tastes in fashion.

Georgie gave her a funny look, wondering how long and how carefully Sarah had been studying her. ''It is convenient,'' she answered, ''but mostly it was Big Bob's doing. He didn't know anything about girl's clothes, so he dressed me his way. Sometimes I think Billy'd like skirts better.''

''Billy likes you fine the way you are.'' Sarah caught Georgie's eye. ''That's an understatement, Georgie.''

Georgie smiled suddenly, the two of them drawn close in the cherry thicket. ''I'll have to wear dresses soon anyway.'' She paused, then looked up brightly. ''I don't think you can wear man's pants when you're carrying a baby.''

Sarah felt a jolt. There it was again, the old familiar tug of happiness, and easier to bear when the body wasn't her own. ''Does Billy know?''

Georgie shook her head. "He ought to have guessed but he hasn't. I wonder about telling him."

Sarah stretched out her hand, noticing suddenly that it was thin and hard and polished, like the hand of Elva Roberts back in Galveston Bay. "You tell him, Georgie. It'll be the making of him."

Sarah asked that they not name the baby after her, although she was delighted when they did. The baby, called Sally to distinguish her from her great-grandmother, had a fringe of spice-colored hair and the wide-set gray eyes of a Chase.

You didn't get a smidgin of yourself into this one, Georgie," Sarah laughed, jiggling the baby in her arms. "She's all Chase and Kincaid."

"Georgie doesn't mind," Billy answered. "Georgie's going to get back at us with the boys, aren't you?"

Georgie nodded vigorously. "That's right. They're all going to look like Big Bob."

She settled back, watching Sarah and the baby, the older woman's movements sure and certain, as if she didn't even have to think them through. How did that happen? Georgie wondered. Had she been born with the knowledge or had there been moments, long forgotten, when Sarah felt as clumsy with her children as she sometimes did with Sally?

Georgie wasn't certain, but she felt a high degree of hope for herself as a mother. She was changing, had changed already from the windmill-climbing tomboy Billy had married. For the first time in her life she had a figure, breasts and hips and a waist that precluded her changing back into men's pants and shirts. She'd worn skirts during the last days of her pregnancy, moving the waistband up as her stomach grew and looking, Billy said, like a ship in full sail as she moved across the yard.

No longer a ship in sail, Georgie had come to a quiet port in her life, a port where skirts and even the flounced, hand-sewn petticoat Sarah had given her seemed desirable. If Sally had changed her that much already, there was no telling where the changes might end.

"Here," Sarah said, handing the baby back to Georgie. "There's something I want to show you."

"Careful," Billy said, mistrusting any transfer of his daughter from hand to hand. "Don't drop her."

Sarah smiled as she turned away from them; the caution, the knitting of eyebrows, reminded her of Creath. Against one wall, where it had always stood, was a wooden cupboard. The family's important things had always been kept there: land titles and deeds, keepsakes, letters from Austin and Fan and Eva; until Hutch's death, when Sarah had buried it with him, the leather bag from the Cherokee had rested there too, far to the back. Now she drew out a white box, a box so new and shining its top looked like glazed ice.

"This is for Sally," It was Billy to whom Eva handed the box. She watched as he opened the lid and plucked, from the tissue inside, a silver cup with the baby's initials scripted on the side.

Georgie's eyes widened. It was the first silver to come into her family that she knew of. "Oh, Sally, you are the luckiest baby, aren't you? Say thank you to Sarah."

But Sarah, sitting down, was looking at Billy. "It's from Eva," she explained. "She wanted you to have something nice."

Billy's eyes darkened and for a moment silence threatened to spread, like ink, across the room. "She sent this?" he asked at last.

"She sent a letter asking me to pick it out," Sarah answered. The letter had been two pages long, as if she didn't trust Sarah to get anything short of a monstrosity without specifically detailed instructions.

Billy stared at the cup in his hand, then set it down on the table. "I didn't know she knew about Sally," he said.

"I wrote to her," Sarah told him. Just as she had written of Billy's homecoming and of all the months in between. Eva's responses were grateful of the news, so full of deep and unexpressed longing they cut at Sarah's heart. She wished, now, that she could make Billy see that. "I've been thinking," she went on, voice mild as she smoothed her skirt with her hand, "of having the Antelope Run folks down to visit this summer. Austin and Meta too. It's my seventieth birthday and I've a mind to see my family gathered while I'm still above ground to enjoy it." She looked up as she finished, daring him to challenge her.

Sarah didn't look seventy, Billy thought, not as he understood seventy to be. Only the iron in her seemed to have taken years to produce.

When they were all gathered, there were too many of them to fit in the cabin. Austin and Meta's two oldest children were married, with children of their own, and despite their immersion in their own lives, they appeared with spouses and children in tow. *Austin must have said something to them*, Sarah thought. Only later, when Austin, with a worried face, asked after her health, did she realize the truth of it, that everyone had hurried to her side because they thought, at seventy, it might be their last chance.

"Are you feeling well, Mother?" her oldest son had asked, and Sarah, grasping the meaning of his frown, had laughed.

"My yes. You don't think . . . oh, Aus!" She looked at him, eyes bright. He would always be her Aus, the grave and serious little body she'd carried through the mud during the runaway scrape. For him she would live forever. "I'm indestructible, don't you know that? Though I do want to talk to you about a will later, in case mortality should get the better of me." He nodded. "Where's Clive?

Clive was Austin's oldest son-in-law, whom Sarah liked immensely.

"He left for Union," Austin replied. "The train ought to be in by now."

In the last year, rail service had extended into the wilds of the Panhandle. Sarah suppressed a wish that Billy had been the one to collect the Antelope Run relatives. But Billy was off showing Joe, Austin's oldest son, the new riding horses he was breeding. He was making himself purposely scarce, she knew, as if he could avoid forever the moment of contact with Eva.

"You slept well in the bunkhouse?" Sarah asked, returning her attention to her oldest son. The bunkhouse had been the

only place to put them. Tonight they'd be joined by Eva and
Johnny and Therese, while Fan and Adelita and the boys
slept in the old Prado cabin across the stream.

Austin chuckled at his mother's question. "The children
thought it was quite the thing. I myself, I'll always be a
town boy."

Sarah reached suddenly for his hand, squeezed it. "So
I've noticed."

They made small talk as they walked along. Under the
shade of elm trees, Sarah saw Georgie and Meta and
Elizabeth, Joe's wife, setting the two long tables that had
been made from sawhorses and planks of wood. From the
corner of her eye she caught the flutter of blue and white,
tablecloths made by Georgie for the occasion.

"I wonder how long it will take them from Union," she
said, thoughts drifting into the conversation.

"With the new road, a little more than an hour, I think."

It was strange, Sarah thought, how much of life was
made of waiting: waiting for Creath to come in from the
field, waiting for the crops to ripen or rain to fall, waiting
for a baby to come, waiting until the boys were asleep so
she and Hutch could sneak out to the cattle barn. And now,
even with changes and improvements and inventions, she
was waiting still.

When Clive drove into view it was Eva's parasol Sarah
saw first, Eva's parasol like an iced and decorated cake,
leaning out to the side beneath the surrey awning. Billy and
Joe had come back by then, and for one wild moment Sarah
was afraid he might bolt at the sight of the surrey. He didn't
though and Georgie, whisking off her apron, came up to
stand at his side, thrusting Sally into his arms.

They looked like prosperous ranchers, Sarah thought as
her kinfolk climbed out of the surrey in a flurry of silk and
satin. But soon they were peeling out of their train clothes,
Fan and Johnny stripping down to their shirt-sleeves and
Adelita kicking off the high-topped shoes she'd bought just
for the journey. Only Eva remained stiff and formal, holding
her bonnet in her hand like a bouquet.

Georgie was the first to speak. "I'm Billy's wife," she
said, stretching out her hand.

Eva looked grateful. "I'm glad to meet you, Georgie." Her eyes wandered past Georgie to her son. "Hello, Billy."

Billy nodded. Except for rustling of trees, everything was perfectly still. *This is terrible*, Sarah thought, *terrible*.

But Georgie, miraculously, was taking Eva by the arm, drawing her forward. "And this is Sally." Billy tensed as if to step back with the baby in his arms but Georgie checked him.

Eva's luminous smile, the smile Billy had never seen before, dawned slowly as she looked down at the baby. "Why, she's beautiful, Billy, just beautiful."

Billy hesitated a moment. Only Sarah saw the nudge of Georgie's knee. "You can hold her if you want."

As Eva took the baby, her arm brushed against her son's, releasing the scent of lilac sachet from her clothes. Billy wondered how it was that he'd hated her so all these years.

Georgie made a point of seating herself and Billy near Eva at the table. When the baby began to cry, Eva offered to take her and Georgie handed her over, this time without any reflexive tensing from Billy. Gurgling, Sally clutched the strand of pearls that hung from Eva's neck.

"Watch out," Billy warned, "she'll break your beads."

Eva smiled. "I don't mind."

She was content, content in a way she'd never expected to be. Eva had held and cared for each of Adelita and Fan's children but they were growing now, the two boys almost men and Therese, nearing thirteen, on her way to becoming a beauty. It comforted her to hold a baby again, and to hold a baby of her own flesh and blood filled her, suddenly, with a sense of completeness. She would have let Sally strip her to the bone, pull away pearls and pins and flesh itself, just for the feeling of that moment.

From her place, the place they'd insisted she take at the head of the table between Austin and Fan, Sarah had seen all of this transpire. It was foremost in her mind when, later, she took Billy's arm, pulling him away from a game of horseshoes. "Walk with me awhile," she said.

They moved down the slope of the yard, past the barns and storehouses and outbuildings that spun off on either side like spume flung from the prow of an advancing ship. When they came to a place where the land dropped, meadows spreading away before them, Sarah released Billy's arm.

"If you stand here," she said, "you can almost believe the land's never been touched. You can't see a fence or fence post, you can't even see the house because of the rise. It was this piece of ground Hutch found first. I've tried to keep it clear for him."

Billy, behind her, was uncertain where this might be leading. "You've done a good job, Sarah."

But it wasn't his praise she was looking for. "One can't keep the land forever, especially when they've as much as we have. My," she was wading now, pushing forward through the knee-length grass, a nimble bark in familiar waters, "I didn't know how much we had until I started looking at the maps. Hutch added here and there; I thought he was buying small parcels. That's a woman's way, maybe, to look at life like a piece quilt. I doubt even if he knew how much he was setting his name to.

"I've been thinking about the Stinking Spring, Billy, and what you said about the oil. And," she continued without waiting for his reaction, "I've talked to Austin and Fan and Eva. This place will go to all of you someday, all of you equally, though what Eva and Fan will do with more land I don't know. But I want you to have the benefit of it now. If you wait for me to die, well," she shook her head, a rueful smile, "I don't plan on it, that's all. Dig on the Stinking Spring if you want, Billy, or another site, if you want to pick one."

Billy was silent for a moment, so silent that Sarah turned to look at him. "I wouldn't want you to think," he said, "that that's what I came back for." It had bothered him ever since he'd first mentioned oil to her.

Sarah waded through the grass to him, took his arm. "I know that, Billy." She smiled, her russet eyes catching the sunlight that reflected off the grass. "I know."

Epilogue

She stood alone for some time after Billy went back to the house, telling him she wasn't so old or so feeble that she couldn't make her way back without him.

The sun was beginning to set and she had a sudden urge to watch it, watch its round globe sinking fast into the solid line of earth. All day long the sun blazed overhead, eternal and slow-moving. But here at the borders, at sunrise and at sunset, a person could see how swiftly its light passed overhead.

She hoped she'd done the right thing in letting Billy have the land. It would change things, no doubt. New men would come onto the land to work for him; men, she supposed, not nearly as mannerly and polite as Hank Andrews and his crew. Oddly, she thought, it was Creath who'd best understand what she'd done, even though he'd been a farmer and even though Billy was more Hutch's kin than his own. Creath, unlike his brother, had reached out to shape the land, to bring somthing up out of it that, stubbornly, it refused to give.

So it was Creath now, she thought, who'd understand her, understand better, perhaps, than she understood herself. For Sarah was not simply ceding land to Billy. In reading the geological survey books she'd formed her own passion, her own curiosity to see what, if anything, the land concealed. Stinking Spring.

It was Hutch who, if he was near her, would not understand. She remembered his resistance to fences, his dislike of the railhead; he'd wanted the land to stay forever as it was when he first laid eyes on it. But that, Sarah thought, wasn't the world's way. Land was so much clay for men to shape and mold and it was what the struggle made of them, as much as what they made of the land, that mattered. And so Billy would have his chance, he would not be denied.

"You've got to see that, Hutch," she said aloud.

The sun was nearly gone now, its light spilling to her in a horizontal flood. Shadows pooled in places where the earth dipped and bearded tufts of grass shot up to stand, suddenly tall, in silhouette.

Sarah turned and started back up the slope to her house, her foot firm against the earth where, below, the oil waited.